The new Zebra Re
cover is a photogra
fashionable regency
satin or velvet riband around her wrist to carry a fragrant
nosegay. Usually made of gold or silver, tuzzy-muzzies varied
in design from the elegantly simple to the exquisitely ornate.
The Zebra Regency Romance tuzzy-muzzy is made of alabas-
ter with a silver filigree edging.

An Intimate Waltz

"Might I have this dance, Miss Lindsay?"

Jane stood up and allowed him to place his hand on her waist. Soon they were mesmerized by the steady pulse of the waltz, as well as by each other. There was some quality about this man, the Devilish Lord Drew Devlin that made Jane lose herself in his embrace.

Jane bit her lower lip nervously as he stared at her. "You are insufferably arrogant, aren't you, Lord Devlin?" she demanded, trying to squelch the lightheaded feeling that was creeping up over her.

Drew merely smiled in response. And then he pulled her closer, scandalizing the starchy matrons that watched. But suddenly Jane didn't care what anyone around her thought. She surrendered to the heady feeling of his closeness. Some part of her remained dimly aware of her shocking behavior, but she had no wish to stop, even though she knew where it would lead her. . . .

THE BEST OF REGENCY ROMANCES

THE Valentine's Day Ball

DONNA BELL

ZEBRA BOOKS
KENSINGTON PUBLISHING CORP.

For my husband Dennis—
My one and only
valentine

ZEBRA BOOKS

are published by

Kensington Publishing Corp.
475 Park Avenue South
New York, NY 10016

First printing: January, 1991

Printed in the United States of America

Chapter One

"How can you be so calm about it, Jane?"

"Because, my dear, it is not the end of the world. You will have many balls when the Season begins."

"Perhaps, but this is the most important! All the Heartland ladies in our family have met their husbands at our Valentine's Ball when they were just eighteen. And here am I, dressed in blacks and stuck behind this blasted screen where *he* cannot even find me!"

The indignant Miss Pettigrew glared at her older cousin whose merriment shone clearly in her green eyes. Miss Lindsay, who often found her cousin's dramatic utterances amusing, held up one hand to stem Cherry's fierce retort.

Swallowing her laughter, Jane Lindsay said sensibly, "Cherry, come now, do not be angry with me. I know this is not easy for you, but you should learn to look on the bright side. After all, we are lucky your mother thought it proper of us to even hold the ball this year since we are not quite out of mourning for Grandmother. And as for being dressed in black, I would never call this gossamer silk of silver gray exactly staid. As a matter of fact, as you well know, it is vastly fetching, which probably accounts for all the young gentlemen who have taken the trouble to come over here, leaving the dancing, to express their delight in your appearance."

This last brought a coy smile to Miss Pettigrew's rosebud lips, and she pressed her older cousin's hand, saying, "Please

5

forgive me, Jane dearest, for being so cross. I am truly sorry."

"I shan't regard it. I remember, too, what it was like to worry about not being able to attend the St. Valentine's Ball when I was your age." Jane Lindsay's quiet laugh sounded, and her younger cousin marveled at the fact that it contained not a hint of bitterness.

As Jane returned her attention to the dancers passing in front of the intimate alcove they shared, Cherry studied her older cousin. Jane Lindsay, dressed in a very simple silk gown of pale lavender, was not a great beauty, she admitted. She was attractive, and to Cherry, who adored her, Jane was the epitome of elegance. How she had reached the advanced age of four and twenty, soon to be five and twenty, without being married, Cherry could not fathom. And so, the only solution, from Cherry's romantic viewpoint, was that Jane hadn't attended the traditional Heartland St. Valentine's Ball when she was eighteen years of age. There had been no ball that year; Jane's mother had died just after Christmas, and the entire household had been in deep mourning. Hence, Jane hadn't met her future husband, as family tradition dictated, at the ball.

And as for Seasons in London, thought Cherry with a frown, Jane had had two. But it had been too late, the jinx had already taken hold, and now Jane was on the shelf. Not in her dotage precisely, but from Cherry's perspective, her cousin might as well be, for she would never marry now.

Resolutely, Cherry turned her smiling visage on the assembled dancers, determined to lure her future husband to her side, whoever and wherever he might be.

Jane Lindsay watched Cherry's face take on that glazed look as the smile became frozen on her face. Ah, she thought, how glad I am that I no longer expect Prince Charming to come waltzing into my life. I shall be glad, positively relieved, she mused, when I may don a cap and no longer play these silly games men think women want to play. Not that I have ever played those games, she admitted. She reflected wryly that perhaps that fact had more than a little

6

to do with her unmarried state. Again, a tiny sigh escaped her lips, but this time, it was not all for her cousin.

A sharp tweak on her skirt brought her abruptly back to the present.

"Look! Who is that? I have never seen him in Bath before. Isn't he divine?" whispered Cherry, her smile never faltering.

Jane obediently turned her attention in the direction of the dancers. Not ten paces in front of them stood a man of great height. She studied his profile as he turned to speak to his companion. The strong chin and jaw were indeed handsome, but in a forbidding way. Jane wondered idly why her cousin would express such interest in this man. Then he turned, his lazy gaze coming to rest on her.

Jane didn't drop her eyes; the coy moves of the debutante were not for her. Besides, she noted cynically, he was too busy surveying her figure to notice where her eyes were directed. She took the opportunity to study his face further.

His mouth reinforced her first impression: here was a man accustomed to getting his own way. His nostrils flared, and she imagined how ruthless and demanding he would probably be. Then she looked into his eyes, eyes so dark they appeared black in the candlelight. Yet there was a definite light of amusement, and Jane realized he was studying her face and looking deep into her green eyes. Again, she regarded him unabashedly, for she had decided long ago never to flinch from the challenge of a man's gaze.

He nodded his head imperceptibly, obviously deciding to dismiss her as he turned to study her cousin.

And who would not? thought Jane, for Cherry was petite, trim, and beautiful. She had golden blond curls that clustered around her face, her china blue eyes shone with mischievous lights, and her rosebud mouth seemed to beg for a kiss.

The stranger smiled at his companion whom Jane hadn't noticed until that moment. Both men turned, and it was with a start that she recognized the companion as her portly cousin, Roland Havelock. Ha! she sniffed; she might have known! Well, if this mysterious gentleman (and she hesitated

7

at the use of the word) was a friend of her despicable cousin Roly, then he was not the future husband for Cherry!

"Here he comes!" whispered that damsel in excitement before smoothing her skirts and sitting up straighter.

The stranger stood back a little as Cousin Roland entered their cozy alcove and bowed, a tremendous creaking noise audible over the strains of the musicians' country air. Jane stifled her smile quickly, but she had the uncomfortable feeling that the perceptive stranger had noticed her amusement.

"How are you, Jane, my dear? And my sweet Cousin Cherry? May I say how beautiful you both are this evening?"

"If you must, Rol . . . Roland," said Jane. "How nice of you to come. I didn't realize Aunt had sent you an invitation, since you were rusticating in . . . You must refresh my memory. Where, precisely, were you, uh, sent?"

"I have been exploring the New World," said Roland in strangled tones. Recovering, he continued, "You must know, Jane, that I would never miss the Heartland Valentine's Ball, especially this one, when my dear Cousin Cherry is to make her debut."

"How gallant of you," said Jane dryly. "We missed you at Grandmother's funeral last April."

"I was sorry to hear about Grandmother." Roland Havelock's florid face turned a deeper shade of scarlet, but his thick lips remained fixed in a syrupy smile. "And how is my charming little Cousin Cherry?" he intoned, his tiny eyes raking Cherry from head to toe.

As on previous occasions, Jane thought privately that if one could take away some of the size of his lips and add this to his eyes, Roland Havelock's face would be eminently more acceptable. Of course, that still left his immense girth, and his taste for wearing shocking colors. His navy breeches were unexceptionable, but the satin coat of puce was revolting, and the rings of perspiration rendered it positively repulsive. Altogether an unpleasant relative; no wonder, as a child, she had nicknamed him Roly.

Again Jane's eyes were drawn past her cousin to where the stranger stood. She was surprised to find his eyes resting on her until she realized his gaze lingered below her chin. Not wishing to appear self-conscious (which she had always been on the subject of her questionable blessing) she shifted slightly and brought one gloved hand up to her chin, striking a thoughtful pose and effectively hiding the display of deep cleavage. Jane chanced a glance in the stranger's direction. Why, he looked positively amused!

But her indignation faded as she became lost in those merry brown eyes. Cherry was right; the man was extraordinarily handsome. And he was moving toward her.

After Roland performed the introduction, Jane defiantly dropped her hand and rose, sweeping an elegant curtsey in answer to his polished bow.

"I'm afraid I didn't quite catch your name, sir," said Jane, her serenity returning now that she was on even footing with this disconcerting and discerning man.

"Lord Devlin, Miss Lindsay." His voice lingered over her name, indicating that he had not been as lost as she in their silent confrontation.

"How do you do, Lord Devlin," she said with a smile, revealing nothing of her irritation.

"Are you newly come to our area, Lord Devlin?" asked Cherry shyly.

"Yes, I've been in London the past six months, but before that I was in the Indies."

"How exciting! I should love to travel to such a fascinating place!"

"Nothing but a nasty, dirty place, I do assure you, Cherry. Absolutely uncivilized. And positively sweltering!" said Cousin Roland.

"You exaggerate, Mr. Havelock," said Lord Devlin. "Certainly, one must look at the islands with an open mind, and then one can see the exotic beauty that abounds there."

If Lord Devlin had not been so blatantly tantalizing Cherry with his words, Jane Lindsay might have fallen under the spell of those piercing dark eyes and that smooth voice. As it was, Jane saw only an accomplished flirt who was trying, quite successfully, to lure her innocent cousin

9

into his web. Quickly, she interrupted.

"And is that where you met one another, rusticating in the wilds of our island colonies?"

"It is hardly rusticating when one chooses to live there for ten years, Miss Lindsay. Of course, I cannot speak for Mr. Havelock. However, in answer to your basic question, yes, we did meet there."

Though she felt churlish, Jane could not prevent a curling of her lip. She was not fooled; she had contacts in London. Hadn't Viscount Drew Devlin's history been the subject of one of her old friend's letters a month or so past? And the gist of it was that the viscount had returned after ten long years of banishment over some scandal. Arriving in London, he had proceeded to create one new on-dit after another. Well, she knew how to handle rakes. And he was probably a fortune hunter, too.

"Perhaps you would care to show me the countryside, Miss Pettigrew," the rake was saying. "We could make up a party and have a picnic, if your cousin, Miss Lindsay, could be persuaded to chaperon." He smiled sweetly in Jane's direction, pretending his words had not been a direct insult.

Jane returned a grimace of a smile. "That sounds delightful; however, since we are not out of mourning, it would be impossible. Perhaps next year."

She extended her hand, which he took in his, bowing over it. He peered up into her triumphant face, his expression a promise that their exchange was far from ended.

As the two gentlemen left them, Cherry sighed loudly. "I have never met anyone like Lord Devlin, so exciting, so worldly."

"What about young Lord Pierce?"

Cherry pouted prettily. "He is well enough, but he hasn't Lord Devlin's ease of manner. Besides, he hasn't even shown up yet."

Jane smiled and shook her head. "Don't worry, my dear, he is too smitten with you to stay away. He'll be here, and the first thing he will do is present himself to you."

Cherry tossed her head as though to say she wasn't at all

certain she would deign to speak to the errant Lord Pierce. Jane hoped fervently her prediction would come true; she certainly didn't want Cherry daydreaming about Lord Devlin. What had Sally Cumberland called him in her letters? Devilish Devlin! And somehow, Jane knew instinctively the appellation was all too appropriate.

Jane Lindsay looked out across the ballroom, her gaze taking in its splendor without truly seeing it. She gave a satisfied nod. Yes, she thought, the ballroom at Heartland had never appeared to better advantage. Clusters of hothouse flowers in all shades of pink, from the palest to the deepest rose, adorned the walls, artfully arranged in the shape of hearts. Her grandmother would have been proud. Cream-colored bows of silk moire adorned the doorways and the musicians' gallery. And presiding over everything were Cupids painted in muted tones on the ceiling. As a girl those naughty figures had both attracted and repelled her; now, she merely wanted to laugh at their foolish antics.

Miss Lindsay sighed and shifted her chair slightly so that she might have a view of the refreshment tables. She lifted her grandmother's brooch which decorated her generous bosom. Touching the tiny spring, she revealed the dainty timepiece.

"Eleven o'clock. I do hope Pipkin has seen to the supper buffet. Perhaps I should check to be certain."

A spark of her usual liveliness leapt into Cherry's blue eyes. "I'll go and see for you, Jane. I must go to the ladies withdrawing room at any rate."

Jane nodded her assent. After all, Cherry was young; her feet still itched to dance. And despite the fact that their year of mourning was not quite at an end, Cherry couldn't be expected to act as mature and staid as . . . well, thought Jane, as I am.

She watched fondly as Cherry's silvery gray gown disappeared amidst the crowd along the edge of the dancers. With her petite figure and open manners, Cherry could afford to miss dancing at this Valentine's Ball. Jane doubted Cherry would pass her first season without becoming betrothed.

11

Unlike you, came the unbidden thought. But Jane Lindsay would allow no more maudlin reflections to cross her well-disciplined mind. Besides, it was not as though she had not received several eligible offers. She smoothed her lavender gown and stood up, stretching her weary limbs.

The lines of the gown she wore were simple, the very latest style from the Continent, with not a single flounce or ruffle to detract from the wearer's figure. Jane had been pleased with the effect earlier that evening when she had studied her image in the glass. Had it been her imagination, or did the simple lines mask her dubious charms? She had thought so, until the unwelcome Lord Devlin had stared at her bosom so conspicuously.

Jane was diverted from these uncomfortable recollections by the entrance of her aunt, a short, squat lady of five and forty years who seemed to float and flutter as she moved. Jane always wondered if Cherry would eventually come to resemble her mother.

"Jane! Where is Cherry? She isn't dancing, is she? She agreed to behave, you remember, if we held the ball as usual."

"Calm yourself, Aunt Sophie. She has gone to see that Pipkin has set up the buffet properly."

"Oh, oh, well, then, that's fine. Just fine. I do hope she will behave," said Sophie Pettigrew.

"You mustn't worry, Aunt. Cherry would never do anything to disgrace herself—not before her first Season in London this spring."

"Of course, of course, you are right, Jane. You are always so wise. Sometimes I think we must be a sad trial for you."

"Nonsense! Now, go and enjoy yourself. I promise you, Cherry has been a pattern card of propriety all evening, demure to the gentlemen and unfailingly polite to every lady. But you can't blame her for wanting to escape this confining alcove for a few moments. It is a trifle boring." And that, thought Jane, is a vast understatement.

But her Aunt Sophie, reassured on that subject, said anxiously, "What about the valentine messages? Has Pipkin

12

gathered all of them? They must be ready to distribute before the supper dance."

"I'm sure Pipkin has seen to it. He's been taking care of it since before I was born, you remember."

"I know, I know. But I can't help but worry. He has some extra ones for the girls who are not sought after, doesn't he?"

"He always does. Cherry and I helped make them ourselves. All Pipkin has to do is place the unfortunate girl's name on the envelope."

"Good, then I can relax. Now, where do you suppose Cherry has gotten to? She should have been back by now."

"She's just putting off returning to our corner. Why don't you see that our guests in the card room are entertaining themselves sufficiently?"

"If you think I should," said Sophie Pettigrew, as she fluttered back into the ballroom where the musicians were striking up a waltz.

It was almost midnight; Jane spied Pipkin, attired impeccably in his black butler's coat. He was looking at her, waiting for her signal before he passed out the elaborate valentines, most of which their guests had spent weeks making with the finest lace and the most sentimental poems.

As the daughter and heir of Heartland, Jane had always received more than her fair share of the gentlemen's offerings. Perhaps that was why one part of her remained detached from this tradition; her lack of self-confidence led her to think that the cards she received were merely polite tokens, whereas the other young ladies looked on their cards as symbols of conquest.

This year would be no better; probably worse, now that she was the mistress of Heartland. But Pipkin still waited, and she nodded to signal to the old servant that it was time to begin that long-awaited tradition of the Heartland Valentine's Ball.

Giggles, lingering sighs, coy blushes: all this and more would follow. Jane chided herself for her cynicism, and she plastered what she hoped was a gracious smile on her face. She stepped into the ballroom to watch the festivities.

13

Cherry, she noticed, was across the room, standing very properly beside her mother.

The music came to an end; Pipkin, aided by several footmen, distributed the eagerly awaited valentines. Jane's long, delicate fingers twisted the heart-shaped locket that hung around her neck. Two Cupids cavorted wildly on its case, and normally she would have found such a piece of jewelry distasteful. But this was the Heartland locket; it had adorned the neck of each mistress of the house at the Valentine's Ball for the past four hundred years. Still, it created a heavy burden for Jane who recalled vividly her grandmother's recollections of how her grandfather would lovingly fasten it around her neck before each ball, saying that she would always be his valentine.

A deep voice sounded close to her ear; Jane managed to remain serene as his warm breath stirred the errant tendrils of brown hair resting on her neck.

"An interesting custom, this, and an interesting piece of jewelry, Miss Lindsay."

Not turning to face him, Jane replied, "Both have been in my family for several hundred years, Lord Devlin. I'm certain you, too, have cherished family traditions."

"I can see you have heard nothing about my family, Miss Lindsay. The only traditions the earls of Cheswicke have followed have been greed, misery, and lust. Not precisely laudable traits."

She turned, then wished she hadn't. Why did he have to stand so near? She struggled to maintain her facade of careless composure.

Lord Devlin lifted the locket from her hand, studying the ornate etchings in the heavy gold. "They seem to be struggling to control the ruby, just here," he said, rubbing his thumb across the heart-shaped ruby. "Is that, perhaps, a reflection of the struggle its beautiful owner must endure?"

"Rubbish!" said Jane harshly, her voice a trifle high.

He smiled, and she wondered how in the world she had been caught up in the typical drivel spouted by a man — especially this particular man. Why did he have the power to

14

rouse such uneasiness in her breast?

"Your valentines, Miss Jane," intoned Pipkin.

"Thank you, Pipkin. Is the buffet ready?" she asked, eagerly returning to her well-maintained discipline.

"Certainly, Miss Jane. Shall I tell the musicians to strike up the supper dance?"

"Yes, I suppose everyone has had a chance to read their cards and try to guess who wrote them."

The butler retreated, and Jane looked at the delicate lace basket in her hands. Valentine cards, some in envelopes, peered back at her. Suddenly, she wished she were anywhere except beside Lord Devlin. Why she should care what he thought of her, she dare not ask herself. Perhaps his referring to her as an acceptable chaperon still rankled. That was it, she decided.

"You must be the most popular lady at the ball, Miss Jane."

She glared directly into his teasing brown eyes. How dare he make free with her name! "They are merely courtesy greetings to the hostess of the ball, Lord Devlin."

He raised his brows at this cynical, and no doubt accurate observation.

"Then there is no one who has claimed you for the supper dance?"

"I do not dance this evening, sir."

"But you must sup," he persisted.

"I must tend to other matters, Lord Devlin, but I do thank you for thinking of me."

With this, Jane made her escape, crossing the floor quickly, and not slowing her pace until she gained the solitude of her own chamber.

She fumed, she raged, she castigated herself for being such a ninny. He was merely trying to captivate the most difficult female at the ball; that was why he had sought her out. He probably had a bet with someone; perhaps her horrid cousin, Roland. Or, more than likely, he was trying to win her approval so he could gain admittance to Heartland, and hence, to Cherry.

Seated in front of her mirror, her maid taking the pins from her hair, she studied herself as she hadn't done in ages. Her eyes were rather pretty, she conceded, but her mouth would never be described as delicate, or a rosebud. Her nose was good—neither too large nor too small. Her hair, as it cascaded freely around her shoulders was her best trait, but it was wasted now that she was past the age for wearing it down.

She grimaced as Tucker worked feverishly to confine one strand of the heavy tresses before another pin slipped its moorings. She couldn't prevent a smile, remembering the time at the seminary for young ladies when her friend Sally had persuaded her to cut her hair short, convincing her that without the heavy length, it would curl. After hours of trying to coax it to curl, they had finally given up, and she had been consigned to months of looking like one of Cromwell's Puritans. What a scold they had had to endure from the headmistress!

"Hmph! That'll do, Miss Jane. You'll last the rest of th' ball now. Have ye met any interestin' people?"

"Men, you mean, Tucker."

"Aye, well, there's no harm in that, Miss Jane."

"No, no harm at all. And as a matter of fact, I have made the acquaintance of one new gentleman, a viscount, if you please."

"Oh, Miss Jane, I'm so happy for you!" said the old servant.

"Don't be too happy. I can't think when I've met a more disagreeable man!"

Jane rose and left the room, while her maid tidied up the dressing table. She would have been surprised to find that her maid's smile had not faded at her last words. Instead, Tucker hummed a quiet song as she worked, for she had seen her mistress dismiss one man after another—nice young men they had been. Mayhap, thought the servant, what Miss Jane needed was a man who was more than a match for her. For her Miss Jane was no milk and water miss!

Still carrying the basket of valentines, Jane paused outside

16

her room and looked down the long corridor that led to the main rooms. She shook her head and headed in the opposite direction, opening a door that led to a narrow staircase. A single sconce of candles on the wall lighted the dark passageway as she hurried up the familiar steps.

She stopped in front of the first door and knocked, entering at the growled command, "Come."

"Hello, Nana," she said quietly, leaving the door ajar as the staleness of the air assailed her.

"Ah, child, so ye've not fergot yer old Nana on this special night," said the ancient servant who rocked incessantly in her low chair, her gnarled hands clutching its arms like claws.

"Of course not, Nana," said Jane.

Mindful of her skirts, Jane perched on the edge of the narrow bed. Its softness enveloped her, for it was of the finest down, the only privilege her old nurse had ever requested. Jane smoothed the covers, smiling gently as she recalled those stormy nights when she had fled the nursery and sought refuge in her Nana's feather bed.

Nana had always pretended to be asleep as she moved her heavy form to one side. It wasn't till morning that the old nurse would scold her for being such a naughty girl. Looking back, Jane realized this was probably because her fears were Nana's fears, and the comfort of a loved one warded off the evils of the storm for both of them.

When Jane had outgrown the nursery, Nana had remained, but she had ordered the windows nailed shut and locks placed on all the doors to ward off the piskies and faeries that haunted her Cornish soul.

And how many times had Jane sat and listened to those old tales of goblins and witches? Even when she was past the age to do so, she would wander up those stairs to Nana's room to hear the stories again and again.

Breaking into her reverie, the old nurse said, "So ye've brought yer valentines to share with Nana."

"Of course, you're better than I at guessing the authors of the anonymous ones."

Jane proceeded to read each verse aloud, telling the names

of the signed verses, and allowing her old nurse to help her guess the nameless ones. Most of Jane's were signed.

> "To the fairest of the fair,
> For fairness lies not in the person,
> But in the soul."
>
> An Admirer

"Mr. Primrose, or whatever the new curate's name is."

Jane laughed. "Right, of course. And here is one from Cherry with a sweet verse about sisters. Shall I read it?"

Nana shook her head. Cherry hadn't grown up at Heartland and was not a favorite of Nana's.

"Let's see, here's a different one; the handwriting is atrocious and 'tis merely written on a blank card.

> "Your beauty at first caught my eye. . . . But every moment that I converse with you steals in some new grace, heightens the picture and gives it stronger expression. . . . By all that's good, I can have no happiness but what's in your power to grant me. Nor shall I ever feel repentance, but in not having seen your merits before. I will stay, even contrary to your wishes; and though you should persist to shun me, I will make my respectful assiduities atone for the levity of my past conduct."
>
> An Admirer

Jane stared at the note, her smooth brow puckered in confusion.

"Can't place it. Doesn't sound like the usual verse. Don't think it can be any o' our local swains."

" 'Tis from *She Stoops To Conquer*," murmured Jane. She looked over at the old nurse and added, "A play by Oliver Goldsmith. Odd that anyone should be able to quote it. And it was obviously written in haste, so it can't have been prepared before the ball. And there's no lace or other decoration."

"Seems ye've a real admirer, dearie."

Jane shrugged off the suggestion and picked up another card, slipping the carelessly scribbled missive into her reticule. She would investigate further; not, she told herself, that she believed its contents. It was just a little mystery that would be amusing to solve. Probably one of Cherry's beaux who felt sorry for the spinster cousin. Perhaps Cherry had even suggested it, hoping to add to Jane's enjoyment of the evening. Yes, the more she thought about it, that was the most likely solution—and they had seen the play in Bath only last month.

"That's all, Nana," said Jane at length.

" 'Tis enough, I think, child. And one or two quite promising."

"Nana!"

"It would be good to see the nurseries at Heartland full with babies."

"I'm certain Cherry—"

"I didn't mean her babies, and well you know it! Now you go back to the ball and find the authors of those verses."

Jane shook her head at the ancient and smiled.

"Ah, so ye've someone in mind," said the nurse, misinterpreting that smile. Her rocker became motionless as she stared into Jane's green eyes.

Shaking off an uncomfortable eeriness, Jane said lightly, "Just an irritating man, Nana, but I assure you, I was not thinking of him. And he certainly never sent me a valentine tonight!"

But the old woman sat forward suddenly and grasped Jane's hands in hers. "Have a care, missy. He's a danger to yer heart, he is. I can feel it."

"What nonsense, Nana! Not to my heart! Perhaps Cherry's, but I'll soon put an end to that!"

"Ah, that one! She can look after 'erself, she can. Just like her namesake—she'll be carried away by a trickster like the King o' the Piskies, mind you!"

"I would hardly describe Lord Devlin in such a manner, Nana."

19

"And just how would you describe him, Miss Lindsay?" said the shadow standing in the doorway. It moved into the room and defined itself as Lord Devlin.

Jane let out an exasperated exclamation and turned to her old nurse who had covered her face with her shawl.

"Don't look at him, Miss Jane!" she whispered breathlessly.

"Now see what you've done with your skulking about! It is all right, Nana; it is only the man I had mentioned to you. He's not a spirit, just a very annoying guest." She glared up at him, and he grinned in response.

"I beg your pardon, madam, if I frightened you. I have an affinity for old houses, and I was merely exploring. I got a bit turned around and went farther than I had supposed." As this speech was administered in a calm, repentant voice, the old woman lowered her shawl and regarded him fiercely.

"Where are you from, boy?"

"Yorkshire."

"You don't sound it," she commented suspiciously, a frown creasing her wrinkled forehead.

"I have spent the past ten years abroad."

"Aye, that explains it." Nana cocked her head in Jane's direction and asked, "What do you want with my Jane?"

The viscount's eyes twinkled as Jane gasped, "Nana!"

With a serious demeanor, he responded, "I had hoped to persuade Miss Jane to return to the ball. I would like to learn more about this fascinating old house."

"Hmph!" said Jane.

"Then that's all right. You two run along. I've got to get my rest, I do. Good night, my lord. Good night, missy."

Jane stood up, looking irresolutely from the viscount's proffered arm to the old woman who had closed her eyes and resumed rocking.

"Good night, Nana," she said, grimacing as she placed her gloved hand on Lord Devlin's sleeve.

He reached past her, his chest brushing against her breast as he retrieved the lace basket and her reticule from the bed. The white card fell from the reticule and he caught it. He picked it up, quickly digesting its contents.

"Goldsmith, I believe."

Jane took the card and pushed it more securely into the reticule as he commented, "It seems you have at least one valentine that you deemed worthy of separating from the others. What a fortunate fellow."

"Poppycock!" snapped Jane.

They had reached the top of the stairs, and Jane paused, waiting for the viscount to go first. He, however, seemed disinclined to release her arm, only tucking it closer, trapping her hand against his side as they descended the narrow stairs.

"The candles have gone out," said Jane as she realized they were in total darkness.

"Are you afraid of the dark, Miss Jane, or perhaps only of me?" asked her companion.

"I am afraid of neither, sir, but I must admit I find the minor irritations of life vexatious."

What a rich laugh he had, she thought, and realized she was smiling. Recovering immediately, she reflected how fortunate it was that they were immersed in darkness.

"I believe we are at the bottom, Miss Jane." She stopped in her tracks and he turned to face her. "What? Unwilling to call our little tête-à-tête at an end?"

Not betrayed into revealing her temper, Jane said quietly, staring at what she believed to be his face, "You are insufferably arrogant, aren't you, Lord Devlin?"

Again that laugh. "Perhaps, Miss Jane, I am merely voicing my own hopes."

"And untruthful, as well."

"Then perhaps I should prove my words." With this, he embraced her, pinning her arms to her sides as his lips sought hers.

"I shall scream!"

"And how will you explain our presence here together? Come, kiss me."

His lips tasted vaguely of liquor, and Jane tried to concentrate on this instead of on the lightheaded feeling that was creeping over her. But the fight was impossible, as his kiss became more demanding, his tongue probing relentlessly, and she swayed, pressing against him. He groaned and released her arms, but instead of using these weapons to pummel his chest as any gently reared lady should have, Jane slipped her arms around his neck and wound her fingers into his dark curly hair.

Some part of her remained dimly aware of her wanton behavior, but she had no wish to stop. It was her turn to groan as she tried to press even closer, an impossible feat, under the circumstances.

Then he was setting her away from him; Jane managed to stifle a whimper of protest, and immediately began straightening her gown.

His breath came in short, rasping waves as he stammered, "I'll escort you back to the ballroom, Miss Lindsay."

So now she was to be called Miss Lindsay. "That will not be necessary, Lord Devlin. You go on without me."

He opened the door behind him and backed out, leaving her weak and confused.

Recovering her wits, Jane hurried to her chamber, shocking her dresser with the state of her hair. Tucker scolded her charge mildly with the privilege of an old retainer. As Jane remained silent, wrapped in her own thoughts, Tucker ceased her diatribe, studying her mistress with a puzzled frown.

When the maid had finished, Jane thanked her and left the room.

The guests were beginning to return to the ballroom from supper, their voices heightened by drink and the excitement and challenge of blooming romance. The musicians began to play a country dance, sets were made up, bows and curtseys performed, and the ballroom came to life once more.

Jane's satin-slippered toes silently tapped the marble floor. An unaccustomed restlessness assailed her, and she forced herself to sit calmly, watching the guests who were viewing the valentine greetings from years past which were displayed between each of the French doors that lined one wall of the grand ballroom.

The tradition of displaying Valentines given at former balls had been introduced by her grandmother. Starting with her own Valentine greetings as a debutante, she had searched the attic trunks for more. The oldest was from a great-great-great grandfather to one of the famed beauties of his day. That faded date read 1691.

And so, their collection had grown, as friends donated their favorite cards, some decorated with lace and velvet, a few decorated with precious gems.

The chaperons' chairs were arranged in little groups, far enough away from the French doors to allow people to stroll beside them.

Where was Cherry? she wondered, thinking that she wished she had found a way to escape this enforced inactivity. Still, she knew she would always do that which was proper. Impropriety was as foreign to her as civilization was to an aborigine.

Jane's thoughts and eyes were drawn back to the dancers. Dark eyes met hers as Lord Devlin promenaded past with Anne Powell, her nearest neighbor; for once, Jane found it impossible to hold his gaze. She dropped her eyes self-consciously.

Rising swiftly, she tried to appear her usual calm self as she moved among the guests viewing the valentine display.

"Jane, my dear, whose billet was this?" asked a rotund matron in a purple satin turban.

"That was one of my mother's, I believe, Lady Tarpley."

"She was such a beauty with that red hair and those great blue eyes." The dame, who had been a great friend, as well as rival of her grandmother, looked Jane up and down. "You always resembled your father's side of the family, Jane dear."

"Yes, ma'am. I am definitely a Lindsay," said Jane dryly. "Did you know we have one of your valentines on display this year?"

"Really?" trilled the grande dame. "Where? I don't remember giving one to dear Janine."

"Actually, Lady Tarpley, I believe Lord Tarpley gave it to

her after last year's ball. He told her it was one he had written before you and he became well acquainted, and he had been too shy to send it to you. He planned to surprise you by having Grandmother put it up with the others this year."

"That naughty man! Show it to me!"

"It is in the next group. There," said Jane, pointing to an elaborately decorated heart with faded writing. The old dame peered myopically at the print before sighing deeply and smiling.

"I must see Herbert," she said, and, with a flurry of purple silk, hurried toward the card room where her husband had remained hidden all evening.

Jane smiled. Lord Tarpley was in for an embarrassing moment in front of his cronies.

Jane drifted back to the stately door on her left and peered into the dimly lighted garden beyond.

A movement on the balcony caught her eye. Odd, she thought, that anyone should have chosen to stroll outside on such a chilly February evening. She rose and moved toward the doors, pressing close to the cold glass. She gaped in astonishment as a woman in a dark cloak hurried across the wide balcony and down the steps. A flash of silvery material was all Jane needed to guess the female's identity.

Quickly, she slipped out the doors. The shock of cold air made her pull her flimsy shawl closer about her shoulders as she stopped, allowing her eyes to grow accustomed to the gloom. There, heading for the summer house, was Cherry, the foolish chit!

Jane muttered a mild oath under her breath before heading for the balustrade. If she took the time to go across the terrace to the steps, she wouldn't catch up in time. In time for what? she asked herself.

Without further thought, Jane hitched up her skirts, climbed onto the railing, and dropped into the flower beds below. A sharp pain shot through her ankle making her pause, gulping down the cold winter air. She closed her eyes, willing the pain to be brief. As it receded, she tested the joint gingerly. It was tender, but she'd only twisted it.

Quickly, she trudged out of the damp earth and onto the gravel pathway. Hurrying as fast as her ankle and skirts would allow, she pursued her quarry. The intricately carved woodwork of the summer house loomed before her; her ankle continued to ache dully. Just wait! she thought, till I get my hands on you, Cherry! Just you wait!

The door was open, and she could hear quiet voices from within as she slowed her pace and finally stopped outside. Pausing to catch her breath, she recognized the deep voice of a man.

The summer house was little more than a large gazebo. In warmer times, Jane loved to escape to its quiet and relaxing atmosphere. It had been built before she was born, and with her grandmother's permission, she had added a fireplace as well as removable glass panels to cover the open windows during the winter months. Somehow, Cherry's deception hurt Jane more deeply since her clandestine meeting was taking place in this, Jane's favorite retreat.

Taking a deep breath, Jane entered. The moon and the light from a lone candle afforded her the great satisfaction of witnessing her cousin's startled expression. Young Lord Pierce nearly threw Cherry's hand back at her as he leapt away from Cherry's side.

"Jane! I can explain—"

"Really? You can explain away your wanton, not to mention disrespectful, behavior? I should love to hear it, but there really isn't time. You see, your absence is no doubt being remarked, as well as mine and Lord Pierce's. I wonder what interesting conclusions our guests are forming," said Jane dryly.

"Please, Miss Jane, allow me to assure you that Cherry, uh, Miss Pettigrew—"

"You cannot explain away ill manners, Lord Pierce" interrupted Jane, stressing his title. No matter if they had known Lord Pierce since he was in shortcoats, she would not allow him to minimize the gravity of the situation. "Cherry, go to your room. I will tell your mother you had the headache and retired early."

"I will not!" exclaimed Cherry, showing her natural spirit finally. "Just because you didn't get to enjoy a Valentine's Ball when you were eighteen, you don't want me to! Well, I'm not going to end up a sour old maid like—"

"Cherry!"

Lord Pierce's startled protest silenced Cherry as nothing Jane might have said could have. She turned horrified blue eyes on the young lord, stammered an apology, and fled.

"Miss Lindsay, she was overwrought. I take full responsibility."

"Never mind, Lord Pierce, I am well aware my cousin regrets her words. She is already forgiven. Please, return to the ball; I would not wish your dual absence to become fodder for the gossipmongers."

"As you wish," he replied, bowing elegantly before leaving her.

Jane sought the nearest chair and collapsed. She had been truthful in telling Lord Pierce she had already forgiven her cousin. Still, she found an unutterable fatigue settling over her, and her ankle was beginning to throb abominably.

"May I join you?"

Now what? thought Jane, as she looked up to find Lord Devlin towering over her.

"What are you doing here?" she asked rudely, not caring anymore to play the gracious hostess.

Taking her question as his cue to join her on the settee, Lord Devlin responded, "I was on the balcony when Miss Pettigrew escaped, and when you leapt the balcony railing, quite gracefully, I might add. I'm afraid my curiosity got the better of me, and I simply followed you. I didn't wish to interfere, so I awaited the conclusion of the contretemps."

"How noble of you, Lord Devlin. Now, if you'll excuse me, I should return to my guests," said Jane, getting to her feet and willing her ankle to hold firm.

Devlin stood also, rising above her as few gentlemen could. He must be well over six feet tall, she thought. Then she shook her head, reminding herself firmly that her presence here with Lord Devlin would be construed in much the same light as Cherry's ill-advised rendezvous.

Jane took one step and her ankle wobbled; she grasped his arms as he steadied her. "Thank you, Lord Devlin," she said, not daring to look up into his dark eyes as a thrill coursed through her body at his light touch.

"You've hurt yourself," he said.

"A mere strain of the ankle. I am quite all right." She took two unsteady steps, clenching her teeth.

"Yes, I can see you are fine. Here, allow me." He swept her into his strong arms as though she were a mere child and returned her to the settee.

He knelt at her feet, lifting her skirts ever so slightly; his manner very businesslike, he began to touch her ankles gently.

"Which one is it?"

"It's the—Ah!"

"Right one," he concluded. "It seems to be a bit swollen, but I don't feel a break."

"Thank you so very much, Dr. Devlin."

"You're quite welcome, Miss Lindsay. Happy to be of service."

He ran his hand a short way up her calf, and Jane gasped indignantly, "You, sir, are no gentleman!"

He laughed, and Jane's treacherous sense of humor threatened to overcome her indignation.

"That, Miss Lindsay, is quite true. I am not a gentleman, not in the sense this insane society defines the word."

Jane thought she detected a note of bitterness in his voice. She tried to read his face, but the dim candlelight made it impossible.

Timidly, she ventured to comment, "You seem almost proud, or relieved, to be able to confess that, sir."

He shrugged and rose. "And you are surprised, because you cannot imagine being anything but what you are, a very proper young lady."

"Hardly a young lady."

"Ah, now you are fishing for compliments. Very well, have it your way: a very proper not-so-young lady."

27

She glared up at him as he reached down and gathered her into his strong arms again.

She began to struggle, saying, "Please, Lord Devlin, put me down!" When he didn't comply, her voice became shrill. "I said put me down!"

He stopped, but didn't release her. "If you wish to scream, my dear, do so. But I believe it would defeat your purpose to have everyone come to your aid."

She flashed him an angry glare before folding her arms. He took a few steps and then faltered, pretending to be losing his grip. Jane threw her arms about his neck.

"Much better," he commented, smiling down into her fuming face. "Now, which door? I don't suppose you wish to enter through the ballroom."

"The library," she said flatly. "Around the side of the house."

They were in luck; no guests had found their way to the library, and their entrance went undetected.

"I suppose I should thank you, sir, for coming to my rescue," said Jane grudgingly.

He cocked his head to one side, fixing her with a wicked grin. "I assure you, Miss Lindsay, the pleasure was all mine."

Jane, who was reclining on a leather couch, tried to throw him a haughty look, but she couldn't. Really, the man was too absurd.

Instead, her eyes flitted about the room, coming to rest on a slim book on the table at her side. Frowning, she lifted it and turned it over.

"She Stoops to Conquer," she read quietly.

"An excellent play, as I recall, though it has been some time since I saw it performed," commented his lordship as he knelt at her feet.

Jane's eyes focused on his position. "What are you doing?"

"Examining your ankle again now that I can see it."

Jane moved her legs as far away from him as possible. "You'll do no such thing! I am perfectly all right!"

"And that is why you walked so gracefully into the house just now," came the sarcastic reply as he reached for her

28

again, one large hand encircling her slim ankle as the other probed gently. Jane winced, trying to withdraw. Lord Devlin nodded in satisfaction. "Just a slight turn; I daresay in two days' time you'll not even feel it."

"Thank you again ever so much!" snapped Jane.

He was grinning up at her from his kneeling position when the door opened silently. Jane closed her eyes. It needed only this!

But it was only Pipkin, Heartland's butler, and a more loyal servant one could not find. Thank heaven for that, thought Jane.

"Ah, Pipkin, the very man!" said Lord Devlin, rising quickly. "Your mistress has injured her ankle — slightly, to be sure — but she will require some assistance to gain her chamber. Be so good as to summon two stout footmen to make her a chair."

Pipkin's properly disinterested gaze swept from his lordship to his mistress, and he nodded regally.

Jane, fuming at the insinuation that the task would require "two stout footmen" snapped, "Just tell Mickey to come here, Pipkin."

Again the butler nodded, saying ominously to no one in particular, "Confess your faults one to another, and pray one for another, that ye may be healed. The effectual fervent prayer of a righteous man availeth much. James 5:16." With this, the butler bowed and left the room.

Jane, who was flexing her ankle cautiously, did not at first perceive Lord Devlin's astounded expression. But as the silence lengthened, she turned her attention from her injury and met his startled gaze.

To say the sober Miss Lindsay giggled might have been too extreme a suggestion, but her laughter did bubble forth uncontrollably for a brief moment.

"What," said his lordship slowly, "was that?"

Still smiling, Jane said, "Pardon me, I forget how startling Pipkin's pronouncements can be to the unsuspecting."

"You mean he is in the habit of spouting biblical dictums?"

"I'm afraid so."

"Why do you put up with it?"

"Because he is Pipkin. He is as much a part of Heartland as I am; more, perhaps, because he's been here longer. I suspect he has Methodist tendencies."

"Fellow ought to be reprimanded for his impertinence at the very least."

"Oh no, I wouldn't dare. Besides he doesn't mean it as an insult. At times, his selection is so apt. Why, I remember once when a half-pay officer was hanging about after my mother. When he called one day, my mother was out, and Pipkin, bless his soul, while informing this roué, added quite appropriately, 'And there shall in no wise enter into it any thing that defileth, neither whatsoever worketh abomination, or maketh a lie.' The fortune hunter never returned."

"Still, he must prove an embarrassment at times," protested Lord Devlin.

"Not at all. Anyone with an entree to Heartland knows Pipkin and makes allowances."

"Then I suppose I must, too."

Devlin smiled down at her, his dark eyes holding a promise—or should she regard it as a threat? wondered Jane.

They both looked expectantly toward the opening door.

"I see, Miss Lindsay that your rescuers have arrived, so I will take my leave of you this evening. I shall call tomorrow to see how you are faring."

"Thank you, Lord Devlin," replied Jane, ever conscious of the eyes and ears of the servants. "Good night."

As the darkly handsome Lord Devlin bowed and exited, Jane stared into the dying embers of the fire and fought the feelings that settled on her shoulders. She closed her eyes and took a deep breath before addressing the footman.

"I hope I shan't be too heavy for you, Mickey."

Looking up at his hulking figure, Jane watched the footman's blank face become wreathed in a smile. "You're nothing but a feather, Miss Jane, to old Mickey."

She returned his friendly, childlike smile, and said, "But that is because you are so strong, Mickey."

Deeming it time to interrupt, Pipkin said firmly, "Take

Miss Jane to her room, Mickey. Then you can go to the kitchen for a snack."

The large man smacked his lips and reached for Jane. Though his movements were often rough, he lifted her as gently as if she were a fragile kitten.

Having attained her bedchamber and dismissed her maid, Jane Lindsay tried to clear her mind of the confusing events of the past evening. Certainly, this Valentine's Ball had been different from any other she had attended. Lord Devlin had seen to that.

And why? She still could not fathom his motives. He had been alternately amused by her, amusing to her, gruff, dictatorial, and . . . yes, and passionate. What did it all mean?

After several Seasons in London, Jane thought of herself as sophisticated, perhaps even cynical. She was certainly practiced in recognizing all the forms of flirtation. But Lord Devlin's actions and attitudes didn't fit any of the patterns she'd encountered before. His wasn't the die-away air of the poet, nor did he shower her with compliments. And though he had kissed her without permission, she didn't feel he deserved the title of rake. Of course, she might be mistaken; she would have to write to her friend Sally. Perhaps he was merely trying to be interesting.

And that was one thing, decided Jane firmly, Lord Devlin was not—interesting!

Just then there was a scratching at the door.

"Come in."

"Jane . . . Jane, I . . ."

Jane opened her arms and the teary-eyed Cherry flew across the thick carpet and into the comforting embrace, babbling apologies all the while.

"You must understand, dearest Jane, I was so very distraught."

"I do understand, but you must be made to realize that if tonight's actions were an example of how you expect to conduct yourself in London, you will quickly be the talk of the town. And not very pretty talk either."

"I know, I know, and I promise you, my behavior will be

31

exemplary."

"Then we will speak no more about it."

Cherry sat up, drying her tears as best she could with the soggy scrap of lace she still clutched in her hand. With her back half-turned to Jane, she said, "You know, it really wasn't as terrible a Valentine Ball after all."

"How is that, Cherry?" said Jane cautiously.

"Well, Lord Pierce did arrive, and it was just as you said. Upon his arrival, he sought me out immediately. It seems his sister Mary made them late, made them all late. He was in a towering rage over it, but I told him very prettily that one could not leave the house with one's hair not perfectly styled."

Jane smiled. "That was very charitable of you."

"I thought so. And then, of course, we also had an interesting new guest."

"Who might that be?"

"Why, my Lord Devlin, of course. Have you ever seen such a handsome man? And fascinating. I do hope he will call again."

"I believe he plans to remain in Bath for some time. I have a feeling," said Jane, "we have not seen the last of Lord Devlin."

Later that evening when Cherry's girlish confidences had wound down, Jane reflected on that last statement. And she wondered if it were true. And then she wondered why she wondered.

It was all so vexing for one such as herself who had always been so logical, predictable, to have these doubts, this curiosity disturbing her peace of mind.

♡   *Chapter Two*   ♡

The day after the grand Valentine's Ball at Heartland was usually as busy as the day before. Guests who had stayed the night rose at their leisure, consumed a huge breakfast buffet, and finally took their leave by two or three in the afternoon.

By that time, the guests who had returned to Bath were beginning to arrive to congratulate the hostesses and offer huge floral tributes that seemed to suck the very air from the stately rooms. Previously, Jane escaped these trying visits by spending her afternoon on horseback as far from the house as possible.

But this year was different. This year, she was the mistress of Heartland, and even her flibbertigibbit Aunt Sophie had seen fit to remind her of her duty. With her own lecture to Cherry still ringing in her ears, she knew she couldn't justify deserting her aunt. She grimaced at Cherry who lost no time in appropriating the first young male caller as a suitable escort for a drive.

For Jane, though, there was no escape, so she received their visitors while reclining on the gold fainting couch in the gold salon, her foot propped up on a pillow, a lace shawl arranged over her lap. And she smiled and smiled, until her cheeks ached, endeavoring to be witty and attentive when all she really longed for was solitude and quiet.

And that was all she wanted, Jane told herself as she stifled a flash of pique when Pipkin announced Lady Tarpley and her mousy husband Herbert. Had all her guests been as insipid last night as they appeared by daylight? She closed her eyes, banishing such social heresy from her mind.

Still, Jane had to admit to herself, the day would have proven less dull if the irritating Lord Devlin had made an appearance. It was not that she wanted to see him, she told herself. It was merely that he had said he would call to see how her ankle was.

That was the problem, Jane assured herself, Lord Devlin was committing a social solecism by not calling. And Jane believed in behaving in a socially proper manner at all times. Really, the man lacked refinement. And she was delighted that he hadn't called.

"Miss Jane," said Pipkin quietly in her ear.

"Yes?"

"A card has arrived for you, and a flower."

Jane looked up sharply. It was unusual for Pipkin to act in such a secretive manner. His very correct butler's expression became more blank, and Jane took his cue. Excusing herself to her aunt and their guests, she leaned on Pipkin's arm as she limped into Heartland's grand entrance hall.

On a silver tray in the reception room just inside the massive front doors lay a single red rose and underneath, a card trimmed in fine lace. Jane again looked to Pipkin for an explanation.

"It was delivered moments ago by a rather grubby urchin who gave it to the footman and ran. He, of course, left it to me to decide if it might be worthy of your attention."

"And you think it is?" asked Jane, unsure of herself for once.

"I thought a mere letter and rose could not harm you, Miss Jane, 'for in the multitude of dreams and many words there are also divers vanities: but fear thou God.' "

With this cryptic scripture, the butler backed away, closing the great double doors.

Picking up the card, Jane recognized the hasty scrawl from the *She Stoops to Conquer* card of the ball. Though the decorations on this card were elaborate, the sentiment was short.

> "If you keep me at this distance, how is it
> possible you and I can be ever acquainted?"
>
> Yours

Jane reread it twice, frowning all the while. Really, this was becoming tiresome. While last night's card had been intriguing, this one was unnecessarily obtuse. How could she become acquainted with a phantom? And why would she want to?

Jane stood up, smoothing her elegant gown with her brows knitted. She had thought it one of Cherry's ill-advised kindnesses, but Cherry had enough sense not to continue such a charade. And from anyone else, a missive like this was pure nonsense. Not malicious, perhaps, but certainly not worthy of her notice.

With this decision made, Jane returned to the gold salon, steeling herself for participation in the social niceties for the remainder of the afternoon.

Finally the steady flow became a trickle, leaving only a few of her aunt's bosom friends gossiping gleefully. Jane pleaded a headache and escaped to the privacy of her room.

Tucker, who had a tendency to fuss any time Jane was indisposed, was soon dismissed, leaving Jane to the latest Gothic novel from Duffield's.

The dressing bell rang; Jane toyed with the idea of calling for a tray in her room rather than face more conversation. But again, she knew what was expected of her, so she donned her pale gray evening dress and descended to the dining room.

Jane participated very little in the conversation swirling around her as Aunt Sophie and Cherry discussed and dissected each person's dress, manners, and speech. Their words were not spoken in a malicious manner; rather, it was merely social conversation — what was expected of them. But neither her aunt nor her cousin truly wished to shred anyone's reputation: they were both too kindhearted.

Since Sophie Pettigrew and her daughter were hopeless romantics, a great deal of their exchange dealt with speculations on the couples who had called that day when only the night before they had not been couples. But through a valentine card, a verse, or a scrap of lace, two lives had suddenly become intertwined. And like matching cards in a game of chance, some pairs were discarded while others were formed.

And finally Cherry hit upon the one name which Jane had managed to dismiss while she had buried herself in that dreadful novel.

"Where was Lord Devlin?" asked Cherry. "Did he call while I was out driving with Mr. Fitzhugh?"

"Oh! You mean that dark-haired man your cousin brought? Such a frightful gentleman!" said her mother, fluttering her shawl as she spoke.

"Frightful? I would say delightful!" sighed Cherry. "And so handsome! Did you know he's spent the last ten years abroad, Mother? Some barbarous island. Cousin Roland was telling me about the place—flowers blooming everywhere, immense beaches of white sand stretching forever, deep blue water. How I would love to go there!"

Her mother smiled indulgently and added, "And no doubt have a handsome husband to guide you, my dear."

Cherry's giggles intruded rudely on the picture Jane's mind had been building of this wondrous island of warmth and beauty. She looked up from her trifle and delivered a repressive frown at mother and daughter.

Laying her fork aside, Jane said firmly, "I must go to bed. My ankle is beginning to throb. I hope you'll not take offense if I bid you good night."

Her aunt and cousin got to their feet and hurried to her side as Pipkin stepped forward, helping her rise. Her awkwardly hasty retreat was accompanied by their sincere expressions of concern.

Jane knew she was behaving strangely, and she felt guilty for worrying them needlessly. Her ankle was not bothering her in the least, just as Lord Devlin had predicted, but she thought she would have gone mad had she been forced to endure one more story about one more guest, especially that particular guest.

Later, as she arranged herself for sleep in the huge feather bed, Jane's mind drifted back to her aunt's original description of Lord Devlin.

"Frightful," she had called him. Jane recalled that she, too, had considered his darkly handsome appearance a bit too forceful at first. But frightful?

As she fell asleep, her only remembrances of Lord Devlin were the sensations caused by the touch of his lips on hers.

As soon as Jane got out of bed the next morning, she tested her ankle and was relieved to find it strong as she took a turn about the room.

Tucker entered with her morning chocolate. "Oh, Miss Jane, do be careful. Why I remember my cousin—you remember my cousin Jim—he got a catch in his neck, refused to go to bed, and now he has to walk with his head layin' on his shoulder."

Jane smothered her laughter and said kindly, "I hardly think an ankle and a neck the same case, Tucker."

"Not exactly, but you can never be too careful."

"I shall be very careful," promised Jane, obediently sinking onto the green chaise lounge.

Tucker placed the tray she carried on the table at Jane's side. Pouring steaming chocolate into the fine Sèvres cup, Tucker asked, "You'll be riding today, Miss Jane?"

"Yes, I think I'll have Mrs. Brown pack a light nuncheon and ride to the Abbey."

"Alone, Miss Jane?" When Jane nodded, Tucker said, "Ain't right, you ridin' all that way without so much as a groom."

"Now, Tucker, it is not as though I am a child."

"Yer a gently bred, unmarried lady and shouldn't be out alone like that."

"On my own estate?"

Ignoring her charge, Tucker continued. "Besides, the abbey's dangerous. Who knows when a good wind will tumble down another wall. Ye might be hurt."

Jane drained her cup and stood up, towering over the rotund little maid. Patting Tucker's arm, Jane said. "You may be right, but it is the one place I can escape where no one will follow me. And after yesterday, dear Tucker, I must get away before I give full rein to my tongue and tell my sweet aunt or cousin to go to the devil."

This absurdity brought a reluctant grin to her servant's face. Shaking her head, Tucker moved to the wardrobe and began removing Jane's black riding habit.

"As if you ever would," she said over her shoulder. "Ye'd best wear your woolen cloak. The sun's out, but there's a frightful winter wind."

Galloping across the home wood, Jane felt the cobwebs blow away. Leaning closer to the sleek sorrel's neck, she urged him on and over the first wooden fence.

Slowing her mount, Jane thought this was what she had needed all along. The worries and stress of the ball were forgotten in the exhilaration of the wind blowing her hair free of the confining chignon at the nape of her neck.

And as for the disturbing Lord Devlin? He was naught but an annoying fly swept from her mind by the freedom enveloping her. His lordship had no strange hold on her; she had merely been suffering from a fit of the dismals.

She stroked Sinbad's glossy neck and pulled him up at the top of the hill that overlooked the stately old mansion with its green lawns and surrounding woods.

"Now, isn't this better, my beauty? I wager you've been feeling miserable, too, confined to the pasture this past week." The horse's ears flicked backwards as he listened to his mistress's voice. "This is where we both belong," said Jane firmly. A gentle touch of the reins sent the horse down the far side of the hill.

It took almost an hour for Jane to reach her destination, the old ruin of an abbey of the eighth or ninth century. The setting had been a favorite of her father's who had fancied himself an amateur antiquarian. He had often taken his small daughter with him when he "researched" the site, and Jane felt closest to his memory when she visited the abbey.

Tying Sinbad inside the wall of what had once been a large stone chapel, she made her way to the altar. This area still boasted four walls, but the roof had burned and fallen in several hundred years before. Indeed, her father estimated the abbey had been abandoned in the fourteenth or fifteenth century.

Out of habit, Jane brushed off the stone slab where she imagined a smooth wooden altar had once stood. Sitting down, she remembered how as a child she had pretended the raised stone platform was her oven and had "baked" all sorts of exotic dishes. She smiled and leaned back on her elbows, staring up at the chilly blue February skies.

Once, when her father had wandered into the alcove and found her reclining on the stone slab pretending to be a sleeping princess, he had rebuked her for defiling a holy place. She had turned her inquisitive emerald eyes on her father and said, "I don't think the monks will mind, Papa; I shan't get it dirty."

He had tousled her long, straight hair and said quite seriously, "Then I suppose it will be alright with them." Jane smiled at the memory.

Later, as a romantic young miss on holiday from school, she had been wont to escape the annoying attentions of her young cousin Cherry, who had by that time come to live at Heartland, by riding to the abbey. This had required slipping the supervision of the groom assigned to her also, because the crumbling abbey had been responsible for her father's death.

One of the outer walls had collapsed on him, trapping his

legs beneath a small mountain of stone. Jane had been away at school when it occurred. In her young mind, she had blamed herself—if only she had been with him, he would not have been pinned underneath. She would have released him in time or, at least, ridden for help immediately. As it was, it was the next day before they had found him. The circulation in his legs had been cut off too long; the bones in one thigh were crushed. He lived almost two years, but being an invalid took the heart out of him, and he was never the same.

Only his daughter had been able to bring a smile to his face. It was he who had insisted she not blame the abbey, saying that he could not bear it if his clumsiness destroyed all the wonderful memories of the place they had shared.

So Jane continued to visit the abbey whenever she could. Her visits brought her comfort, rather than grief, for she never failed to visualize her father stepping through the grassy, stone-strewn cloisters.

On this day, as on all others, Jane felt only a deep peace settling on her troubled spirit. When she closed her eyes to the clouds floating across the sky, she could almost hear her father say, "Well, my sleeping princess, can I wake you with a kiss, or will that turn me into a toad?"

After an hour of solitude, the very proper Miss Lindsay said good-bye to her special retreat and remounted, her equilibrium once more restored.

Jane pulled back on the reins as she and Sinbad reached the top of the hill overlooking Heartland. She surveyed the valley and the road leading to the house. The drive was lined with trees, and she could not decide if that was actually a carriage she had glimpsed moving toward the house.

She shrugged; it didn't matter now, she felt quite capable of playing the gracious hostess. She sent the horse down the hillside at a gentle trot.

Where the trees reached the vast lawn, they stopped, and the drive of crushed seashells turned to the left, before dividing, one path leading toward the front door, and the other to the stables behind the house.

There was a carriage approaching the house, a rider at its side. Who could it be? she wondered. Surely all of Bath had been to Heartland the day before; there could be no one else left to call.

Even as this thought crossed her mind, Jane realized there was one guest who had not visited the previous day. She studied the rider and horse carefully. It was a huge horse, possibly seventeen hands, yet the rider was not dwarfed by the giant steed. Yes, she thought sourly, it had to be he; he sat so casually in the saddle, seemingly relaxed, though the horse crab-stepped back and forth, trying its best to run away with the bit. She was too far away to see his face, but she felt certain it was Lord Devlin.

Jane gave an impatient exclamation and slowed her restive mount to a walk. Perhaps, if she dawdled, she wouldn't be forced to endure this particular visit. It was cowardly of her, Jane admitted, but she felt unwilling to surrender her peace of mind, and another encounter with Lord Devlin just might produce that effect.

She watched as the rider leaned over, evidently speaking to the occupant of the carriage before turning his horse in her direction.

Jane also turned her horse — nonchalantly, she hoped — and headed back into the line of trees on the top of the hill. Moments later, she heard the rapid approach of a horse and muttered, "Drat the man!"

"Why, Miss Lindsay, avoiding me?" said Devlin's deep voice.

"Not precisely," she lied.

"Ah, then you mistook me for someone else."

The self-satisfaction in his tone made Jane want to grind her teeth. Instead, she shook her head, determined to be civil to this arrogant lord.

"Not at all, Lord Devlin, as a matter of fact, I did not see you; I merely decided to extend my ride."

"Then how fortunate for me, Miss Lindsay." He smiled, but the expression failed to reach his eyes, leaving Jane to

41

wonder at his meaning. He turned his attention to the view of the house and its grounds below.

Jane grimaced, then stole a glance at his profile. He seemed almost forbidding. Perhaps this is the side of Lord Devlin her aunt had witnessed, which would account for Aunt Sophie's strange opinion of the man.

But why should she care one way or another? she asked herself. And why did he have to show up now? Why did he always surface just when she had said something or had done something that was not quite the thing, for he obviously did not believe her story about extending her ride.

Truly, he was a vexing man with extremely poor timing. He had witnessed her disastrous leap over the balcony; he had overheard her tirade against Lord Pierce and Cherry, and most of all, and certainly worst of all, Lord Devlin had been the cause of that most improper kiss. Of course, she thought objectively, he had not experienced that kiss alone.

All these thoughts flashed through Jane's mind as she carefully placed a smile upon her face. In tones reminiscent of her cousin, she said, "La, Lord Devlin, it was just that I was enjoying this beautiful day, so rare for February."

His handsome face became set in an odd expression, his nostrils slightly flared, his eyes hooded, and his sensual mouth drooped at the corners. "I quite know how you feel, Miss Lindsay," he drawled. "But as it happens, I was not on a solitary ride; I was calling to see how your ankle fares. I see, however, that my concern was quite unnecessary. You have obviously recovered from your indisposition."

"Yes, I am much better." Jane deemed it time to change the subject. "Who was with you in the carriage, Lord Devlin?"

"Your cousin, Mr. Havelock. I happened upon him as I was strolling in Bath, and he insisted on my accompanying him in his phaeton." Jane arched one brow at the implication that he had not planned on coming to call at all. "Unfortunately," continued the viscount, "there was not room enough for the two of us to be comfortable."

Unbidden, a small bubble of laughter came to Jane's lips, and this time, when she looked at Lord Devlin, his smile lighted his dark eyes with warmth.

"Just so," he said, his tone adding to her amusement.

"You are too bad, sir." She tried to sound severe, but she fooled no one.

"Not at all," he responded. "And to be quite truthful, I thought a ride by myself infinitely preferable to being cooped up in a carriage on such a beautiful day. I invited your cousin to return to his lodgings and get his own hack, but he informed me that he doesn't ride."

"No, I'm afraid Cousin Roland does not favor this mode of transportation; he never has. I believe it is due to the fact he had an unfortunate accident as a child."

"Took a nasty spill?"

"So to speak; he mounted his pony one day, and the poor beast just lay down and died."

She was rewarded for this revelation by Lord Devlin's rich laugh. Jane decided it would be rude not to join in.

Finally, wiping tears from her brilliant green eyes, she admitted, "It was a very old pony."

Lord Devlin dissolved into laughter again. When he could speak, he turned merry brown eyes on her and said, "You are roasting me, Miss Lindsay."

"On my honor, I promise you it did happen. Poor Roly never recovered from the embarrassment."

Suddenly, she eyed him uneasily. Her voice was filled with concern as she said, "I should not have told you, sir. I can't fathom why I did; I do hope you will not repeat—"

"Let me assure you, Miss Lindsay, the story will go no further," said Devlin, very much on his dignity.

They continued to ride along the rim of the small valley, the silence lengthening awkwardly.

Jane's mind turned over various topics of conversation, but they had already dealt with the weather and Lord Devlin's reason for coming to visit.

Jane wondered uncomfortably why she suddenly found it

difficult to engage in trivial social conversation. She had never experienced such a problem before. True, she did not flirt and sparkle like some young ladies; she never had, but neither had she been known to struggle to keep a conversation flowing.

Finally, though of course she had no real interest in his response, Jane asked, "What brings you to Bath, Lord Devlin?"

He hesitated before answering, "I am looking for a home for my mother."

"Does she live in London now?"

"No, York."

"Goodness, that is quite a distance from here. Wouldn't a house in London be better?" Now why, thought Jane, did I ask such a personal question?

"No, my mother does not like London society. I think Bath will suit her admirably."

"Yes, I suppose many older people prefer the milder climate here."

"Mother is hardly old; I daresay she's not even turned fifty yet."

"Don't you know for certain?"

He waved an impatient hand. "I have only seen her for a week in the past ten years. And before that, I was too young to think of such things."

"Then she has been living alone all these years. How dreadful for her."

His bark of laughter had nothing to do with amusement. "She has had my uncle for company, the illustrious earl of Cheswick."

Jane recalled vividly his harsh descriptions of the earls of Cheswick, their only passion being for money and power. She shivered.

Putting on her best social expression, she said kindly, "You must bring her to visit when she arrives."

He pulled his horse to a stop; Jane followed his lead, easily holding Sinbad still despite the horse's preference for action.

"I shall do that," said the viscount quietly. Becoming brisk, he added, "I suppose we should be returning now."

For an instant, Jane felt a stab of disappointment. Impatient with herself, she said, "Yes, we wouldn't want to ruin your reputation." She regretted the churlish words immediately. Why did this man have such an unfortunate effect on her manners? And morals, a wicked voice echoed in her mind.

He bent a sardonic gaze on her and said, "My reputation? I told you at the ball that I am no gentleman, so we need have no fear on that score. Are you perhaps telling me you are no lady?"

Knowing a blush would be her response, Jane plied her riding crop to Sinbad's rump quite unnecessarily, and sent him flying down the hill to the stables.

The Viscount Devlin followed at a leisurely pace.

By the time Miss Lindsay and Lord Devlin entered the gold salon, the refreshments served to Cousin Roland and her aunt and Cherry had been consumed. Jane knew well that Cherry could never resist the delicious cakes Cook prepared, but she rightly attributed the emptiness of the tray to Roland.

"Jane, how naughty of you to monopolize Lord Devlin," said Aunt Sophie, extending her hand to the viscount who bowed over it gracefully. The round little woman sighed audibly.

"We thought you had decided to ride back to that dreadful abbey with him," said Cherry, her words spoken a trifle sharply despite her trill of laughter.

"I should think you know me better than that," said Jane. She might have added more, but Lord Devlin asked, "Abbey? What abbey is this?"

"Just some old ruin on the edge of the estate. It is hardly worthy of a second glance, but Jane sets great store by it," said Cherry, eager to engage the elegant lord in conversation.

Jane poured out the fresh tea Pipkin had brought and handed a cup to Lord Devlin. Aunt Sophie pressed the new tray of cakes on their guest before passing it to Roland again. Jane rolled her eyes; she was getting hungry and would have appreciated one of those light biscuits, but she didn't wish to call attention to herself by getting up and fetching it. And as usual, her Aunt Sophie never had a thought for another female, except Cherry, when there was an eligible bachelor in the vicinity.

"I would enjoy visiting such an interesting relic, Miss Pettigrew. Perhaps you would consent to accompanying me on a ride and show it to me."

Cherry looked a bit dubious despite the attractive offer, and Jane bit the side of her jaw to smother her amusement. Cherry disliked riding every bit as much as their Cousin Roland did, though she dearly loved dressing in an elegant riding habit and being the center of attention. Jane wondered how she would handle this problem, but she reckoned without Aunt Sophie.

"I don't like the idea of your riding so far without a chaperon." She turned a simpering smile on Lord Devlin, and added apologetically, "My daughter is not out yet, formally, though it is but a matter of weeks before we journey to London, sir. Perhaps Jane and Cousin Roland would care to go also."

Jane was opening her mouth to reject such a proposal when Roland began to cough, his napkin not quite catching the crumbs that spewed forth. Lord Devlin, who was seated beside him beat him forcefully on the back until the spell had passed.

Jane watched the proceeding with a frown. She could have sworn Lord Devlin's heel landing none too gently on Roland's slippered foot had precipitated the coughing spell. But she must have been mistaken, she decided.

When Roland Havelock had been soothed with sympathy and tea, he said hoarsely, "We'd love to go on the outing, providing, of course, I can take m' phaeton. I'm quite an out and outer with the ribbons, but I don't care for sitting on top of some boney nag."

"I'm sure that can be arranged, though it will make your outing much longer to go around by the road. Why don't I have Cook pack a picnic basket, and you young people can make a day of it," added Sophie Pettigrew with an ingenuous glance at Jane.

All eyes then turned on Jane. She would have felt ungracious had she vetoed their plans, so she reluctantly agreed. Lord Devlin and Roland Havelock exchanged satisfied looks as the outing was slated for the following day.

The gentlemen took their leave shortly afterwards.

Lord Devlin pushed away from the table after consuming a delicious meal in the small breakfast room of his hired house in the elegant square called Laura Place.

The house was spacious for a townhouse, but it was not the home Lord Devlin sought for his widowed mother. Not that she would disapprove; she never questioned anything her son or husband did, and in the past ten years, living with the despotic earl of Cheswick, her brother-in-law, she had learned total submission.

This was why Lord Devlin sought other lodgings, outside of town, so his mother might have her privacy yet still be close enough to socialize if she wished. There was the key word, thought Drew; her wishes were to be respected at all costs. He ran a distracted hand through his already disordered hair. God! how she must have suffered locked away with his uncle, a selfish, vicious old man who cared for nothing but money and power.

Each time Drew thought of his sweet, timid mother, the guilt of neglecting her during his banishment hit him anew. His hands formed into fists, but his helpless anger was directed at himself more than his uncle. He could have sent for her. He had made enough money in his own right to be self-sufficient.

Still, the fact remained: he simply hadn't thought of her sorrow or loneliness. But now he meant to set her up in style. In Bath, she would be accepted as she never had been in London. The daughter of a country curate, she had married his father, the Honorable William Peterson, for love. But life had not proved easy for them. His father had enough money to make their lives comfortable, but this had not been sufficient. Eventually, his father had grown weary of explaining his wife's humble background; he had held it against her that she had not brought property or a dowry to their marriage.

When Faith Peterson had begun to apologize for her very existence, the love that had fostered their match was forgotten by both. Drew's earliest memories of his mother were her tears as his father slammed out the door. Those same tears had sent him off to the Indies, an unhappy, bewildered young man.

But now he was back, summoned by his uncle. Through an unfortunate accident that had taken off his twin cousins at once, he was now heir to the title earl of Cheswick and all the wealth and responsibility the name entailed. And never again would his mother be made to suffer humiliation.

There was a knock on the door. He was expecting no one, and it was with impatience that he gestured to the footman to admit the visitor.

"My Lord Devlin, I count myself fortunate to find you at home."

"What do you want, Havelock?" said Drew, his impatience showing as he motioned to the servant to withdraw.

Roland Havelock lowered his considerable bulk into a dainty chair, and Devlin cringed lest it break. A smile flashed across his features as he recalled Miss Lindsay's revelations about her cousin's pony. He could still recall the music of her laughter. He wondered if she knew how sensuous she was. Too bad she was a lady; he wouldn't mind a bit of a romp with such a handful. But, though the viscount protested that he was not a gentleman, he drew the line at trifling with young ladies of good *ton*. And he refused to consider marriage; someday he would have to set up his nursery, but not yet.

Reluctantly, he turned his attention to his guest. "I believe I am doing you a favor tomorrow, Devlin, and I wondered what was in it for me."

Devlin could barely keep a look of distaste from darkening his features. This man before him was just the sort he normally avoided, and he had to remind himself that he might need the man's services.

"As I told you before, Havelock, I wish to see the area surrounding Bath, and Heartland is as good a place to start as any other."

"Yes, so you told me. You're looking for a place to buy for your mother. But I can tell you you're wasting your time at Heartland. My cousin would no more sell it than the Prince would go back to his wife." A wheezing laugh accompanied this witticism, and Drew frowned.

"Perhaps, but since I find Miss Lindsay and Miss Pettigrew quite charming, I continue to look forward to our proposed picnic. I find myself curious about something, Havelock."

"What is that?" said his guest, accepting the proffered glass of port Devlin extended.

"How is it that Miss Lindsay inherited Heartland? The property must not be entailed."

"No, not entailed, but it may as well be," said Havelock, his voice filled with bitterness. "Heartland has been handed down to the eldest daughter of each generation. Hence, there is no perpetual family name associated with the estate. Supposedly, the tradition got started because of some connection to the original St. Valentine. In order that the eldest daughter of the family might always marry for love, she received the estate, or some such nonsense. Heartland was inherited by my grandmother when she was only sixteen. She married at eighteen after meeting my grandfather at the Valentine's Ball. He was the younger son of a baronet. All he brought to the marriage was a small estate in Sussex. But I am boring you with family history," said Havelock, his snake-like eyes peering intently at the viscount as though trying to ferret out the reason for his host's interest.

"Not at all, I find it fascinating. Tell me, how are you cousin to the Misses Lindsay and Pettigrew?"

"Grandmother produced three children: Jane's mother, the eldest daughter; Cherry's father; and my mother. Jane's mother, had she lived, would have inherited Heartland; therefore, it passed to Jane on my grandmother's death last year."

"And the small estate in Sussex?"

"Went to Cherry's father, then to her. An estate manager has been handling it the past ten years; it's enough to give Cherry a respectable dowry, but not like Heartland."

Each time Roland Havelock pronounced the name of the estate, he couldn't keep the envy and bitterness from his voice.

Lord Devlin's devilish sense of humor led him to ask innocently, "Miss Lindsay is not exactly in the first blush of youth, and she's still unmarried. What happens when she dies? There'll be no daughter to pass it on to."

Havelock appeared much struck by this question and took several minutes before responding thoughtfully, "I suppose it would go to the only other female descendant."

"Miss Pettigrew?"

"No, she's only the daughter of a son of the family. It would have to go to my mother."

"Who would probably no longer be among the living by the time Miss Lindsay consents to meet her maker."

Havelock, who had been speaking as if to himself, looked up sharply at the viscount's penetrating eyes. He laughed self-consciously and shrugged. "I suppose then it will be a matter for the solicitors to decide. But I have kept you too long, sir. I must be going."

"Very well. Just remember we leave at ten."

"I look forward to it, Lord Devlin."

Devlin sat staring at the fire for some time after the oily Mr. Havelock had left him. But his thoughts were not on their late conversation. Instead, he puzzled over Miss Lindsay.

How, he wondered, had such an intriguing young woman managed to escape matrimony during her Seasons in London, for surely she had had at least one Season since Miss Pettigrew was to have hers. Did Miss Jane Lindsay not care for gentlemen? But that was impossible! Though she might deny it, she had certainly enjoyed their encounters, even that passionate kiss they had exchanged.

And though he had been able to tell she lacked experience, still, she must have been kissed before, or she would have been too shocked by his passion to return it. And she had definitely returned his kiss.

The viscount drank deeply of his port. He would have to quit thinking about Miss Lindsay; she was too unsettling, both to his mind and his body. Standing, he set his glass deliberately on the mantel and strode from the room and out of the house, startling his new butler.

A brisk walk by the river would soon cure his physical and mental preoccupation with the enticing Miss Jane Lindsay.

"Jane! What are we to do?" shrilled Cherry as she flung open Jane's door quite unannounced.

Jane looked up from her dressing table and exchanged an amused look with Tucker who was arranging Jane's long, straight hair in a becoming snood.

"Do sit down, Cherry, and tell me what has occurred to make you so out of breath. You look positively blown."

Anxiously, Cherry bent down and surveyed her beautiful face in the mirror. Satisfied that she still appeared to advantage, she pulled up a nearby chair and said quite seriously, "The most dreadful thing has happened; Lord Pierce and his sister Mary have come to call."

"Dreadful? Is that really you speaking?"

51

"Surely you can't have forgotten!" exclaimed Cherry. "We are to have a picnic today, this very morning, with Lord Devlin!"

"And Cousin Roland," added Jane dryly.

"Yes, yes, of course," said Cherry impatiently. "What are we to do with Lord Pierce and Mary?"

"We could lock them out and not let them in," suggested Jane.

"Now you are making fun of me," said Cherry, the pout on her lips only enhancing her beauty.

"Pray don't be goosish. We shall invite them along, of course. I feel certain Mary would like to go, and you know how Lord Pierce feels about being in your company."

Cherry frowned, considering this new situation.

"Besides," said Jane knowingly, "you have nothing to fear in the way of competition from the sweet (but let us be frank), plain Mary Aubrey." Jane let this bit of information sink in before continuing. In Jane's opinion, the addition of two more people on their outing could only improve it. "Furthermore, I should think you would revel in the attentions of two handsome bachelors vying for your consideration all day long."

There! That had done it. Cherry's frown vanished and was replaced by an expression that could only be compared to the cat who had drunk the cream.

"I shall send word to Cook so she may add to the feast, and then I'll go and ask Lord Pierce and Mary. They will be delighted with the scheme!"

Jane shook her head as her cousin's tiny form disappeared in a flurry of silk.

"You know how much I love my cousin, Tucker, but I daresay it will be much more peaceful around here when she and my aunt leave for London next month."

"Amen to that," said the old retainer.

When Jane entered the gold salon fifteen minutes later, she found all their guests waiting. She was conscious of all eyes turning her way and felt relieved she had chosen her hunter green riding habit; its manly cut masked her generous bosom and gave her confidence.

Greeting each guest in turn, she seated herself beside Mary Aubrey. "You are looking very elegant these days, Mary. I must compliment you on your choice of color; it is very becoming."

Mary Aubrey might be plain, but she was neither vain nor stupid. She smiled at Jane and thanked her, adding, "I do hope we are not intruding, but Peter would go, you know." She nodded to the window embrasure where Cherry was seated, Lord Pierce standing over her, hanging on every word.

Jane laughed quietly. "I am happy to have you, for now I'll have someone to talk to at luncheon."

Lord Devlin, who had been following their conversation, said with exaggerated gallantry, "Fie, Miss Lindsay, as though you would be neglected. I swear you are fishing for compliments."

Jane silently thanked him for not saying "again," for she would not have put it past such a one as Devilish Devlin to embarrass her.

"Now we need not worry about anyone feeling neglected," said Jane briskly, rising to her feet. "We had better be going. I do hope the weather holds."

"It must," pronounced Lord Pierce dramatically, then blushed as all eyes turned toward him and Miss Pettigrew.

Somehow (Jane felt certain it was Cherry's doing), it was decided that Miss Aubrey and Cousin Roland should ride in his phaeton while Cherry accompanied Lord Pierce in his equipage.

Both Jane and her horse stood impatiently as all this was arranged. She chanced a look at Lord Devlin and his lips were twisted in a sardonic smile. He caught her eye and raised a brow, issuing a silent invitation as he raised his riding crop and pointed at the hillside.

Jane caught her lower lip between her teeth, debating. Should she ride to the abbey cross-country, even though it meant being alone with Lord Devlin? Or would it be wiser to endure the tedium of following the road behind two phaetons, one driven by her ham-handed Cousin Roland.

She looked from the carriages to the viscount. With that wicked raised brow he challenged her to accept his invitation.

"You enjoy your drive. Lord Devlin and I are going cross-country. We'll meet you at the abbey," called Jane as she quickly signaled Sinbad to be off, not risking anyone questioning the propriety of what she was doing, especially her own conscience.

Once again, Lord Devlin had led her into acting in a manner contrary to her true nature. What was it about the man that she ceased to be herself?

The question haunted her as she galloped up the hill and sailed over the first fence. She could hear Lord Devlin's horse right behind her. It dawned on Jane that she was running from the man, and she deliberately slowed Sinbad to a sedate trot, letting his lordship come abreast of her.

"You are an intrepid rider, Miss Lindsay. Not many women I know would even attempt such a jump, downhill as it is."

"I have gone over it so often, I suppose I have forgotten the times when I didn't quite make it. I notice you didn't hesitate, Lord Devlin."

"And have you think me a coward as well as ungentlemanly? I should think not!" She caught the gleam in his eyes and shook her head.

"You can't fool me, Lord Devlin, you enjoyed that run, and the jump. I believe you enjoy many things that others might consider dangerous, or even outrageous."

"Analyzing me, Miss Lindsay? I didn't realize you were so intrigued."

Jane glared at his back as he sent his mount forward in a mighty leap. She jerked back on Sinbad's reins, then rubbed his neck to apologize. "Sorry, old boy, but I want to see how far he'll go before he realizes he has no idea which direction to take."

As soon as the words left her mouth, she watched the aggravating Lord Devlin pull up his horse. He turned in the saddle, bowed to her, and arched that brow in inquiry. She could not refrain from a smirk as she sent Sinbad forward.

They rode in silence for some time, but it was not an awkward silence. Jane glanced at Lord Devlin's profile; it was obvious that he was enjoying the morning just as she was. The beauty of the countryside, the warmth of the sun, and the glory of being on horseback always filled Jane with an unsurpassed contentment.

Even, she thought, with the odious Lord Devlin at her side. But perhaps odious was too harsh, she corrected herself firmly. After all, his sense of humor did seem in harmony with hers most of the time.

And perhaps he had sensed her reluctance to join the others on the circuitous route mandated by the vehicles. His suggestion that they ride by the more direct route had been very welcome.

"How is it that you are unmarried?"

So much for thinking Lord Devlin a kindred soul, thought Jane crossly. "I was wondering the same thing about you, Lord Devlin," she responded sweetly.

He laughed. "I suppose I deserve that, but you were forewarned not to expect the usual social drivel from me."

"Was I? How careless of me to forget. That accounts, no doubt, for the fact that I decided to ride to the abbey with only your conversation for company."

"Touché! But you still have not answered my question. Never asked?"

"Of course I was asked," snapped Jane. "Any female standing to inherit a lucrative estate like Heartland receives countless proposals."

"All honorable, to be sure. Perhaps that accounts for your single state?"

"You, sir, are insufferable! Did you ask me to ride with you only to insult me?" Immediately, Jane regretted the question, for one could never tell how the viscount might respond.

He seemed poised to attack, but didn't. Jane realized she had been holding her breath, waiting for his response.

"Actually, no, but I could tell that you, like myself, were not looking forward to a slow, dusty ride. Was I right?"

"Yes, Lord Devlin, and I should thank you instead of attacking you." Jane smiled, pleased with her self-control; she was once again the calm, poised Miss Lindsay. But she was being premature; she reckoned without the maddening Lord Devlin who positively enjoyed provoking her.

"You appear quite bitter about your unmarried state, Miss Lindsay. But not everyone is a fortune hunter. And I fear you underestimate your personal charms."

"I know enough to realize when I am being offered Spanish coin, Lord Devlin. I do own a mirror, and I am able to see that while my looks do not repel, I am hardly a suitable model for a Dresden figurine like my cousin Cherry."

He pulled up his horse to take an impersonal inventory of Miss Lindsay while she fumed silently.

"Are you quite finished?" she said after a moment.

"Yes, and I do believe you exaggerate the matter, my dear Miss Lindsay. As a man, give me leave to tell you your charms alone would be enough to make many a man choose to shackle himself for life."

"I have given you no such leave, sir," said Jane. "But perhaps I might make just a small observation about you?"

He nodded, his demeanor serious, but Jane suddenly had the feeling he was laughing at her. Nevertheless, she plunged ahead with what was intended to be a scathing set down.

"While your appearance might be well enough, Lord Devlin, your manners leave a great deal to be desired. I would suggest that you engage a tutor who might help you remember how a member of the *Ton* should comport himself. After your lengthy — shall we merely say journeys? — you have perhaps forgotten what good manners are."

The viscount's face hardened.

56

"Ah, I see we have hit a tender spot, but I am certain you admire my candor."

The smile he turned on Jane was anything but admiring; she found it difficult not to shiver. Inwardly, she cursed herself for stooping as low as he had, but her outer aspect gave no indication of this.

His eyes glittered dangerously, and his voice held a deceptive sweetness. "You know, Miss Lindsay, you are an unusual female. If you were not so wealthy, you would have made an excellent headmistress. I wonder, have you instructed Miss Pettigrew in the detection of fortune hunters? But I may be in error; perhaps Miss Pettigrew's case is different. Is she also an heiress? If so, I wonder that you are allowing her a Season in London."

When Jane had found words again, she said quietly, "Never mind about Miss Pettigrew, Lord Devlin. She is only wealthy in charm and beauty. And despite the impression she gives, she is an extremely good judge of character."

"Oh, that is a relief. Still, I believe I'll just keep an eye on her when I go to London."

He rode ahead; Jane urged Sinbad to catch up with the other horse. She leaned over, grabbing his reins. Lord Devlin quickly halted his mount, his eyes never leaving her offending hand.

"No need for theatrics if you wish a word with me, my dear Miss Lindsay."

Through gritted teeth, Jane said, "Cherry is not for you, Lord Devlin, fortune hunter or no. Stay away from her."

"Is that an order?" he asked complacently.

"Yes," she replied, then added, "And I am not your dear Miss Lindsay!"

To Jane's relief, the abbey was in sight, and she could ride ahead, leaving Lord Devlin to follow along at an easier pace.

Jane had known all along what Devlin's motives were, despite his seeming attention to her. He was digging for information about Cherry. Well, now he knew; Cherry would not bring wealth to her marriage. Hopefully, this would deter

57

him from making a nuisance of himself. Jane wondered if Lord Devlin stood to inherit wealth along with the title of the earl of Cheswick. She devoutly hoped not, for Cherry would be less likely to be intrigued by a penniless Lord Devlin, despite his delightful smile and his ability to charm when he wished.

Jane left a thoughtful Viscount Devlin in her wake. He had not meant to nettle Miss Lindsay; quite the opposite. But she was so infuriatingly sure of herself, he simply hadn't been able to resist.

And now he had lost ground. He had meant to charm her. She loved Heartland; she would never consider selling it to someone she despised. And despite what Havelock had said, the viscount felt certain he could convince her to sell; after all, what woman would enjoy the aggravation of managing such a vast estate alone? And despite his gallant assertions to Miss Lindsay that she was a "young lady," she was still old enough to be considered on the shelf. It was unlikely there was a husband in her future.

But now he would have to retrench, try another tact. If he couldn't charm the belligerent Miss Lindsay, perhaps Miss Pettigrew might provide some useful weapon in his campaign to gain Heartland.

Besides, Miss Lindsay had clearly issued a challenge, and he had never failed to pick up the gauntlet, even when it had meant a duel. Lord Devlin set aside that particular remembrance; it, too, had been issued by a lady. No, he reminded himself; the title hadn't really applied to that female.

By the time Jane reached the abbey she was willing to admit she had spoken harshly when Lord Devlin had clearly been in a jesting mood. While apologizing went against the grain, Jane promised herself she would act as though nothing had happened.

Therefore, as they waited for the others to arrive, she explained what she knew about the abbey to his lordship who gave every evidence of being sincerely interested.

"The abbey dates back to the times of the Saxons. It was

built around the time of the original Abbey Church of St. Peter and St. Paul in Bath."

"How can you be certain?"

"My father discovered a sealed underground crypt. It contained not only the remains of this abbey's most distinguished monk, but also some important documents. Most had rotted away, but there was enough evidence to lend credence to my father's theory about the age of the structure. It was quite exciting; my father was so thrilled when the Antiquarian Society sent members down here to investigate. And when they agreed with him, he was in high alt."

"Then your father was an antiquarian?"

"Only as a hobby. His other hobby was horses, and I was more able to share that with him. Although I was happy about his discovery of the crypt, I didn't want to see it."

"So you have never been in it?"

"Yes, I finally agreed to go down there after the group from the university left. It had been cleaned up by then, and the rats removed."

"Where is it?" asked Lord Devlin, looking around expectantly.

"If I remember correctly, it is over here." Jane climbed up on a small pile of stones and pointed to a mass of shrubbery on the other side. "Father had it locked after they took all the papers away and had examined it thoroughly."

"What happened to the papers?"

"They are on display at Oxford or Cambridge, I forget which."

He laughed at her nonchalant manner. "I thought you loved this place so much."

Jane's fine green eyes looked about her; then she shook her head and smiled. Lord Devlin could have told her that at that moment, she was as beautiful as any woman he had ever seen, but she wouldn't have believed him.

"I love the abbey, but not because of its history. When I am here, I am with my father. My memory of him is strongest when I walk among these crumbling stones."

"You are lucky to have such memories. My own father was killed in a curricle race when I was seven years old. I grew up under the thumb of my uncle — and my two older cousins."

The bitterness in his voice was overwhelming, and Jane might have been moved to comfort him had not the two phaetons chosen that moment to arrive.

They ate the magnificent offerings of Mrs. Brown in the bright sunshine by the remaining walls of the ancient ruin, sheltered from any breeze that might spring up. Lord Devlin was at his most bewitching self as his tales of the exotic Indies wove a spell around the listeners.

In response to Miss Aubrey's query about the natives of the island, the viscount looked about himself furtively and whispered, "Voodoo."

Cherry shivered deliciously. "Do tell," she almost whispered.

Lord Devlin's previous stories of pirates and scenery were as naught compared to his next tale.

"Their superstitions are many, intertwined with their native religions, as well as bits of Christianity. It was a well-known fact to the landowners that on certain nights of the year it was best to simply lock one's doors and not venture outside until daylight." Lord Devlin's narrowed eyes moved from one listener to another. Cherry breathed an "Ohhh." He quirked one brow when he saw Jane's sardonic smile, but he continued his tale with an ominous laugh.

When his story was told, Devlin's smile broke the spell for his listeners.

"A fascinating story, to be sure," wheezed Havelock, who promptly settled himself for a little snooze.

After putting away the remains of their cold collation, Jane settled herself beside Mary Aubrey. Mary was twenty years old, the veteran of two Seasons in London, and still unmarried. It was rumored that she would not be averse to receiving the attentions of the local curate, Mr. Primrose, but her mother wanted better things for the eldest of four daughters.

Mary was often overlooked at social functions; her appearance was neither striking nor repulsive. And her wit was sharp and, at times, biting. Jane preferred Mary's company to women closer to her own age.

"It is just as you predicted," said Miss Aubrey quietly, her nod indicating her brother and Lord Devlin dancing attendance on Cherry who smiled and flirted with her bewitching blue eyes.

Jane smiled. "I hope you don't mind, Mary. Cherry isn't deliberately rude; she doesn't realize one shouldn't monopolize the only two eligible partis at such a small gathering."

Mary stretched her lanky frame and leaned against the stone wall at her back. "Don't forget, one of those eligible partis is my brother. I've grown accustomed to that puppy dog look. He's been making a cake of himself since the day Cherry turned the tables and quit tagging along behind him."

They shared a quiet laugh before Mary continued. "Of course, Lord Devlin is a different case entirely, but I have no interest there. He seemed almost annoyed when we arrived and interrupted your tête-a-tête."

"And it was of such a personal nature," scoffed Jane. "I was merely relating the history of the abbey. While I do not care for Lord Devlin's manner, he does seem possessed of a more lively intelligence than the average spoiled darling of the *Ton.*"

Without thinking, her eyes came to rest on her Cousin Roland who snored quietly, his head listing to one side as he leaned against a large stone. Jane's mouth twisted in distaste; no wonder he slept after the vast quantities of food and wine he had consumed.

Not knowing what turn Jane's mind had taken, Mary said, "Still, he was very solicitous to me, serving my plate, seeing that I was comfortably seated."

Jane frowned and opened her mouth to speak; "Cousin Ro—? Oh! You mean Lord Devlin."

"Yes, Miss Lindsay. May I be of service?"

Jane blushed painfully as she peered up at the tall viscount who had wandered their way while she was woolgathering.

"No, Lord Devlin. I . . . I was speaking to Miss Aubrey." He nodded, but she felt a fool.

To the group in general, Lord Devlin said, "I propose that we see this crypt Miss Lindsay was telling me about earlier. Who wants to join us?"

Cherry shuddered delicately. "I wouldn't go near such a horrid place!"

Mary shook her head, also. "You must count me out, I'm afraid. There are probably mice and perhaps bats."

"Lord Pierce?"

"I saw it many years ago," he said, never taking his eyes from Cherry. "But I wouldn't mind venturing down there again."

"Oh, no, Peter, you mustn't leave Mary and me alone up here!" breathed Cherry, clutching at his sleeve.

The young baron swelled with pride and patted her hand. "Of course I shan't leave you, if you don't wish it. Or Mary either!"

"Very well," said Lord Devlin. He nodded to the oblivious Roland Havelock and added, "Looks as though Mr. Havelock declines, so that leaves only you and me, Miss Lindsay."

All eyes turned on Jane who sat fidgeting with her gloves.

"Miss Lindsay?"

"What? Oh yes, of course, only I don't have the key," she hedged.

"But Jane, the key is by the bottom step," said Lord Pierce. "Don't you remember? You dared me to go down there and—"

"How silly of me to forget," trilled Jane. Peter, Mary, and Cherry stared at her, speechless. None of them could believe what they had heard. Jane never forgot. Never!

Suddenly, Cherry giggled. "I know what it is! You're afraid to go down there because of that monk being buried there! Afraid you'll anger his spirit! It's listening to that crazy

62

old nurse all these years!"

Now everyone turned expectantly to Cherry for details—everyone except Jane.

"What rubbish," said Jane, her voice as firm and certain as usual. "Come along, Lord Devlin. But I warn you, you will very likely ruin your coat."

"Hardly a deterrent, Miss Lindsay," he said, removing this garment and placing it neatly on one of the blankets.

As they moved away from the others, Cherry's plaintive voice rose. "I am cold, Peter. Will you accompany me to the carriage so I can get another blanket?"

Jane stopped in her tracks and turned around. Mary waved her on, saying loudly, "What a good idea, Cherry. I'll go with you."

Jane looked up to find Lord Devlin's questioning gaze on her.

"I had to make sure Cherry wouldn't forget her manners, but Mary will take care of it. She is wise beyond her years."

"Hmm. And nearly as ancient as Miss Lindsay." He reached down and picked up a sturdy stick. Taking out his handkerchief, he tied it around the end. "I took the liberty of equipping myself with a tinderbox from the picnic basket."

Jane led the way, talking all the while to bolster her courage. "There is one monk buried in the crypt. His name was Brother Valentine, which is why, so the legend goes, my ancestor who built Heartland named it as he did. It is also why St. Valentine's Day has held a special place in our family's tradition."

"A lot of superstition and poppycock, in other words, for this can't possibly be the burial site of the St. Valentine who was supposed to have lived in the seventh century."

Jane laughed. "Perhaps, but the key to what you said is 'supposed to have lived.' No one knows for certain, and I choose to believe that our monk is the original St. Valentine."

They had reached the entrance to the vault's staircase. The rough steps had been hidden by a well-placed shrub. The viscount pushed aside the foliage, lending a dim light down to the door.

"I'll go down first. Where did you say the key was?" said Devlin.

"Next to the last step. There's a recess in the wall on the right, I think it is." Jane took a deep breath and followed slowly. Over and over in her mind, she repeated, "I am not afraid; I am not afraid."

"Ah! Here it is."

Jane could hear the rusty lock protest as Drew tried to turn the key. Please, she thought, don't let it open.

But her luck was out. The lock groaned, but gave way. Lord Devlin took out his tinderbox and proceeded to light his makeshift torch. He took Jane's limp hand and led the way into the tomb.

The doorway was low, and Jane didn't bend over enough; the snood confining her long, heavy hair was plucked from her head.

"Oh dear!"

"What is it? Oh, never mind, I've got it." He stopped, his head cocked to one side. His voice was silky as he murmured. "You should always wear your hair down. It is beautiful."

Jane was disconcerted by his manner; she took the net and shoved it in the pocket of her habit. "Shall we go?"

He took her hand again, sending exquisite tremors up Jane's spine. Almost, she forgot her fear.

Once inside, Lord Devlin found a candle someone, probably one of the university researchers, had left behind. He lit this, let hot wax drip on a nearby rough table, and stood the candle in the wax.

"There, now we can see even if my torch goes out."

Jane's shiver communicated its way to his strong hand as he once again lead her farther inside.

"Cold?" he asked, turning from his perusal of the room.

Jane shook her head, hoping her teeth wouldn't start to rattle. Devlin drew her arm through his, never letting go of her hand. Jane made no protest, leaning on him quite openly. Under other circumstances, she would have been appalled to act so familiarly.

"You are afraid. I shouldn't have forced you to come."

Lord Devlin's concern was evident, and he turned to lead her out, but Jane said quietly, "No, sir. I wanted to come."

"Why? What are you trying to prove? It is obvious you have an unnatural fear of this place."

Jane's tiny laugh was too sharp, but her voice was strong as she explained. "I do have an unnatural fear, as you call it. I am ashamed to admit it, but it is true. But this is one fear I can face. I'll be fine. You see?" She released his arm and walked toward the far wall.

"Now this tomb is where our Valentine is buried. You see the birds—all in twos—that are carved all over it?"

Drew, standing beside her, held his torch closer. "Yes, if memory serves, St. Valentine's Day became associated with lovers because it is supposed to be the day when birds choose their mates."

"Quite right," said Jane. "So you see why I think our monk is the true St. Valentine."

"I must disagree. I think it much more likely this monk—who was no doubt quite distinguished since he has his own vault—this monk simply took the name Valentine. By the time he was alive, St. Valentine's Day had become associated with lovers because of the birds choosing their mates on February fourteenth. And so, this monk, this Brother Valentine, had those birds carved on his tomb."

Jane's laugh sounded quite normal as she protested. "And I cannot agree with you, Lord Dev—My God! What was that!" Jane's breath was suspended as they heard a low creak. The slam that followed was anything but quiet. Jane let out a shriek.

"Shh! Who's there!" Drew thrust the torch into Jane's hand, closing her lifeless fingers around its handle. Hurrying to the closed door, he called again. "Who's there? Hell and . . . ! The door's locked."

"L—l—locked." Now Jane's teeth were rattling. He hurried back to her, catching the torch as it fell from her fingers.

"Miss Lindsay! Jane! That's enough!" He jammed the torch between the crumbling mortar on the brick floor and paused to be certain it would remain standing.

Jane's saucer-shaped eyes remained fixed on his face, her mouth rounded in an astonished O. Devlin put his arms around her to still her trembling. There was no passion in his embrace. Jane accepted this comfort passively. She was incapable of either speech or action.

When her teeth had stopped chattering, and the violent shudders ceased racking her body, Drew said sensibly, "Someone will come soon. Remember Jane, Lord Pierce has been down here; he will know there can't be too much of interest and will soon wonder at our protracted absence. They'll get us out, even if they have to break the door down."

Thankfully, it didn't occur to Jane how Lord Pierce and her Cousin Roland could break down such a thick and sturdy door without the proper tools.

"Who could have closed it?" whispered Jane, her face still buried in the viscount's coat.

"Wind, no doubt. I thought it had begun to shift. We're probably in for some more cold weather. At least it is dry and relatively warm down here."

Jane nodded against his shoulder. "And also, Mary was wrong."

"About what?"

"At least we're not sharing quarters with mice or bats."

Jane's mild attempt at humor wasn't lost on Drew. Taking her firmly by the shoulders, he looked into her face and said, "I knew you'd come about. You've got bottom."

He released her carefully and set two stools to rights beside the door.

As Jane sat down, she couldn't help but think on the viscount's warm comment. Warm, but hardly romantic. Yet the last thing she desired from Lord Devlin was romance or flirtation, wasn't it?

"So, Miss Lindsay, do you go to London with Miss Pettigrew?" he asked, his conversational voice more suitable to the drawing room than a dark crypt.

Snapped back to the present, Jane frowned. Why was he back on Cherry's visit to London? "No. This is to be her time. Her mother is accompanying her."

"I should like to see Miss Pettigrew in London, holding court at her first ball."

"Holding court?"

"Certainly! With her beauty and her pleasing personality, I predict she will be the reigning belle of the Season."

Jane was torn between pride in her cousin and her desire to protect Cherry. She certainly didn't wish to encourage the pretensions of rakes like Lord Devlin. Finally, she compromised.

"I hope you may be right. Cherry is a dear child, and she deserves to be able to have her choice of eligible suitors."

"What about you, Miss Lindsay? Were you one of the belles of the Season at your come-out?"

"Hardly. My entrance into the *Ton* was quite brief and quite uneventful. My mother had been ill in the spring, so I went to London for the Little Season in the fall. I stayed with my friend Sally—now Lady Cumberland, perhaps you know her?" Lord Devlin shook his head. "It was great fun—the shopping, the invitations, the rides in the park."

"I imagine you shone to advantage on those rides."

Jane smiled at him—a brief, intimate smile that never failed to captivate her audience. Lord Devlin was not immune; he leaned forward to see her better in the dim light.

"Then the parties and balls actually arrived. I was suddenly stricken with shyness. I couldn't talk or laugh. And dancing, which will never be my forte, was a disaster! From that standpoint, it was a relief when my grandmother wrote, calling me home."

"Your mother?"

"Yes, there was nothing the doctors could do. She made it through Christmas—she always loved that time of year—and died at the end of January."

"I am sorry. I can tell you still miss her."

"Oh yes. My grandmother passing away last year brought it all back—quite painfully."

"So, you never had a Valentine's Ball when you were Cherry's age."

"No, and she bemoans the fact regularly," laughed Jane.

"She does? Not you?"

"No! It meant I didn't have to attend any balls and attempt to dance for a whole year!"

"But why should Miss Pettigrew care so vehemently?"

"Ah! Cherry may tease me about being superstitious, but she truly believes Heartland's tradition that the children of the house, sons and daughters, will meet their future spouse at the ball when they are eighteen."

"So you are unmarried because there was no ball that year."

"Exactly! And no matter what I say, Cherry will insist it is true."

"Perhaps it is. After all, I'm sure you eventually came out of hiding and had a Season."

"True, but I have never felt truly comfortable on the dance floor, though I manage."

"I find that difficult to credit. You are made for dancing, so tall and graceful."

Again Jane delivered that smile, and Drew was moved to rise, bow, and take her hand. "I believe I hear the first strains of the waltz. Will you do me the honor, Miss Lindsay?"

Jane shook her head at his absurdity, but she stood up and allowed him to place his hand on her waist. He began to hum a waltz tune, guiding her easily through the steps of the dance. At first, Jane's movements were stiff, but as she relaxed, she felt the rhythm through the touch of his hands.

The torch fluttered and burned itself out, leaving the task of lighting the small chamber to that single candle. Lord Devlin drew her closer until his arm encircled her waist; her long hair tickled his hand. Jane raised her chin, her eyes coming to rest on his mouth.

Drew's humming ceased as he returned her gaze. With the music suspended, their movements stopped, also. The silence was broken only by their breathing, which seemed to be getting louder.

Jane's tongue licked her lips, and she caught her lower lip between her teeth. The hand holding hers came toward her mouth, soothing that nervous gesture with a gentle touch of his thumb. Slowly, Drew lowered his mouth to hers. His lips brushed hers, his tongue tasting that full lower lip. His eyes opened; Jane stared at him, mesmerized.

She loosened her hand from his and slipped it up, joining her hands around his neck. She pulled his face back down and kissed his lips.

Drew's arms closed around her waist as he pulled her against him. His mouth kissed and teased, pleading and persuading, his tongue exploring her mouth, her tongue answering, darting nervously. He had somehow backed her against the wall—or was it the tomb?—she didn't care so long as the rhythmic movement of his hips continued to caress her just between the tops of her thighs.

Dimly, she grew aware of the pounding on the door, and the pulsing of her blood and breathing began to slow down. Drew stepped away from her, his dark eyes puzzled, even overwhelmed, by their exchange. He took a deep breath before dropping her hands—she couldn't recall giving them to him—and turning toward the door.

The pounding from the outside had ceased. Someone was putting the key in the lock and turning it. Jane quickly smoothed her riding habit, staring down in surprise to find three buttons unfastened. Correcting this, she flipped her long hair behind her shoulders and joined Lord Devlin by the opening door.

In the general hubbub that followed, Jane's unnaturally high color and Lord Devlin's abstracted manner were put down to agitation of the nerves, a natural result from their harrowing experience. And if Miss Lindsay snapped at her crying cousin to quit being a ninnyhammer, she was easily forgiven.

As for Lord Devlin, his continuing silence might be wondered at, but perhaps his nerves were more highly strung than anyone suspected.

Lord Devlin's nerves were anything but high-strung at that moment. In truth, he held his emotions under a tight rein, but not because of being locked in a dark crypt for almost an hour. Nor was it because of Miss Lindsay's extremely provocative body. What struck the viscount quite forcibly as he reached ground level was the absolute stillness of the air. There was no possible way the wind could be held responsible for that door closing. And if not the wind? He studied the small group of people, his eyes coming to rest on Miss Lindsay.

No, he told himself firmly, she would not have arranged for someone to close that door in the hope she would be compromised, and he would be forced to offer for her. It was unthinkable! Yet, the thought remained.

And who, of that innocuous group would have wanted to do a mischief to either him or Miss Lindsay? It was a puzzle, a rather nasty one, at that.

It was a weary Miss Lindsay who rode at Lord Devlin's side in front of the carriages on the way home. She had felt unequal to the cross-country ride with its numerous jumps. But mostly, the thought of a private ride with Drew Devlin had made her insist on taking to the road.

And Lord Devlin hadn't protested, she realized. He probably had no wish to be private with her, either. Her cheeks flamed at the thought of her behavior. She squirmed uncomfortably in the saddle, remembering that feeling of hot urgency as he pressed her against the wall. The thought alone made her feel uncomfortably warm.

How could she ever look him in the eye again? He had no doubt found her behavior repelling. She had to know; she stole a glance at his forbidding profile. The corner of his mouth was turned down. His brow was furrowed. Suddenly, he turned to face her, the full force of his frown hitting her like a blow. Jane's color rose, but this time it was due to anger and indignation.

How dare he! she thought. How dare he look down his thin, aristocratic nose at her when she had only responded to his advances! Had he left her alone, she would never have kissed him! Not in a million years!

In high dudgeon, she lifted her riding crop; a slight touch sent Sinbad careening down the road. Lord Devlin prepared to follow, but he pulled up suddenly.

Let her go, said a voice within. She's nothing but trouble for you.

♡ *Chapter Three* ♡

Jane stretched and opened her eyes, blinking at the bright morning light. She turned over and burrowed into the pillows.

"You asked to be waked up at nine, Miss Jane," said Tucker sympathetically. She could always tell when her mistress had trouble sleeping; the covers were twisted and pulled every which way, and this morning, they were a fright.

Jane let out a groan, but sat up and leaned against the pillows. "I know, but I do wish I could sleep a little longer this morning." She accepted the cup of steaming coffee from Tucker. "Still, I do want to go to the library, and I will be glad of Cherry's company on the long ride." I suppose you had best come along, Tucker; I can't trust her young maid to keep her out of mischief."

"If you think it's best, Miss Jane, though Mrs. Brown did ask for my help." At Heartland, a request from their formidable housekeeper/cook was tantamount to a royal summons, and the maid was obviously torn.

"Then you must stay; surely I can trust Cherry now that she is eighteen." Jane's voice held a world of doubt, but she brushed aside the maid's protests. It seemed neither one of them could forget that time last fall when Cherry had slipped out the back door of the best modiste in Bath to meet secretly with Mr. Fitzhugh. She had been found in the Pump Room two hours later, no less than five young swains swarming around her as she parceled out smiles and coy looks. Jane had dealt with the matter without telling Cherry's mother who would have swooned in horror, predicting the dire consequence of social ruin for the entire family.

"I think I'll be daring and wear the burgundy carriage dress this morning, Tucker. I confess, though I wish no disrespect to my grandmother's memory, that I shall be glad when March arrives, and I may wear real colors again."

"Your grandmother, rest 'er soul, wouldn't want her girls unhappy, I'm thinkin', Miss Jane."

Jane swung her legs off the bed and scratched her rib cage in a most unladylike fashion. "That's true, so I'm sure she'll forgive the wearing of burgundy if she happens to look down and see."

"Miss Jane!" exclaimed the shocked maid. Jane tried to look remorseful, but her eyes twinkled. Fortunately, Tucker had leaned over to find the matching slippers and didn't see.

Jane's tongue often got the better of her; she would say the wrong thing to the wrong person. If she had made such a statement to her old nurse, that good lady would have made the sign of the cross and nodded in agreement. Talking with ghosts was an everyday occurrence for Nana.

"Is Miss Cherry awake?"

"I believe so, Miss Jane. I think I saw her goin' downstairs before I came in to wake you."

"So early?" asked Jane, though she expected no answer.

Cherry usually had to be dragged out of bed even when presented with the prospect of a morning shopping in Bath. Heaven help them all if the girl was up to more mischief. Jane had seen to it since that last incident that Cherry never visited Bath without one of the older, more sedate servants along.

But surely she wouldn't jeopardize her reputation just before her departure for London.

"There you are, Miss Jane. And pretty as a picture, too,"

said the loyal maid.

Jane gave her appearance a cursory glance before thanking Tucker and hurrying downstairs.

There was Cherry, alone in the small sitting room they had turned into a family dining room; eating breakfast and luncheon there was much more cozy than either of the other formal dining rooms.

Cherry had also opted for a change from their usual gray and lavender mourning gowns. She wore a rich blue, not quite navy, but close enough to be respectful. On the side board was a fetching bonnet in a matching color.

Swallowing, Cherry greeted her older cousin cheerfully. Doing it too brown, thought Jane suspiciously. But she could be subtle, too, and she returned the greeting enthusiastically. In her mind, however, Jane vowed to not let Cherry out of her sight. It would mean curtailing her visit to the library, but it was necessary. Please, she added to some undefined Fate, let March arrive quickly so I can be rid of what is becoming a burdensome responsibility.

"Where shall we go first?" asked Jane a few minutes later before taking a bite of toast.

She encountered a sharp look from her cousin before Cherry masked her annoyance. "First? I thought we would go to Duffield's first so you may choose some books."

"If you wish. Then we should really proceed to the dressmakers. Mrs. Warner gets so busy later in the day. Besides, it is only logical to start with the gown and then select the accessories."

Her voice a little too disinterested, Cherry asked, "Are you planning to order some new gowns now? I had thought you would wait until we are officially out of mourning."

"By the time they are ready, we will be. Now, finish up, so we can leave soon."

"I'm finished," grumbled the girl.

Jane hid a smile, congratulating herself on effectively spiking Cherry's guns. There'd be no clandestine rendezvous that day!

The morning promised just as beautiful a day as the one before. Jane forgot her worries about Cherry and gave herself up to the pleasure of the pleasing landscape. As they passed Lord Pierce's modest manor house, Cherry, too, leaned out the window. She sighed audibly.

"Is anything the matter, dear?" asked Jane.

Cherry almost managed to keep the whine from her voice and the pout from her appealing lips, but Jane had known her cousin too long not to recognize the signs of frustration. Jane turned back to the window.

A few moments later, Cherry sighed again, quite dramatically. Aha! thought Jane; she has come up with a plan.

"It is just that I wanted to shop for a gift, a very special gift."

"I shall be happy to accompany you," promised Jane.

"No! I mean, well, you see, you cannot see the gift. It would spoil the surprise. Remember, you do have a birthday coming up." Cherry delivered her most winning smile. Unfortunately, it had no affect on Jane.

"Very well," she began, and Cherry's smile broadened. "However, I know you wouldn't wish to appear to be alone in a shop, for no matter what anyone says, ladies do not go out unattended—ever."

Cherry sighed again, and Jane had to restrain herself from giving her young cousin a lecture on deportment and respect for her elders. But she relaxed against the squabs and closed her eyes. Somehow, the outing she had been looking forward to had turned into a battle of wits. She wished she'd stayed at home to help Cook and let Tucker go in her place.

But as they entered Bath, Jane's spirits lifted. It was always more amusing to shop with someone else, and Cherry would soon be gone to London. She had best enjoy her company while she could.

Thus, as they neared the library, Jane instructed the footman to pass it by and continue to the fashionable shops in Milsom Street.

Mrs. Warner greeted them by name and bade them be seated while her minions scurried to do their mistress's bidding. In moments, Cherry and Jane had been served a cup of tea and were debating the merits of the latest fashion plates in *La Belle Assemble*. Mrs. Warner was consulted on styles and fabrics, and this good businesswoman shortly had her clerks bringing forth all manner of cloth: linens, silks, satins, wool crepes, delicate muslins, and the finest lawn for those unmentionables.

After selecting two morning gowns and a new carriage dress to wear the day she journeyed to London, Cherry wandered about the parlor looking at the strategically placed displays in the window.

She was just contemplating her ruined plans, a delicate pout on her lips, when she looked outside and saw her co-conspirator. He saw her as well, and started across the street. Cherry put up one gloved hand to warn him off. Then, glancing behind her to where Jane and Mrs. Warner were in deep conversation, she moved slowly toward the door. With another quick check to be certain her cousin's attention was still occupied, she slipped outside.

Grabbing the surprised Lord Pierce by the hand, she practically dragged him to the nearest side street and around the corner to freedom.

Jane looked up moments later, her eyes taking in the emptiness of the parlor while her mind denied the truth. Surely Cherry wouldn't be so selfish! But that, of course, was foolish of Jane. Cherry, who could be so thoughtful at times, was basically self-centered.

"Miss Lindsay, is there something wrong?" asked the modiste.

"No," Jane assured her. "My cousin, who was meeting friends, must not have wanted to interrupt our business. I see she is already gone. Unfortunately, we neglected to set a time and place for our departure this afternoon. If she should return here, please tell her to meet me at Goodnight's pastry shop at two o'clock."

Fortunately, Jane knew she could trust Mrs. Warner to remain silent, and their little charade should fool any other listening ears.

The least Cherry could have done, thought Jane sourly, was to pick a different location for her disappearance. Mrs. Warner made a great pretense of promising to deliver Jane's message to Miss Pettigrew, but predominant in both ladies' minds was the remembrance of Miss Pettigrew's indiscretion the past autumn.

When I get my hands on her! thought Jane as she stalked down Milsom Street, giving each shop front a cursory glance as she passed. Jane paused at the entrance to the Octagon Chapel; it was a possibility, so she entered. And so Jane's afternoon proceeded with her anger, frustration, and worry growing every minute.

She was approached by tradesmen hawking their wares, rollicking bucks already in their cups, and beggars, as she made her way gradually toward the Pump Room. This was her last resort, yet Jane hoped Cherry had not been so foolish as to go into such a public place in the escort of a solitary gentleman. But there was nowhere else to search; it was almost two o'clock, and she would need to return to Milsom Street to meet the coachman soon.

Jane paused as she entered High Street, her gaze traveling quickly from the White Lion Hotel and Guildhall on her left, past the Orange Grove and Abbey, and down to the Pump Room. She flipped open her grandmother's watch that was pinned to her bosom. Two o'clock, already.

The clatter of a carriage made her look up again.

"Jane! Oh, Jane! Come and see Lord Devlin's spanking team! Aren't they splendid?"

Jane's furious glare was met with a quizzical expression from the viscount.

"Splendid," she said through clenched teeth.

Lord Devlin's tiger had gone to the horses' heads, and the viscount threw him the ribbons. He helped Cherry descend before turning to face Jane.

Cherry continued to chatter alarmingly while Jane dueled silently with Lord Devlin. Then he laughed and lifted Cherry's hand to his lips.

"I think, Miss Cherry, that your cousin would like to be private with me so that she may ring a peal over me. Is that not right, Miss Lindsay?" Jane said nothing, and the viscount turned to his tiger. "Drive to Milsom Street, Piglet, find the Lindsay coachman, and tell him to come to the White Lion immediately. We'll be having tea."

"No, we will not," said Jane.

Devlin smiled; Miss Jane had to be terribly upset to be so rude in front of a servant. He nodded. "Tell him to come here."

"Yes, m'lord," said the happy tiger proudly. He climbed into the driver's seat and was soon gone.

"Now, Miss Lindsay?"

"Oh, no, Jane, please! Lord Devlin . . ." Her voice dwindled to nothing, and Cherry moved away from them, her face a bright red.

Drew Devlin took Jane's arm and propelled her toward the Collonade. He turned to her with twinkling eyes.

"Let me have it."

"What do you mean, sir, making assignations with a young lady old enough to be your . . . your little sister! Have you no conscience?"

"I suppose not."

His admittance of this only angered Jane more, and she found her entire body was shaking with the effort of maintaining some semblance of control in this public place.

"Well, let me tell you, sir, that here our gentlemen know better, and if you intend to live up to your reputation as Devilish Devlin, then I suggest you leave Bath! Why don't you leave England altogether and go back to that island of yours!"

If there was one thing Drew had learned in his years of exile, it was patience. But he still possessed a healthy temper, and this unjust attack on his character was almost more than he could bear. And then to suggest he leave his own country? It was too much!

"May I suggest madame (and I use that form of address because you are acting like a stupid mother hen), that you keep your opinions of my character to yourself until you have learned what really transpired? You are nothing better than a termagant with your ranting and raving. It is no wonder your cousin behaves with a lack of decorum with you as an example!"

With this, he turned on his heel and stalked away. Jane remained fixed like a statue, unable to take in Cherry's babbling explanations.

Some moments later, Jane took a deep breath; her eyes focused on her cousin's tear-streaked face with surprise.

"What is it, Cherry?"

"You don't understand!" sobbed the girl. "It wasn't Lord Devlin at all! It was Peter, Lord Pierce!"

Horrified at Cherry's words, Jane felt the pavement reel beneath her feet. What had she done? Her tongue, her wretched tongue!

She took Cherry's elbow with one hand to guide her to their coach which had just arrived. Once inside, she bade the distraught girl to dry her tears and blow her nose and tell what had really happened.

"It was my idea. I wanted to go to the Pump Room today. That frightful Annie Hawthorne is always telling me how wonderful it is to go every day and hear the gossip and have the men dangling after her. She makes me feel like such a baby. And I knew you would not consent, for you're always saying it's such a waste of time."

Jane agreed, and told Cherry to continue.

"So I told Peter we would be shopping and asked him to come to the dressmaker to rescue me."

"And you didn't want to ask me because you knew I would forbid you to go there with only Lord Pierce for escort."

In a very small voice, Cherry said, "Yes." Then the rebellion returned to her tones as she added, "And you know it's true!"

"So Lord Pierce agreed even though he knew it was improper; you should have more pity on the man, Cherry. But where does Lord Devlin come in?"

"He saw us on the steps to the Pump Room and asked us if he could join us. He even sent a servant to find you and tell you where we were."

"I received no messages, but I suppose he couldn't find me. I was out walking all over Bath by that time."

Cherry chose to ignore Jane's sarcasm and continued.

"Anyway, once inside, he introduced me to everyone I didn't know, including a duchess!"

"Now you are roasting me!"

"No, truly! And I sat with her the entire time. Actually, she is the dowager duchess of Wentworth. She was most kind. I believe she has known Lord Devlin forever. She warned me that he was a wicked man, but she was only teasing me. And she said she thought I would be the darling of the coming Season!"

Jane couldn't help smiling at this childish boasting, but her thoughts returned to her encounter with Lord Devlin, and she blushed, shocking her cousin.

"Jane? What is it?"

But Jane refused to be drawn, and sank into her corner of the carriage, her spirits completely downcast. There was no help for it; she would have to write a letter of apology.

It was time for tea when they reached Heartland, but Jane was still too distraught to be able to relax and enjoy this respite. Her solicitor was waiting in the study, Pipkin informed her, his expression dour and forbidding.

"Did he say what it was about?"

"No, Miss Jane," said the butler as he opened the study door for her to enter. His next words were spoken like a preacher warming to his subject. "And he said, 'Woe unto you also, ye lawyers! for ye lade men with burdens grievous to be borne, and ye yourselves touch not the burdens with one of your fingers.' "

Crankshaft, who had been the family attorney for many years, ignored Pipkin's pronouncement, and bowed low over Jane's hand before explaining his visit.

"Miss Lindsay, I know you have never thought of Heartland as a burden," he paused as they both recalled Pipkin's biblical pronouncement. Clearing his throat, the plump Mr. Crankshaft continued. "But someone has brought to my attention the fact that it might be so, and that person has offered to, uh, relieve you of the burden. For a very generous sum, I might add."

Jane smiled. "Are you saying someone has offered to buy Heartland?" He nodded. "I hope you told him it wasn't for sale?"

"I did indicate that it was unlikely. But the sum —"

"I wouldn't take all the money in the Treasury. No, nor all the jewels either!"

"I do understand, Miss Jane, but I did tell the gentleman I would approach you."

Jane shook her head. What next? How could anyone think she regarded Heartland as a burden? It was her home! It was her life! She turned sharply, her shrewd eyes on the discomfited lawyer.

"Who was it? It couldn't have been anyone from Bath. Who would think I might want to sell?"

"I did promise to keep his identity confidential."

"Mr. Crankshaft, you have worked for my family for the past twenty years, I know. I hope you have been happy in this association and wish it to continue." Jane's face was blank; she was only bluffing, but the man in front of her had no clue to this.

"It was Lord Devlin. He was wanting to buy it for his mother."

"Devlin! I might have known! And all these visits have only been to inspect the property!"

"I beg your pardon, Miss Lindsay?"

"Never mind, Mr. Crankshaft, never mind. You will join

81

us for tea before you go back to Bath, won't you?"

Lord Devlin stretched his stiff limbs before picking up the morning mail and papers. He sifted through several envelopes before coming to the one he had been expecting. A smile was on his lips as he opened it. Yes, it was from Miss Lindsay, her apology.

Dear Lord Devlin

I must apologize for jumping to the wrong conclusions the other day. I want to thank you for saving my cousin from her own foolishness.

Also, I want to thank you for the very generous offer for my house. Heartland is not now, nor will it ever be, for sale. Especially to you.

Most truthfully,
Jane Lindsay

The smile faded from his lips. She was the most maddening female he had ever met. If he were in the market for a wife, he would marry her just to have the right to teach her how to go on. But he was not in the market for one, of course. Someday, perhaps, but not until his odious uncle was dead. And when he did choose a wife, it would be a sweet, unspoiled girl, perhaps the daughter of a respectable curate like his mother, someone who would be biddable and calm. It certainly wouldn't be some high and mighty spinster with more hair than wit.

No, that wasn't fair. Jane Lindsay was anything but stupid. Arrogant, pushy, self-righteous, and prudish, perhaps. Well, he corrected himself again, not prudish, not deep down. His mind wandered as it frequently did to their encounter in Brother Valentine's crypt. Passionate was the word for Miss Lindsay, though he doubted very much if Jane would agree with him. She wouldn't admit to such an improper characteristic. It was no wonder she intruded into his thoughts so often.

Pushing his chair away from the table roughly, he walked to the sideboard and poured a glass of port. Sipping it thoughtfully, he was interrupted by his valet.

"What is it, Samuel?"

"Mr. Havelock wishes a few moments of your time, my lord."

"Send him in." Just the man I need to see, thought the viscount. He liked a woman with spirit, but Miss Jane Lindsay was a shrew; she needed taking down a peg. And if what he had in mind resulted in her selling Heartland to him, then so much the better.

"Devlin, old man. So good of you to see me so early in the morning. I do believe the rest of the world sleeps till noon, but I knew I could count on you." He took the seat indicated by the viscount.

"Samuel, get Mr. Havelock some coffee. And a plate?" he asked his visitor.

Roland Havelock was never one to turn down food, especially when offered by such an august personage as Lord Devlin. Perhaps he had been wrong in thinking the viscount only just tolerated his company.

When they had both been served generous helpings of grilled kidneys, eggs, and toast, Havelock said confidently, "How about joining me this evening in a hand of cards? I'm meeting friends for dinner and then cards, dice, and so on."

"Yes, thank you for inviting me." Drew waited a few minutes before asking casually, "Tell me, have you had any more thoughts about that little puzzle we discussed recently?"

"What puzzle is that?"

"Who will inherit Heartland when Miss Lindsay is gone."

"I did ask a fellow about it, you know. And he said it sounded like my mother. Of course, if she's gone, it would be a matter for the courts to decide."

"I daresay. You know, your cousin is not in the ordinary way."

"Jane? Lord, you don't have to tell me! She cares nothing for the gentler arts. Do you know she can shoot, drive, hunt, fish, and even fence a little bit?"

"Is that so? A regular fellow, eh?"

"Just about. Of course, I doubt she could best you or me in any of those things, but she's good, all the same."

"Still, she does have her foibles, if Miss Cherry is to be believed."

Roland Havelock stopped chewing and looked inquiringly at the viscount.

"I understand she is extremely superstitious. So much so that she won't walk near a graveyard at night."

"I suppose that could be true. That old nurse of hers was from Cornwall and filled Jane's head with all sorts of nonsense. I think she's batty—the nurse, I mean—and I told Jane she should turn her off when she outgrew her usefulness, but Jane wouldn't hear of it. Just another example of how wrong it is to have a woman in charge of an estate like that."

"Exactly! You know, I offered to buy Heartland from her?"

Havelock choked on his coffee, spilling some down the front of his brocade waistcoat. Recovering, he asked, "Did she take your head off?"

"Oh, I spoke to her lawyer. She did write me though. Most unpleasant."

Havelock snorted. "No doubt! She got a viper's tongue."

Momentarily diverted by a very different remembrance of that tongue, the viscount fell silent. But after all, what he was going to propose was just a prank, just a little joke to get back at Miss Lindsay for her impudent letter.

With this in mind, he leaned closer to the distasteful Roland Havelock, pretending an interest in his guest's conversation.

It was the next morning, and Lord Devlin had a dreadful

headache. Probably from that wretched liquor he had consumed the night before while attempting to be an agreeable guest, he thought miserably. But it would be worth it. Everything had gone as planned.

He knew Roland Havelock was a dreadful card player and a reckless gambler. While he himself rarely indulged, he was generally quite lucky. And even if he hadn't won, which he had, he was certain Havelock would lose, spreading his vouchers around the table. As luck would have it, Lord Devlin now held most of those vouchers in his dressing gown. They would be sufficient to win Havelock's cooperation in the little prank he intended to play.

"Mr. Havelock, my lord," announced the valet.

Lord Devlin took another sip of the strong black coffee and tried to appear more sharp-witted than he felt.

"Your servant, Devlin," groaned Havelock. The viscount had thought his own appearance sadly rumpled, but compared to the unfortunate Roland Havelock, he was in excellent shape.

"Have a seat," said the viscount, producing a handful of crumpled vouchers from his pocket and spreading them on the table. "I assume you've come to take care of these."

"Well, I, uh, you see, there is some difficulty. . . ." Devlin raised a brow and waited mercilessly. "I've had some setbacks recently and must beg your indulgence for a short time."

"How short?"

"A matter of two or three weeks, at most."

"Let me understand this, Havelock. You played an entire evening, losing all the while, and had no way to redeem your vouchers." His discomfitted guest nodded slowly. "Very bad form, old man."

"I do apologize, Lord Devlin. I expected my run of bad luck to end."

"That's what all bad gamblers say. Still, there is a way."

"Yes?"

"You could do a small favor for me, and I would be will-

85

ing to forget all these."

Havelock watched as the viscount lifted the pile of notes, letting them slip through his fingers. Havelock slipped a nervous finger inside his wilted collar and licked his fat lips.

"What is it?"

"A trifling matter. I have a score to settle with your cousin, Miss Lindsay. It is but a prank, but I believe it would take her down a peg. Of course, I will understand if you feel you cannot help me out of family loyalty."

Havelock, who could boast not a loyal bone in his body, hesitated all the same. His cousin would be a formidable enemy and if she ever discovered his part in this . . .

"Well?"

Roland Havelock's beady eyes returned to the pile of vouchers by the viscount's hand. "Very well, as long as it doesn't harm her."

"She won't come to any harm, I promise you. The first thing I want you to do is to see to it she discovers this note." He handed over a small notecard which Havelock read quickly.

"I don't understand. What are you doing with a note to my cousin Cherry from Pierce?"

Clearly, the man's understanding was limited. "It is not really for Miss Cherry; nor is it from Lord Pierce. I wrote it so that Miss Lindsay would feel it necessary to go to the graveyard just past the Heartland gardens. She would only venture to such a spot at midnight if she thought she were saving her cousin."

"That's true enough. Still, I don't see what good that will do you. It's not as though there is going to be a ghost to scare her or anything."

"Oh, but I can assure you there will be."

How her Cousin Roland had engineered an invitation to dinner, Jane couldn't be sure. He had probably flattered her Aunt Sophie dreadfully, for as a rule her aunt disliked

86

him. But here he was, and they were stuck with him for an entire evening.

It was not as if her evenings were exciting without his presence. Quite the contrary, but while the ladies of Heartland lived quietly most of the time, their evenings were never boring. And boredom was what Jane was experiencing at that moment. She forced herself to pay attention to her company once more.

"And then the duchess said—"

"Which duchess?" asked Cherry quickly. "Was it the duchess of Wentworth? I am acquainted with her, you know."

"Why, yes, yes, so it was. Anyway, she said, 'Roland, you scamp, I believe you've the devil's own luck with cards!' Of course, she was right, and she was soon into me quite heavily."

"Oh, I didn't realize she gambled," said Cherry naively.

"Lord, child," said her mother. "All the ladies play, though mostly silver loo. Why, we must teach you before we go up to London, so that you will know how to go on."

"I should be happy to be of service," said Cousin Roland gallantly.

But Jane thought it time to intervene; she had heard rumors about her Cousin Roland's skill at the tables—or lack of it.

"I will teach you, Cherry." She received a glare from Havelock. "After all, you want to know how ladies play, not an expert, neck-or-nothing player such as Cousin Roland is reputed to be." With this, Jane rose from the table, leading the way to the gold salon.

"I'll just bring my port along if you ladies have no objection. Nothing worse than sitting all alone at a huge table with only a glass of spirits for company."

The gold salon was so named for the color of its draperies, but also for the delicate white Louis XIV furniture which was trimmed in gold. Jane led the way to an intimate grouping consisting of two couches and two chairs. The sofas faced one another and she quickly claimed one of these, pulling Cherry down by her side. Aunt Sophie sat on the opposite couch while Cousin Roland prepared to seat himself on one of two dainty chairs.

As he lowered his considerable bulk, Jane wondered irreverently where she would find another to match the set. She wasn't certain if the subsequent creaking emanated from the chair or Cousin Roland's corset, but the chair remained intact.

Roland leaned toward Cherry and began to tell her slightly scandalous tales of London and its better-known inhabitants. Cherry blushed delicately at his boldness, but Jane recognized the stories as being two or three Seasons old and quite exaggerated.

Trying to draw Roland's attention away from Cherry, who was obviously uncomfortable, Jane asked, "How is your mother, Roland? You have been to see her since your return to England, haven't you?"

"Actually, I intend to go next week. She has been ill, and I didn't wish to visit on account of that."

Aunt Sophie was shocked. "But surely you must realize, my boy, that the best thing for an ailing mother is her child? You should go to her at once and beg forgiveness!"

"There's no need for that. Mother understands only too well my delicate, susceptible constitution. She would be terrified lest I contract some deadly disease from her." He patted Aunt Sophie's plump hand on the arm of the sofa on his left.

Their conversation drifted haphazardly here and there for the next hour. Jane found her mind had a tendency to wander, and she was caught several times without the appropriate rejoinder to a query. She shook her head to clear away the cobwebs and endeavored to pay attention.

Yawning, she wondered desperately if it were too early to send for the tea tray.

"What we need is music," she announced during a lull in conversation. "Cherry, why don't you play something; you perform much better in company than I do." This was certainly true; whereas Jane's playing was more inventive, (a tactic she employed to cover mistakes), Cherry's skill could easily be appreciated by any audience.

Under cover of Cherry settling at the pianoforte, Roland Havelock slipped the folded note from his coat pocket and placed it casually in Cherry's vacant seat. The listening trio smiled at one another as Cherry began a flawless introduction.

Jane settled back on the sofa to enjoy the performance, one hand leaving her lap and coming to rest on the upholstery at her side. Her fingers touched paper, and she looked down at the notecard. In bold, masculine handwriting, she read Cherry's name on the outside. Unobtrusively, she picked up the note, easily holding it in her palm.

Jane looked about to be sure everyone's attention was elsewhere while she opened the notecard slightly and digested its contents. Then she slipped it between the cushions.

That I have been reduced to this! she thought bitterly. And if I didn't read notes addressed to someone else, notes found accidentally, I would have no clue about Cherry's little peccadilloes, she reminded herself. Obviously, Cherry would soon announce that she was retiring. Hadn't she said earlier she needed to write letters to her schoolgirl friends in London? Probably invented that tale just so she could escape and meet Lord Pierce! In the graveyard, thought Jane, stifling a shiver. Still, the message in the note held a desperate ring to it; perhaps they were planning an elopement! She had to go. Oh, she could confront Cherry now, but that would only lead to more subterfuge. She would have to speak to Peter, too.

Cherry's piece ended, and Pipkin entered with the tea tray. Bless his pious heart, thought Jane; he had read the boredom in her eyes at dinner and was trying to hurry their guest's visit along.

"These cakes are wonderful, Jane. There must be a new

cook here since I was a boy."

"No, it is still Mrs. Brown," said Jane, knowing that Mrs. Brown had never deemed it necessary to serve her best to such a rude and naughty little boy. "Do have another."

He helped himself to the last cake, spilling crumbs as he leaned over. Jane wondered again how such a mousey woman as his mother could ever have produced such a great lug of a man.

Then she turned her attention to Cherry; she had no wish to be up all night, so she would help Cherry make good on her escape. "Cherry, didn't you tell me you hadn't written those letters yet? You know, to your friends, apprising them of your arrival date in London."

"That's right," Cherry replied. "I really should make a start tonight."

What an excellent thespian she would make, thought Jane.

"You mean you haven't even written to Emily Bingham?" asked Aunt Sophie.

"I'm afraid not. I hate to be rude. . . ."

"We quite understand," said Cousin Roland, dusting off his hands and returning his cup and saucer to the tray. "I, myself, must be going. It's quite a long trip back to Bath. Still, at least we have a full moon tonight."

It was half past midnight when Jane slipped out of the house by the back stairs. The note had instructed Cherry to meet Peter at half past one. With any luck, Jane would send Lord Pierce packing before Cherry even left the house.

The family graveyard was located past the large, well-manicured gardens at the back of the house. One of her ancestors had built a small chapel on the grounds when she had grown too infirm to make the journey to services at the village church. This formidable matron had also engaged the services of a full-time clergyman. When she had died, she had instructed that she be buried beside the little stone chapel at Heartland. Since that time, all of the family had been interred there. The chapel itself was kept in good repair, but it was never used.

As a child, Jane had been locked in the dark building all of one afternoon. She had been playing hide-and-seek with Roland who was visiting. She had hidden in the chapel, and the door had been mysteriously jammed shut with a large stick. She was sure Roland was responsible, but no one would believe her. The hours spent in that stone chapel had been terrifying for a superstitious little girl, and she rarely went there afterwards.

These memories came flooding back as she made her way out of the garden and past the small stand of trees that shielded the chapel and its graveyard from the house's view.

She half-expected to see Lord Pierce's horse tied up by the fence, but the area was deserted. Jane paused, gathering her courage before opening the rusty gate. Its hinges creaked, rending the still night air like a knife.

I must tell the gardener to oil those, Jane told herself firmly.

Keeping to the center of the path, her eyes never straying to the graves on the left or right, she approached the chapel. The door was open. Odd, it was always kept closed, usually locked.

She hesitated, her fear overwhelming her boldness. Then a whisper of white appeared just at the corner of the building. Not on the ground, but higher up, as though floating. Jane turned and the apparition floated to the ground, coming closer, closer . . .

"Jane! My God, what have I done? Jane! Jane! Wake up; it is I!" Devlin sat on the ground and pulled her into his lap. He threw the gauzy white material off his body with one hand while gently patting her face with the other.

He hadn't expected this! He had expected her to put up

some sort of fight, some argument. But when the full moon had shown him her look of sheer terror, he had realized his mistake. Miss Jane Lindsay was a brave, strong woman when she faced another human being, but her own fears of the supernatural could vanquish her without so much as a whimper.

She hadn't even screamed; she'd just fainted dead away. If Drew hadn't been so busy rubbing her wrists and unbuttoning the top buttons of her woolen gown, he would probably have taken a whip to himself.

Let her be all right, he prayed. When he had climbed up that ladder he had found at the back of the chapel, he had felt clever and enterprising. He was pleased with the result as he swung down from the top rung, holding onto a rope, and waving his fluttering white costume in the moonlight.

Then she had fainted.

He was a cad, a cretin, a nincompoop! How could he have—

"Oh-h-h."

"Jane, my dearest, are you all right? Tell me."

"I . . . Where am I?" She struggled against his embrace and looked around. "Oh! what happened? How did you . . . ?" Her eyes came to rest on his discarded costume; his dark eyes followed her gaze, and he shifted uncomfortably.

"You! It was you!"

"Now, Jane, calm down, and I'll explain."

"Explain? Of all the low, despicable—the note, that was yours, too!"

He nodded, though it hadn't really been a question. "I was only trying to teach you a lesson," he began.

"A lesson? Hah! You did it to humiliate me! I never want to see you again, Lord Devlin!" She made his name sound like a curse, and he winced.

Jane struggled to rise, shaking his hand from her arm as he steadied her. Without another word, she walked away, her head held proudly, her steps firm and sure.

"At least let me escort you back to the house."

She ignored him, but Drew continued to walk by her side.

When they reached the kitchen door, Jane stopped and turned.

"I was quite in earnest, Lord Devlin. I never want to see you again. If we meet in public, I shall not cut you, for I wouldn't wish to stir up curiosity, but you are never to set foot on Heartland again."

The next morning, Jane took her bruised and battered pride and drove out before her aunt or cousin had risen. In the gig she packed food, medicines, and small treats to distribute among her tenants and the invalids in the parish.

Returning just in time to dress for tea, she was greeted by her maid.

"This came while you were out, Miss Jane," said Tucker, pointing to a single red rose on the dressing table. Frowning, she opened the attached card.

In the now-familiar scrawl was another quotation from *She Stoops to Conquer.*

"I'm so distracted with a variety of passions that I don't know what I do. Forgive me, madam."

                                                    Yours forever

Really! thought Jane, Cherry was carrying this too far! But Jane's temper quickly cooled; Cherry was leaving in a few days and she felt sure her cousin was the culprit. When Cherry left, the bogus love notes would cease.

Jane then decided she might just see if she could speed their departure along.

Two days later, Bath saw the leavetaking of two of its more lively inhabitants. Jane, who had had quite enough of

Cherry's escapades, had suggested to her aunt that they should depart quickly for London before the best dressmakers became too busy. Aunt Sophie had gasped in horror at the thought and insisted that they leave immediately. It had taken only two days for them to be ready.

Lord Drew Devlin hadn't exactly bolted from Bath, but he did decide rather quickly that his mother must be moped to death at his long absence, and he, too, left town.

Jane, who was basking in the sudden tranquility of her life, soon heard of the viscount's departure. She ignored the tiny flicker of distress that this news produced, and returned to her novel.

It was by Jane Austen, titled *Pride And Prejudice*. The characters were quite entertaining, decided Jane, but in reality, no one could fail to recognize such strong feelings as Mr. Darcy and Miss Elizabeth Bennet were having.

A week later, a disapproving Pipkin announced her cousin Roland Havelock.

"Jane, I feel fortunate to find you at home."

She eyed him curiously and bade him be seated.

Dressed in a dark blue morning gown of modest cut, Jane's appearance was at odds with Havelock's bright yellow pantaloons and puce waistcoat. He looked the perfect fop against her quiet elegance.

But Roland saw nothing amiss as he smiled coyly and produced a gold, heart-shaped box from behind his back.

"I'm going to visit my mother, and I wanted to bring you these to thank you for your hospitality during my visit."

"How kind of you, Roland. Thank you so much," said Jane, surprised by the gesture. Perhaps Roland had finally grown up, she hadn't believed him capable of such thoughtfulness — never mind that she broke out in a rash every time she ate chocolates.

She slipped the satin ribbon off the box and offered one to her cousin, saying, "I believe I shall wait, but do have one, Roland."

He gave a wheezing laugh and held up his pudgy hands. "No, I mustn't indulge. Must watch my figure, you know. But there is a small favor I must ask of you, Jane."

Ah, here it is, thought Jane.

"Since I'm going home, I will have no need of additional servants. But I do hate to leave this one chap high and dry, as it were. He's been with me several years; he's acted as my butler, valet, footman — even a groom, if needed. Just an all-around decent fellow. I was wondering if you might have a place for him here?"

Jane had to admit she had misjudged her cousin. Here he was, concerning himself with a servant's plight. To make amends, she said, "Of course. Have him come out in the morning; I'll tell Pipkin to expect him."

"You won't regret it!" He reached across to pat her hand and knocked the cutwork table scarf to the floor. "So clumsy of me," he said amidst a creaking of corsets as he bent to retrieve the scarf.

"What's this?" he asked, holding up a piece of jewelry.

"Oh, it is Grandmother's pendant. I was wearing it earlier when the clasp broke. I must take it to have it fixed."

"It must be very valuable."

"I suppose so; the stone is very fine, but I value it because it's such a part of Heartland tradition. It's my good luck charm; it could never be replaced."

"No, it certainly couldn't. Now really, I can't stay. I have other calls to make before I leave tomorrow."

"Be sure to give your mother my best."

"I certainly shall. No, no, I can see myself out. Good-bye, Cousin."

"Good-bye, Roland."

Later, when Jane left the room, she picked up the box of sweets and took them to the kitchen.

"Mrs. Brown, could you do something with these? You know how I am about bonbons, and I really don't want them."

"Certainly, Miss Lindsay," said the austere woman.

"Thank you." Jane smiled at her and received naught but the tiniest lift of the lips in return. Mrs. Brown must be in a good mood today, she thought wryly as she left.

Tom, the pot boy, stared open-mouthed at the pretty box as Mrs. Brown opened it.

"Nothing but trouble," she announced. Tom frowned and watched in mounting horror as the formidable woman opened the back door.

Mrs. Brown would have been indignant had anyone called her vain, but the truth was she could not bear the thought of anyone under her domain consuming food prepared by anyone other than herself. If the family wanted to go to dinner somewhere else, that was their business; they were quality. But the lesser servants knew better!

With the wide-eyed pot boy watching in agony, Mrs. Brown stepped to the edge of the kitchen yard and threw the chocolates as far as she could. Tom stifled a gasp.

"You, Tom, close your mouth and get back to work!"

He did as Mrs. Brown bade him—everyone did—but he sniffed quietly as he bent over his scrubbing.

Jane encountered Pipkin as she retraced her steps to the morning room. "Pipkin, I told Mr. Havelock that we would be able to help him with a slight problem he has."

"Yes, Miss Jane?"

"It seems he no longer requires the services of a servant who has been in his employ several years. He asked if we might have a place for him, and I told him we did."

"Yes, Miss Jane? In what capacity has he served?"

Jane frowned. "He said the man has acted as his valet, butler, footman, and even groom. Surely you can find something for the man to do. He seems quite versatile."

"As you wish, miss." When Jane had nodded, he turned, raised his eyes, and said, "Though I walk in the midst of trouble, thou wilt revive me: thou shalt stretch forth thine hand against the wrath of mine enemies, and thy right hand shall save me."

* * *

The next morning, Tom came shuffling in from the pump outside, carrying two dead pidgeons.

"What's that?"

"I found 'em, ma'am, in the yard."

"Well, get those nasty, diseased things out o' here before I take a switch to you! They're of no use to me!"

Tom hurriedly took the dead birds beyond the yard to dispose of them.

Jane, dressed for her morning ride, hailed the boy.

"What do you have there, Tom?"

"Two dead birds, ma'am," he answered, shuffling his feet at this unusual attention from his mistress.

"Did you trap them?"

"Oh, no, ma'am. I wouldn' do that! I found 'em in th' garden, honest I did."

"What could have killed them do you suppose?" Her question was rhetorical, but Tom was ready with his answer.

"Choc'lats! See?" He lifted one of the birds for her inspection and there, on the beak, were traces of dark chocolate. "That's wot did 'em in. Mrs. Brown threw out th' box wot ye gave 'er yesterday, ma'am. I guess choc'lat poisoned t'birds."

"So it would seem," murmured Jane. Then she smiled down at the boy and said seriously, "Thank you for taking care of this, Tom. You must make sure the rest of those chocolates are picked up and thrown away. No eating any, mind you. They must have been spoiled, and we don't want you getting sick."

He promised, "Cross me 'eart an' spit in yer eye."

Jane continued on her way to the stables, putting the matter of chocolates and dead pidgeons from her mind.

♡ *Chapter Four* ♡

Jane's life slipped into a tranquil routine. Mornings were for rides and household duties. Afternoons were for estate business or receiving and making calls.

In the weeks since her aunt and Cherry had departed for London, there had been no anonymous notes or gifts. Jane was glad of it, for it proved to her that Cherry had been behind it all along. With this little annoyance out of the way and her new spinster status firmly settled, she would be much more content.

Jane avoided confronting certain facts, however, when she told herself how happy she was. No matter what she did, the viscount was never far from her mind. The most frustrating occasion had been when she visited the ruins. The abbey had always been a source of solace and peace for her. But her mind had betrayed her; her eyes saw only his face when she walked among the fallen stones. Even her remembrances of her father couldn't erase Devlin's image for long. It had been more than a month, and she could not bring herself to return.

Many of her neighbors left for London for the Season, so there were very few dinners or country balls to attend. This suited Jane at first; she was tired of the rush and inconvenience. Still, she was feminine, and she longed to show off her new, colorful gowns now that her period of mourning was at an end.

She dined with the rector and his wife; she attended a

small card party at Lord Pierce's house—his mother and sisters hadn't gone to London yet. But she couldn't bring herself to attend the assemblies in Bath alone. Tucker urged her to go, but the thought of arriving by herself was daunting; she supposed Cherry's presence hadn't been all negative.

But April was drawing to a close, and the Ashmores were giving their yearly "breakfast," a curiously named event which began at three in the afternoon and ended in the small hours of the next morning.

Jane planned to wear an apple green gown with a lace overdress. It was cut more daringly than most of her gowns, but now that she was well and truly on the shelf, she could dress as she pleased. She had experienced some doubts about the neckline which seemed to show an alarming amount of bare bosom. Mrs. Warner had declared it was quite high compared to other ladies', but then other ladies hadn't Jane's generous cleavage. Still, Jane had allowed herself to be persuaded.

The chip straw bonnet with matching green ribbons gave her a girlish look that belied her advancing age. She planned to change the bonnet for a dainty pearl and emerald tiara before the dancing began in the evening. And Jane planned to dance; even if she was not a good dancer, she would enjoy herself.

Finally the first of May arrived, a beautiful day for the traditional May Day festivities. It was also Jane's birthday; she was five and twenty. A quarter of a century, she told herself in the mirror after popping out of bed with her usual morning vigor. Jane grinned and stuck out her tongue at the impish image.

"Happy Birthday, Miss Jane," said Tucker, entering through the dressing-room door.

"Thank you, Tucker. What a beautiful day it is!"

"Always is for your birthday, miss. There are flowers and baubles all over downstairs, Miss Jane."

"Then let's make me presentable and get on with it. No," she said, "just leave my hair down this morning. I want to act like a girl today."

99

"Too bad Miss Cherry and Mrs. Pettigrew couldn't be home for your birthday."

"True, but I shan't pine, not with the Ashmores' al fresco breakfast and all my friends around me. And of course, you, Pipkin, and Nana are family, too."

Tucker took a deep breath and said softly, "Thank you, Miss Jane; you're that kind, you are."

Jane squeezed the maid's hand, then Tucker set to work and soon had her mistress ready to face the day.

Jane stopped by each bouquet of flowers, carefully reading the cards. She thought how wonderful it was to have so many friends; one didn't have to be married to be happy. Beside her plate at the breakfast table was a small mountain of packages — a shawl from Lady Tarpley, handkerchiefs from the Ashmores, a porcelain bird from her aunt, and . . . Jane blushed and quickly stuffed the pair of pink silk pantalettes back into the box. Cherry! Would she never cease to be a source of embarrassment?

Jane was down to the last box. There was no card on the outside, and Jane opened it quickly, her curiosity piqued. Inside lay a slim leatherbound volume. She turned to the title page cautiously. *"She Stoops to Conquer,"* she breathed, and read the scrawled inscription:

I have taken the liberty of underlining two passages on page 22 — would that I possessed as much audacity as brave Marlow.

Ever Yours

Hastily, Jane turned to the page and read,

"By coming close to some women, they look younger still; but when we come very close indeed. . . ." (Attempting to kiss her.) "I protest, child, you use me extremely ill. If you keep me at this distance how is it possible you and I can be ever acquainted?"

Underlined twice were the stage directions: "Attempting

to kiss her."

"Pipkin," said Jane sharply, and the butler appeared at her elbow. "From whence did this package come?"

"A clerk from Duffield's on Milsom Street delivered it this morning personally, Miss Jane."

Jane pushed away from the table; a footman leapt forward to remove her chair. With book in hand, she entered the morning room and sat down by the window, falling into a brown study.

Obviously, her surmise had been incorrect; Cherry was not behind the mysterious notes.

Then who was?

She knew of no one who would wish to pull such a prank on her, except Cherry. But Cherry would never go to such lengths to continue it when she was in the middle of her first Season in London. It had to be someone else, and since no one else had reason to try to trick her, the notes must be sincere. But who could have formed such a strong, and, thought Jane, peculiar attachment to her? And why not come forward?

There was no one. . . . Well, there was Mr. Primrose, the shy curate. Still, she hadn't seen him since dining at the rector's.

Unable to answer her own questions, Jane rose and wandered out of the room, ascending the stairs slowly. She stopped by the corridor leading to her room. Turning, she opened a door, revealing the narrow staircase leading to the nurseries.

Her old nurse greeted her warmly.

"So, ye've turned a year older, m'dear." The shriveled old lady cocked her head to one side, studying Jane carefully. Jane knew what was coming—Nana had been saying the same thing every birthday since Jane could walk. "You don't look any different from when I saw you yesterday."

They both laughed at her familiar jest, and Jane sat down on the edge of the feather bed.

"What did ye come to see yer old Nana about, love?"

"I can never keep my thoughts from you, can I? Still, I've

no desire to, for the truth is, I need your help."

Jane was so clearly troubled, her old nurse gripped the arms of her rocker, her wrinkled face pursed attentively.

"Do you remember the valentine I received that wasn't signed?" Nana nodded. "I received several afterwards. I showed you one or two, remember?"

"Yes, and ye was convinced they were from Cherry, or that she was behind it."

"I was, and when they stopped after Cherry left, I felt positive I had been correct." Jane held out the leather book. "This arrived this morning — delivered personally from one of the local booksellers." Jane read the note and the passages to her mentor.

Nana shook her head thoughtfully. "That's not from yer cousin, missy. Just like the others. 'Tis from some man who's too shy or backwards to speak for hisself, so 'e writes down what 'e thinks. Why, 'e can't even think for hisself. 'E lets some book say what 'e means."

"I just don't know. If you're right, then which gentleman of my acquaintance is so awkward?"

"Why d'ye care, missy? That's what I'm wonderin'."

Jane looked annoyed. "I want these silly notes to stop, and that's all I want. I'm quite happy the way I am, and I certainly wouldn't be interested in someone so strange."

"Then it's not romance yer searchin' for?"

"Certainly not!"

"Hmm. I've an idea who it is," said the old woman dramatically. "There's only one man who could write such nonsense, and that's that silly Mr. Primrose."

"That's who I thought of, too. But remember, Nana? Mr. Primrose sent another valentine on the night of the ball. Why would he have sent two?"

"Just t' keep ye wonderin'."

"He does often seek out my company, but it is always about some church project."

"Just an excuse."

"I suppose." Jane stood up.

"What are ye goin' to do about 'im, lass?"

"I must talk to him to be certain he is the author of these aggravating notes, and then I shall insist he stop." Jane bent to kiss the wrinkled cheek, but her mind was already wrestling with the task ahead.

Jane stood on the edge of the Ashmores' terrace overlooking sloping green lawns. The Ashmores were relatively new to Bath, having lived there only fifteen years. They had built their house in the style of an Italian villa with a large quantity of open spaces, columns, and smooth marble.

Mrs. Ashmore had declared herself tired of the huge open tent they had erected in the past, so her amenable husband had ordered large circular umbrellas in rainbow colors. Mrs. Ashmore had arranged these in groups of two or three with seating for a dozen or so under each.

The result was quite inviting, thought Jane, as she surveyed the grounds. The colorful gowns of the ladies added to the beauty of the scene. In the background was the River Avon; two or three punts had already been launched with gallant, if unskilled, gentlemen rowing their ladies.

"So good to see you, Jane dear, and many happy returns." said Mrs. Ashmore as she toddled across the terrace. The two women were a study in contrasts: one tall and stately, the other short and round, looking rather like a spinning top as she rolled along. But no one dared belittle Mrs. Ashmore's appearance; this lady was, Jane always thought, one of the truly sincere people in the world. Jane could not recall ever hearing so much as a mild rebuke cross Mrs. Ashmore's lips.

"I want to thank you for the lovely lace handkerchiefs," began Jane. "And I must compliment you, Mrs. Ashmore. You have outdone yourself this year. The gardens are beautiful."

"I'm glad you think so. Mind you, Mr. Ashmore said I had windmills in my head when I told him no big tent, but he is such a dear. Spoils me dreadfully! Now, come along; we'll see who we can find." She reached up and took Jane's arm, leading her down the broad steps, talking all the while.

103

"Lady Pierce is here with her girls. They leave for London in a day or two, but they are always so obliging to stay for my little breakfast."

"They wouldn't wish to miss the best entertainment of the year!"

"Best in the spring, perhaps," laughed Mrs. Ashmore. "We all know Heartland's Valentine Ball is the central entertainment of the year. Only think of all the little romances that begin that night! Why, even this year, Mr. — uh, but I am being premature." She winked at Jane. "I shan't say another word!"

Jane shot her a puzzled frown, but didn't have time to comment as Mary Aubrey greeted her.

Mrs. Ashmore excused herself, and Mary took over as Jane's guide, seeming to stroll aimlessly among the other guests.

"We leave in two days' time," said Mary with an obvious lack of enthusiasm.

"Don't you want to go?" Jane was surprised; Mary was hardly a social butterfly, but she had never avoided doing the Season.

"Let us say that I am not anxious to exchange Bath's quiet round of family and friends for the tedium of hourly social obligations. Surely you can understand that."

"Yes, I do."

"Unfortunately, Mama can't." Mary looked around, spotting the shy Mr. Primrose, and they moved to join him beneath a large pink umbrella.

"Ladies, I am honored," he announced breathlessly as he looked nervously at Jane. He returned to his own chair after seating them, his eyes straying to Mary occasionally, but he restricted his conversation to Jane.

Amos Primrose was aptly named; he had blond hair and a pale complexion. The least attention made him blush a bright pink. But he was a man of strong convictions, and the few times he had delivered a sermon in the village church, his passionate words had stirred the congregation. Socially, however, his conversation was stumbling and awkward, as it was with Jane and Mary.

Safety lay in conversing about church matters, and to this end, he addressed Jane. "I shall send you a note about the Spring Bazaar. You organized it so well last year, I hope we may count on you again, Miss Lindsay."

"Yes, I'd be happy to do so."

"You know I would help, Jane, if I were going to be here," said Mary wistfully. Jane was about to make a sympathetic rejoinder when Mary's seventeen-year-old sister hurried up to them.

"Mary, Mama needs your help."

"In a minute, Margery."

"She said now." Margery, who was trying very hard to sound sophisticated, only managed to appear a talebearer.

"Very well, if you'll excuse me."

Mary departed, leaving Jane alone at the table with Mr. Primrose. Despite her resolution to discuss with him his peculiar note-writing habits, Jane was distracted by his agitated manner. He began drumming his fingers on the wood.

To end this irritating noise, Jane asked quickly, "What is it, Mr. Primrose?"

"I . . . uh, that is, I . . ." She smiled at him, and he plunged ahead. "It is unbearable that it should continue as it is, Miss Lindsay."

When she didn't reply, he put his head in his hands, then sat up and looked around self-consciously.

"I fear I owe you an apology."

"So it is you," said Jane, glad to have her suspicions confirmed.

He frowned. "No, that is, I did tell Mary, Miss Aubrey, to fetch you here, that there could be no occasion for gossip if the three of us were here together."

"Mr. Primrose, I should tell you that I guessed your secret some time ago. I wasn't certain, mind you, but today has proven my suspicions correct."

"You did? But how?"

"There are not many other people who would have resorted to . . ." Jane paused. She had been about to say "sub-

105

terfuge," but that was, perhaps, too harsh. "Shall we just say writing instead of calling?"

"But I wasn't allowed to call — except on church business."

Now it was Jane's turn to frown in confusion. "Who told you not to call? I'm certain I never said such a thing, Mr. Primrose. And I assure you, though I cannot return your regard, your suit would have been looked on with the greater respect, had you but spoken."

Mr. Primrose was obviously baffled. He had spoken, and Lord Pierce had warned him away, as had Mary's mother. But perhaps Miss Lindsay meant she was willing to intercede on his behalf.

Hopefully, he said, "Would you speak to Lady Pierce for me?"

Jane's mouth dropped open. The awful realization of her misunderstanding hit her like a blow, and she sat back, too stunned to speak.

"I realize I am being presumptuous, asking too much, but . . ." His blush deepened as he looked up to discover another guest standing close by, evidently awaiting the end of his conversation with Miss Lindsay.

"But here is Lord Devlin. I'd no idea you were returned to Bath, sir. Welcome back." Mr. Primrose stood up and bowed deeply, his usual pale color returning.

"Thank you, Mr. Primrose. It is good to be back. I had forgotten some of Bath's more charming qualities during my journey north. Actually, I was wondering if I might steal your attractive companion."

"Of course, Lord Devlin."

"Miss Lindsay, will you honor me with a stroll?"

"Thank you, Lord Devlin," said Jane, recovering from her contemplation of a narrow escape. She rose quickly, anxious to be gone, but she paused and said softly, for Mr. Primrose's ears alone, "I will do what I can."

He pumped her hand energetically, his complexion turning that bright pink once again.

Lord Devlin appeared disinclined to talk, and this suited Jane admirably. What a fool she had made of herself — al-

106

most. She and Mr. Primrose had been speaking at cross-purposes; she didn't think her words had registered with him. She devoutly hoped not!

But no, he had been too busy considering his own plight with Mary. Evidently, their attachment was a relationship of some time — and depth. And that was Mary's reason for wanting to forego the trials of another Season in London.

What was Lady Pierce thinking? Mary had turned down at least two offers of which Jane was aware, and now she had found a man to love. What matter if he had little money. He wasn't penniless; neither was Mary. And Lady Pierce had three more daughters to launch!

Out loud, Jane muttered, "Matchmaking mothers can be so foolish!"

Drew stopped and turned to her, that familiar twinkle in his dark brown eyes. "Since I know you can't be referring to me, I shan't take offense at that comment. But judging from your fierce expression, someone is in your black book."

Jane's laughter bubbled forth and her smile was warm and intimate. "Dreadful man! Where have you been?"

"To York first, to take my mother from the castle tower, at great risk to myself, I might add."

"I must admit I'm glad the dragon didn't win, sir."

"Are you? I was afraid you might be cheering the dragon on after our last unfortunate encounter."

"Unfortunate?" Jane said loudly. Then she looked about her and lowered her voice. "A mild word for such an abominable prank, Lord Devlin."

"Drew, my name is Drew," he said, looking down on her.

"How nice for you, Lord Devlin."

"You insist on torturing me, Jane?"

"I insist on being respectful and respected, sir."

"Hmm. How dull, but I shall leave it at that for now."

Jane let it pass; she didn't wish to argue with anyone — even Lord Devlin — on her birthday. But she couldn't refrain from asking, "Where are you taking me?"

He laughed. "We are making progress, you and I. Two months ago, you wouldn't have taken two steps without questioning my motives. As a matter of fact, I want to introduce you to someone very special to me."

Jane felt a vise close over her heart. Not only had she guessed wrong about Mr. Primrose, but even Lord Devlin was about to defect. Where had he met this special someone? Not that she cared; she couldn't care less. . . . Could she?

But Jane had no time to answer this disturbing question as they were fast approaching a chattering group of older people seated on chairs in the shade of a towering oak.

Two matrons sat a little apart from the others, and it was here that Drew stopped.

"Your Grace," he said, nodding to one lady whom Jane recognized as the dowager duchess of Wentworth. "I believe you said you had met Miss Jane Lindsay several years ago."

"So I did, my boy, though I daresay Miss Lindsay has no recollection of it. It was during your first Season in London."

"Thank you for remembering, Your Grace."

"And this is my mother, Faith Peterson."

Jane felt an immediate warmth from this lady as she looked into dark eyes that were so like her son's. Jane smiled and dropped a curtsey to both ladies.

"Won't you join us, Miss Lindsay?" said Mrs. Peterson. Her voice was soft, though Jane had no trouble hearing her. She was an attractive woman of fifty years or so; her dark hair, barely touched with gray, matched her eyes.

When Drew had seated Jane, the dowager duchess barked, "Now, my boy, run along and bring me some of that iced champagne punch."

"My pleasure, Your Grace." He grinned at Jane as if to apologize for abandoning her.

But Jane was rarely discomfited in social situations. Actually, *never* was the correct word — with the exception of any situation that included Lord Devlin. But he was gone for the moment, and Jane began to enjoy her conversation with her new acquaintances.

"Drew has been telling me about your house, Miss Lindsay. He made me curious, so I looked it up in the guide books. It has quite a romantic history," said Mrs. Peterson.

"Yes, we are rather proud of that history."

"It's fine to be proud of one's ancestors, but it's the present that matters, I always say," said Her Grace.

"Now, Martha, we mustn't be rude," temporised her friend.

The duchess laughed and said to Jane, "Faith Peterson is another Dolly Ashmore. You will never hear a harsh word from her; she is always agreeable."

"She is exaggerating, Miss Lindsay."

"Not a word of it. Sometimes it makes me feel so cross, I just try to goad her into a temper. But it has never worked, I promise you, not even when we were girls together." With this, the duchess excused herself and turned her attention to the conversation at the next table.

"I have had my moments, I assure you, Miss Lindsay. No one could be as saintly as Martha says."

Jane smiled. "I do hope not; I would feel quite downcast to think anyone was that perfect. I myself sometimes have the most dreadful temper."

"So I have heard," said Mrs. Peterson, her gentle tones and friendly expression robbing her words of offense.

"No doubt," responded Jane.

"Yes, Drew has been quite vocal, but then he always was. At times, I was very put out living in a household with several obstinate males, though Drew was as nothing compared to my brother-in-law, his uncle. How I have missed Drew!" Tears sprang to the older woman's eyes as she spoke of her son.

Jane wondered how he could have left her all those years without so much as a thought. No wonder he was trying to make it up to her now. She thought she could almost forgive him for trying to buy Heartland.

"You were very glad to see him again."

"Glad? It was like a dream come true when I received his letter. He wanted to take me away immediately, but I told him to go to London and reacquaint himself with society first. If they had rejected him, I would have—"

"But surely there was no question of his acceptance? As

the heir of an earldom, he would be accepted everywhere."

"Perhaps, but there was that incident—though it occurred so long ago. I have found many people have very long memories." A shadow crossed her eyes briefly before she shrugged it off and smiled at Jane again.

"Let us speak of happier times," suggested Jane, afraid their conversation was taking too personal a turn. After all, she told herself, she had no wish to know about Lord Devlin's personal history. "Are you here on a visit, or are you going to live in Bath?"

"Drew has taken a charming house in Laura Place. I am quite satisfied with it, but he, of course, wants something better for his mama. But we shall see," she added, smiling in a way that led Jane to believe her wishes would be granted in the end. "You must come to tea one day."

"I would love to, Mrs. Peterson. And perhaps Drew will bring you to Heartland for a visit."

"We'll just have to see to it, Miss Lindsay."

"See to what?" asked the viscount as he handed each of them a glass of punch from the footman's tray. Drew waved the servant toward the other tables and joined them.

"Miss Lindsay has kindly invited me to Heartland, and I said I would see if you might be persuaded, if you don't mind, to take me one day soon."

He raised a brow and said, "Are you certain I am included in Miss Lindsay's invitation? I seem to recall . . ."

Jane blushed, but the viscount couldn't tell if it was anger or embarrassment that had brought the becoming color to her cheeks. But he wouldn't complete what he had been about to reveal about her previous ultimatum.

"Of course you are included!" said his mother. "Miss Lindsay is too gracious to exclude you, Drew, no matter what you may have done."

"Thank you, Mrs. Peterson. Shall we say Thursday?"

"Lovely, I shall look forward to it."

"Now, I really must go and pay my respects to Lady Pierce. She will be going up to London in two days' time, and I must say good-bye. I'm very glad I met you, Mrs.

Peterson."

"And I you," she responded, smiling kindly, but with that same merry twinkle in her eyes.

Drew, however, seemed to have slipped into a dark mood. He stood up and bowed, but didn't say a word of farewell.

"She is lovely, Drew," said his mother quietly.

"Yes, she is, but too damned self-possessed," he muttered.

"Drew!"

"I beg your pardon, Mother. I forgot myself."

"You wouldn't want some empty-headed miss to share the cold evenings with, my dear."

"Who said anything about sharing cold evenings! I only made that observation because it's true. Sharing anything with Miss Jane Lindsay is the last thing on my mind!"

"If you say so, but it is odd how often she creeps into your conversation."

"Nonsense! If I have mentioned her at all, it has been because of my desire to buy her estate. Since there's no hope of that, I haven't given her a moment's thought," he growled.

"Of course not," she said, smiling into his scowling face.

"Bah! There's no talking to you about it. You see orange blossoms every time I even mention a female's name. I'll leave you to your friends."

Stopping here and there to greet other friends and to thank them for their birthday remembrances, Jane slowly made her way to Lady Pierce's table. She was not looking forward to her conversation with that estimable lady, but she had promised Mr. Primrose, and she was always one to keep her promises.

Lady Pierce was seated under a bright yellow umbrella. Her hair was flame red, though everyone agreed this was due to art rather than nature. Her gown was of bright purple satin. On her feet, she wore silver shoes with red lacquer heels, a fashion some thirty years before. Surrounding her were half of the younger guests at the breakfast. Lady Pierce was what some people called eccentric. In reality, she simply loved bright things: bright colors and bright young people. She greeted Jane warmly and offered a heavily rouged cheek

111

for Jane to kiss.

"Lady Pierce, I had to speak to you before you leave. It will be dull around here without you and your family."

"How kind of you to say so, Jane. But, of course, I know how you must be missing that darling girl Cherry. I know I miss her myself. And Margery is devastated until she can rejoin her childhood friend."

Jane made a suitable reply to this. In truth, she suspected Miss Margery was simply devastated because Cherry had a headstart on her in London.

"I understand Mary doesn't want to leave just now."

"No, she has some strange notions, but as I told her, as soon as we get to London, and she starts receiving all those invitations . . . Well, you know what it is like!"

"Perhaps you are right, but I thought Mary might enjoy staying with me at Heartland. I know I would love the company, for as you just said yourself, it is terribly quiet without Cherry."

The older woman appeared much struck by this, but she wagged a plump finger at Jane and whispered, "There is one problem with that, my dear. Mary has made an unsuitable attachment here in Bath, and I think it best if she distances herself from that young man."

"Unsuitable? I see."

"Oh, perhaps you don't. It is . . ." She looked around at the bevy of young people laughing and talking, and she lowered her voice even further. "It is Mr. Primrose." She sat back and nodded wisely, waiting for a shocked expression to appear on Jane's face. None did, and Lady Pierce thought it best to impress upon Mary's friend exactly how unfortunate such an attachment was. "He is in the clergy, you know. And they are always poor. Mary has a small annuity, but it would not be enough to live on."

"True, but Mr. Primrose is hardly a pauper. And have you ever attended services when he gave the sermon?"

Lady Pierce, whose idea of a good sermon was a short sermon, rolled her eyes and nodded.

"Personally, I thought he was magnificent," whispered

Jane. "I thought to myself, why, this lowly curate may just one day be a bishop — a wealthy and powerful bishop."

Jane awaited the effect of this disclosure patiently. Lady Pierce frowned, pondering this possibility.

"I wonder if the wife of a bishop receives many invitations from influential people."

"Undoubtedly."

"But he isn't a bishop now," countered the older woman.

"No, but that really doesn't matter. It won't matter until there are children, grandchildren, to launch in society."

"I don't know. I would miss her so. In London, I mean."

"Then why not announce an engagement today — tonight at the ball? Mary would be delighted to go to London then. She would need to go to London to shop for her trousseau. And you would have the pleasure of introducing only one unattached daughter."

"I must think about this, Jane. Not a word to anyone, mind, until I've made up my mind."

"You know I won't breathe a word, Lady Pierce." Jane rose said and curtseyed before moving away.

"Look at her," said Lord Devlin under his breath as a group of ladies entered the Ashmore's open ballroom some hours later. Had anyone been listening, they would have known instantly to whom he referred, for his eyes followed Jane Lindsay's movements as she crossed the room.

He moved to intercept her, but stopped as that curate claimed her. Mr. Primrose didn't appear to be leading her into the dance; instead he led her to a sofa and seated himself by her side. He was going to take her hand in his! thought Devlin, clenching his fists. No, Primrose shook her hand firmly and dropped it. He was leaving her.

"Miss Lindsay, do say you've saved a dance for me," said the viscount, his voice softer than he had intended.

She laughed. "I have confessed to you my reputation for dancing, Lord Devlin. So does everyone else. I have almost all my dances left."

"This one, I hope?" The musicians were beginning a waltz.

Jane nodded. "Don't say you haven't been duly warned."

"You forget, I have danced the waltz with you once before."

Jane looked up quickly, expecting the familiar twinkle to be in those dark eyes. She was unprepared for the passion mirrored there, and her breath quickened in response. She dropped her gaze as they took the floor, concentrating on her steps.

It was even easier than before, she thought in wonder as they glided around the room, twirling and turning until she felt quite giddy. They didn't speak, but a dreamy smile formed on her lips, and she leaned back in Lord Devlin's arms and studied his face.

The music ended, and Jane felt as though she had awakened from a sweet sleep. The smile froze and faded as the ballroom and its other occupants came into focus.

She was passed from one partner to another after that. Jane had always been popular, but it had been her ability to put people at ease that accounted for this, not her prowess on the dance floor. Not, she told herself, that some miracle had made her graceful. She was still too stiff, but she felt capable of following the dance creditably after her success with Lord Devlin. He was quite a teacher, she told herself.

Surreptitiously, Jane watched the viscount's performance with other ladies. He was certainly at ease, but she failed to see any of his other partners lose themselves in his arms the way she had. She stumbled and her partner had to catch her up to prevent a mishap. Jane, she addressed herself sternly, pay attention to this dance, this partner, or you'll soon find yourself a wallflower.

Before Jane knew it, supper was being served. It was a buffet, a sumptuous array of meats and vegetables, poached, sautéed, stuffed, and braised to perfection. Fresh fruits had been arranged artistically between platters of cheeses and delectable pastries. Servants made certain wine glasses were never empty.

114

Jane's presence had been requested at several tables, but Mary Aubrey took her arm and guided her to a table of young people. Mary was sitting, Jane noted happily, between her mother and Mr. Primrose. It took little effort on her part to discover that Lady Pierce had approved Mr. Primrose as her future son-in-law.

In such a merry group, Jane had only to lend half an ear to the conversation. There were no deep literary or philosophical discussions to ponder, so she was at leisure to observe other tables. She turned after agreeing that yes, the Prince Regent was the kindest of hosts, and encountered Lord Devlin's lazy gaze. How long had he been watching her? He continued to stare, never smiling precisely, but with a pleasant expression. He didn't nod or acknowledge her in any way. Finally, Jane turned back to her own table.

A few minutes later, she looked again, but Lord Devlin's table was empty. Jane waited impatiently for her own group to return to the ballroom. She wasn't certain why; Lord Devlin hadn't even spoken to her since their first dance. He had very likely gone home without giving her another thought.

She didn't care if he had, she told herself, looking this way and that to locate him among the many guests. She was becoming much too concerned with the viscount. She would simply ignore him for the remainder of the evening.

"Miss Lindsay, I have heard a rumor about your friend Mary Aubrey. It is said that she is to marry Mr. Primrose."

Jane pivoted and found herself looking into Lord Devlin's dark moody eyes. "Yes, I believe we may wish them happy."

"We? So you wish them happy, also? I had thought—"

"Yes, Lord Devlin, what did you think?"

"It appeared this afternoon that you and Mr. Primrose were on intimate terms."

"How dare you?"

"I said it *appeared*. Apparently I was mistaken."

"I should think so! I even agreed to speak on his behalf—but I shouldn't be telling you this. It is none of your concern, Lord Devlin."

"Probably not, but I couldn't help overhearing you speak of writing or some such thing."

"That was a misunderstanding on my part." The music began again, and Jane looked wistfully at the couples taking the floor. She had been longing to dance with him again, she freely admitted this to herself. But it was only because he made her feel so graceful; she didn't even have to mind her steps when she was in his arms. But Jane Lindsay was only too aware of social conventions; she would never dream of asking the viscount to dance.

Lord Devlin's eyes followed her gaze. Did she really want to dance with him again? Two dances to one gentleman invited public speculation. It was not improper, but in someone with Miss Lindsay's impeccably spotless reputation, it would be noticed. Still, he found it impossible to deny what she obviously wanted. "Might I have this dance, Miss Lindsay?"

"Certainly, Lord Devlin," she answered eagerly, then chided herself for sounding like a gauche schoolgirl. What was the matter with her lately?

Jane found thinking impossible as they became lost in the heady steps of the waltz. There was some quality about this man, this Devilish Devlin that made her lose herself in his embrace. She had never felt so free.

Jane looked up and smiled dreamily. Devlin was about to pull her closer, then berated himself. She would be outraged at his making a spectacle of them. He looked at her beautiful green eyes, the creaminess of her silky skin, the generous swell of her breasts. He remembered how she had tried to hide her magnificent figure at the Valentine Ball; he had laughed, letting her know he had guessed her embarrassment. Yet here she was in his arms, more than willing to have him look at her, study her. He could do nothing less than oblige her, he decided.

Jane bit her lower lip nervously as he continued to stare. She was not embarrassed, though she had always abhorred the way men ogled her. But on this occasion she was neither angry nor embarrassed, and she refused to question the reason for this. But she did so want to thank him, to tell him . . .

"When you do that with your mouth," he whispered, "I want very much to kiss you, Jane."

Forgetting entirely to be outraged by his remark, Jane asked, "Do what?"

"Nibble at your lip in that bewitching manner."

"You shouldn't say things like that, Lord Devlin. I wanted to tell you something, but now—"

"Tell me; I promise I'll behave."

"I wanted to thank you for making me feel at ease when we dance. And it's not just when we dance; I feel more confident when I dance with anyone now." She blushed, and Drew watched with interest the way the color spread downward from her cheeks.

"You can thank me by calling me Drew."

"We have already discussed that, sir."

"Ah, so the deed I have done, the wonder I have wrought, for which you are eternally grateful, whatever it is, is not worth that one forfeit?"

"No . . . yes. Very well, but only when we are alone."

"Such as now, Jane?"

"Such as now, Drew."

And then he did pull her closer, scandalizing the more starchy matrons that watched. Jane saw their faces out of the corner of her eye, and suddenly she didn't care what they or anyone else thought. She gave herself up to the heady feeling of his thighs touching hers, his arm circling her waist. Boldly, she let her cheek rest against his chin and closed her eyes.

The music ended and the spell was broken. Drew led Jane to a chair beside his mother. Deliberately, he bowed and left her, seeking someone else, anyone else for the next dance. He wanted to laugh at himself. It was a new experience for him, protecting a lady's virtue from gossiping tongues. In the past, he had associated himself with demireps or ladies with shady reputations; there had been no need for discretion.

Even before his exile to the Indies, when he had thought himself passionately in love with Cynthia, it had been she who had kept him at a proper distance, much against his will.

He couldn't understand Jane. She was all that was proper. When he had first met her, he had thought her a veritable prude. Since then, she had changed. Perhaps she had drunk too much champagne. He couldn't recall ever seeing her drink to excess, and it was possible that an entire day spent socializing was more than she could handle.

This theory, however, was improbable, admitted the viscount as he watched his mother and Jane conversing. Jane appeared to be completely at ease, having no difficulty keeping up her end of the conversation.

The intricate movements of the dance brought him back to his partner, and he forced himself to be agreeable to Miss Whatever-her-name-was.

As for Jane, she was growing weary, weary of the black looks she was receiving from jealous young ladies and their gossiping mothers, weary of the speculative leers from several gentlemen who had heretofore considered her too proper, and most of all, weary from the way her body betrayed her every time Drew Devlin came into view. At the earliest opportunity, she found her hostess and said goodnight.

Still dressed in her bedclothes the next morning, Jane went up the stairs to the nursery to tell Nana about the Ashmores' picnic and ball. She described the dresses, the decorations, the food.

Finally, the old nurse grew impatient and asked, "What about Mr. Primrose? Did ye ask 'im about th' notes?"

"Yes, Nana. That is, I nearly did, but fortunately I realized he hadn't written any such notes to me. He's in love with Mary Aubrey!"

"Miss Aubrey? Why, I never would 'a guessed it, Miss Jane. I'm that sorry, I am."

118

Jane patted the gnarled hand. "Never mind, dear. You know very well I wasn't interested in him. But I think I was able to help them. Mary's mother was against it, but I believe I was able to persuade her otherwise. Perhaps they'll name their first child after me."

" 'Tis yer own babes ye should be namin'. But never you mind, dear," said the old woman. "Ye'll find the man who's been writing those notes. Mayhap 'twill be someone ye can love."

Jane laughed; her worries about the letters seemed trivial. She would no longer let them bother her.

"I'm going into town today, Nana. Is there anything I can bring you?" Jane knew the nurse would say no, and that she would end by bringing her of the some sweetmeats the old woman dearly loved.

She was about to leave when she spied a straight pin on the floor. "You've dropped a pin, Nana."

Jane was about to pick it up when the old woman said sharply, "No! I dropped 't, and I must pick 't up. Remember, 'twould be bad luck if I didn't."

"Of course, I forgot. I'll come see you when I return."

With her habit of shopping early, Jane was one of the first customers at the booksellers. While she no longer felt driven to discover who had sent the notes, she was curious. She asked to speak to the senior clerk and was whisked to a tiny office in the rear of Duffield's.

"How may I help you, Miss Lindsay?"

"I received a letter and a book yesterday. The book, a copy of *She Stoops To Conquer,* was from your establishment and one of your messengers delivered it. The note was unsigned, and I was hoping you could tell me who purchased the book."

"I remember the transaction. One of our new clerks helped this customer, and he required a little assistance. However, I'm afraid it would be impossible to tell you the name of the buyer. Whoever it was had merely sent a servant in with the note and asked that it be delivered with the book.

Naturally, we didn't ask the writer's name."

"Oh dear."

"I do hope this hasn't hurt our relationship with you, Miss Lindsay. You know you are one of our most valued customers. It is just that we often are asked to send small gifts to beautiful women, and to handsome men, for that matter, and the sender is usually quite careful to guard his or her anonymity."

"I quite understand, Mr. Fairfax. Do not distress yourself that I blame you in any way. I am glad to be considered one of your valued customers, and I must confess that I don't know where I would turn without Duffield's."

"You are most kind. If you wish, I will call the clerk to my office, and you may question him."

"I doubt it would be illuminating, but thank you anyhow. Now, I must see what you have that is new. Good day, Mr. Fairfax."

"Good day, Miss Lindsay."

From the booksellers, Jane went to the bootmaker. She had finally been forced to admit her favorite riding boots were past hope. Taking the well-worn pair with her in hopes of duplicating them, she placed her order. Both feet were carefully measured, the dimensions noted, and she was soon on her way again.

Her next stop was to the milliner where she spent an hour trying on the latest bonnets.

"I shall take the straw one with me, and you may send the green velvet shako when it is ready."

"Very good, Miss Lindsay," said the clerk, handing the velvet cloth Jane had brought in to a servant. "Will there be anything else?"

"Not today, thank you."

"And thank you for your patronage, Miss Lindsay."

"You're welcome." As Jane started through the door, she bumped into another customer just entering.

"Excuse me, ma'am," Jane said automatically.

"It was my fault. Why, Miss Lindsay, I didn't expect to meet you again so soon."

"Mrs. Peterson, how nice to see you."

"My dear, I am so glad we met. I hate to impose, but if you have the time, that is—"

"I am at your disposal, ma'am. If I may be of service to you in any way, it would please me to stay."

Mrs. Peterson smiled and asked, "Would you please help me choose a new bonnet? I can never find one that suits me." Jane protested, but the older woman waved away her compliments on the hat she was wearing. "You see, in the shop, they all look delightful, but once I get them home, they are never quite right."

"I'd be happy to, Mrs. Peterson, though I'm no expert on the latest fashion. I myself tend to wear whichever style pleases me the most."

"And the results are very agreeable, I assure you. The hat you wore at the Ashmores' breakfast was so becoming—light and frivolous, but eminently suitable. And today, that poke bonnet you are wearing is also flattering. Perhaps I wasn't meant to wear headdresses," concluded the doleful matron, seating herself in front of a mirror and untying the ribbons on her navy bonnet.

"I doubt that! Come, Mrs. Hill, show Mrs. Peterson that lovely straw bonnet, the one with the cherry red ribbons."

There is no more empathetic activity than trying on a wide variety of hats. One gets the chance to giggle at the absurd, gasp at the frightful, and exclaim over the beautiful. After an hour of such activity, Jane and Faith Peterson were well on their way to becoming fast friends.

After this successful expedition into the world of fashion, it was only natural that one lady should invite the other to a hot cup of tea, and that the other should accept. Jane's coach took them both the short distance from Milsom Street, across the River Avon to Laura Place.

The bright salon looked out on the street, affording its occupants a pleasant view. The furniture was upholstered in pale yellow chintz; the draperies and thick carpets were a blue-gray. There were green potted plants and vases of fresh flowers everywhere.

"What a delightful room, Mrs. Peterson."

"Thank you, Miss Lindsay. I'm a bit embarrassed by it every time I enter it."

"Why would you be embarrassed?"

The older woman laughed, a light girlish sound. "I've been here little more than a week, you know. It is a rented house, but when I first saw this room it was bright purple! I was horrified, and I'm afraid I let it show. Drew whisked me away to the furniture warehouses, draperymakers, rug dealers, and so on. Within one day's time, he had the room transformed to what you now see."

"But I fail to understand why you should feel embarrassed."

"But I do! I made Drew feel dreadful that he had chosen this house. He did so want me to like it."

"But you do, don't you?"

"It is lovely, now. But I felt like such a demanding mother, a veritable shrew."

"And I have told you at least a dozen times that you are no such thing, Mother!"

"Drew!" exclaimed Faith, her face alit as she watched her son enter the parlor. "You'll join us for tea, I hope."

"I wouldn't miss it, Mother. Hello, Jane. What brings you to Bath?"

"Shopping, Lord Devlin," she said, stressing his title.

He laughed as he pulled his chair closer to the sofa where Jane and his mother were seated.

"Jane is reminding me, Mother, that she only promised to use my first name when we were alone together."

"Quite right," said Mrs. Peterson. "But we are alone; I promise I am every bit as discreet as my son."

Jane glared at the viscount; he returned a wide-eyed stare.

"Jane and I are quite the best of friends, Drew."

"Are you?" he asked, accepting the cup of tea Jane passed him.

"Yes. Jane very kindly helped me select three new bonnets this morning. I don't know what I would have done without her."

"You exaggerate, ma'am."

"No, I'm not generally given to exaggeration. More than likely, I would have chosen the three ugliest hats in the shop, only I wouldn't have discovered it until I got home with them!"

The viscount laughed. "She's quite right, Jane. And then she would have kept them in the cupboard, too embarrassed to return them."

They were all laughing by now. Jane finally asked, "How do you know it won't happen again? You haven't tried them on at home yet."

"You're right. I'll do that right this minute!" She rang for the footman and told him to fetch all three hatboxes from her room.

When he returned, Faith Paterson picked up one hat. Standing in front of the fireplace which had a fine gilt mirror hanging above it, she carefully set the frothy confection of ribbons and organdy netting on her dark hair. Satisfied with the angle, she turned to her audience.

"Lovely, Mother, most becoming."

Jane seconded his verdict. While his mother was busying herself with the next bonnet, the viscount turned his attention to Jane.

"Did you meet Mother by accident?"

"Yes, as I was leaving the milliners', she was going in. She asked me to stay."

"I appreciate your helping her. She always seems so self-assured, even reserved, but it only masks her timidity. She is so eager to please, afraid of offending—especially those for whom she cares."

"Like you."

"And now you, I think. She wants to be a part of Bath society."

Their quiet conversation was interrupted as his mother requested their approval once more.

"With her girlhood friend the dowager countess and you to support her, she should do quite well."

"Your mother would be accepted anywhere, Lord Devlin."

He grimaced at the title, misinterpreting her meaning. "I don't want her accepted because her son will be the earl of Cheswick someday. That sort of thing can change to ridicule in the blink of an eye," he said bitterly. "I want her accepted for herself."

"She will be, I assure you, Drew," said Jane, placing her hand on his sleeve.

His eyes softened, and he took her hand in his own, holding it gently, almost reverently. Jane studied his face, her eyes questioning, wondering.

"What about . . . ?" Faith Peterson smiled and turned back to the mirror. She was very pleased indeed that she had happened upon Jane Lindsay earlier.

She cleared her throat loudly, and turned around again. This time, her query was met by two attentive listeners.

Jane took her leave not long afterwards, shyly reminding Drew and his mother that she was expecting them at Heartland on Thursday. On the ride home, Jane tried not to think about how many hours there were until teatime on Thursday.

♡ *Chapter Five* ♡

The evening of the same day she and Jane Lindsay had bought hats, Faith Peterson was attending a musicale the dowager duchess of Wentworth was giving. Drew had been included in the invitation, but he had declined emphatically. Her Grace believed those in her position were responsible for supporting the arts. Unfortunately, she had no ear for music, so the singers and musicians she collected as her protégés were often mediocre, if not terrible. Since only these performers comprised the duchess's musical evenings, her guests often left with the headache.

In the coach, however, Drew's mother asked him once more to join her.

"No, no, no, Mother. I see no reason to subject myself to such caterwauling. I much prefer a quiet game of cards."

"Very well." She was silent for a moment. Then, having gathered her courage, she said timidly, "Drew, what do you intend to do about Jane Lindsay?"

"Do? Why, Mother, must I do something?" he said haughtily.

"You can't trifle with her affections; she is too fine, too special."

"I assure you, Mother, I am not trifling with Miss Lindsay."

"Then you are serious, Drew?" she said, her delight showing in her voice. "When may I wish you happy?"

"Not so fast, Mother. Until we met again at the Ashmores—just yesterday, might I remind you—I would have sworn Jane Lindsay despised me."

"She couldn't!"

"Oh, she had good reason; I saw to that."

"Drew, what did you do?"

"Never mind, Mother. Evidently, Jane has forgiven me, but that doesn't mean she would welcome my suit. And for that matter, I've not yet made up my mind. Jane Lindsay is not like you, Mother. She is headstrong and opinionated, not precisely wifely traits."

His mother clutched at his arm; in the dim light of the carriage lamp, she peered at her son. "Drew, you mustn't consider meekness the most important trait in a wife. Love and respect for each other mean more. Without that, a marriage is empty, and bitterness grows." The anguish in her voice filled the air.

"Mother?"

"No, I've said too much already, Drew. I'll say no more. Ah! Here we are now."

"Enjoy the music, Mother."

She laughed. "Wretched boy!"

It was as well his own destination was but two streets away. His mother's revelations about her marriage had been unsettling. But it was what she hadn't said that disturbed him the most, and his own thoughts would take some time to sort out.

He was greeted warmly by his host Giles Stanton. They had met as mere boys at Eton. Being young and far away from home, they had formed a time-tested alliance. Drew, who was tall and strong even then, had protected Giles from the older boys until they had both been accepted. Giles, who possessed a sunny personality, won friends easily and shared them with the quiet, studious Drew.

"Drew! It's good to see you! Come in, come in! You know Harry Routh and Farley. And you remember m' brother Andrew? And this gentleman is Roland Havelock."

"Mr. Havelock and I are acquainted. How are you,

126

Havelock? Didn't know you'd returned to Bath."

"Nor I you, Devlin. Yes, I just got in today. Just here for a day or two, then on to London. What about you, old man?"

"I'm settled here for some time. I've brought my mother from York."

"How is she, Drew?" asked his old friend Giles.

"As sweet as ever, thank you. Now, what are we playing?" Lord Devlin seated himself as Farley dealt the cards.

Six hours later, the play broke up. Farley and Routh, who were slightly to go, offered Drew and Havelock a ride. Havelock could barely stand and accepted immediately. Drew declined, bade his host good night, and walked home.

He rarely drank to excess, and the cool night breeze soon refreshed him, sharpening his thoughts. And his thoughts returned to his mother's advice.

When he had left for York, he had been confused. His anger at Jane Lindsay's harsh condemnation had quickly faded, mainly because he knew she had been justified. And knowing she never wanted to see him again had helped his decision to put her out of his mind.

Miss Jane Lindsay wasn't made for dalliance, even though her figure made such an idea dizzying. But marriage had been the last thing on the Viscount Devlin's mind since he returned to England and visited his malevolent uncle in York the past summer.

Lord Cheswick had never been a pleasant man, always seeking more power, more money. But fate had rendered him bitter with the death of two sons and the knowledge that his title and estate would go to his despised nephew. His only pleasures now came from exercising his power over his relatives.

The old man's frustration grew during his nephew's brief visit; he had no power over Drew. The estate and title were entailed; Drew would succeed to both, no matter what. Worst of all, Drew had been wise in his investments during his ten years abroad. A thriving plantation and shipping business had given his nephew financial independence.

The cunning old man had discovered his one weapon—Drew's feelings for his mother. Faith Peterson had served as an unpaid housekeeper for the earl's sprawling home since Drew's exile. Cheswick never mistreated his widowed sister-in-law; instead, he had ignored her. Any pin money she had was carved from the meager household expense account which the earl picked over like a vulture once a month. Still, Faith Peterson never complained; at least he didn't ridicule her humble beginnings. Until, that is, the earl discovered how angry this made her son. That was his weapon, and he had wielded it with malicious glee.

After two weeks, Drew's mother had begged him to leave, telling him the insults would stop once he had departed. He had reluctantly agreed. She urged him to visit London and face the society that had shunned him ten years before. He had been only one and twenty when the *ton* had laughed him out of London. He had to face them.

And his mother had been right about everything. She had also told him he would be welcome everywhere now that he was heir to an earldom. He had tried not to be cynical when veritable strangers toadied him, but he was only human.

This had been his reason for selecting Bath for his mother's new home. Her lack of illustrious ancestors wouldn't matter as much. And with the dowager duchess of Wentworth to help launch her, Faith Peterson was assured of acceptance. And not just because her son was a wealthy peer.

So, after dallying in London, he had visited Bath and taken the house in Laura Place. And he had brought his mother, vowing to make up to her for the years of emptiness. Her gentle patience would finally be rewarded, and she would never be lonely again.

He was surprised to see the lamps lit in his mother's sitting room as he made his way down the corridor. He put his head in the door and said, "What is it? I warned you

128

about the headache."

She laughed, put her embroidery on the table, and motioned for him to enter.

"I do not have any aches, I assure you. The music was quite . . . passable."

"Then why are you still awake? Not waiting on me, I hope?" His voice held a note of reproach.

"No, not in the way you think. I wanted to continue our conversation about Jane Lindsay."

"Mother, what I do or don't do is for me to decide," he warned.

"I agree, but in order to make a decision, you must have all the facts."

"And I don't?"

"No, you're under several misapprehensions, darling. First of all, please don't use my marriage or my personality as a guideline for choosing a wife."

"You said something earlier to that tune, Mother. What do you mean?"

"Drew, you think the past ten years of my life have been unbearable for me." He nodded, and she continued, choosing her words carefully. "They weren't. Yes, I was lonely, and I missed you and worried about you, but I wasn't miserable. Your uncle lives like a hermit, but I didn't. I attended church and made a number of friends."

"My uncle is a monster, Mother. Don't try to defend him!"

"I'm not, but he was never cruel to me. Why, he hardly even knew I was there."

The look he gave her was disbelieving, but he didn't contradict her again. "What has all this to do with Jane?"

"I'm coming to that. You remember when your father was killed in that race? Everyone said I was so brave—I never cried. Drew, it wasn't bravery; one simply doesn't cry for a stranger."

"He was your husband! My father!"

"Yes, and he was a good man. A little weak, perhaps, because he let other peoples' opinions influence him. It was that weakness that turned him away from me. And I was weak, too. I couldn't abide scenes, and I would stay home, hidden away from society so I wouldn't embarrass my husband. I was too afraid to stand up for myself. I was everything you think you want in a wife—docile, humble, retiring."

"Did you hate Father so very much?"

"No, I could never have hated him. I only despised myself for my weakness."

"But Mother, surely it isn't weakness to be agreeable."

"When one is always agreeable, don't you think it shows a lack of self-respect, self-confidence?"

"I never looked at it quite like that."

"It is difficult to love someone who doesn't love himself. Now, your Jane, she has self-respect."

"Yes, she has that," he laughed, not thinking to correct his mother's calling Jane "his."

"I'll say no more. But think on it, Drew, think very carefully."

Lord Devlin realized suddenly he didn't need to think about it. He loved Jane Lindsay—every delectable, hardheaded inch. He wondered why he hadn't seen it before. From that first kiss . . . No, from the moment he had first laid eyes on her at the ball, when she had raised her chin, defying him to look her over like a horse at Tattersall's. He smiled at the remembrance, but his next thoughts were far from sunny.

"Mother, I don't know if she'll have me."

"She's not indifferent to you, Drew. Anyone can see that."

"I know, but she may think I'm only after her estate. I did try to buy it once. And she detests fortune hunters."

"The future earl of Cheswick a fortune hunter?" she asked, incredulous. "A discreet inquiry or two would reveal your own rather impressive prospects. And once that fact is established, you need only woo her, my dear."

"You make it all sound so simple, Mother. I must win her trust first, and that may be the most difficult part."

* * *

"Mr. Havelock to see you, my lord," said the wooden-faced butler.

"Tell him I'm not in. No, wait. I'll see him in the library." Drew finished his morning coffee and strolled out of the breakfast room.

"Havelock, what brings you here?"

"A slight problem, Lord Devlin," said the other man, wiping his brow nervously.

"Yes?"

"You know I lost over two thousand pounds last night, Devlin."

"I remember, but I'm surprised you do. Do you always drink so heavily?"

Havelock flushed an ugly purple, but he swallowed his anger. "I haven't the money to redeem my vouchers right now."

"It seems we've had this conversation before. But I fail to understand why you're here. You should be telling Farley and Stanton: I don't hold your IOU's. I lost, too, last night."

"True, but I thought you might see your way clear. . . ."

"Not a guinea."

"I have a bit of information. . . ."

"Nothing you say could interest me, Havelock."

"Not even a bit of advice about those notes you sent to my cousin?"

"I have no idea what notes she may receive," lied Drew, quelling his curiosity.

"Of course you do, Lord Devlin." Havelock smiled, his thick lips curving like two fat slugs.

"If that is all, Havelock, I have better ways to occupy my time."

Havelock wiped his brow again; he was getting nowhere. Desperately, he said, "Then I'm afraid, Lord Devlin, I must tell my cousin about that little prank—"

He could say no more since Devlin had grabbed his cra-

131

vat and thrown him into the nearest chair, twisting the starched fabric until Havelock's beady eyes began to bulge. Sneering with distaste, Devlin released the man.

"Get out, Havelock. You can tell Jane, but your blackmail won't work. She already knows. And she has forgiven me. As a matter of fact, you may soon be wishing us happy. And then all those points we discussed about who will inherit Heartland will be moot. I'll see to it Heartland is overflowing with heirs!"

"You'll pay for this," said Havelock when he had reached the relative safety of the door. "You're not married to my cousin yet, Devlin. And remember, it will take time to produce an heir, a female heir, to continue the tradition!"

"Get out."

Havelock hurried away; Lord Devlin tried to regain the calm he had felt upon rising. It was impossible to remain in the confines of the house, and he strode out the door, walking briskly toward Sidney Gardens. After half an hour, he was able to reflect on Havelock's visit without anger clouding his mind.

He couldn't get Havelock's obscure threat out of his thoughts. He had hoped to pursue Jane unhurriedly, giving her time to trust him. Still, from what he had seen of Roland Havelock, the man was all talk. He couldn't possibly act on his threat; the very thought was laughable.

"Miss Lindsay, you shouldn't be doing all that climbing and stretching!" scolded Heartland's scandalized cook. "That good-for-nothing footman ought to be doing that! Sims! Where is he?"

"I'll fetch 'im, ma'am," offered Tom the pot boy, scrambling to his feet and fleeing before Mrs. Brown could turn her frustration on him.

"Now, Miss Lindsay, let me help you down." With the cook's help, Jane descended the stepladder, a jar of strawberry preserves in each hand.

"These are from two years ago, Mrs. Brown. They must

have been overlooked when we sorted through the larder last year."

"Not overlooked, Miss Jane. We decided you would take them to old Mr. Jenkins. Then he passed on, and we forgot about them."

"You're quite right! I don't know how you remember everything, Mrs. Brown."

A ghost of a smile was the only evidence that the stern cook was pleased by her mistress's observation. The title of Misses was strictly a courtesy; the cook had never married, having dedicated her life to Heartland at an early age. No one dared to cross swords with Heartland's Mrs. Brown, from the pot boy to the wily old butcher in the village.

"There you are, Sims," she snapped as the footman hurried into the cool larder. "We've got to make room for this year's canned goods. Mr. Pipkin says you can read."

"Yes, ma'am."

"Good, get up on the ladder and read the labels on those jars to me."

He did as he was bid, handing down some jars as directed. Jane worked on the lowest shelf, collecting jars in her sturdy work apron.

"The raspberry jam, Mrs. Brown, should we save them? We ran out year before last, remember?"

"True, we'd best save them." Mrs. Brown took the jars in her own apron into the kitchen and arranged them on the table.

"That's all, Mrs. Brown," said the footman.

"Good, Sims. You may go back to your other duties."

"Yes, ma'am."

The footman climbed down and left.

Jane asked, "Wasn't that the man my cousin sent?"

"Yes, Miss Lindsay."

"Is he working out?"

"Mostly, but Mr. Pipkin doesn't trust him."

"You know Mr. Pipkin," said Jane, not unkindly, but they all knew Pipkin's puritanical judgement.

"No, it's not that." Mrs. Brown looked around guiltily; it

was unlike her to gossip.

"Mr. Pipkin has twice found Sims upstairs, but he never has a reason for being there."

Jane smiled. "I appreciate your telling me, Mrs. Brown. He probably has a crush on the upstairs maid."

Mrs. Brown sniffed and returned to her tally.

With her filled apron gathered in one hand, Jane grabbed the top shelf to pull herself up. As she did, it gave way, glass jars and wood collapsing on top of her.

"Miss Jane!" screamed the cook, rushing into the larder.

"I'm all right, Mrs. Brown," said Jane, her voice a bit shaky. "Most of it landed in front of me and then toppled over on top. Ouch!" Jane lifted a bloody hand, and Mrs. Brown pulled her out from under the wreckage.

"It should have been me down there! Oh, Miss Jane! I'll never forgive myself! You, Tom, run get the surgeon. Ann, fetch Mrs. Tucker! The rest of you—out!"

"Really, Mrs. Brown, I'm fine. Just a small cut and a few bruises, I'm sure," protested Jane as the anxious cook hovered over her. She was sitting at the kitchen table, looking into the demolished larder. "All that food and work gone to waste. I wonder what made it fall. It didn't even feel loose when I was working up there."

"It's old; I've been telling Mr. Pipkin he needed to see to it."

Tucker bustled in with Jane's case of medicinal supplies. In no time, the cuts on Jane's palm had been cleaned and dusted with bacillum powder.

"I think you should let me wrap it up, Miss Jane, so you won't use it."

"It hardly calls for that, Tucker," said Jane, looking into her maid's concerned face. "Oh, very well. Do what you will."

An hour later, Jane was seated in the cheery morning room, her feet propped up on a stool, and within easy reach of her uninjured left hand was a cup of tea, a plate of Cook's buttery biscuits, her embroidery, and the latest novel. Many ladies of the *ton* would have been in heaven;

Jane, however, found such enforced inactivity little short of unbearable. Still, when she had tried to help sort out the mess in the larder, Mrs. Brown had exclaimed in horror, her protests backed up by the village doctor who had arrived expecting nothing less than a corpse.

So, Jane had retreated to the morning room. One compensation, she told herself, was her solitude. She didn't have to listen to someone's mournful sigh each time she lifted her hand.

Pipkin looked in occasionally, but he was different. He had sniffed at Mrs. Brown and the surgeon and said, "The soul of the sluggard desireth, and hath nothing: but the soul of the diligent shall be made fat. Proverbs 13:4."

Jane opened the letter from Cherry that had arrived in the morning mail. It contained the usual exclamations and nonsense—until the last paragraph.

> I have asked Mama if we may go to Paris in June. Everyone is going now that we are at peace again. It would be DREADFUL to miss such an opportunity. You could come, too, Jane dearest. Perhaps if you write to Mama, together we can persuade her.

Jane reread the passage again. She smiled; surely Cherry knew better than to try and cozen her! The prospect of a trip to Paris was tempting, but not in June. In June she would begin planning Open Day at Heartland. It was always held on the fifteenth of July. Perhaps afterwards, in August.

Pipkin entered and handed her a calling card, the corner turned down to show that the caller was actually present.

"Lord Devlin? Show him in."

Jane straightened up; just as she was pushing the footstool out of the way, Drew entered.

"Here, let me help," he said, pushing it back in place. Jane grinned.

"Actually, I was removing it."

135

"You shouldn't be! Are you all right?"

"I'm fine, but how did you find out?"

"I met Dr. Harrington as I was entering the drive, and he told me about your accident. I must confess, I had expected to see you lying senseless on the couch. I was surprised when Pipkin let me in here."

"I must remember to thank Pipkin," Jane said, smiling up at him until she began to feel self-conscious. She took refuge in the social banalities.

"Won't you be seated? Isn't this beautiful weather we are having lately?"

"Indeed," he said, turning to find a chair so she couldn't see his amused expression. Since Jane's chair was placed away from the others, close to the windows, the viscount picked up a chair and placed it beside hers. Pipkin entered with more refreshments.

Jane picked up the teapot awkwardly in her left hand. Drew sat forward, taking it from her.

"Let me do that. What happened, precisely? I see your right hand is bandaged."

"It's nothing, really. And as for the bandage, I merely let Tucker, my maid, bandage it to ease her worry. You know how these old family retainers are."

"No, I don't; my childhood didn't included a warm home. But I'll take your word for it, providing you promise me you'll be able to dance by tomorrow evening."

"Tomorrow evening? But I—"

"You are going to the Assembly in Bath with my mother and me. At least, I hope you will come."

"But you're to come to tea tomorrow."

"Yes, but we would like for you to dine with us instead, and then go to the Assembly. It will be the first one for Mother, and she was so hoping you'd join us to bolster her courage."

This last was said in such sincere, pleading tones that Jane doubted he was being completely honest. But it did sound like a delightful outing, and she had been longing to wear her new scarlet gown.

"Very well," she agreed slowly.

"Good! I'll come out here to escort you."

"There's no need for that. I shall be perfectly safe with our coachman and Mickey along. It's not as though we're at opposite ends of the world."

"No, we're not, are we?" His dark eyes held hers.

The morning is growing uncomfortably warm, thought Jane. "Would . . . would you care to take a walk in the garden, Lord Devlin?"

"Drew," he said.

"Drew," she echoed, taking his hand and standing up. He was so close to her their bodies almost touched. And still he stared, his hand holding hers. Jane's breath came faster; there didn't seem to be enough air; her breast rose and fell rapidly.

"Drew?" she said tentatively.

He stepped back, tucking her hand in the crook of his arm. The morning room, like the library on the opposite side of the house, boasted French doors. He opened one, allowing her to pass through it.

"Is your mother enjoying Bath?" asked Jane, after searching for a safe topic.

"Yes, she loves it. She goes to the Pump Room every morning, and she already has a small circle of friends."

"Is she taking the waters?"

"She tried them once, but she enjoys the very best health, so she has no need of them. A fortunate circumstance, since she told me in no uncertain terms she would never drink them again. To be precise, she told me she thought the hot mineral springs must arise out of the very depths of Hell—an extreme observation for the daughter of a curate."

Jane laughed. "So she attends the Pump Room to socialize, like most of its patrons."

"Yes, and then she shops or reads or walks in the gardens. She is an amateur gardener."

"Laura Place is the perfect setting, being so close to Sidney Gardens, as well as the shops and the Pump Room."

"Yes, Mother swears she much prefers it to the country."

"Then I suppose you're glad I wouldn't sell you Heartland."

"Definitely. And this way, I can visit its beautiful mistress."

Jane frowned. She was unused to receiving such fulsome compliments from Lord Devlin. Such comments in the past had been delivered in a taunting manner. She was unsure how to respond.

"Why so serious, Jane? Normally, a lady responds when she receives a compliment."

"I'm sorry, Lord Devlin. I thought you were teasing me."

He stopped and scanned the immediate vicinity. The gardener was working nearby, and Drew pulled Jane behind a row of shrubbery. They were quite alone except for the buzzing of a bee.

He took her in his arms and murmured, "I was in earnest then, and I am now, as well."

With this, he lowered his lips to hers. Returning his kiss eagerly, Jane was surprised when he raised his head and released her. He took her hand and placed it on his arm again before leading her back by the garden.

Drew would have explored the garden further, but Jane said, "Let's go back in. I am tired."

The viscount left soon afterwards. He was feeling very pleased with himself. He had shown Jane that he cared for her reputation, that he respected her; he was not simply trifling with her. And she had been disappointed by his brief kiss; that meant she cared for him, he hoped.

Yes, he thought, she must care. She didn't go about kissing every man who spoke to her! That was absurd! That first night she had only kissed him because . . . Why had she kissed him at the Valentine Ball? She hadn't liked him above half. So why?

He urged his gray stallion to a gallop. He was going crazy; his jealousy was rendering his judgement faulty, and he admitted he was jealous at the thought of Jane kissing anyone else. He slowed the big horse to a walk, controlling it easily as the animal shook its head to protest. He tried to remember that first kiss. How had she returned his kiss—expertly or inexpertly? It had been sweet, he remembered that very well. Her response had been tentative, and then she had given full rein to her passion, molding her body to his.

"Damn!" he said aloud. Why hadn't he kissed her like that in the garden when he had the chance? The devil take chivalry and gentlemanlike behavior! He would escort her home after the Assembly, and he would kiss her as she had never been kissed before!

As for Jane, she was restless. She didn't know why precisely, but since her walk in the garden with Drew, she'd found it impossible to sit still.

She lifted her grandmother's brooch and noted the time. If she forgot about tea, she would have time for a good ride before dinner.

Jane made her way upstairs cautiously. If she met Tucker along the way, she could forget about riding. Tucker would be incensed. Jane changed as quickly as possible, folding her discarded gown and placing it in the back of the wardrobe. She removed the loose bandage and picked up her tan leather riding gloves. Then she made her escape down the backstairs.

Once she was clear of the grounds, Jane let Sinbad fly. Bending low over the horse's neck, her billowing hair appeared to be one with the long mane. Over all the fences, high and low, they sailed. Finally though, the run had to end, and she eased back on the reins. Jane was too good a horsewoman to think about anything for the next fifteen or twenty minutes but gradually cooling her horse.

Then she was ready to think, to ask herself some very difficult questions. In her usual logical manner, she first reviewed the facts. First, Drew's kisses were very enjoyable for her. Second, he seemed to enjoy kissing her, too. And third, he had never indicated he wanted anything further

139

of her. Certainly love had not been mentioned, nor marriage. Even Jane hadn't thought about such a possibility.

What did Lord Devlin want with Miss Lindsay? He couldn't believe she would accept a carte blanche. But what other possibility was there? she asked herself. Perhaps he found her innocent passion amusing. But that couldn't be it either, or he would have kissed her, really kissed her, in the garden earlier.

Jane's experience with men in social situations was limitless, but her experience in romance was nil. The closest thing to romance she could recall had been nothing but business—fortune hunters hoping to contract a lucrative future for themselves by marrying her. She hadn't even been kissed—except once, at fourteen, by the old rector's son. And that had been wet and disgusting.

Jane knew her behavior hadn't been ladylike. What if Drew felt she had been too free, too fast? Perhaps he'd had her kisses and that was all he wanted. But at five and twenty, Jane knew there was more between a man and a woman. She could recall every word of her friend Sally's vivid description about what happened on her wedding night. That had been informative, and only last year hadn't she interrupted the stable boy with one of the local village girls under the haystack? She remembered how they had been moaning, unaware that she was riding by. The girl's dress had been around her hips, and the boy—

Jane trembled, trying to rid herself of the painful longing flooding her body. She shifted in the saddle, but it didn't help, so she turned Sinbad around, urging him to a canter as she headed home.

Tomorrow night, she vowed, I will ask Drew to accompany me home in the carriage. I will tell him my maid was ill and unable to travel to Bath. It will be late; such a request won't seem unusual. And then I will make him kiss me!

Jane stretched like a cat as Tucker laid out her clothes

for the morning. Tucker was very much on her dignity with her mistress after Jane's secret ride the day before.

"Which dress will you be wearing tonight, Miss Jane?"

"The new red and silver one."

"And your hair?"

"I wish I could wear it down; it is so much easier." And Drew likes my hair down, she thought. "Getting it to stay up takes so many pins, I can hardly hold up my head."

Fashion debates always loosened Tucker up, and she laughed, "Yer exaggeratin', Miss Jane. But I think I've an idea. I have some of the silver braid left over from the reticule I knitted to match the dress. Why don't I thread it through the white net and make a snood? It would be very becoming and wear much better."

"What a clever idea! Tucker, you're a genius! I'll feel so elegant."

"Because you will be, Miss Jane," said the loyal maid.

"Of course, I shan't be fashionable. Catching one's hair up in a net, no matter how becoming it may be, is just not fashionable."

"Do you care so much?" asked Tucker, bewildered by her mistress's sudden infatuation with current fashions.

"No, not really. I was just making an observation. Do you think you might have time to sew some seed pearls here and there on the net?"

"I'll see to it."

"Oh, Tucker, I'd forgotten! One reason I chose this fabric was because it would match Grandmother's ruby pendant. But the catch is broken."

"I'll get Mickey to leave for Bath right now. He'll be back quick as the cat can lick her whiskers." Taking up the heart-shaped pendant, Tucker hurried away.

Jane had never felt more beautiful as she studied her image in the cheval glass. The dress was in the prevailing empire style, made of a deep scarlet silk. The neckline and short puffed sleeves were edged with tiny ruching in white

141

organdy, trimmed with a row of delicate silver braid. A strand of pearls, bound on either side by the silver braid, separated the deeply cut bodice from the full skirt. The bottom of the skirt measured a full four yards around, another unfashionable detail, but Jane had insisted. She loved the way it flared as she twirled this way and that, imitating the movements of a waltz.

Only one detail was missing—the heart-shaped pendant. She had ceased asking if Mickey had returned yet. Finally, her unfashionable but flattering snood decorating her brown hair, Jane picked up her reticule and Norwich shawl. She heard a commotion at the bottom of the stairs, and picking up her skirt, she ran down the steps.

"Mickey! What happened? Pipkin?"

With the entrance of his mistress, Pipkin jumped up from his undignified position on the floor beside Mickey and began clearing the entrance hall. The hysterical maids vanished, leaving several footmen, Jane, Tucker, Pipkin, and the unfortunate Mickey.

"Take him to my quarters," said the butler.

Pipkin's rooms were nearby, being located on the first floor with a view of the front door. It took four stout footmen to lift the huge servant. Tucker brought the case of medicines and began to clean Mickey's wounds. Jane waited patiently in the background.

"Now, Mickey, tell us what happened."

His eyes glistening with tears, Mickey moaned repeatedly, "I lost 't, Miss Jane. I lost 't."

"Lost what, Mickey?"

"Yer necklace. Please, Miss Jane, don' send me away."

"I should say not, Mickey! Tell me, how was it lost?"

"This man, a bad man in a mask and with a long cape, 'e made me give 't to him. 'E 'ad a gun. I said no! But 'e said, 'I'll shoot yer horse.' I couldn' let 'im shoot Toby."

Jane smiled. Mickey would have died before giving in to the highwayman, but he had to protect the old, broken-down horse Jane had given him.

"You did the right thing, Mickey. You and Toby are

142

more important than a necklace." Even as she reassured him, Jane felt close to collapse. Her grandmother's pendant, the one worn by all the Heartland women—gone! She took a deep breath and asked, "How did you get hurt, Mickey?"

"I tried to chase the bad man, but I fell off. I hit my head. I didn' wake up for hours."

"How do you feel now?"

"My head hurts, but I'm all right. It was awfully bloody; it scared me."

"I know; a head bleeds very badly. We're all happy you're better, Mickey." She smiled into his childlike eyes and turned to go.

At the door, she paused when he asked tearfully, "Do you still like me, Miss Jane?"

"Yes, Mickey, I still like you very much." Wearily, Jane climbed the stairs. She looked through her remaining jewelry and selected a necklace of perfectly matched pearls. They would go with her new dress, too.

It was a subdued Miss Lindsay who was ushered into the yellow salon in Laura Place. Drew crossed the room and led her to the sofa. His mother greeted her warmly. Jane replied suitably, but her manner was listless.

"I hope you like duck, Jane," said Mrs. Peterson. "I hesitated to serve it; it seems to be one of those dishes one either loves or abhors."

"Duck is fine, ma'am. I'm looking forward to it."

"That is a beautiful gown, Jane," said Drew.

Jane turned a weak smile on him, and her eyes filled with sudden tears. Drew sat down by her side and put a comforting arm around her, saying, "What is it, Jane? What has happened?"

"I'll go and get some brandy." His mother rose and hurried from the room.

Jane fumbled with her reticule for her handkerchief. The viscount thrust his own into her trembling hands and

143

asked again, "What is wrong?"

"My necklace, my grandmother's pendant . . ." She blew her nose.

"The one you wore to the Valentine Ball?"

She nodded without stopping to wonder why he would remember such a detail. "It's gone, stolen, a highwayman—"

He grabbed both her arms and spun her around to face him. His black expression was frightening.

"Did he hurt you? Touch you?"

Jane frowned, then she realized his mistake. "No, it wasn't stolen from me! I had sent it to Bath with Mickey to have the clasp repaired." Drew released her arms and relaxed against the back of the sofa. "A highwayman stopped Mickey and demanded the necklace. He threatened to shoot Mickey's old pony, so he gave it to the thief. Then Mickey tried to follow the scoundrel and fell off. He hit his head and was unconscious for several hours."

"Is Mickey all right now?"

"Yes, for the most part. He was afraid I wouldn't like him anymore. He's such a sweet boy."

"Hardly a boy. He's as old as you, my dear."

"You know what I mean."

"Tell me, when did the robbery occur? On the way to Bath or on the way home?"

"On the way home, I think. I didn't think to ask. Why?"

"Think about it, Jane. A highwayman who stops servants on old horses? He would soon die of malnutrition. How could he know Mickey was carrying something of value? There are two possibilities: either the highwayman is connected to Heartland or he was in the jeweler's shop. I assume you have notified the local magistrate?" She nodded. "Good. I will inquire tomorrow at the jeweler's to see if there were any strange characters standing about when they returned the repaired pendant to your footman. You talk to Mickey to ascertain when the robbery took place. If it was on the way to Bath, that narrows the list of suspects considerably."

"Oh, Drew, it couldn't be one of our servants. They're practically family."

"No one new of late?"

"Well, there is Sims. He came to us from my cousin Roland. But he seems a decent fellow." Jane paused. "Although Pipkin doesn't trust him."

"If your Pipkin doesn't trust the man, I wouldn't either." Especially if the man worked for Roland Havelock, added the viscount silently.

"I'll keep an eye on him. But first I'll ask Mickey if he ever made it to Bath."

"Good! Feeling better?"

"Yes, it feels good to be doing something. I'm sorry for turning into a watering pot, Drew. I didn't realize how upset I was about losing the pendant. I never cry—at least not in company."

"You need never cover up your feelings from me, Jane." Drew's voice was as soft as a caress, and Jane leaned forward expectantly.

"Here we are!" said Mrs. Peterson brightly as she entered carrying a tray with glasses and a decanter. Jane straightened up as the older woman continued, "I thought wine would be more suitable. Are you feeling more the thing, my dear?"

"Yes, thank you," said Jane, accepting the goblet.

"Good! Now, tell me what to expect at tonight's Assembly."

"There will be dancing, of course, and some rather bland refreshments. As far as the company? I haven't been to the Assemblies in over a year. so I'm afraid I'm no help there."

"Of course, I had forgotten. Drew told me you were in mourning. I'm so sorry, dear."

"Thank you. The Assemblies are not as rigidly controlled as they once were, as you may be aware. When Beau Nash ruled Bath's social scene, all Assemblies ended at eleven o'clock sharp. When the Princess Amelia asked Nash for just one more dance at eleven, she was refused.

145

Back then, every Assembly began with the minuet, one couple at a time. It took two hours!"

"How tedious, especially if one didn't particularly care for one's partner."

"That's what I thought, but no one dared to suggest that to Mr. Nash," laughed Jane.

"Dinner, my lord, ladies," announced their very proper butler.

Jane grinned, wondering which scripture Pipkin would have chosen to elaborate on this announcement. She caught Drew's twinkling eyes on her. He had guessed her thoughts.

After seating his mother at one end of the table, the viscount escorted Jane to her chair. Leaning over, he whispered, "Perhaps, 'For the kingdom of God is not meat and drink; but righteousness, and peace, and joy in the Holy Ghost.' "

Jane giggled, then she bit her lip in embarrassment. Drew's mother, however, was smiling benignly on both of them. For the first time, Jane wondered why she was the only guest. It was almost as though Faith Peterson considered her one of the family.

Reinforcing this suspicion, Mrs. Peterson said, "I do hope you'll forgive our being so casual, Jane. The formal dining room and table are so large, we would have been reduced to shouting at one another. This had been a small sitting room, but I thought it ideal for a family dining room. It is close enough to the kitchens that our meals are even hot."

"It is lovely, Mrs. Peterson. You have an eye for colors."

Faith Peterson beamed and urged Jane to try the turtle soup.

"I haven't asked you about your hand, Jane. How is it today? Ready for dancing?" teased Drew.

"Healing nicely, thank you."

"Drew was telling me about the accident. It's a wonder you weren't hurt worse! And all those hours of work wasted!"

"Now that is exactly what I said!" agreed Jane. "You must make your own preserves, too."

"Yes, my specialty is peach."

"Do you know, I have never made peach. Mrs. Brown, our cook, makes it, but even she admits it isn't exceptional."

"I'll write down my recipe for her, if you don't think she would be insulted. I know how sensitive cooks can be, and the last thing one wants is an angry cook."

"I think she would appreciate it."

Through all this, Drew sipped his wine and observed. He was feeling very lucky to be in company with his two favorite ladies. And the fact that they enjoyed one another's company only pleased him more.

He watched Jane over the top of his glass, studying her objectively, as a work of art. She was so elegant in the deep red gown. And that hair net — whatever it was called — added to her timeless beauty. His eyes strayed to her deep décolletage, and his thoughts lost their ethereal quality. He wanted her as he had never wanted any other woman. He wanted to be with her, to comfort her when she cried, to kiss her and hold her when she was weary. He wanted, quite plainly, to love her, to make her feel loved.

"Drew, have we put you to sleep with our domestic talk?"

"Certainly not, Mother. I was merely woolgathering." He turned to Jane and smiled. "I was wondering if I might persuade Jane to ride with me tomorrow."

It occurred to Jane that Drew's thoughts must have been centered on her since his invitation was issued so suddenly. She returned his warm smile and accepted.

"Good!" The viscount looked toward the end of the table to find his mother's fond gaze resting on him.

As they entered the Upper Assembly Rooms, a country dance was in progress. It had been over a year since Jane had attended one of Bath's Assemblies, but it was as if the clock had been turned back. The last time, she had been with Cherry, surrounded by young men vying for Cherry's next dance. And Jane had been forced to play duenna, an unenviable job.

But tonight was different; Miss Lindsay on the arm of an eligible bachelor, in company with his mother, was an entirely different matter. She couldn't help but be pleased by the looks of envy in other ladies' eyes as they progressed around the ballroom, speaking to friends and acquaintances. It was not a common occurrence for Jane. Oh, she had been envied for her wealth, her poise, or her social position before, but tonight produced a different effect. She had a glimpse of the power women such as Cherry possessed. It was a heady sensation.

But the pleasure she gleaned from such envy was shortlived. Her old lack of confidence reasserted itself, and she was left to wonder and doubt. Why, she asked herself, was she on the arm of Lord Devlin? Why had he singled her out? He was handsome, charming—when he wished to be—and appeared to be wealthy. His future held an earldom, so he certainly wasn't trying to raise his social status.

Perhaps, whispered a frail, inner voice, he is truly in love with you. At this preposterous thought, the sensible Miss Lindsay raised her eyes to his.

But his lordship's attention was elsewhere. She followed his fixed stare, her green eyes coming to rest on a silvery young matron of average height and a slim, girlish figure. Her décolletage was so low, it seemed her ivory breasts would escape at any moment. Lord Devlin had stopped, too infatuated to take his eyes from the fairylike vision before them.

And Jane found she couldn't face seeing the desire in his eyes, not when it was directed at someone else. She murmured something about the ladies' withdrawing room and vanished in the opposite direction.

Drew turned to follow her, a frown wrinkling his brow. "Drew! Dearest Drew! How are you?"

Jane stopped and looked across the dizzying array of

colorful dancers. She could neither hear their words nor see the viscount's face. She could only see the sensuous, purring beauty, her long fingers resting on Drew's shoulder. And that frail little voice within her head appeared to be cowering, promising never to raise such hopes again. Jane lifted her chin and pasted a smile on her face. He would never know how close she had come to believing in him.

"Lady Cynthia, you are unchanged after all these years. What is it? Ten? Eleven?" Lord Devlin sneered at the lovely vision. He noted with grim satisfaction the brief flash of hardness in her eyes.

Then she giggled. It was the same tinkling sound that had so intrigued him at the tender age of nineteen. Now, the sound produced a cold chill.

He bowed and turned away, but delicate, beringed fingers touched his sleeve. He looked into her eyes — eyes that were now glistening with unshed tears. She was a beautiful and accomplished actress.

"Perhaps we could talk, Drew? A dance?" she breathed.

A waltz was beginning. He scanned the room for Jane, but she was nowhere to be seen. So he nodded.

He took her in his arms, holding her very properly. They made a superb couple with her silvery blond hair and alabaster skin and his dark hair and tanned complexion.

"I have grown up, Drew, changed from that horrid debutante who treated you so cruelly," she whispered.

Her voice was so quiet, he had to bend his head to catch her words. Jane watched from a row of chairs filled with the partnerless. Mr. Primrose appeared before her and stumbled through a request to dance. Jane smiled upon him as though he were a long lost beau, startling the shy Mr. Primrose no end.

"I have grieved so over the pain I caused you, dearest Drew."

"Is that so? I understand you are on your second husband. Ah no! I forgot. My condolences, Lady Cynthia, on

149

your late husband's death. Six months ago, wasn't it?"

Briefly she stiffened in his arms; then she purred, "But it was you I dreamed of when the lights were out, my dearest."

His merry smile lighted his face, and as Jane swept by in Mr. Primrose's arms, she had to suppress a longing to touch his lips.

Lord Devlin was enjoying himself. He had known his return to England would stir the coals of old gossip; he had prepared himself to face this. And he had known he would one day come face to face with Cynthia, but he hadn't been certain how he would react. His anger had long since died out, but would that youthful passion also be dead?

He looked down at her again. Not a flicker of passion, neither hate nor love. It would be amusing to let Cynthia think he was still bewitched, to exact some measure of revenge, petty though such an idea might be. But there was Jane to consider; he was doubtful she would understand.

Drew spied Jane and Mr. Primrose who were busy laughing and talking as the music ended. He escorted Lady Cynthia from the floor, returning her to her eager admirers. Then he turned on his heel, searching for Jane.

He found her surrounded by her many friends, both male and female. The musicians were striking up the complicated Boulanger. She would come to him now, he thought, smiling as Jane did indeed draw nearer.

"Lord Devlin," she said, nodding to him and smiling as though she were highly amused by her escort's anecdote.

"Miss Lindsay," he responded as she continued past him.

What was going on? he asked himself, frowning fiercely. A large matron in a purple turban was staring at him, brows raised and lips pursed. The devil take her, he thought, and Jane Lindsay!

Without further thought, the viscount stalked up to the first unpartnered young lady he saw and asked her to dance. She leapt to her feet and practically dragged him onto the dance floor.

The next few hours were a fever of dancing and laughing. Jane thought she had never worked so hard at having a wonderful time while being so completely wretched. The viscount had shared three dances with Lady Cynthia—two of which had been waltzes. He had danced with Jane once—a country dance that kept them apart more than together. She was miserable.

The viscount was furious. At first, he had only been puzzled by Jane's behavior. Then the anger had overtaken his good judgement, and he had asked himself why he was avoiding the beautiful Lady Cynthia. It couldn't be for Jane's sake! She was too busy to notice!

It was a silent, tense carriage ride back to Laura Place. Even Mrs. Peterson felt the strain and fell silent after one attempt to engage Jane and Drew in conversation.

The carriage stopped in front of the town house, and the matron quickly descended. "Good night, Jane, my dear. I hope to see you again soon."

Automatically, Jane replied, "Thank you for a lovely evening, Mrs. Peterson. Good night."

And then they were alone in the comfortable new carriage Drew had purchased for his mother. Jane could just see his features in the dim light from the carriage lamps. He was frowning. His entire aspect was forbidding; he sat ramrod straight, his arm folded across his broad chest.

And earlier she had been planning to kiss him, practically seduce him, she thought, managing not to laugh hysterically.

It was out of the question now, of course. His thoughts were elsewhere. A sob, quickly masked as a yawn, escaped her. Jane began to count out the rhythm of the horses' hooves as they took her closer to Heartland.

If he would only explain, she thought; any explanation would suffice. Perhaps this Lady Cynthia had cast a spell over him. Or even if he would make up some story about getting travel sickness when he rode backwards too long. Then he could move beside her. And if he touched her in the romantic, velvety darkness of the coach, it would break

151

the spell the wicked fairy had cast.

But that was absurd! Jane chided herself. Lady Cynthia was not a witch. Drew was thinking about her because he wanted to do so, and she couldn't change it. Perhaps Drew had been just a little bit in love with her, Jane. But Jane wasn't a widow, an experienced matron who would be only too eager to take the viscount to her bed. And evidently, she and Drew were old friends—perhaps they had been lovers in the past.

Mentally, Jane castigated herself for a fool. She should never have allowed herself to believe. . . . She would simply forget about Lord Devlin! Of course, it wouldn't hurt to write to her old friend Sally to learn what on-dits circulated about Drew and Lady Cynthia—past or present.

As for Drew, he wasn't thinking about Lady Cynthia. Oh, her image flitted across his thoughts occasionally on that long carriage ride to Heartland, accounting for his queasiness, no doubt.

For the most part, however, it was Jane's image that occupied his mind, images of her dancing every dance, quite gracefully, without him. No wonder she was so grateful to him for teaching her to feel at ease on the dance floor. She could dance with anyone she wished now, and evidently, she wished to dance with anyone but him. Drew refused to consider the country dance they had shared; Jane had talked to the couple beside them more than to him. Consequently, in a fit of pique, he had danced with Lady Cynthia more often than propriety dictated. This had certainly set the old tabbies' tongues to wagging! But after three dances with Cynthia, Lord Devlin had been terminally bored. How had he ever been interested in such a creature? She might be able to recite one hundred on-dits, but she probably hadn't two original thoughts to rub together. And her interest in snaring him had become patently obvious: as though it was a sweet nothing, she must have sighed a dozen times and murmured into his ear, "An earl, fancy that."

They turned into the gate of Heartland. A half-mile of

drive, and she would descend.

"I'm feeling a trifle off, sitting backwards all this way," said Drew, moving across the carriage to sit beside Jane.

"You should have moved sooner," she whispered, not daring to look up. Didn't he realize his nearness was almost impossible to bear? But she wouldn't, couldn't, forgive him.

A gentle hand raised her chin.

"Drew?" she breathed.

"Shh." He leaned toward her, and kissed her awkwardly. The angle was all wrong. Time was running out. Impatiently, he pulled her onto his lap, slipping his arms about her.

As he began to kiss her in earnest, Jane's hands crept up his chest and around his neck. Her fingers played with the dark curls touching his collar. She turned in his lap, pressing her pounding breasts against his chest. His lips left her mouth and traveled downward, leaving a trail of kisses from her chin to around her neck. He kissed her ear, his tongue teasing until Jane moaned. Then his mouth traveled down to her bare shoulder. Locked in his embrace, Jane arched her back, her breasts ached to receive his attention. Drew paused; he was going too fast, too far. He should be wise for both of them. Jane shifted in his lap, her hands pulling his face down to those soft, white mounds. He surrendered; his hand cupped one breast, and he kissed it, then the other. He nuzzled the fabric of the gown, coaxing forth a dark nipple. His lips descended. . . .

The carriage slowed; it came to a halt. Footmen with lanterns hurried down the steps of Heartland to light their mistress inside. The carriage door was thrust open.

Gathering her shawl and reticule in her shaking hands, Jane said rather loudly, "Thank you for a lovely evening, Lord Devlin, and thank you for seeing me home safely."

"My pleasure, Miss Lindsay," he replied, not bothering to follow her out of the carriage. Drew looked up the steps to the massive front door. There was the severe Pipkin.

What the butler would say if he saw the viscount's present state didn't bear considering!

Then Jane was gone, and he signaled his driver to proceed.

♡ *Chapter Six* ♡

Jane lay awake long into the night, and when sleep finally overtook her, it was a turbulent rest. Even sleep could not erase the warring emotions in her breast.

She rose at ten. Her eyes were red; her body weighed a ton. She forced herself to eat a nourishing breakfast, hoping to regain some of her usual energy. Next, she wandered out of the cozy breakfast room and stood uncertainly in the hall.

"Shall I send word to the stables, miss?" asked Pipkin, upon discovering her, hand on the bannister, staring into space.

"What? Oh, no. Lord Devlin and I are riding this afternoon, I think."

"Just so, miss. The morning mail has arrived."

Jane took a deep breath and turned to the table by the stairs. She shuffled the envelopes, pocketing one from Cherry and another from Aunt Sophie.

"I'll be in the summer house, Pipkin, should anyone need me."

"Very good, Miss Jane."

Jane was soon settled on the chintz-covered chaise longue. A delicate breeze ruffled her hair. It was her favorite spot. In winter, the glass panels and fireplace kept the summerhouse warm and inviting. But in the spring, with the panels removed, the fragrance of flowers filled the air. From her position, Jane could look across the garden to the house. The sight always brought a deep contentment to her soul. Today, she yawned and closed her eyes.

Not to sleep, not yet. She shut out the beauty of her surroundings so she could think about the viscount. But more importantly, she needed to investigate her own actions and motives.

Introspection wasn't a common practice for Jane Lindsay. She was the kind of person who had to be reminded that she must be freezing before realizing that she had indeed grown quite chilled. But her behavior in that coach had surprised her. It was as though she'd had no control over her body. It was not a pleasant thought. And every time the remembrance of the way she had arched her body and pressed his face to her breast. . . !

She reminded herself that, in all fairness, she had planned to kiss the viscount. And due to her lack of experience, she'd had no idea a person could so entirely forget herself when passion flared. There had been that kiss in the crypt, but she hadn't really realized what she was doing. In the carriage, she had been all too aware; she simply hadn't cared. And that was shocking in itself.

It wouldn't be quite so disturbing if she hadn't been angry with Drew. But she had been—angry and disgusted. And he'd offered no apology, no explanation. All he had to do was touch her, and she had been lost.

What would he have to say when he arrived that afternoon? Would he apologize for his behavior, begging for forgiveness? The image of a contrite Lord Devlin was ludicrous, and a tired smile curved her lips. He would probably act as if nothing had occurred—no kiss, no Lady Cynthia. She certainly wouldn't refer to either.

Finally, she slept.

The remainder of Lord Devlin's night had passed more calmly than had Jane's. He had been in the habit, through the years, of forcing himself to empty his mind of disturbing thoughts, in order to sleep peacefully.

He rose at eight, dressing hurriedly before making his way to the jeweler Jane employed. He was the first customer of the day, and there were no curious ears to overhear his rather strange interrogation.

Drew was somewhat disappointed to discover that Jane's footman Mickey had indeed arrived at the jeweler's to have the pendant repaired. The crime would have been much easier to solve if the suspects could have been narrowed to the people at Heartland. And, of course, his favorite theory included the guilt of Roland Havelock's former servant.

As it was, the possible suspects were limitless. The innocent Mickey might have told any number of people that he was in Bath for his beloved mistress to get her pendant repaired. And the jeweler couldn't recall any suspicious people in the shop who might have witnessed Mickey leaving with the valuable pendant.

When he returned to Laura Place, he breakfasted with his mother. He blessed her silently for not chastising him on his foolish behavior the night before. She must be at least part saint, he decided.

Afterward, he accompanied his mother to the Pump Room. She was very shortly immersed in conversation with a group of her contemporaries.

"Drew, darling! How wonderful of you to come this morning," called a familiar voice. He frowned as Lady Cynthia glided to his side and slipped her arm through his. "You remembered I was going to be here," she said, her voice a trifle shrill as she flashed a triumphant smile to the interested audience.

Gently, but firmly, he detached her cloying hand from his arm and made her a stiff, formal bow.

"No, Cynthia. As a matter of fact, I had forgotten you said you were coming to the Pump Room this morning. I merely escorted my mother."

"How gallant of you," she simpered, ignoring the cut he had just delivered.

"If you'll excuse me . . ."

He took two steps away, and she trilled that infamous laugh. He turned, raising one dark, questioning brow.

"I see how it is. You don't wish to anger your little heiress. Or should I say *big* heiress?" She laughed and spoke in a loud aside to her small group of admirers. "Have you ever seen a female, a lady, that is, with such large — Ouch! You're hurting me, Drew!"

Drew propelled her to a lone chair against the wall. Glaring down at her, he said quietly but distinctly, "If I ever hear you, or hear about you, insulting Miss Lindsay in any way, form, or fashion, I will kill you. Not a duel, mind you. An execution, *Lady* Cynthia." He pivoted and left her there, her beautiful eyes wide with astonishment and fear.

Drew waved to his mother, signaling his departure. Before he could escape, however, he spied his old friend Giles Stanton.

"Drew, it's good to see you are in good spirits this morning, full of vinegar, as usual," said Giles quietly. "Thought you might have fallen prey to the divine Cynthia again."

"Devil take you, Giles. You know me better than that!"

"Yes, besides, you and the other one were just as much a topic of speculation last night."

"Other one?" drawled the viscount.

"No need to get on your high ropes with me, old man. Only repeating what the green-eyed tabbies were saying. I wasn't even there! What's 'er name? Miss Lindsay?"

"Your information is correct, Giles, and I would appreciate it if you wouldn't speak in such a cavalier manner about her."

"Ah, sits the wind in that corner? When may I wish you happy?"

His friend's grin was infectious and Drew laughed. "Not yet, but soon, I hope."

"Excellent! I shall be your second."

"You mean best man."

"Now, that depends on one's view of marriage." Both men laughed. Then Mr. Stanton said, "By the by, I had a visit from Roland Havelock this morning."

"Havelock? I thought he'd left Bath."

"Said he was on his way out of town. He stopped by to redeem his vouchers."

"Redeem his—Odd, I wonder where he found the money."

"I've no idea. I thought I'd never see the ready. I mean, the fellow's a bit on the seamy side, if you ask me. Farley's the one who brought him the other night. You know Farley when he's had a drink or two."

"Yes, we all know Farley. Well, I'd best be going, Giles. It was good to see you."

Giles Stanton said good-bye to thin air; the viscount was already striding toward the door.

Pipkin signaled the footman to open the door as Lord Devlin raised his hand to knock. The viscount handed his riding gloves and hat to the footman and smiled at the butler. Pipkin, of course, displayed no emotion.

"Hello, Pipkin."

"M'lord. Miss Lindsay is expecting you. If you'll just step this way?"

The viscount followed the butler through the great hall, past the gold salon and the state dining room, to the long ballroom. Crossing the shining marble floor, Pipkin opened one of the French doors and stood aside to let Devlin pass.

Drew stopped. "Where is she?"

"In the summer house, I believe, m'lord. Right this way."

"Never mind, Pipkin. I know the way. I'll announce myself."

The butler's chest swelled, and he turned to study the viscount. Lord Devlin met his gaze; he could have rebuked the servant for such insolence, but he said nothing.

Then Pipkin intoned, "He that diligently seeketh good procureth favor: but he that seeketh mischief, it shall come unto him. Proverbs 11:27."

"I am familiar with that passage, as I am sure you are with, 'The steps of a good man are ordered by the Lord; and he delighteth in his way. Psalms 37:23.' Your mistress will come to no harm from me, Pipkin."

With the glimmer of a smile flavoring his dour expression, the butler said, "Very good, my lord."

Jane was dreaming of being alone, locked in a tomb, but the tomb was made of glass. It was her funeral, and there was a great crowd looking down at her. But they couldn't see her, couldn't tell she was watching them. The droning of the rector filled her ears. Then, suddenly, it was silent; the crowd evaporated. Only two people remained—Drew and Lady Cynthia. They were kissing and touching, writhing on the top of her glass casket. Jane screamed, "Stop! Stop! Oh, please, Drew, stop!"

She sat up, chest heaving, eyes wild.

"Jane! It was only a nightmare! Shh, Jane, shh." Drew sat on the edge of the chaise longue, his arms around her, comforting her.

Jane stiffened and pushed him away.

"Are you all right?"

"Yes, I'm fine, Lord Devlin."

His countenance puzzled, he said quietly, "Lord Devlin? What were you dreaming, Jane?"

"I don't remember," she lied, swinging her feet to the floor on the opposite side so he couldn't see her face. She rose, straightening her gown as she regained her composure. "I didn't mean to go to sleep. I'll have to change before we ride."

"I don't mind waiting," he said quickly, suspicious that she would use this inconvenience as an excuse to avoid their ride.

Jane only nodded and began walking toward the house. Drew caught up with her easily. After a moment of her continued silence, he asked, "Has something happened, Jane?"

160

She stopped and faced him. She read the concern in his dark eyes and steeled herself against it. He really had no idea how his defection to Lady Cynthia had shaken her. Nor did he realize how difficult she found it to keep a proper distance between them; if he touched her, she might cast away her resolve to keep him at arm's length.

Shaking her head, Jane did permit herself a slight smile. "I'm just a bear when I awake." She took his arm, and they continued to the house.

"By the way, I stopped in at your jeweler's this morning."

"Thank you! I talked to Mickey, just as you said. He told me he was robbed on the way back to Heartland."

"Yes, and unfortunately, the jeweler couldn't recall any suspicious-looking characters in his shop."

"I would have been surprised if he had. I sent a messenger to the local magistrate, just to warn him about a highwayman in the neighborhood. He wasn't very encouraging about finding the culprit. I daresay I've seen the last of the Heartland pendant."

"I would have another made for you, Jane, if I thought it would help. But I know it is the sentiment attached to it that you miss."

"That's true, but I thank you for helping me, Drew." They walked in silence for a moment. Climbing the steps to the terrace, Jane asked, "Did your mother enjoy the Assembly?"

"Definitely. I escorted her to the Pump Room this morning, and she was quickly taken over by her new friends."

"I'm not surprised. She is a lovely person."

"Yes, I'm finding out how kind she really is. When I was younger, I couldn't understand her."

"You weren't close when you were growing up?"

"No. Mother always tried to excuse my uncle's cruelty. For me, there was only black or white, nothing in between."

"A common malady of youth, I believe. But you and she appear to enjoy each other's company now. You're very lucky to have her."

Drew opened the French doors. "I know. I've always believed a person made his or her own luck. But sometimes, good luck just finds you." He smiled into her eyes, then allowed her to enter the house.

Jane knew his words had a double entendre, but her new resolve made her dismiss his remark as mere flirtation.

Soon they were riding through the home wood; the path they had chosen would eventually lead to the ruins of the old abbey.

Lord Devlin's mood continued to be flirtatious which suited Jane very well. She had no trouble keeping up with his light banter. There was no tension—physical or emotional—to discomfit her. She was relieved, she told herself, that he hadn't referred to the previous night.

They dismounted when they reached the ruins. It had been several weeks since Jane had visited the abbey, and she spent some time wandering through the fallen stones with the silent viscount following. And this time, she found her memories of her father were as vivid as ever.

"It must have been difficult for you, Jane, coming here the first time after your father died."

"Yes, I still remember that visit. I could almost hear my father's words vibrating amidst the stones."

"And now?"

"Now it is silent, peaceful."

She turned and smiled at him. Leaning against one of the three remaining walls, Drew looked incredibly handsome and rugged. Jane thought it wise to change the subject.

"I received letters from Cherry and Aunt Sophie today. They are each convinced the other one is unreasonable and obstinate."

"About Paris?" he asked. Jane nodded, and Drew observed, "Don't we all when we don't get our way?"

"No, at least I hope I may not have such a narrow view." She looked up at the clear blue sky and frowned. "That sounded like thunder."

162

Drew moved closer to her. "Have we reverted to the weather for a topic of conversation?" he teased.

Jane shook her head. "It must have been my imagination. What were we discussing?"

"How narrow-minded some—" Drew glanced up and cried, "Watch out!" With this, he shoved her away from the wall, knocking the breath out of her as he dove on top her. She then heard a thunderous crash.

Trying to catch her breath, Jane could only stare in horror at the huge stones scattered where she had just been standing.

"Jane! Are you hurt?" demanded the viscount. She shook her head, and he leapt to his feet, running around the wall to the crumbling staircase on the other side.

Jane followed, clutching her ribs. Gradually, her breath returned, and she shouted, "What are you doing? You can't go up there! It's not safe!"

Drew turned, his eyes lighted by cold-blooded determination. "Someone must have managed to climb these steps. I intend to find out who it was."

"Drew! Don't be ridiculous! Why would anyone wish to harm us?"

"Not us—you." He continued to climb while Jane watched in fear. He lost his footing and sent a shower of small stones to the ground as part of the stairway collapsed.

"Drew!" screamed Jane. "Please come down! There's no one there. The abbey is old; it's tumbling down about our ears."

"Quiet!" he commanded, and Jane glared at his back. He stepped onto a narrow walkway that ran the length of the wall. In the past, it had been a corridor leading to the monk's chambers. Now, it was little more than a ledge.

Jane closed her eyes, whispering a quick prayer. When she opened them, Drew had disappeared. She ran along the wall, looking up, searching for some sign of him. Suddenly Jane gasped.

"Easy!" said Drew, grabbing her arms as she tripped

over another fallen stone.

"How did you get down here?" she asked.

He held up a rope. "This was tied around the tower up there. I simply swung myself to the ground. It took only a matter of seconds."

Jane paled, and the viscount led her to the shade of a nearby tree, seating her there. Jane shook her head and said, "But who would want to do harm to either of us? I have no enemies."

Her frown touched his heart; he wanted more than anything to protect her. He hesitated. If he started enumerating the suspicious events that had occurred to Jane, or near her, since he had met her, it would only distress her. And he had no real proof. For all he knew, the shelf in the larder falling, the highwayman, their being locked in the crypt, and even today's near-fatal disaster were only coincidences.

He smiled down at Jane, and she visibly relaxed. "The rope was probably left there by some local boys. Their tying it around the tower no doubt loosened some of the stones. We shouldn't let it bother us, but I don't think it would be wise to visit the abbey alone in the future."

"No, I doubt I shall."

He pulled her to her feet, but made no attempt to embrace her. Jane tried to convince herself that she wasn't disappointed.

"Come, let's go home. I could stand a glass of ale; it is terribly warm today," said Devlin.

"What? Reduced to making conversation about the weather, my Lord Devlin?" Grinning, she hurriedly returned to the horses. As he threw her into the saddle, she yelled, "Race you to the first fence!"

Monday morning dawned bright and clear. Jane dressed in a severely cut carriage dress of hunter green. Her hair was pulled back in a tight chignon at the nape of her neck — she called it her schoolmistress look.

Tom Summers, clad in his red and black livery, drove the open landau at a spanking pace to Laura Place. The young groom James, also dressed in his handsome livery, hung onto the back, smiling and winking at the pretty servant girls as they rolled along.

Jane was shown into the soothing salon at Laura Place where Mrs. Peterson joined her only moments later. They lost no time going out to the carriage. James hopped to the ground and assisted them into the well-sprung vehicle.

"It is so kind of you to show me around the countryside. You shall be much better company than a mere guidebook, my dear."

Jane laughed and said, "I should hope so. I always imagine guidebooks being written by musty old dons who are bent on boring schoolboys to death."

They both laughed causing Tom Summers's weathered face to break into a smile. Nothing prettier than the sound of his mistress's laugh, thought the old man.

As they crossed the Old Bridge, Faith Peterson commented, "What a beautiful Judas tree."

"That path leads to the Chapel of St. Mary Magdalen; it was built in the Middle Ages. For a time it was a house for lepers, hence the significance of the blood red Judas tree blossoms. We are going up to Beechen Cliff. It is an excellent vantage point for viewing the city and all the countryside beyond; it is four hundred feet high."

A short time later, Tom Summers pulled up on the ribbons. "Will you be wanting to walk about, Miss Lindsay?"

"Yes, Summers." The groom jumped down and ran around to open the carriage door. After helping each of the ladies to alight, he stood rigid as a soldier.

"James, would you set out that basket and some carriage rugs?"

"Yes, Miss Lindsay," he said, bounding into the carriage and gathering the items Jane wanted. He spread the rugs under a tree, placing the basket on top of one.

"Will there be anything else, miss?" asked Summers.

"No, we'll do. You may come back for us in about an hour."

"Very good, miss."

Jane led Faith Peterson along a rock-strewn path, closer to the edge of the cliff. "If you look across the valley, you can see the Royal Crescent and Lansdown Hill beyond."

"It is beautiful. Now, what is that hill?"

"That's Solsbury Hill. Below it is Swainwick, a delightful little village. It was the first site of civilization in the area, though I'm not certain how civilized it was. Bath has been occupied by the Romans and Danes, as well as the native population. It was originally called Aquae Sulis, so it has long been known for its healing waters. Legend has it that a British king named Hudibras had one son named Bladud. This son contracted leprosy and was expelled from the village. In order to survive, Bladud became a swineherder. He gave his pigs the disease, and it was they who found the healing waters."

"Very believable! Have you tasted the famous waters? They taste like swine have been bathing in them."

Jane chuckled. "The other version of Bladud's legend is that he built a temple to Minerva, the Roman goddess of medicine. According to this legend, Bladud used black magic to make the healing bath."

"Oh, I much prefer the swineherd theory."

"I must confess I do, too. As a little girl, I would beg my father to tell the story over and over. I could just see Bladud, a future king of Bath, cavorting in the pigsty!"

They shared a laugh over this tale. Then Mrs. Peterson asked, "Where is all the limestone found for which Bath is so famous?"

"Most of it is in the quarries on Combe Down. Ralph Allen, who patronized the revival of elegance in Bath, owned it. The architects Wood senior and junior used it for many of their buildings. Those massive columns on the fronts of the houses in the Royal Crescent are all Bath limestone. The houses, so magnificent in front, are quite dull in back. This led to a saying in the past century,

166

"Queen Anne in front and Mary Ann behind."

"There now! You see what I mean! A guidebook never gives one such interesting tidbits!"

"Would you like to return to the blankets and have some of Cook's pastries now?"

"That sounds delightful! I didn't have time for breakfast this morning. I slept too late after Martha FitzSimmon's literary evening. I'm just not accustomed to these late nights yet."

"Do you think you'll stay in Bath, Mrs. Peterson?" asked Jane as she opened the basket.

"Yes, you can't imagine how heavenly it is to have nothing to do all day but visit with people. My brother-in-law's estate in York was too isolated to allow daily contact with the outside world."

"That must have been difficult for someone like you who seems to enjoy people."

"It was, at times. I had a small circle of friends who would visit me on occasion, but nothing like this. Of course, I shan't allow myself to become an idle fribble entirely. I have spoken to your rector—Hall, I believe is his name—about helping with the parish poor. I suppose once a clergyman's daughter . . ."

"So you are well and truly settling in. Does Drew plan to make his home here, also?" asked Jane—casually she hoped.

"For the time being. But even if he doesn't like to think about it, someday he will be earl of Cheswick. His responsibilities will require his spending part of the year in York. And then, if he chooses to take his seat in the House of Lords, London will be his residence when Parliament is in session."

"I didn't realize he was interested in politics."

"Not politics—government. He feels very strongly about helping the poor, regulating the factories springing up all over the country. But, of course, you wouldn't know that about Drew. That's hardly a topic he'd choose to take up with a pretty young lady."

167

"I don't see why not! I am interested in such things. It is the duty of all of England's citizens, men and women, to take an interest in the less fortunate."

"True, but as women, you and I do all we can through our church work. That is the way of society. And never belittle the importance of the work we do, Jane. Our work is more personal; we have the satisfaction of seeing the children happy and smiling, rather than hungry and sullen."

"You're right, of course. How is it, just the mention of Drew's name, and I am all up in arms?" said Jane.

"I wouldn't dare guess, Jane. But I do think it's an excellent question for you to ponder. My, but your Mrs. Brown makes the best teacakes I have ever put in my mouth!"

Tactfully changing the subject, the two ladies debated the efficacies of one ingredient over the other when baking teacakes.

That same afternoon, Lord Devlin again rode to Heartland, but he entered the grounds through the back pasture. He guided his big gray stallion into the woods, circling the green lawns until he had a view of the driveway. Then he dismounted, tethering his horse in the shelter of the trees, away from prying eyes.

His mother had told him she and Jane intended to go sightseeing that day, and he didn't want to miss the opportunity Jane's absence would provide.

Drew hadn't discussed the incident at the abbey with his mother when he returned to Laura Place, but it was foremost in his mind. That night he had declined an invitation to join his friends at cards so that he might set his thoughts in order. This had long been his way of dealing with problems. And he felt certain these accidents represented a very real problem — protecting his Jane, preferably without her knowing.

Donning his green brocade dressing gown, the viscount settled himself in a comfortable chair in his sitting room.

168

His mother had gone out, and he had sent the servants to bed, preferring to be completely alone with his thoughts.

The first incident had been the mysterious shutting and locking of the crypt door with him and Jane trapped inside. Havelock had been present on that occasion, but Drew hadn't seen that as a threat, and he hadn't interrogated Havelock. The other people at the abbey that day were all in London, so he couldn't question them about Havelock's movements.

The shelf falling in the larder did represent a threat to Jane, and he would need to question Mrs. Brown about that. True, it hadn't proven to be life-threatening, but the accident was suspicious.

The robbery by the highwayman hadn't harmed Jane physically, but it had stunned her emotionally. Devlin would have Pipkin question the footman about the thief's appearance. If it had been Havelock, the description would be enough; few men were as large as Jane's cousin. If it had been the footman Sims, perhaps Mickey could remember some distinguishing mark. The viscount felt certain Havelock was connected to that robbery. How else had he found the large sums of money necessary to pay off his gambling debts?

And the last "accident," the one that had come so very close to ending Jane's life? His own, also, when he had tried to save her. There was no way he could prove Havelock or his henchman Sims had been up there. The best he could do was see to it that Jane didn't go to the abbey alone again. She had said she wouldn't; he would have to believe her and do the best he could to protect her anywhere else.

And so, at first light, he had sent to Bow Street in London, requesting a discreet Runner, an investigator who would be willing to work privately for some time. Next, he had roused Jane's lawyer, Mr. Crankshaft. He had had to explain a great deal to the close-mouthed solicitor before the man had agreed to answer his questions concerning Jane's heir. In essence, Heartland was up for grabs when

Jane died if she hadn't produced any offspring. At present, the logical heir was her aunt, Roland Havelock's mother.

And Drew had only himself to blame for having set Havelock's curiosity and greed to work. Heartland was one of the richest estates in England; certainly a prize worth murder if one had few scruples. And Roland Havelock had never struck Lord Devlin as a particularly scrupulous man.

Drew watched as Jane's coachman drove the landau down the long drive to the road; at least her groom was perched up behind, he thought grimly.

He waited ten more minutes before mounting and turning his horse toward the house.

"My lord," said Pipkin, bowing. "Miss Lindsay is from home at the moment."

"Yes, I know, Pipkin. Actually, I came to see you. Is there someplace we could be private?"

Pipkin nodded and led the way to the study. Drew knew he had shocked the old man, though Pipkin had given no indication of such. But after Drew's rather pointed remarks about Jane the day before, perhaps the butler thought he wanted to ask permission to pay his addresses to Jane. But the viscount's amusement was quickly banished as he recalled the serious nature of his visit.

"I'll be brief," began the viscount as soon as the door was closed. "I very much fear someone is trying to kill Miss Lindsay."

The butler turned a sickly green, and his prim mouth drooped. Drew took the servant's arm and led him to a chair. He turned, his gaze searching out a decanter of port. He gave a full measure to Pipkin before seating himself in front of the butler. Pipkin seemed to have aged before his eyes.

"Are you all right? Should I send for someone?" Pipkin shook his head and sipped the strong liquid. "I've shocked you; I'm sorry. I would say I was mistaken, but the matter is too grave for such weakness."

"Please, my lord, I want to hear what you have to say.

I'll be fine. Please continue."

"We visited the abbey last Friday on our ride. Just as Miss Lindsay was standing by one of the remaining walls, several huge boulders fell. I managed to push her out of harm's way. Then I ran up the old steps. Someone had tied a rope around the tower, presumably for a quick escape."

"Village children?" asked the butler weakly.

Devlin shook his head. "Jane thought she heard thunder just before the rocks fell. The sky was clear as a bell; I believe she heard someone pushing the stones that last little bit to make them fall. A child, even a youth couldn't have moved those stones. I daresay I would have had trouble. Someone wanted to harm your mistress."

"What does Miss Lindsay say about this?"

"When I suggested such a thing, she became so upset that I dropped the matter entirely. I can understand. She has always been so well loved in the neighborhood; she cannot fathom why anyone would wish her harm."

"No one would, my lord. I can't imagine why. . . ."

"Perhaps in the hopes of obtaining Heartland?" said Lord Devlin quietly.

"Mr. Havelock!"

"He is my favorite suspect, but that may be because I do so dislike the man. And how about this Sims Jane mentioned?"

"Yes, I can see him involved in such a nefarious scheme. I'll sack him immediately!"

"No! You mustn't, Pipkin. Think, better the devil we know than one we don't. If he is here, you can keep an eye on him; tie his hands, so to speak."

"True. But we must do something. Miss Jane, why, she's . . ." The butler stood up, his demeanor as proper and unrelenting as ever despite his misty eyes.

"I would like to speak to Mrs. Brown, your cook. And also to Miss Lindsay's maid. Those two, I think, will be our greatest allies."

"There is not a body or soul on Heartland who wouldn't

give his life for Miss Lindsay, my lord."

"No doubt you're right, Pipkin. But with all that protection, we would never be able to catch the blackguard. And believe me, I have every intention of catching him."

"Amen," said the butler, bowing his head. "Mrs. Brown sent that Sims fellow out on an errand not thirty minutes ago, with Mickey along, so we needn't worry about him. I think, m' lord, perhaps it would be best if you accompanied me to the cook's sitting room. Mrs. Brown coming to the study when everyone knows the mistress is out would appear strange. Let me go first; I'll see to it the scullery maids are busy elsewhere."

Moments later, Lord Devlin found himself sitting in a cozy parlor just off the kitchens. There was a tidy desk against one wall, a comfortable chair, and a small sofa in front of the spotless fireplace. Pipkin entered, followed by two middle-aged women. The viscount inclined his head to them.

"Mrs. Brown?"

The woman dressed in unrelenting black curtseyed and came forward. "Yes, my lord," she said in a deep, stringent voice.

"Mrs. Tucker?"

The other woman curtseyed and smiled. "Your servant, my lord. How may we help you?"

Lord Devlin felt better already. With such calm, capable people helping, surely they would be able to protect Jane. He indicated that they should be seated on the sofa and took the chair himself. Pipkin remained by the fireplace.

"I suppose Pipkin has given you the bare facts, that Miss Lindsay may be in danger, and we must protect her." They both nodded, their faces filled with determination. "Good, Mrs. Brown, tell me what you can about the accident in the larder."

She flushed at the unhappy memory, but said firmly, "Miss Lindsay was helping sort through last year's canned goods. Sims was reading the labels on the top shelf while Miss Jane was on the floor, going through the ones on the bottom. I shouldn't have let her do it; I should have been the one in there."

The cook produced a capacious handkerchief and dabbed at her eyes.

"Please, Mrs. Brown, you shouldn't blame yourself. I daresay Miss Lindsay insisted on helping."

"Yes, m' lord, she always does," sniffed Mrs. Brown.

"You say Sims was working on the top shelf?"

"Yes, and then he left, and when Miss Lindsay reached up and grabbed the shelf to right herself, it all came crashing down."

"Pipkin, did you look at the wall afterwards?"

"Indeed I did, my lord."

"What did the wall look like? Like the bolts had pulled out?"

"Why, no, my lord. Now that I think on it, the plaster was as neat as could be. Those bolts must have been loosened!"

"Perhaps. We should be wary of our Mr. Sims, at the very least. Now, Pipkin, I would like for you to question Mickey about the highwayman's appearance. If our suspicions are correct, either Sims or Havelock was the robber. Perhaps Mickey noticed something that would give us a clue. Send word to me in town if he can help."

"Lord Devlin," said Mrs. Brown, "I just remembered, when you said Mr. Havelock's name. He visited Miss Jane some time ago and brought her a box of chocolates. Miss Jane loves them, but she gave them to me to get rid of them. She always breaks out—"

"Emily!" said Tucker indignantly.

"Never mind, Mrs. Tucker," said Drew, smiling at the maid. "Please go on, Mrs. Brown."

"It's probably nothing, but young Tom—he's the pot boy—he brought in a dead pigeon after I threw the sweets out in the yard. He swore it was the chocolates that killed it."

The smile had long since faded from Drew's face. He looked from one anxious brow to another. They waited expectantly for his next words.

"I wish we had those sweets now; we could have them tested. But we don't, so it's still a guessing game. And perhaps I am all about in the head, but I fear I'm all too right. Miss Lindsay must not be left alone where the servant Sims is. Mrs. Brown, you must keep a close eye on any dishes prepared for Miss Lindsay. Once they leave your care, Pipkin will make certain no one tampers with them."

"What do you want me to do, m' lord?" asked Tucker.

"I know that Jane relies on you heavily, Mrs. Tucker. You've been with her for many years, I understand."

"And with her mother before her."

"Try to guide Miss Lindsay away from any invitations where she will be out alone at night. Or in the daytime, for that matter. You might suggest that the highwayman is still on the loose, and you would feel better about her if she took an extra footman with a loaded blunderbuss anytime she leaves Heartland."

"But what about riding? Miss Jane rides every day by herself, all over the estate."

"I shall take care of that. I'm hiring someone who will follow her, at a discreet distance, whenever she goes out alone. When he isn't there, I will be. Oh, yes, Pipkin. Will you speak to the gamekeeper about the man? I wouldn't want this fellow getting shot for poaching."

"Is there anything else, m' lord?" asked Pipkin.

"No, just keep your eyes open and don't hesitate to send for me if you feel there is the least cause."

"Thank you, m' lord. I'm sure we all feel better knowing you are helping."

"Believe me, Pipkin, I feel the same about the three of you."

Jane and Drew's mother returned to Bath just in time for tea. As Jane accepted the older woman's invitation, she wondered if Drew would be present. She had not long to

174

wonder, for there he was, in the parlor, his nose in a book. He stood up when he heard them enter.

"Did you enjoy yourselves, ladies?"

"It is a beautiful scene, Drew. You should have Jane take you up there some time," said Faith, a slight smile curving her lips.

Drew grinned at his mother, warning her to be careful. "Perhaps I shall. Thank you for showing Mother the countryside, Jane."

"It was my pleasure. And informative for me, also. I learned a great deal about you."

"A day of tedium!" he laughed. "Mother, do tell me you didn't drone on about me the whole time."

"I think now would be a good time to go upstairs and refresh myself before tea. Jane?"

"No, thank you. I'm fine."

"Good. Oh, Drew, do ring for tea. I won't be a moment!" Faith Peterson winked at her son before gliding from the room.

"Won't you sit down, Jane?" he said, as he walked across the room and pulled the bell.

"Thank you."

He rejoined her on the sofa. "Now, what could Mother possibly have told you about me that was interesting?"

"Only that you plan to have a go at the government when you become an earl."

"Oh, that. Well, I intend to see if I can lend my support where it will do some good. Things aren't working the way they are now."

"I think that's very noble of you; if only more of the nation's influential people would take an interest."

"I couldn't agree more. But it may be years before I have a chance to put my plan in force, as mean as my uncle is. I fear he won't oblige me by dying any time soon."

"Drew!"

"Ah, I have shocked you again. But why should I pretend an affection for a man who has made my life miserable at every turn?"

"I suppose you're right, but one simply doesn't voice such a thought in polite society."

"I thought you and I were beyond the polite niceties, Jane," he said softly.

Fortunately for Jane, who was becoming transfixed by his steady gaze, the butler entered with the tea tray. Mrs. Peterson followed on his heels.

After pouring everyone's tea, Drew's mother picked up the book he had laid aside. *Pride and Prejudice* by Jane Austen."

"An excellent novel, Mother. Much better than the ordinary drivel, I'm told. You would enjoy it."

"I didn't even know you read novels, Drew," commented his mother.

"I haven't before, but I was given this one and decided to try it."

"You know Miss Austen resides in Bath?" said Jane.

"Really? I had no idea."

"Perhaps you are acquainted with Miss Austen's models for her characters, Jane?" teased Drew.

"No, I don't think so; however, I might guess you were the model for Mr. Darcy. If I remember correctly, you would fit his physical description."

"Foul my dear! The novel was written sixteen years prior to its publication date. I was far too young at the time. Do you find me as arrogant as Mr. Darcy?"

"Not very often, Drew. At least, not as often as I used to do."

"Mother! Are you going to allow this?" he laughed.

"Needs must, my dear. I haven't read the book. Now, do quit squabbling. It isn't good for the digestion."

"Yes, Mother," said Drew with mock docility.

Jane remained longer than the prescribed thirty minutes, owing, she told herself, to the excessively hot temperature of the tea. It took much too long to cool, and she simply didn't care to add milk to speed the process.

Though it was dusk before she left them, Jane didn't notice the coolness of the evening. She continued to feel wrapped in the cozy warmth of the yellow salon at Laura Place.

When Jane returned from her visits, Mickey was loitering in the hallway. He smiled bashfully when she spoke to him.

"Did you want to talk to me, Mickey? Or were you waiting for Mr. Pipkin?"

"You, Miss Jane."

"I see. Why don't we go into the study?"

When he stood awkwardly before her, Jane prompted, "What did you wish to tell me, Mickey?"

"I saw that Lord Devlin today."

"Today? I think you mean yesterday, Mickey. Lord Devlin and I went riding yesterday."

"No, Miss Jane. It was today. It was when I went out with Sims to find some berries for Mrs. Brown. I had to go with him because he doesn't know where to look. So we left, and I saw Lord Devlin waiting in the woods."

"Waiting?" asked Jane, her smooth brow creased with puzzlement.

"Yes, Miss Jane. I didn't tell anybody, not after that highwayman the other day. Why would he be watching you leave?"

"So it was while I was leaving," she murmured. Mickey nodded.

"Did I do right to tell you, Miss Jane?"

"Indeed you did, Mickey," she said, smiling as she dismissed him. Before he left the room, she said quietly, "Mickey, don't tell anyone else about this. Promise?"

"Yes, Miss Jane. I promise. And if I see 'im again, I'll come and tell you."

"Good, Mickey. Thank you."

Jane remained in the study for the next hour, ostensibly working on the household ledgers. In reality, her mind was occupied with the puzzle Mickey had presented to her.

Why would Lord Devlin be watching for her departure? And where had he gone afterwards? Had he followed her? She didn't think so. Her groom had been with her, and he would have noticed someone trailing after them, even if she hadn't.

And she didn't believe Drew was so infatuated with her that he couldn't bear the thought of four and twenty hours passing without setting eyes on her. Why then, was he observing her movements? An ugly suspicion, one she couldn't believe, flashed across her mind. She dismissed it immediately.

But, thought Jane, it was disturbing that Mickey's story about Drew should make her recall his suggestion of danger. She had scoffed at the idea of someone trying to harm her at the time, but that tiny grain of uncertainty had remained.

Wearily, Jane acknowledged to herself that she would be wise to be cautious. She rose and went to the window, staring at the peaceful landscape with unseeing eyes. Impatiently, Jane twitched the curtains closed and left the room.

A week later, the viscount was feeling rather foolish when he contemplated all the measures taken to insure Jane's safety. Despite his best efforts, she had twice wandered away from the house at Heartland without anyone knowing. The Bow Street Runner, an older man named Wilbur Bailey, had stationed himself on one side of the massive house commanding a view of the stables and the front drive. But on the other side of the house, the library's French doors allowed anyone to exit without being detected. This, Mr. Bailey told the viscount, made his job impossible.

Still, Drew's other precautions had enabled him to sleep nights. At Tucker's request, Jane had begun to take a groom with her any time she drove out or went riding. Tucker didn't pause to wonder why Jane had fallen in with

178

this suggestion so readily. Pipkin kept an eye on Sims, and Mrs. Brown made certain Jane's meals went directly from her safe hands to the table.

"They're on t' us, Mr. Havelock."

"The devil, you say, Sims! How could they be?"

"I don't know, sir. That Lord Devlin's always hangin' around. I saw 'im comin' toward the stables yesterday, out of the woods, beside the house."

"What of it?"

"That's th' second time I've seen 'im doin' that. So last night, when everyone was asleep, I sneaked out there and guess what I saw!"

"Tell me, man!" said Havelock, sweat beginning to run down his fat jowls.

"There was this man sleepin' in th' woods. He's all comfortable like with a fire an' food, a little tarp set up t' keep th' rain off."

"Who is it?"

"I don't know for sure, Mr. Havelock, but my guess is Bow Street."

"A Runner," breathed Havelock, his face turning white.

"That's my guess. And I think Lord Devlin is behind 'is bein' there. Plus the fact that I'm never left to my own devices anymore. Finding a time to get away 'ere was almost impossible."

"You made sure you weren't followed, didn't you?"

"Of course I did. But what do you want me t' do now?"

"Nothing, absolutely nothing. And I shall go away for a time."

"I say! Yer not goin' t' leave me there! What with that looby of a footman Mickey and that Bible-quoting butler, I'm ready to murder the whole lot of 'em!"

"Restrain yourself, Sims. For the time being, anyway. Don't worry; I won't forget about you."

"No, you don't dare forget about me," mumbled Sims.

"Here now! I've paid you well plus what you're earning

179

working at Heartland."

"Yes, but it's not like it is in London, is it? In London, there were all sorts of ways to get me 'ands on a spot o' money."

"Someday, Sims, you shall have all the money you need. I'll make you my estate manager—someday."

Three weeks passed; nothing untoward occurred, and the Bow Street Runner was inclined to disbelieve there was a danger. Bailey never relaxed his vigilance, but as he told Lord Devlin, "Ain't nothin' t'see."

Drew found himself more often in Jane's company, but they were never alone. Even when they went riding, the groom accompanied them. Drew didn't ask Jane why this was so; he assumed Jane was merely following her maid's advice. Since he was keeping such a close watch over her, and trying to keep her ignorant of the surveillance, he felt doubly responsible for her. If anyone suspected how often he could be found in or about Heartland and its mistress, Jane's reputation would be in shreds. So, he often took his mother or invited Jane to Bath, joining a group of friends at cards, attending the Assemblies, and once, even persuading Jane to go to the Pump Room.

If the viscount had paused to consider the nature of their present relationship, he might have been puzzled by Jane's behavior toward him, especially if one recalled their previous stormy encounters—encounters that often included fire and passion.

As for Jane, she was content with the comfortable friendship she and Drew had found. She was more than willing, she told herself, to forego passion—it was much too disturbing to her peace of mind. Their more relaxed relationship allowed her to trust him, and to trust her judgement of him. After all, Jane was accustomed to having male friends; it was only the passionate suitor she had come to mistrust over the years.

Jane decided it had been the idea of Drew paying court

to her that was so disturbing. She had realized Drew didn't fit into the two categories of her past suitors—fortune hunter or social climbing cit. Then she had received a letter from her friend in London which upheld Drew's claim to personal wealth. Sally had been quite emphatic: Lord Drew Devlin was as rich as Goldon Ball in his own right, never counting what he would inherit with his title, earl of Cheswick. And socially, it was he who would be raising her to his level, not the other way around.

This tidbit of information would have gladdened the heart of a more self-centered lady. But to Jane, the news was unsettling. If Drew wasn't a fortune hunter, then why was he at such pains to make love to her? Could he truly love her? Jane didn't dismiss the idea, but she was unable to accept this unequivocally. The possibility that he was merely trying to win her approval to buy Heartland was doubtful; she was sure he had accepted defeat on that question. Lurking in the back of her mind, the thought that he wished to do her harm for some unknown reason seemed too ludicrous to examine.

So Jane welcomed the cooling of their relationship to friendship. This was something she could accept from a man. Late at night, when trying to arrange the covers for sleep, perhaps she allowed herself to miss his kisses, but her life was certainly more calm, normal.

Under Drew's subtle nurturing, Jane found her social role changing. She had always been the consummate guest or hostess at any social event, but she looked in disdain at what she termed "silly flirtation." Her own manner had been perpetually reserved. Now she laughed more easily; she even flirted with Drew's friends. Giles Stanton demanded at least two dances at each Assembly or ball, and Farley began to neglect the card room and its libations in order to fetch her punch or other refreshments. Drew silently surveyed this unusual spectacle, a slight smile curving his lips.

* * *

Jane sang softly to herself as she bathed. She really hadn't allowed enough time to dress before her guests arrived, but she refused to rush. Drew wouldn't mind. He no longer found anything she said or did worth starting an argument. He had changed toward her.

This change had aroused her curiosity at first. Then it had piqued her pride. How she had baited him with outrageous comments on a myriad of topics, but to no avail. He would occasionally raise one of those wicked brows. Let's see, thought Jane, it's his left one, I think. She smiled again as she remembered, and her hand paused, letting the warm water from the soft sponge trail down her breasts and stomach. Now, after a week or two, she had grown accustomed to this new situation and accepted it.

The door opened, and Tucker entered, carrying a warm towel. Holding out the towel, the maid teased, "Thinkin' of Mr. Stanton, perhaps, or Mr. Farley?"

Jane stepped out of the tub and was enveloped in the soft cloth.

"No, not Mr. Stanton. Or Mr. Farley. Oh, they're both handsome men, and quite charming, but neither one touches my heart."

"Who does?"

Jane laughed. "No one, as you well know."

"Not even a very tall, dark man?" asked Tucker, busying herself in the wardrobe.

"If you mean Lord Devlin, Tucker, you may say the name. I promise you I shan't swoon. Lord Devlin is a friend, only a friend. And I am quite content to have it so."

"As you say, Miss Jane," said the maid. Jane restrained a childish urge to stick out her tongue at the maid's back.

"You'll be wearing the yellow silk?"

"Yes. And you had better put up my hair. Though it's to be an informal evening, I mustn't let our guests think my appearance too casual."

The entertainment was informal enough, thought Jane. She had invited nineteen people for an afternoon of croquet followed by an enormous buffet and dancing, should anyone wish to dance. The rector and his wife would be attending, and Mrs. Hall liked nothing better than playing a lively tune for the "young people."

Also on the guest list were Mary Aubrey, who was a guest at the rector's house while her family extended their stay in London, and Mr. Primrose, her fiancé. Drew was bringing his mother and his two friends. The rest of the guests were neighbors like the Ashmores, who had just returned from a brief stay in London. It would be an amiable group, all the guests acquainted with one another, and the atmosphere relaxed. It was, in short, just the sort of evening Jane enjoyed most.

Jane descended the long, curving staircase, carrying her straw bonnet by its yellow satin ribbons. Her thoughts were occupied with last minute details, and she failed to notice Drew watching her progress.

"Oh! Drew, you startled me," she said as her foot touched the bottom step.

He held out his hand, his gaze warm as he looked her over from head to toe. Jane shifted from one foot to the other, that old feeling of hot breathlessness building under his relentless scrutiny. Then his quick grin put her at ease, as it always did. It was odd, she thought, how intimidating his expression could seem until he smiled. It was like a transformation.

"I do believe that pale shade of yellow is prettier on you than on anyone else I have ever seen. It does something strange to those green eyes of yours. They look rather like a cat's eyes; I shall expect you to purr instead of speak."

"I suppose that is meant to be a compliment, Drew," said Jane. "But I must warn you, if I wished to take it the other way, I could."

"Yes, I suppose I could have meant it as a subtle insult, only you know me better than that. I am never subtle when it comes to abuse." With another of his disarming smiles, he tucked her hand into the crook of his elbow.

She laughed and moved along the corridor, saying, "Yes,

I am only too aware, though you seem to have turned over a new leaf." Drew paused and turned to face her. Did she read some challenge in his eyes?

"Perhaps," he began slowly, "I am only lulling you into a false sense of security. Then, when you least expect it, I shall ridicule you unmercifully."

"Thank you for the warning, my dear sir. Forewarned is forearmed, so they say," quipped Jane, hoping her face wasn't becoming flushed under his disturbing gaze.

"Drew, do quit beleaguering Miss Lindsay and let her join her guests," called his mother from the doorway of the gold salon.

He extended his arm again, and Jane laid a gloved hand on his sleeve. She was surprised by the fluttering of her heart this simple courtesy produced. She was over that unsettling childishness, surely. She looked up at Drew and returned his smile. It must have been their lively exchange.

The games began, and several times Jane caught Drew staring at her, his eyes lighted by an unidentifiable emotion. Each time, she frowned, unable to satisfy her curiosity. Had the moon changed? Or had he slept in a room with an open window, the moonlight falling on his face? Nurse had told her either event could change human emotions. It was nonsense, of course, but what other explanation could there be?

Hitting the ball through the first wicket, Drew looked up quickly before Jane could avert her eyes. What was the matter with her? He could have sworn she'd come to trust him, yet she continued to regard him as though she were appraising his motives again. Could she still be suspicious of him?

Jane bent over, swinging her mallet expertly. She was rather good at the game, having played it often with her grandmother. She had had to learn the rules anew when she'd grown up; as a child, her grandmother's rules had been structured to let Jane win. Though the game was old, it wasn't yet a traditional entertainment in the days of the Regency, so Jane often had to teach new guests how to play. But Drew knew how; he had told her it was often played in the Indies.

"Miss Lindsay, I say, tell me again where I'm supposed to hit the thing with this stick," said Mr. Farley, his tones making him sound like a whining little boy.

"Through this hoop, Mr. Farley. No, no, one doesn't hold the mallet like a billiard cue. Hold it like so," said Jane, placing her hands over his on the mallet. Out of the corner of her eye, Jane saw Drew take a step in her direction. Then he stopped and turned his back. Jane was unaware Mr. Farley was grinning as he peered at Drew over the top of her head.

"He's got more hair than wit if he means to anger you, Drew," said Giles Stanton quietly. "Pay him no mind."

"I shan't. He's just being annoying because he didn't have anything but tea before he began to play. Farley a bit on the go is much worthier than a cold-sober Farley," laughed Drew.

"Glad you understand. But Drew, one other thing. Not that I wish to advise, but—"

"Then don't."

"Yes, well, but I must," said Giles. Drew shook his head and then nodded. "Aren't you taking things a little too slowly with Miss Lindsay. I mean, you've nothing to fear from me or Farley, but there are others who might not be so agreeable."

"I appreciate your concern, Giles, but I believe you can trust me in this. Miss Lindsay is not one to be hurried along. I'll know when the time has come."

"I hope you're right." Giles moved away to make his next play.

"I hope so, too," murmured Drew.

The late afternoon was mercifully cool as they finished their games and entered the house. Jane had turned the ballroom into a comfortable, inviting oasis for their evening of dining and entertainment. The French doors along the back wall had been thrown open, and in the gathering twilight, Chinese lanterns had been lit outside, should any guests feel inclined to take a stroll. One end of the huge ballroom held a buffet table that groaned under the weight of chilled lobster, pork tenderloin, duck à l'orange, tender asparagus and artichokes, tomato aspic, cheeses, fresh fruits, and Mrs. Brown's delicate pastries. Keeping the seating informal, Jane had brought in an oval table large enough to accommodate the entire party. Farther along the length of the room, there were groupings of comfortable chairs and sofas with plush Aubussan carpets underfoot. Next came game tables for those who wished to play cards. The pianoforte stood between the card tables and seating areas, facing the remainder of the ballroom. This portion had been left uncarpeted, its gleaming marble floor ready for the first dancers.

"What a delightful idea," said Mrs. Ashmore, surveying the ballroom. "Now I can keep one eye on my daughter while having a comfortable coze with my friends."

"Very wise of you, Jane," put in Mrs. Hall, the rector's merry wife. "And I will so enjoy playing for you young people if you wish to dance. How kind of you to arrange the instrument so I can watch. Wasn't that considerate of Miss Lindsay, Gerald?"

"Gerald," better known to his parishioners as Rector Hall, nodded solemnly. Jane took no offense; Rector Hall—she'd always thought the name sounded like a girls' school—rarely displayed any emotions. Somehow, his countenance made his fire-and-brimstone sermons seem more effective.

Jane steered her guests to the buffet table where several footmen hovered to serve the guests or carry plates. Pipkin presided over this operation with his usual aplomb.

The guests seated themselves randomly around the huge table. Mr. Farley secured the chair on Jane's right, and said loudly, "Rather like King Arthur's, what?"

From her other side, Giles Stanton smiled gallantly and said to Jane, "I daresay they didn't have the pleasure of such beauty at the knights' table."

"How kind, Mr. Stanton," responded Jane. She flashed

him a smile; then her eyes drifted across the table.

Directly opposite was Drew. He was looking especially handsome in his gray superfine coat and black waistcoat. Nestled in the folds of his snowy cravat was a single ruby; the jewel winked at her, and Jane blinked, looking up from the ruby to those sensuous lips and the patrician nose. As she studied his dark eyes, gleaming like onyx in the candlelight, Jane realized Drew was returning her scrutiny. She raised her chin, refusing to be cowed. Someone spoke to Drew, and he turned reluctantly to answer his neighbor, Lydia Ashmore. Jane addressed some inane comment to Mr. Farley and took a bite of marinated artichokes. She wrinkled her nose in distaste; she hated artichokes.

Six couples took to the dance floor as Mrs. Hall tried the keyboard with an energetic introduction to a country dance. The squire's round wife sent her daughters off with a smile and settled her considerable bulk on a nearby sofa. She was soon joined by Mrs. Ashmore and Drew's mother.

Sir Humphrey, the neighborhood's scholarly widower, had been eying Mrs. Peterson, but as she quickly became engrossed in conversation with the other ladies, he sighed and turned away.

Drew leaned against one of the six fireplaces, an excellent vantage point for observing the dancers while he conversed with Mr. Ashmore and the squire. Sir Humphrey soon joined in as words became heated regarding Parliament's latest efforts to deal with the postwar poverty and starvation.

"What do you say, Devlin?" asked the tall, bony squire.

"I'm afraid I haven't studied the situation as deeply as you gentlemen. I returned to England only last year, but I do feel very strongly that we should take care of our former soldiers."

"Here, here!" said the squire.

"But you can't just give them things," protested Mr. Ashmore, a tough-minded businessman despite his noble ancestry.

"It has been the same throughout history," said Sir Humphrey. "The aftermath of war is poverty. But surely, at this stage of civilization, we can find ways to help, to rehabilitate these fine men into our society."

"I agree," said Drew. "Something other than charity. Factories are sprouting up here and there—"

"Yes, and their damned machines throwing honest men out of work!" declared the squire.

"For a time, perhaps, but in the long run, more machines mean more goods, profits, and therefore, factories," asserted Mr. Ashmore.

The conversation rose and fell along with the strains of the country dances and the waltzes. Drew found his mind pulling away from politics across the room where Giles and Jane glided around the dance floor. Next it was Farley's turn, a country dance. Then the rector's foppish cousin, Nigel Hall, claimed her for the Boulanger.

The squire proposed a hand of cards, and Drew moved to the card tables. Taking the seat facing the dancers, he was able to continue his observation.

What was it about Jane that held him captive? He could name a number of females who were more beautiful. But there was something, some quality that held him as firmly as the bars of Newgate. He knew he loved her. But why?

"I say, Devlin, are you playing?" inquired Sir Humphrey.

"What? Oh, yes, of course." Drew promised himself he would pay attention to the game, but his mind was soon wandering again.

Finally, Mrs. Hall began another lilting waltz. If he weren't so far away, he might have swept Jane into his arms, forgetting his resolution to remain aloof. Drew didn't bother to tell himself he could have handled being so near to her; he knew he would have held her much too close. And Jane? Would she have rested her head on his shoulder?

But this was all conjecture, for the squire's puppy of a son had stammered out his request for Jane's hand in the waltz. Jane accepted, of course; it was all a polite hostess could do. Yet, as she placed her gloved hand in the young man's, her green eyes sought out Drew. She smiled; oh, it was ever so slightly but Drew knew they had shared one of those silent, infinitely intimate moments when two people's thoughts are so closely atuned, no words are necessary.

He would speak to her, that night, before he left.

Mrs. Hall abandoned the pianoforte when tea was served, but she promised to play one last waltz afterwards.

The perfect opportunity, thought Drew as he moved toward the sofa where Jane chatted with Mary Aubrey and Lydia Ashmore. He accepted the cup of tea Jane offered, but he didn't interrupt their conversation about indispensable items for setting up one's household.

Giles Stanton and Farley wandered over and engaged him in conversation, but Drew kept an eye on Jane.

Pipkin entered the ballroom, moving silently across the thick carpets and standing behind Jane. She paused and looked up expectantly.

"Yes, Pipkin."

"Might I have a word, Miss Lindsay?"

"Won't you excuse me, ladies?" said Jane as she rose.

Drew left his friends and followed in time to hear Jane exclaim, "Oh no! Have you sent for the doctor?"

"Yes, Miss Jane. Half an hour ago."

"What is it?" asked Drew.

"Nana is ill. My old nurse," explained Jane, hurrying from the room.

Drew again followed as Jane slipped down the corridor and up the narrow flight of stairs to the third floor. He paused outside the servant's room, watching as Jane sank to the floor, clutching the limp hand of the figure lying on the deep feather mattress.

"Nana, we have sent for the physician; he'll soon make you feel better."

"Don't need a doctor. I've seen th' little people; they'll be back t' take me up wi' 'em."

"No, no, not yet, Nana. You can't leave me yet! Why, you've got to stay and be nurse to my children." Jane did her best to keep her voice from trembling. Drew entered the room and placed a reassuring hand on Jane's shoulder.

The old woman was mumbling under her breath, frowning in her efforts to remember. "Children? I . . ."

"Nana, please. Remember? You told me you'd be here to help nurse my children when I have some."

The wrinkled brow cleared. "Ah, so I did, dearie, so I did." The nurse's faded eyes focused on Drew; she frowned, her confusion growing once again. "What's 'e doin' 'ere?" she asked fearfully.

"It is Lord Devlin, Nana, my friend. He has come to see how you are."

"No! No, Miss Jane, make 'im go away!" said the old woman, clutching frantically at Jane's hands.

"But why, Nana? I don't understand."

"Never mind, Jane. I'll wait outside."

Jane bit her lip, trying to hold back tears as the servant's hand relaxed its grip. She watched Tucker move closer, her expert fingers feeling for a pulse.

"She's jes' sleepin', Miss Jane. Mayhap, she'll rest awhile now. I gave 'er a taste of laudanum when I got up here. She was ever so restless."

"How long before the doctor arrives?"

"Shouldn't be long now. We sent for 'im straight away. We didn't want t' bother you, Miss Jane, if we didn't have to."

"I know, but I'm glad you did."

Drew put his head in the door again and said, "Jane, why don't I go down and explain what's happened? Everyone will understand."

"Thank you, Drew. I would do it, but I don't want to leave Nana right now."

"No, you musn't leave her now. Don't worry, I'll set everything to rights and send them on their way."

Drew was as good as his word. As soon as he had sent the other guests away, he suggested quietly to his mother that she might like to get rid of Giles and Farley for him. The speaking look he gave her made his mother smile and

190

pat his hand. Then she stifled a huge, entirely false yawn and asked Giles and Farley if they wouldn't mind escorting an old lady home. Both men vehemently denied agreeing with her choice of adjective, insisting they would be honored to accompany her back to Bath.

As Drew handed his mother into the coach, she whispered, "The best of luck to you, Drew." He grinned, but vouchsafed no reply.

"Could I bring you something, my lord?" asked Pipkin as Drew reentered the house.

"Yes, a stout glass of whiskey, please. I'll be out on the terrace."

As he waited, staring across the gaily lighted garden, Drew sipped the potent liquid cautiously. What was it called? Dutch courage? But surely he had reason to be confident of Jane's answer. He didn't expect her to act grateful precisely, but he did think she had had time to decide in his favor. She couldn't help but know how he felt about her, had felt almost since that first night he had met her at the Valentine Ball, when she had stared at him so defiantly. He had been sidetracked momentarily by the porcelain beauty of her cousin Cherry. But that had been fleeting. How could mere beauty compare to Jane's elegance and spirit?

What was that family tradition Jane had once explained to him? All the ladies of Heartland met their future husbands at the Valentine Ball. He looked forward to reinforcing the legend of Heartland.

Drew heard a movement behind him and turned toward the house. Jane stood in the doorway, the candlelight from the ballroom illuminating her shapely silhouette. He watched as she glided across the limestone terrace; God, but she was beautiful! His pulse quickened as she neared him.

With a wan smile, Jane peered up at his face. The lanterns in the garden went out one by one as Mickey extinguished them, leaving the couple in near darkness.

"She's asleep. The doctor arrived. He said it was a fit of

apoplexy. He thinks she will recover, but only time will tell."

"He didn't bleed her, did he?"

"No, he rarely suggests that. I wouldn't have let him anyway. Nana was always terrified of that." Jane looked around, as though expecting her other guests to materialize. "Did everyone understand?"

"I daresay they did, but it makes no difference whether they did or not."

The old Jane might have denied such a social solecism; this Jane said only, "Where is your mother?"

"She was very tired. I sent her back to Bath with Giles and Farley," said Drew, unaccountably self-conscious of his conspiracy to be alone with Jane.

"Jane, there is something I . . ." He placed his long fingers over her hand where it rested on the balustrade. A single tear fell from her eye.

"Jane?" he said, turning her to face him. He touched her moist cheek. "Jane, my love."

"Oh, Drew, not now!" she exclaimed, pulling out of his embrace. Jane backed away warily. She was too tired to wrestle with any more emotions tonight. Couldn't he understand how she felt? Was he so self-centered that he couldn't see how distraught she was? Well, she certainly wasn't going to explain it to him!

"What is it, Jane?" Drew found it impossible to keep the irritation out of his voice. What was the matter with her? Was she angry about something? He couldn't recall anything he had done or said in weeks to which she might have taken exception.

"I'm tired," was all Jane could think to say, and she began her retreat toward the darkened ballroom.

"So am I," growled Drew, catching her hand before she could escape. "I'm tired of waiting around here, walking on eggshells, trying to win your approval!"

"I didn't ask you to wait around here!" she snapped indignantly. "And I would thank you, sir, to release me!"

"The devil!" he exclaimed, pulling her into his embrace.

192

That would show her!

But Jane was well and truly angry by this time, an anger that was too weary to turn to passion. Pushing away from him, she slapped his face with all the force she could muster.

Immediately, Drew released her. He sketched a quick bow and hurried across the terrace, down the limestone steps, and strode toward the stables.

Jane stared into the darkness for several minutes. No tears fell; she felt only emptiness inside. Later, she might feel remorse, guilt, or pain, but not yet.

Pipkin, who had not exactly eavesdropped, but had the uncanny knack of knowing when his mistress was distressed, brought her shawl, placing it around her trembling shoulders with great tenderness. Although he didn't touch her, the gesture was like the loving comfort a parent bestows on a troubled child.

Jane turned slightly and gave him a small, grateful smile.

"The Lord also will be a refuge for the oppressed, a refuge in times of trouble," said Pipkin quietly.

"Thank you, Pipkin," replied Jane. "I shall stay out here a little longer. You may tell the staff to go to bed."

"Very good, Miss Jane."

"And Pipkin, I shan't be receiving Lord Devlin again." Not that he is likely to call, she added silently.

"Just so, Miss Jane."

Chapter Seven

"Isn't receiving? What rubbish is that, Pipkin!"

"I'm sorry, my lord. Those are Miss Lindsay's instructions."

"Tell me, Pipkin. If my name were Ashmore, or even Farley, would your mistress be receiving?" Drew's eyes peered intently into the butler's, but not a flicker of emotion was revealed by the servant.

"That is difficult to say, my lord."

"I see. You didn't need to inquire if she would receive me; she has already said she wouldn't. But for anyone else, it is still in question," Drew concluded. He had stayed at Heartland until after midnight; he had risen early to repeat the long ride out that morning. And Jane refused to see him. She was an ungrateful wench!

"I couldn't say, sir," came Pipkin's stately reply.

"I could force my way in," said Drew. This fierce statement did produce a reaction in the butler. With a mere flick of his finger, Mickey appeared behind him.

Drew laughed bitterly. "That won't be necessary, Pipkin. What I should do and what I shall do are two different matters. You may tell your mistress I shan't trouble her again."

The old butler unbent enough to say sadly, "I will inform Miss Lindsay, my lord; such is the nature of my duty."

"I know, I know. By the way, I've sent the Runner, Mr.

Bailey, back to London. I suppose that, too, was a waste. I've been tilting at windwills."

Drew settled his fashionable beaver hat on his head and strolled out the door.

Jane, watching from her bedroom window, let the curtains fall when the figure on horseback had receded to nothingness.

During the two weeks that followed, Jane divided her time between her old nurse's room and planning Heartland's annual Open Day. Nana was improving daily, though her mind sometimes wandered. She would speak vaguely about seeing a vision of danger to Jane, a vision that contained a man, and Jane couldn't help but wonder if the man were Drew. But for the most part, she wouldn't allow herself time to dwell on thoughts of Drew.

She received regular visits from her new friends, Farley and Giles. They would often bring Lydia Ashmore along. It was apparent that Giles Stanton was head over heels about Miss Ashmore, a lively, but kind young lady. As for Mr. Farley, Jane was beginning to wish him gone. He rarely drank, but his personality was tinged with unpleasantness, like a slightly distempered drunk. Drew could have explained to her, had she inquired, that Farley's disagreeable disposition stemmed not from drinking, but from a lack of alcohol.

Twice, Drew's mother called, once alone and once with the dowager duchess in tow. She invited Jane to tea, and Jane accepted cautiously when Mrs. Peterson let slip the fact that there would be a prize fight that day and all the gentlemen of Bath planned to drive out to see it.

At the end of June, the Season in London drew to a close. People returned to their homes surrounding Bath, and Jane put the finishing touches on her plans for the Open Day to be held the third week of July.

Mrs. Peterson called during that last week of June to ask Jane to journey to London with her.

"I know it sounds absurd, Jane, but Martha, the dowager duchess, you know, insists it is the best time to shop. You shan't believe it, but she is frightfully parsimonious." Drew's mother gave her girlish laugh as she revealed this tidbit of information.

"But Mrs. Peterson, I really can't go. I must see to all the final preparations for Open Day. It is quite an event. There must be something for everyone, from the oldest tenant farmer to the youngest girl or boy. And I am expecting my Aunt Sophie and Cherry next week."

"Very well. If I can't persuade you, I shall have to make the best of it. I was so hoping my fashion adviser could go with me."

Jane laughed. "You know very well the dowager duchess will tell you exactly what you must purchase!"

"No doubt you are right!"

Jane ventured timidly, "Will Drew accompany you?"

"No, he refuses to leave Bath. Especially, he said, for steaming, dirty London. Now, I must be going. Martha wants to leave tomorrow. I do hope she plans to make the journey in one day. I dislike staying at strange inns."

"Have a pleasant journey, and a successful shopping expedition," said Jane as she ushered Mrs. Peterson out the door.

When Jane awoke the following morning, she felt restless. She reviewed her plans for the day and could find no reason for uneasiness. As she sampled Mrs. Brown's coddled eggs, she wondered if perhaps she was coming down with something. She pushed the eggs away; the footman pulled back her chair as she rose.

"Miss Jane," said Pipkin when she entered the hall. "Nurse wishes a word with you. Mrs. Tucker said she is quite agitated."

"Thank you, Pipkin," said Jane, hurrying toward the stairs. So this was the problem! She must have sensed that her old nurse had taken a turn for the worse.

Jane hurried into the tiny room, her gaze searching the bed before she realized it was unoccupied.

"So ye've come, missy!" said the wizened figure in the rocker.

"Nana! What is it? Pipkin said you were worse!"

"Worse? Not me!" Jane sank onto the bed, her head resting wearily in her hands.

Tucker came in and scolded, "Miss Jane! Pipkin was supposed to ask you to see me first. There was no reason to upset you! Nana is much improved physically, as you see." The maid stressed the word "physically," and Jane understood her meaning.

"Thank you, Tucker. That will be all."

As if to deny the maid's implication, the old woman said tartly, "Yes, send 'er away. What I 'ave t'say, is for yer ears only, Miss Jane."

Jane nodded to the indignant maid, and Tucker left, closing the door with a decided snap. Jane turned to her old nurse.

"What is it, Nana?"

"Th' man, Miss Jane. I have t' warn ye about th' man."

"What man, Nana?"

The old woman clutched the arms of the chair. "I don't know. I kin see 'im ever so clear in my dream, but when I open m' eyes, 'e's gone. It's them piskies; they're cloudin' m' vision!"

"Now, Nana. Start from the beginning and tell me." Jane's gentle prompting calmed the old woman's agitated spirit, and she began her tale anew.

"I've 'ad th' same dream for months now. Oh, since just after th' Valentine Ball. 'Tis always th' same. Yer there, an' me, but ye can't hear me. This man—I've tried 'n tried t' remember 'is face—this man wants t' take ye away from me. 'E's tryin' t' kill ye, Miss Jane! An' I scream 'n scream, but ye can't hear me!"

"It's only a dream, Nana."

"No, no! I've 'ad 'em afore, I tell ye. Ye remember th' year you got th' fever. I knew ye would, 'an I watched ye

197

like a hawk, but it didn't 'elp. Ye got sick anyway!"

"But, Nana, that was a coincidence. The fever was bad that year; of course, you were worried I might become ill."

"An' when yer mother—rest 'er soul—died. I knew it was comin'. An' yer grandmother—rest 'er soul. I kin see things, Miss Jane, things other people can't see."

This last was spoken with an eerie conviction, and Jane shivered. Shaking off the strange atmosphere, Jane said, "I can't think who it could be in your dream, Nana. No one would want to harm me."

"That's what I thought, too, but since I've been down in m' bed, th' dream comes all th' time—every time I close m' eyes. But I can't remember th' face. 'E's a big man, tall and fierce, but that's all I know."

A big man, thought Jane. Drew certainly fit that description; he was tall even to one of her statuesque proportions. And she had met him at the Valentine Ball. But as before, when the suspicion had arisen in the back of her mind that Drew might wish to harm her, Jane balked at the notion. Then she recalled her old nurse's reaction to Drew, the night Nana had suffered the stroke. Was it possible?

"Miss Jane," repeated the old woman. "Ye must be careful, d'ye hear? I've no wish t'see my girl's funeral afore m' own."

Jane smiled automatically. "Don't worry, Nana. I'll be careful, and you'll see, I'll be fine."

Jane tried to shake off the feeling of gloom that had settled over her. She ordered out Sinbad and went for a long ride, avoiding the small tenant farms that dotted her land, but staying in view of her groom.

Still, she remained troubled, feeling that something, somewhere, was amiss. Heavens! I'm getting as bad as Nana! she told herself sharply.

With a determinedly cheery smile, she greeted Pipkin. The dour-faced butler bowed and presented her with an envelope as she entered the main hall.

"An express from Mrs. Pettigrew. It arrived by special

messenger an hour ago."

Jane felt her knees turn wobbly and sat down abruptly on the hard wooden bench against the wall. A host of butterflies began cavorting wildly in her stomach as she broke the seal and read:

My Dearest Niece,
The most *dreadful* thing has occurred. Cherry, with no *regard* for my feelings, has run away to *France!!* You can imagine my *shame* when I read her note. That a daughter of mine could sink to such *depths!* She is accompanied, of course, by Lord Pierce! I'm prostrate with *grief!* What shall I do? I depend on you, dearest Jane, to set everything to rights.
Your loving aunt,
Sophie Pettigrew

"Of all the . . . !" Jane left the words unsaid, adding only, "The foolish girl! Pipkin! Have my traveling coach brought round in an hour — the fastest horses, mind! Tell Tucker to start packing. Where's that messenger?"

"The kitchens, miss."

"Good! Give him money and a fresh horse. I'll have a note to send my aunt in fifteen minutes!"

Jane strode to her office and penned a quick note.

Dear Aunt,
Leave London immediately. Go visit your sister in Sussex. I will tend to Cherry. If anyone asks, she is with me at Heartland. Tell no one about this disaster, and we shall all come about!
Jane

An hour later, trunks packed and loaded, Jane set out in the elegant traveling coach. Tucker, who was an indifferent traveler, slept peacefully in the opposite seat, her laudanum-induced doze untroubled by the swaying of the huge carriage. As for Jane, she occupied her mind by running over a mental list of necessities, reassuring herself that nothing had been forgotten.

Drew turned his large stallion into the gates of Heartland. As he traversed the last mile to the house, he tried not to think how he would react to another rejection. If Pipkin told him his mistress wasn't receiving . . .

But no, before his mother had left Bath that morning, she had been quite emphatic. Jane had asked if he, too, planned to go to London. She had asked, his mother insisted, in longing accents.

And so, perhaps foolishly, Drew was once again going to Heartland to see Jane. If anyone had told him six months before that he would be so devoid of pride as to chase after any woman—especially one as maddening as Jane Lindsay—he would have called them insane. But here he was, he thought, smiling grimly, as the front door swung open.

Pipkin bowed. "Lord Devlin."

"Pipkin, I've come to see your mistress."

"I'm afraid—"

"I'll brook no interference this time," declared Drew, flexing his hands as Mickey took a step closer. Pipkin shook his head, and the gentle giant stepped back.

"That will not be necessary, my lord. Miss Lindsay has gone away."

"The devil you say! She told my mother only yesterday that she couldn't even venture to London at this time."

"Nevertheless—"

"Jane! Jane! Come down here this instant!" roared Drew. When there was no response, he started up the stairs, taking two at a time, shouting "Jane!" as he progressed.

"My lord! My lord!" puffed Pipkin, trying to keep up.

Drew threw open one door after another. Finally, he surprised two of the upstairs maids who were restoring order after Jane's hasty packing.

Drew stood on the threshold, taking in the scene, the

wind effectively knocked from his sails.

"As I told you, my lord, Miss Jane left not more than fifteen minutes ago." Drew stared at the wheezing butler as though trying to comprehend some foreign tongue. "Perhaps your lordship would care for a drink while I explain." Pipkin stepped aside, letting Drew precede him down the corridor.

Drew hurried down the steps of Heartland not ten minutes later. Pipkin nodded his head as he watched. He was well satisfied with Lord Devlin's reaction to his story. His lordship would see to it no harm came to Miss Jane.

Jane's carriage was just outside Trowbridge when she heard the shot. Tucker bolted up and peered out at the bright sunlight. Jane's hand went to the pocket of her carriage dress; her long fingers curled about the handle of her pistol.

"Tom Summers!" she heard a familiar voice yell. "Don't fire! It is I, Lord Devlin!"

Jane jerked the door open, and leapt to the ground as the groom belatedly scrambled down from his post. Forgetting her promise to her old nurse that she would be careful, she demanded, "What the deuce do you think you're about? Shooting a gun and stopping my coach! Not to mention the fright you've given my horses and my people!"

"Actually, miss, I fired th' shot," admitted her coachman sheepishly.

"Well, no doubt you had just cause!" exclaimed Jane after an instant of frustrated silence. She turned back to Drew, ready to berate him on the other charges when she was struck dumbfounded once more. Drew's small tiger was hefting bags up to her groom who was stowing them in the boot.

"Have you lost your mind, James?"

The groom caught the last bag and turned beet red.

"Of course he hasn't," said Drew, turning to his tiger. "Take the team back to Laura Place. And remember, I took the stage to York." Drew flipped the boy a gold coin.

"Right ye are, guv'ner!"

Drew strode toward the carriage and prepared to help Jane inside. "Miss Lindsay," he said, his dark eyes twinkling.

"I'm not going anywhere with you, you . . ."

"Jane, think of the servants. Get inside, and you can berate me all you wish. Tucker, I'm certain, will not mind."

"Of course not," came the reply from within.

Disdaining his extended hand, Jane climbed inside the coach, spreading her skirt out to force Drew to sit beside the maid in the facing seat.

Chuckling, Drew moved Jane's skirt aside and sat down. He gave the office to start, and the coach moved along while Jane fumed.

Finally, Drew asked, "You wished to question me?"

She glared at him but said nothing. Drew shrugged and turned to the maid.

"You can imagine my own surprise, Tucker, to find myself journeying to France on such short notice. But when Pipkin told me of your mistress's flight, why, 'twould have been unchivalrous to abandon her to such a treacherous journey!"

"Indeed, my lord," murmured the maid, unable to keep her face schooled to polite interest.

"And you can imagine my dismay to find such a lack of appreciation from the distressed damsel!"

"Enough!" snapped Jane. "Why you have decided to plague me with your presence, Lord Devlin, I can't fathom. But let me assure you, at the first posting inn, I fully intend to be rid of you!"

"That might prove a difficult task, my dear," said Drew quietly.

She turned to face him. "Why are you here?"

"Have you any idea what a spectacle you would present in Brighton? An unmarried female, traveling to Paris with only her maid?"

"I hope I may catch Cherry—" Jane stopped, aghast at

what she had revealed.

"Pipkin allowed me to read your aunt's letter." As Drew suspected, this revelation produced another indignant gasp. "Now, before you sack the fellow, think about the poor man's predicament. Even if you had no idea of the impropriety of your traveling to foreign shores alone, Pipkin was fully cognizant of the dangers, both physical and social. You might be set upon by robbers. At the very least, you would be open to the unwelcome advances of every young buck on the way to Paris. And there are hundreds of them!"

"And I suppose, sir, traveling under your protection will improve my social standing," said Jane in scathing tones.

He chuckled. "No, but no one will question a Mr. and Mrs. Davies traveling to Paris together."

Jane's horror-filled eyes stared at him. "Have you taken leave of your senses?"

"No, I don't think so. I considered traveling as brother and sister, but with my dark coloring, I was afraid our identities might be called into question. So, husband and wife it is!" he concluded cheerfully.

"And if I refuse?"

"Then I shall be forced to tell every landlord, discreetly, of course, that my wife is enciente and suffering from hallucinations."

"Enciente! You wouldn't dare!"

"Wouldn't I?" he said, smiling sweetly.

Jane settled into a frustrated silence that lasted until they reached the first posting inn. She treated her unwanted escort to a cold stare as he ordered her lemonade and sandwiches. He settled her in the private parlor of the inn and went out to confer with her coachman.

When Drew returned, Jane was pacing the floor.

"I told Summers we'd rest the horses for an hour before continuing. He insists they'll do to the next stage, and I must confess, I prefer that to hiring post horses so soon."

"Drew, surely you see we cannot go on with this farce?"

"If you mean you have decided to accept the inevitable—"

"Certainly not!"

"Jane, it is for your own good."

"Rubbish! You're only doing this to get even with me for slapping you!"

"Nonsense, indeed! If I had wanted revenge for that I would have taken you in my arms and carried you away."

"You couldn't have! My servants . . ." Jane grew quiet. Her servants had shown themselves only too susceptible to Drew's charm.

"Your servants, my dear Jane, would have applauded. However, my reasons for journeying with you to France have nothing to do with that forgotten event. And cheer up, Jane, perhaps we will catch up with Cherry in Brighton."

"And if not? Will you persist in this charade?"

"We shall take the first packet to Dieppe—with Tucker along as chaperon, in case you have any fear that I have designs on your virtue." He had moved behind her, his breath ruffling the stray hairs on her temple.

"I daresay I could withstand such an assault," said Jane, more gently that she'd intended.

"But would you want to?" he whispered. His hands traveled along her arms with a feathersoft touch.

" 'Ere we are, sir," said the landlord, his broad backside pushing open the door as he entered with a large tray.

Jane retreated to the table. She hadn't realized how hungry she was. As she filled her plate, the landlord beamed. "Now, that'll put the bloom back in those cheeks, Mrs. Davies!"

Jane turned beet red, choking on her lemonade. The landlord made a hasty retreat, apologizing profusely.

"How could you! How could you tell him I was . . . was . . ."

"With child?"

"You said you'd only do that if . . ."

"I know, but I tried it out, and I find it quite makes up for the fact that I am a plain 'mister' and not a lord. Besides, I didn't tell him you were unhinged."

"Perhaps you should have warned the man that you are!"

"Oh, come now, Jane, surely you can appreciate the fun of a bit of play-acting. You can't be so stuffy as that!"

"So now I'm stuffy!"

"Well, you do have a tendency to see the serious side of everything."

"And it seems you can never treat any subject with the dignity it deserves!"

"You're probably right. I once was young and foolish and viewed the world quite differently. But I have learned not to take anything too seriously, especially myself." His tone was light, but Jane was not deceived; his dark eyes mirrored a long-ago pain. Jane touched his hand and broke the spell; he clasped her hand in his, giving it a grateful squeeze.

"We'd best eat, Jane, if we intend to leave within the hour."

Their next stop was at The Bear Inn in Devizes. While the horses were being changed, Drew endeavored to be agreeable by telling them the story of Miss Burney, the famous author of *Evelina*, who had stopped at the Bear years earlier and had met the innkeeper's son, a young boy named Thomas. The innkeeper had offered his son as entertainment, asking if Miss Burney would like to have her portrait taken. The child had grown up, of course, to be the famous portrait painter, Thomas Lawrence.

Jane looked out the window and said, "I believe they have finished."

Tucker rose, giving Lord Devlin an apologetic look, and followed her mistress to the carriage.

The post horses from The Bear proved to be as fast as Jane's own horses, and they made excellent time to Reading. Changing horses at The George, they continued, but their progress was slowed.

Jane stared out the window, unable to focus on the passing countryside. Drew slouched in one corner, sleeping fitfully. Across from them, Tucker's snore augmented the noisy rattling of wheels and harnesses.

A full moon rose, and still they drove, pausing only to change horses as they neared Brighton.

Jane remained alert, her muscles too tight and her nerves too much on edge to allow her the comfort of sleep. She was bored. Enduring an entire day in an enclosed carriage with no distractions or conversation was punishment indeed. She peered at Drew in the gathering darkness and sighed.

"Bored?" he asked, his deep voice startling her.

"Dreadfully!" she admitted.

"Sorry I haven't been very good company."

"Many people prefer to sleep through a journey."

"Normally I don't, but I took the coward's way out. I was afraid you would continue to harangue me about forcing myself on you." He expected an indignant rejoinder, but Jane only laughed.

"You were probably very wise. I wouldn't have given you a moment's peace, and we would now be at daggers drawn."

"No doubt."

A comfortable silence fell between them. Jane supposed Drew to be dozing again when he said, "It shouldn't be too much longer now. When we reach Brighton, I'll ask the landlord if my wife's sister and brother have arrived yet. That should suffice."

"I'll ask," said Jane, trying to achieve some control over her own destiny once more.

"Very well, if you wish," he said doubtfully. "And if they aren't at that inn, I shall go about to the others. Someone will have seen them."

"Is it possible they could have sailed already, Drew?"

"It's not likely. From my experience with the Channel, it is rarely so cooperative."

"But it might cooperate with them just to discomfit me," said Jane.

He laughed at her foolishness. "You really are superstitious!"

Jane turned her face toward the window. She felt tears start to her eyes. Now she really was being foolish to let such a teasing remark upset her so!

"Jane, I didn't mean to hurt your feelings," said Drew. He moved closer, and, placing a gentle arm around her shoulder, he pulled her back against his broad chest.

"You are tired, my dear. You should rest." Stroking her hair, he felt the tenseness leave Jane's rigid body, and she relaxed against him, leaning her head on his shoulder. Gradually, sleep overtook her, and she turned slightly in his embrace as he carefully cradled her weary body.

The sudden stillness of the carriage awoke Jane, and she sat up automatically smoothing her hair and gown. Tucker peered out the door at the bustling yard of the Ship's Inn in Brighton. Drew sprang to the ground and held a quick conference with the innkeeper. The groom hurried to help Jane and the maid from the carriage.

Jane yawned and stretched her cramped muscles, not caring that Drew was speaking to the landlord in her stead. He returned to her side.

"The landlord says he's not seen Cherry, but he did verify that the packet crossed the Channel this afternoon. We may have missed them, but I'll check the other inns just in case.

The landlord, a keen judge of money and people, came forward at Drew's signal and made a low bow to Jane. "If madam will follow me?"

Jane and Tucker trudged into the inn while Drew had a word with Jane's coachman. They were shown into a spacious room, and Jane eyed the big bed hesitantly. Turning to the landlord, Jane asked in her most imperious manner, "And where is my husband's chamber?"

"The next room, madam." He crossed the room and unlocked a heavy door that joined the two chambers. "Mr.

Davies has ordered a cold collation to be set up in his room, madam. Will there be anything else?"

"No, you may go." As soon as the obsequious landlord had bowed his way out, Jane ripped the silk bonnet from her head and threw it on the bed. "Can you imagine that, Tucker? Expecting me to dine in his room! I'll not set foot in that place!"

Tucker looked dubious and offered, "Perhaps 'is lordship is short on funds, Miss Jane, and couldn't afford a private parlor."

Jane dismissed such an idea, saying, "He must know I am prepared to pay for one! Never mind, I simply shan't eat. Help me prepare for bed, Tucker, and then you may go downstairs and eat."

Jane was soon tucked up in bed. Her stomach rumbled in protest as she heard the covers being set in the adjoining chamber. There was a timid knock on the inner door.

In answer to Jane's "Come in," a young maid stepped inside and bobbed a curtsey.

"An' it please ye, mum, yer supper's ready."

"Thank you, you may go."

Sketching another quick curtsey, the maid vanished, closing the door as she left. Jane heard the outer door to Drew's room shut soon after. She listened to the silence for a moment. Drew must still be downstairs, she thought. She could slip next door, fix a plate, and be back in her own room in a trice.

Looking down at the shimmering silk of her nightgown, Jane said, "Blast!" She couldn't risk Drew returning while she was filling her plate, not dressed as she was. Why had she been so quick to disrobe? Now she would be forced to remain in her room!

Resolutely, she retrieved her book from the night table and began to read. After a paragraph, she grimaced and closed the slim, leather-bound volume of sermons. She wished she had been more careful when selecting the book from the shelves in the library at Heartland. It had been shelved accidentally with her novels, and Jane hadn't bothered to read the title before slipping it into her pocket.

She heard Drew enter his room. Judging from the sound of his movements, he was disrobing. That thud could only have been a boot hitting the floor. Jane grinned at the thought of him struggling with the second boot. Thump! There it went. Drew was probably already regretting not bringing his valet. She heard him stride across the floor and held her breath, waiting for his impatient knock on the joining door.

Instead, it was a quick tap and a whispered, "Jane, Jane, are you asleep?"

"No."

"Are you ready for supper?"

"A supper à deux in your room? Never!" she said tartly. She heard a muffled exclamation, and then the lock was tested.

Jane pulled the covers up under her chin as Drew strode into the room. He stopped at the foot of her bed and glared at her.

"Why the devil aren't you going to eat? What maggot have you got in that pretty head of yours now?"

"Maggot? I'll thank you not to be insulting, sir!"

"You can thank me all you wish, but you will come next door and eat!"

"I will not! How dare you think that I would dine with you in your bedchamber!"

"For pity's sake, Jane! Is that what this is about? Weren't you listening earlier when I said I had no designs on your virtue?"

"Of course I was, and that was why I was surprised that you would think I'd—" She gasped as he advanced toward her, his demeanor menacing. "What are you doing?" Jane felt a tremor of excitement tease her body.

"If you won't get up of your own accord, I shall carry you to supper!"

"You wouldn't. . . ." Jane left the bluff hanging. Raising her chin, she returned his fierce scowl. "Very well!" Letting the counterpane fall, she picked up her wrapper from the foot of the bed. Drew acknowledged a moment's hesitation as he glimpsed her rounded breasts practically spill from the top of her nightdress.

Jane knew he was gaping at her—let him! She couldn't help it if Mother Nature had been overly generous when passing out bosoms! It served him right! Jane slowly pulled on her wrapper.

She is deliberately teasing me, thought Drew, sudden anger with his own naivite springing forth. She knew the effect her body would have on him. No woman was that innocent! She raised one slim arm to free her long shiny tresses. His strong fingers curved into fists in his effort to appear untouched by her provocative body. Why was the room so warm? What had happened to the air?

"Drew? Aren't you coming?" asked Jane. She was standing beside him, her modest flannel wrapper covering her charms. Her long, silky hair tumbled around her shoulders. Drew closed his dark eyes to deny the overpowering temptation to take her in his arms.

When he opened his eyes again, Jane was frowning and her lips were pursed. She hadn't any notion how disrupting he found her body. Suddenly the truth hit him full force. She was an innocent. Her slow, deliberate movements had been prompted by anger, not a desire to tease or ridicule. How wise he had been to restrain his instincts!

Still, he had to tell her. "You are very beautiful, Jane, very desirable."

"Now you are offering me Spanish coin, Lord Devlin; I don't care for flattery. Can we not return to our original topic—supper?"

Drew inclined his head. Lightly, he said, "Your wish is my command."

As though dressed for a formal ball, he extended his arm and escorted her to the adjoining room. Jane smiled at the boots and coat left willy-nilly where they lay.

"You should have brought your valet."

"To paraphrase Poor Richard, 'Three may keep a secret if one of them is dead,'" said Drew as he picked up his boots. He studied them carefully, then said doubtfully, "I suppose I could put them outside the door and let the pot boy polish them."

Jane laughed and sat down at the table. As she served herself with cold ham and turkey, rich cheddar cheese, and some cherries, she said, "How do you hope to get along on such a long journey?"

"I am accustomed to dressing myself. I have only had a valet since returning to England. Of course, I did have someone to take care of my clothes." Drew frowned as he retrieved his coat of navy serge and smoothed it with one hand. The wrinkles remained.

"There is nothing for the boots but to allow the inn servants to tend to them, but I will ask Tucker if she will tend to your clothes."

"Will she mind terribly?"

"I doubt it; she thinks very highly of you, Lord Devlin. Though I couldn't venture a guess as to why."

"Couldn't you? And what of her mistress? Does she think highly of me?" There was no mistaking the twinkle in his eyes as he asked this, and Jane answered in kind.

With a coy smile, she replied, "At times."

"Minx!" he laughed, sitting opposite her. "I am starving!"

It was some time later before their hunger was appeased, and conversation was remembered.

"Jane, I want to explain why I had the landlord set up our supper in my room. We must do all we can to keep a low profile on this journey. And what could be more natural than for Mr. and Mrs. Davies to dine alone, especially since the hour was so advanced."

"I understand. I wish you had explained."

"There wasn't time. I only thought of it as the landlord asked me if I wished a private parlor so late. In the long run, I was glad of it. When I strolled down the street, asking for Cherry at three other hostelries, I encountered no less than three men I knew from London."

"Did they see you?"

"No, I was able to avoid them."

"Drew, surely you will admit now that this charade cannot continue. We are bound to meet people we know on the packet."

"That is why I was so relieved you had the good sense to dress in blacks."

"Then my blacks will be protection enough."

"Not against the more desperate type of villain. But I will try to be as unobtrusive as possible. You and Tucker had best go aboard the packet without me. I'll join you when we are certain it's safe."

Jane was too weary for further arguments. Choosing not to eat her fruit, she stood up and began to pace the length of the room.

Drew began eating the cherries as he studied her. Several minutes later, he suggested, "Perhaps you should sit down, my dear; your pacing is detrimental to the rug."

She looked down at the rug in surprise. Smiling ruefully, Jane returned to her chair where she accepted a cherry from Drew. She chewed it thoughtfully.

"It is just that I am so angry with my cousin! How could she do such a nonsensical thing? Every time I think about it, I want to shake her!"

"Perhaps it's a good thing she isn't here," said Drew. He met her startled gaze. "I can't imagine her submitting quietly to such an indignity, and the awfulness of such a scene would have been the talk of the town. We would all have been ruined. I can see the scandal sheets now—Lord Devlin died trying to separate Miss Jane Lindsay and Miss Cherry Pettigrew. One can only speculate what circumstances brought this odd trio to Brighton."

"Then I would simply have choked her so she couldn't scream and throw one of her temper tantrums."

"How is it, Jane, that you have been placed in this position as guardian to Cherry? That's certainly an unusual arrangement."

"Actually, it was my father who was her guardian. And while I have no official authority over her, I am the only one my aunt can turn to for assistance."

"And has there often been need to call on you?" asked Drew, his sympathetic voice caressing her.

Jane met those dark eyes; she felt she might disappear into their depths, leaving behind all the cares and concerns of her mundane existence. Involuntarily, she tilted her head as he leaned forward; his hands traveled to her shoulders, urging her closer.

"Miss Jane, did you need anything else?" called Tucker from the adjoining chamber.

Jane snapped to attention. Standing, she held out her hand and said, "Good night, Lord Devlin."

"Good night, Jane," said Drew. He ignored her hand, and she turned on her heel. Gathering her dignity, she returned to her own room, closing the door quietly.

Had it all been in her head? Jane wondered. Had he really planned to kiss her? Or had she made a complete fool of herself, wearing her heart on her sleeve?

As Jane allowed Tucker to fuss over her, her mind pondered these questions. After blowing out the candle, she lay sleeplessly in the black silence.

Over all other considerations, that one confession dominated her thoughts. "Her heart on her sleeve." When had that physical longing turned to love? Had the love always been there, but she had been too blind to see it? Never mind when she had fallen in love with him, she admonished herself silently. What should she do about it? She could hardly tell him! That would be too forward, too ill-bred! And Miss Jane Lindsay never did or said anything that was less than proper!

Jane ignored the nagging little voice that chided and teased—then why are you, an unmarried female, only footsteps away from your lover's room?

Her eyes red and swollen from lack of sleep, Jane boarded the packet the next day. Tucker, whose stomach had begun to churn while waiting on the quay, was persuaded to make herself comfortable in the cabin Drew had secured for their use. Jane waited on deck, her heart beating faster when she spied Drew's dark hair and handsome face amongst the crowd. She restrained the impulse to meet him at the gangway and turned resolutely away.

She had only spoken to him for a moment that morning when he had delivered the tickets for herself and Tucker. He hadn't lingered to chat, and Jane had been relieved her self-control hadn't been put to the test. For now that she had admitted to herself that she loved him, Jane wanted to shout it at the top of her lungs, to smile and sing and dance!

He would think her mad! Worse still, he would discover her secret. And secret it would remain! Her grandmother always said, "A true lady never admitted to a gentleman that she was interested in him until he had shown interest in her. And most of all, ladies never admitted to loving a gentleman one iota more than he loved her." Her grandmother had known about such matters. Unlike Jane, she had reigned as the belle of the Season for three years before agreeing to a match. So Jane would have to be patient and discreet—traits that had once been ingrained in the very fiber of her being. Surely she still possessed enough strength of will to remain cool and aloof in Drew's presence!

On this thought, Jane turned to greet Drew. He was deep in conversation with a squat little man of some fifty years of age. In a gold brocade coat and white powdered wig, he might have been dressed for a masked ball. Drew appeared to be engrossed in the man's conversation, and Jane started forward. This movement earned her a frown and a casual wave of the hand. Jane paused. Then it dawned on her! She whirled and hurried below, not pausing until she had bolted the cabin door and stood panting from excitement.

"What's toward, Miss Jane? I knew I shouldna' let you stay on board by yourself! No good will come of it, I says to myself!" Tucker tried to sit up.

214

"Nonsense!" said Jane, moving to the small round window. She gazed outside for a moment before turning back to the ashen-faced maid. "Tucker! Sit back down, do! Here, let me wet a rag to cool your brow."

The maid's weak protests were ignored as Jane settled Tucker upon the narrow lower berth.

Jane pulled a chair closer and very gently began to chafe the maid's wrists.

"There is a man on board I must avoid at all cost. He is quite wealthy and powerful, and his hobby is mischief. He was speaking to his lordship just now."

"What's 'is name?"

"Mr. Tuttle. He sounds harmless enough, even appears harmless in his outdated wig and long coats, but he is a gossip of the worst kind. If there is no gossip to be had, he makes it up just to see what effect it might have. And the effect is usually disastrous."

"Horrid man!"

"Exactly! We must do all we can to avoid him."

"But you said Lord Devlin and this man were in conversation?"

"Yes, I do hope Drew is careful!"

There was a knock on the door.

"Yes?" said Jane cautiously.

"With th' captain's compliments, madam. I've brought some tea and biscuits for ye."

Jane opened the door and allowed the fresh-faced cabin boy to enter. When he'd left, she bolted the door and inspected the tray. Tucker waved away all offers of nourishment, and Jane poured out a solitary cup of tea. As she lifted the creamer, she noticed a folded scrap of paper; intrigued, she opened it.

"What's that, Miss Jane?"

"A note from Lord Devlin, warning us about Mr. Tuttle. When we arrive at Dieppe, we are to go directly to Le Poisson Rouge, a small inn just outside town. Lord Devlin will go ashore with Mr. Tuttle and see him settled elsewhere."

"But won't we run across him on th' road to Paris?"

Jane took her lower lip between her teeth as she was wont to do when pensive. She stirred her tea a moment before shrugging her shoulders. "We shall deal with that later. I'm certain Lord Devlin will have some idea on the subject."

The maid's eyes opened wide at this unexpected observation. Never had she heard Miss Jane give up when wrestling with a problem; she wouldn't even allow anyone to advise or help. This was a switch indeed!

When packing, Jane and Tucker had decided that a lady in mourning attire would attract less attention than a solitary lady in fashionable dress. Accordingly, Jane was dressed in dreary black, complete with bonnet and veil, as she and Tucker disembarked at the bustling port of Dieppe.

The jumble of languages, the shouts of the sailors, made it difficult to locate transportation. Suddenly, however, a dirty urchin appeared and told them proudly to follow him. Aided by any equally dirty companion, the boy began to load their baggage into a sturdy dogcart. With Tucker riding behind and Jane on the seat, they had soon left the noise and confusion of the dock behind.

Jane repeated the name of the inn several times, trying to sound as French as possible. The child reassured her impatiently, adding that the "monsieur" had given him his orders for the two "Anglaises."

Gaining the refuge of Le Poisson Rouge, Jane spoke to the landlord in her best schoolroom French. Her husband, she explained, had been detained, but they would require two rooms and a private parlor, plus accommodation for her maid.

The landlord, an emaciated figure with one arm missing and sly, beady eyes, began to shake his head. *"Non et non, madame!* I have only one room left. All the inns are bursting at the seams! You must settle for one small room. And

216

a private parlor? Out of the question!"

Jane lifted her veil and, with one raised brow, deliberated over his appearance from head to toe. Regardless of the fact that the innkeeper was French, he was no different from other dishonest tradespeople she had dealt with in the past. He began to squirm under her scrutiny.

"Monsieur, you are lying; you hope, no doubt, that you may raise your fee, but I am not so easily taken in. You will show me to my room, and you will prepare another for my husband."

"But, madame . . ." protested the landlord weakly, his backbone crumbling before her implacable authority.

"Now."

"Very well, madame. There is one small suite of rooms." He was beaten, but he had one last ploy. "But I will be forced to break my promise to another patron, one who has paid well for the rooms." The gleam in his shifty eyes was back.

"Then do so."

His shoulders slumped, the man mumbled, "Yes, madame."

"Monsieur, I am sorry, but I have no more room."

Drew grinned at the surly landlord. "Not even for an old friend?"

"I do not know you, monsieur."

"I suppose I have grown, but surely my old friend Jean-Francois DuClaire remembers his fellow pirate—Captain Savage!"

The Frenchman studied Drew with his beady eyes for a moment before recognition and remembrance lighted his face.

"Drew! My old friend! Welcome!"

Drew received the obligatory kiss on both cheeks and slapped Jean-Francois's back.

"Enter, enter! You will stay in my apartment, yes?"

"Actually, no, my wife should already be here."

"Your . . . wife?"

"Yes, an English lady with her maid."

Some of his host's jocularity faded. "Yes, she is here. In my best suite. Had she informed me who her husband was . . ."

"I didn't tell her I had spent an entire summer here when we were boys. I wanted to surprise you."

"Ah, well, never mind! Tell me," said the Frenchman, "how are your parents?"

"My father died not long after our stay here."

"I am sorry."

"My mother, however, remains in excellent health. I know she would like to see you again. And your parents?"

"Both gone. It was the war; it aged them."

"And you?" Drew couldn't help but look at Jean-Francois's empty sleeve as he posed the question.

"Yes, me, too. I was in the artillery. A charge exploded prematurely. It was, perhaps, for the best. I had had my fill of death and destruction. But it is over now."

"Thank God. So, have you a family?"

"Yes, my good wife Lucie, two daughters, and three sons."

"You're a lucky man."

"You and your wife, you have children?"

"Uh, no. Not yet."

"The little ones, they make the marriage worthwhile, especially when one's wife is—"

"Jean-Francois!" A voice called from another room.

The landlord bellowed out a response to his wife's summons.

"Wives! A mixed blessing. My wife, like yours, is a woman who knows what she wants and demands to be heard."

"Jean-Francois!"

"A moment, woman! Come, Drew, I will show you to your rooms."

* * *

"For pity's sake, Jane, what did you do to the unfortunate Jean-Francois? I have just endured a five minute speech of commiseration about the cruelty of wives." Leaning against the closed door to their tiny sitting area, Drew's eyes held a distinct gleam of admiration which Jane missed entirely.

"Then you should have told that weasely man to keep his opinions of your *wife* to himself!"

He laughed, and Jane returned a sheepish grin. She indicated the chair opposite hers, and Drew sat down.

"I should have told you to mention that your husband was his old friend Drew."

"That certainly would have made things easier!"

"Sorry, my dear."

"How did you two meet? He seems an odd sort of friend to me."

"He was not always so. I spent the summer here when I was nine or ten. It was the happiest time of my life. My mother and father were here, too, like a real family. And away from the social pressures of London, my father treated my mother like a person of worth. Mother was ill; I think she'd had a miscarriage although they never told me so. But it was wonderful to be here. Mother speaks fluent French, and my father, who was not very learned, depended on her to get by. I picked it up rapidly with Jean-Francois as a playmate. We spent hours on the beaches playing pirates, hunting for buried treasure."

"So you do have some pleasant childhood memories."

"Yes, but it didn't last. Mother got well, and we returned to London. Father was worse than ever. It was as though he was embarrassed for being nice to his own wife. I didn't realize at the time, but it signaled the beginning of those wild, reckless ways that led to his being killed in that curricle race."

"I'm so sorry, Drew."

He smiled. "Before going to the Indies, when I made such a cake of myself in London over . . . Anyway, my first thought of refuge was this place." He looked around the comfortable room. "But we were at war with France, so it wasn't to be considered."

Drew stretched his long legs toward the fire, shifting position and mood. "I say, unseasonably cold for this time of year. I understand it's been raining almost every day for the past three weeks. Until two days ago, the roads were all but impassable."

Jane sat forward. "Then perhaps Cherry is still in Dieppe."

"No, I've asked at every inn. No one even remembers seeing such a couple."

"But surely they landed here!"

"Yes, there's no doubt about that. The captain of one of the packets said he remembered her quite well from yesterday's voyage."

"They must have taken coach for Paris immediately. Perhaps they feared they were being followed. Cherry would love to think that she was being pursued; it would add to the excitement. Drat the girl!"

Jane's bitter tones made Drew long to comfort her. Instead, he looked around the cozy chamber and asked, "Have you ordered our supper? I'm starved."

Jane welcomed this return to a sane conversation; dealing with menus and guests was part of the real world for her, something tangible.

"Yes, but I wasn't certain when you'd arrive, so it will be a little later than usual—another hour or so. Perhaps you'd care to rest. That is your room; mine is on the opposite side."

Drew stood and said, "No, I'm not tired, but I shall order a bath. I feel as though I've got salt and sand everywhere."

Jane blushed at her own thoughts, and Drew's grin gave warning that he was not about to let such an invitation to mischief pass unnoticed. He moved to her side so that he could look down on her, but she couldn't see his face without screwing her head about and looking directly into his eyes.

"Back home on the island, where the water is clear and warm, I would have gone down to a little cove, shed my clothes, and had a delightful swim. But here, I would freeze to death."

"As well you should," squeaked Jane, trying to keep her tone light, but failing. Perhaps he would think she was outraged instead of bewitched by his words.

Drew, however, ignored her words. Resting his hands on her shoulders, he added quietly, "Do you know how to swim, Jane?"

"No," she lied, deeming this the safest response.

"I would be happy to teach you. Perhaps—"

Tucker's knock was a welcome interruption, and Jane almost shouted for the maid to enter. By the time Tucker opened the door, Drew stood by the entrance to his own room.

"Yes, Tucker?" said Jane, quickly regaining her outward composure.

"I came to see if you needed anything, Miss Jane, m'lord."

"Remember, Tucker, it is 'madam' and 'sir' now. There are too many ears about," said Jane.

"I forgot, Mi . . . madam. I'm sorry."

"Just remember in the future. And I am settled for the night unless Mr. Davies has need of you?" Jane turned to Drew. "I asked Tucker if she would look after your clothes, and she readily agreed."

"That's very kind of you, Tucker."

" 'Tis the least I can do for you, sir."

Drew gave the maid a warning glance. Jane frowned. What debt could her maid possibly owe Drew? She would tax Tucker with this very question when they were alone.

Ending the awkward silence, Drew disappeared into his room, mentioning his intention to bathe before dinner. Before Jane could protest, Tucker slipped out the other door, telling the viscount she would have the landlord send up hot water.

Meanwhile, Jane was left with her own uncomfortable

221

thoughts for company. She tried to be angry with Drew for provoking her with his suggestive flirtation. Teach her to swim indeed! Why, a true gentleman wouldn't even mention such an activity as swimming in the ocean—sans clothing! He was horrid! A bounder!

She heard a splash as the hot water was poured into the porcelain tub. Resolutely, she opened her book of sermons.

The sermons had been divided into topics. She had finished reading those about stewardship. She turned the page. "Adultery," she read. Jane skipped to the back sections of the book and began reading at random.

"And let me urge you, sinners all in this wicked world . . ." Jane paused as she heard more splashing from the next room. This time, it sounded like someone rinsing. Drew rinsing himself, she thought. She took a deep breath and returned to her book. "Read ye the gospel according to St. Mark, in the fourteenth chapter, eighth verse, 'Watch ye and pray, lest ye enter into temptation. The spirit truly is ready, but the flesh is weak.' "

Another large splash as Drew stood up.

Jane closed the book with a snap. She peered over her shoulder to see if dear Friday-faced Pipkin had materialized in the room. She was just being foolish, she told herself. She would go below stairs and find Tucker. She had to find some activity that would take her away from the tiny sitting room with the thin walls—anything to keep her wanton thoughts occupied.

Tucker was just unrolling a large cloth with a white shirt inside it when Jane finally located her. It was a laundry room; a hot fire smoldered in the fireplace where irons were heating.

"Madam, what is it?"

"I just needed to speak to you, Tucker."

"Ye should have sent one of th' maids, madam," said Tucker, cocking her head significantly toward an open door to her right. Jane could hear other servants, mostly French, talking as they worked. Jane closed the door before continuing.

"I wanted to ask you why you told Lor . . . Mr. Davies that to do his laundry was 'the least you could do.' What did you mean by that? Are you in his debt?"

Tucker was a good woman, a virtuous woman. It took only a moment for her to decide, however, that total honesty would not be wise in this instance. For if Miss Jane found out how she, Pipkin, and Cook had conspired with Lord Devlin to insure her safety . . . Whew! It would take more than a closed door to contain the ruckus Miss Jane would raise!

"I meant, madam, that I'm grateful to him, though ye may disagree, but I'm grateful to him for coming wi' us. I can't help but feel safer for 'is bein' 'ere."

"Yet it was I who secured a suite of rooms for us," said Jane. Remembering it had been Drew who had arranged for their transport to the out-of-the-way inn, Jane said briskly, "Never mind. What are you doing there?"

"Ironing a shirt for Mr. Davies, madam."

"It is rather large, isn't it?"

"Large enough. He cuts quite a figure," said the middle-aged maid with a knowing smile.

"Tucker!"

"Only funning wi' ye, Miss Jane," she whispered. "Now, ye'd best scoot upstairs before the whole world and 'is brother begins to ask himself what a grand lady is doing in the laundry room of an inn."

"Yes, Tucker," said Jane, smiling despite herself.

As Jane opened the doors, Tucker said, "I'll be up later to ready you for bed, madam."

"I'm so hungry I could eat snails!" said Drew as he joined Jane at the small table in their sitting room. He looked over the assortment of dishes and said doubtfully, "There aren't any here, are there?"

"Escargots? No, only a rich stew of sorts—lamb, I believe. And here we have steamed potatoes with garlic," Jane added, her nose wrinkling as she tested the aromas.

"Tomatoes with basil, some fresh greens au vinaigrette, and the mandatory French bread."

"Good!" Jane nodded as he served her plate first, but her mind wasn't on the food. With Drew occupied playing waiter, she was at leisure to appreciate his fine appearance. He wore a black brocade dressing down in place of a coat, and an informal neckerchief instead of a starched cravat. He had apologized for this bit of informality, saying it was too troublesome to shrug his shoulders into one of his tailored coats for an hour or two's wear. Jane had readily agreed. The result was devastating.

He hadn't shaved either, and the day's growth of beard looked manly, but not forbidding. His wet hair was combed, but as it dried, it curled endearingly about his collar and ears. One curl fell across his forehead; Jane longed to push it back into place, but, of course, she didn't. Instead, she sat primly, hands folded in her lap, a socially acceptable smile set on her face. A proper little voice said in one ear, "Very well done, miss. Very well done, indeed."

The little voice advised her to ignore those most improper longings that were flaring up here and there throughout her body.

What would it feel like to sit in his lap? asked the wicked voice.

Never you mind, said the proper one.

Remember the last time you sat in his lap? In the carriage? You remember what it felt like to sit in his lap, don't you, Jane? But of course you can't remember. You were both too busy elsewhere, taunted the naughty voice.

Yes, she remembered that, thought Jane, her breasts tingling at the memory.

"Jane? Jane, are you going to eat?"

Jane started at Drew's puzzled voice. Ah yes, reality, she told herself. Smiling and nodding absently, she lifted her fork. Somehow, the food had lost its appeal.

Little conversation troubled their digestion; both parties were too engrossed in their own thoughts. It was not until

224

after the maid took the covers away that Jane noticed Drew's abstractedness.

Wanting to set aside her own disturbing ruminations, Jane asked, "Penny for your thoughts?"

He looked at her a moment before her query registered. He hesitated before smiling—a faraway smile. "I was remembering the last time I dined in the private suite of an inn with an unmarried lady. My God, it seems centuries ago," he groaned.

Jane leaned across the small table and placed her hand on his, giving it a gentle squeeze before her hand returned to her own lap.

"I fancied myself in love, a boy of nineteen, an innocent lamb running full tilt toward the slaughter. Lamb is an apt metaphor, for I was no more than a sacrificial lamb for their twisted game of love."

Jane feared to make a comment, or even the slightest movement; it might bring an end to these confidences. She breathed slowly, evenly, willing Drew to continue that she might understand his bitterness.

"The lady—and I use the term lightly, meaning no disrespect to you, Jane—" So he realized she was still present, thought Jane. "—this lady had led me to believe she returned my vows of undying love and devotion. She even suggested we elope, explaining that her guardian would never countenance a match with me, a nothing in society at that time. I planned it all, every detail, down to the last change of horses. From the beginning, things went awry. She insisted we stop at the first posting house outside London for a late supper. I agreed. I would have agreed with any request she made."

Drew stood up and began to pace the floor. Finally, he stopped; leaning against the mantel, his dark eyes sought Jane. He held out a hand and she went to him. As he seated her in the chair, his gentle smile warmed her heart.

"She was nervous during the meal; I put it down to maidenly shyness. I was such a gullible fool! As we finished our meal, the door to the parlor flew open. It was her guardian and eight or ten of their closest friends. I know now they were an ill-sorted lot of hangers-on and gossips. I moved to protect my 'lady'! She would have none of it; you may imagine my bewilderment. Through her laughter, she told everyone how stupid I was, how utterly childish to think that she could love me! Then she walked past me and into her guardian's arms. I knew then! It was all some hideous game they played—had played before and would do so again, even after they were married. The laughter filled the room; it was a nightmare, but I couldn't escape! I walked up to her and slapped her face. The guardian wanted to kill me; I could see it in his eyes. That, at least, would have been merciful. But she stopped him, with just a little shake of her head; such was the power she held over men. With that trill of laughter I had once loved so well, she announced to everyone that I had issued her a challenge to a duel and that she would meet me at dawn."

"Oh, Drew," breathed Jane, unable to keep silent in her distress over his pain. "How could Lady Cynthia do such a thing? How could anyone?"

"So you've guessed the identity of my first love. How indeed? But she did, and we met at dawn." He seemed anxious suddenly to put his tale of woe to rest. "I deloped, of course, but not Cynthia. I never asked where she was aiming, but she shot my hat off my head. The jerk of the pistol knocked her down, and our audience—it had grown from the night before—rallied round the poor damsel in distress. I left the country shortly afterwards on the orders of my uncle. I took over my late father's only property, a run-down sugar cane plantation in the Indies. Best thing to come out of the whole fiasco."

"And you danced with that jade!"

Drew looked at Jane in surprise. She stood in front of her chair with a ferocious expression on her face, her fists clenched, her feet braced.

He chuckled at her, his bitterness overtaken by amusement. Placing his hands on her shoulders, he said sympa-

226

thetically, "It's all right, Jane. I had to be certain she had no hold over me."

Jane studied his face for a moment before nodding, satisfied with what she read there. Then a shadow of suspicion crossed her face, and she said, "But you danced with her three times."

"Yes, my dear, and I'm surprised you noticed since you were dancing with every man at that blasted Assembly. As I recall, I wanted to shoot all your partners and throttle you."

"You only asked me to dance once—a country dance!"

"You didn't give me a chance, short of clubbing you over the head to get your attention."

"And what about all the other balls? You hardly danced with me at all; you turned me over to Mr. Stanton and Mr. Farley."

"Hardly, my love. You were safe with them; they knew you were mine."

"Yours?" whispered Jane.

"Always mine." His arms slipped around her waist, pulling her into his warm embrace. A thousand thoughts and questions she wanted to ask him, but these disappeared as he tenderly kissed her lips. He lifted his head and repeated, "Always." Jane gave herself up to his kisses, joining in just as much as he was—no more, no less—exactly as her grandmother had advised her.

There were no sofas in the room, so Jane soon found herself seated in Drew's lap. She didn't question how they had become so situated, she merely returned his kisses with renewed ardor since she no longer had to worry about her legs collapsing.

Some time later, Drew kissed the base of her throat and mumbled, "Where's Tucker when we need her?"

"Who?" gasped Jane as he kissed her neck again.

He chuckled and raised his head. While Jane tried to entice another kiss from his lips, Drew said with mock severity, "You are not paying attention, Miss Lindsay."

Jane stopped trying to kiss him and, taking stock of her

situation, scrambled to her feet. She shook out the folds of her dress and looked in the tarnished mirror over the mantel. Most of her hairpins had slipped and her hair was down completely on one side while the other side looked even more ridiculous with only a few strands tucked up. She raked her fingers through the long, straight locks and bent to retrieve the fallen pins.

"What are you doing?" asked an amused viscount.

"Trying to set myself to rights before you completely disgrace me!" she replied tartly.

"*I* disgrace *you?* It seems to me I had more than a little cooperation from you, my dear. Always have had."

Jane blushed a dull red and bent her head to continue her search. Drew took her arms and raised her to a standing position. Her blush deepened, but he refused to release her.

"Look at me." She hung her head. "Look at me, Jane." She lifted her head. "That's better. I must apologize for letting this happen."

He read the fear in her eyes and smiled, shaking his head slightly. "No, I'm not sorry it did, anymore than I could be sorry for loving you. But my timing is deplorable. No, don't speak. Let me finish. This trip was difficult enough before; now it will be unbearable. How can I keep from kissing you when I know how willing you are? And you are willing, aren't you, Jane? You do care for me?"

His uncertainty was so endearing; Jane hastened to reassure him. "Yes, Drew, I do care for you. I . . . I may even love you."

"Shh. I know you do, or I've hoped so, but you mustn't put it into words. I might ravish you on the spot. Now," he began, setting her away from him at arm's length, "we mustn't do anything to tempt one another. Not by word or deed. Or look, Jane. If you look at me so, how can I keep from making love to you?" She lowered her shining eyes obediently. "I know you're bound and determined to find Cherry, so I won't suggest we return home right now. But while we're together on this journey, we must be very careful of one another. Agreed?" Jane nodded, and Drew solemnly shook her hand, sealing their agreement. Then he said firmly, "It's late. We both need to get some sleep if we're to leave early in the morning. Good night." Then he vanished into his own room.

Jane stood rooted to the floor. Slowly a displeased frown spread across her features. Well and good for him, all his ideas and plans! What about her? What about her wishes? From that first kiss in the darkened corridor on the night of the Valentine Ball, he had ignored her protests! Traveling to France with her had been his idea entirely, with no regard for her wants and desires!

Well! She would just rectify that problem this time!

Upon entering his room, Drew sank against the closed door. It was going to be a long, painful journey.

All his decisions to take things slowly had backfired. They might have been betrothed by now, perhaps even married. This trip could have been their honeymoon. Instead, it had become an exercise in self-control! And he felt certain Jane had very little self-control over her passions; he would need to be strong for them both.

Suddenly it hit him! He hadn't even asked Jane to be his wife! He pivoted; with hand on the door handle, Drew paused. Slowly, he walked back toward the empty bed. He couldn't risk returning to her. He'd resisted temptation once; he didn't dare tempt nature again tonight.

He looked at the bed again. With little effort, his fertile imagination conjured up the vision of Jane, lovely, ripe Jane, waiting there for him, impatient for him to join her. Groaning, Drew hurried to the other doorway, the one leading to the corridor. He would find his old friend and share a bottle. There would be little rest that night!

Jean-Francois had a sympathetic ear, aided by an excellent bottle of wine. The bottle would become two before Drew felt numb enough to be able to sleep.

"So, my old friend, how did it happen?"

Drew looked at Jean-Francois in surprise. "What?"

One of the landlord's beady eyes winked. "How did you win such a beautiful lady? She is the type of woman makes a man . . . eh?"

Drew cautioned, "Be careful, my friend. You speak of my wife."

"Ah, you English, always so proper. Am I not a man? Can I not see with my own eyes how desirable Madam is?"

Drew's laugh was hollow. "Anyone who is a man could see. That's the problem. I am a man, and I see all too clearly."

"But she is your wife."

Drew was feeling the effects of his wine. He was not past hope, but his natural caution had relaxed. He needed to tell someone, someone who would understand the nobility of his sitting up all night drinking instead of seducing the woman he loved. He needed someone who would sympathize with the terrible longing, the aching in his loins.

"She is not."

The sly grin that appeared on Jean-Francois's face sobered Drew.

"Don't misunderstand. She will be — soon, I hope. It was like this . . ."

Over the second bottle, his story was told, and the Frenchman was sworn to secrecy.

To repay Drew for these shared confidences, Jean-Francois stood up, raised his glass, and toasted the beautiful, stubborn Anglaise. Then he pledged his willingness to aid Drew and his cause. Misty-eyed, Jean-Francois grasped Drew by the shoulder with his one arm and kissed his friend's cheeks before bidding him good night.

His tread a trifle unsteady, Drew negotiated the staircase and found his way down the darkened corridor to his room. He stumbled to the bed, managing to throw off his clothes before crawling between the sheets.

♡ *Chapter Eight* ♡

Jane hummed to herself as she watched Tucker laying out a fresh carriage dress. She sipped the steaming chocolate and sighed. She had slept peacefully, untroubled even by the worry of her cousin's shocking flight.

"Madam, the maid has brought up breakfast for you and Mr. Davies."

"Very well, Tucker. I suppose I should dress first; I hope my husband" — Jane savored the word — "will forgive me for being late."

"I don't think Mr. Davies is awake yet."

"Not awake? That's odd. He doesn't strike me as —" Jane stopped speaking as Tucker delivered a warning look toward the open door to the sitting room where an inn servant was setting a table. "That is, he's not usually such a slugabed."

"Mayhap ye should wake 'im, ma'am."

Jane's eyes widened. She shook her head. Tucker shrugged her shoulders. Jane frowned, taking her lip between her teeth as she waged an inner debate. Being sensible won out.

"Tucker, I'll dress after breakfast. Do you go downstairs and eat now."

"Yes, madam."

Jane stood up and slipped on her wrapper; it was not the sensible covering she had worn when supping with Drew at the Ship's Inn in Brighton. It was pale yellow, of gossamer silk with touches of lace across the bodice. Resolutely, she marched through the parlor, past the curtseying maid and tapped gently on her "husband's" door.

"Drew, dear, are you awake?"

Silence.

She opened the door and peered into the gloomy room. To her mind, the bed, with its rumpled occupant, dominated the room.

"Drew," she whispered, closing the door against the servant's rattling of cups and saucers.

She hesitated on the threshold. If she startled him, he might leap out of bed. What would he look like in a nightshirt? Jane's face became flushed at this indelicate thought, and she chided herself for acting so missish. Still, she approached the bed cautiously.

Her heart beating rapidly, she stretched out her hand to touch his shoulder. As she realized he was completely submerged beneath the blanket, she thought, "Please, let it be his shoulder."

She touched him gently.

No response.

Again, she put out her hand.

It was closed in a viselike grip! She was jerked forward and found herself staring into the barrel of a silver pistol.

"What the. . . !" The gun disappeared, but Drew retained her wrist. They stared at each other, panting from fearful thoughts of what might have happened.

"Jane, never, ever, do that again. Call my name! Something!"

"I did," she sobbed, tears beginning to fall.

"Jane!" he said, his fear giving way to exasperation. He could never predict her reactions! Relaxing his hold on her wrist, he sat up and pulled her onto the bed, cradling her in his arms until her sniffling subsided.

Jane slowly grew aware of being held against a naked chest. The realization had an alarming effect on her hands; she ran her fingers through the springy mat of black hair, so soft to the touch against the hardness of his chest.

232

Drew's arms tightened about her, and Jane lifted her damp face; he smoothed the tears from her cheeks.

"You shouldn't be in here at all."

She ignored his comment and rubbed her cheek against his stubbly chin.

"You are a heartless wench," he groaned, trying to push her away, but Jane's arms had encircled his neck, and she refused to be moved. Not that Drew tried too hard.

"My mouth tastes like cotton," he protested weakly, turning his head as she tried to kiss his lips. Jane smiled and kissed his ear instead. Drew lay back against the pillow, pulling her on top of him. Jane continued to tease him, raining kisses on his cheeks, his neck, his ears.

Suddenly, Drew rolled over, and Jane was trapped beneath him, his body dividing her legs. Holding her hands on either side of her head, he raised up, looking down at her white breasts, confined by the sheer material.

Jane followed his eyes; her taut nipples straining against the fabric screamed for his mouth. He slid farther down in the bed; the pressure of his body against hers sent a thrill coursing downward. Through the thin silk, he kissed her breasts, teasing her erect nipples. Jane felt ready to explode with desire as he released one hand and freed one breast, taking the dark nipple in his mouth and pulling on it, the sensation this caused traveled elsewhere. She moved her hands, both free now, across his naked back, pressing his hard body against her stomach as his mouth teased her breasts, awakening heightened waves of ecstasy. He moved against her rhythmically; Jane's breathing quickened. Then the world stopped. She emitted a small cry, and Drew's movements became slower, harder, until she whimpered in exhaustion.

Giving pleasure to one's beloved provided one an incredible sense of satisfaction, thought Drew, as he raised himself and gazed down at Jane's Mona Lisa-like smile.

And an incredible amount of discomfort, was his second thought. He rolled off of her, willing himself to achieve a patience of almost superhuman magnitude. How he wanted her!

"Drew?"

"Yes, love," he said, one arm tucked behind his head as his free hand replaced the damp material across her breasts. She shivered at his touch.

"What does this mean?"

He grinned, his sense of humor aroused. "It means you are too trusting and too passionate for your own good, and I had best marry you before we consummate our wedding prematurely."

"Then we didn't just—"

"Consummate our wedding?" She nodded. "Not in the strictest sense. But then, I have never been that strict." He ran his hand lightly up her arm; Jane shut her eyes.

"We must get up before Tucker comes looking for you." This possibility sent Jane scrambling to her feet. Drew remained discreetly in bed.

"Hurry," she called, "or your breakfast will be cold."

"Won't be a moment," he said, waiting until the door had shut behind her before crawling out of bed and gathering up his breeches and dressing gown.

Jean-Francois sent them off in his best coach-and-four, his eldest son proudly serving as their coachman. They traveled by back roads to Paris to avoid any acquaintances. The largest vehicle they passed all morning was a dogcart filled with fruit. Drew halted the carriage and jumped out. He bargained with the farmer a moment and returned with a dozen peaches and some strawberries.

At the next tiny village, he purchased a bottle of wine, some mellow cheese, and a loaf of bread. They were halfway to Paris when they stopped beside a meadow blooming with wildflowers. Drew and Jane insisted Tucker join them as he spread carriage rugs for their picnic. The maid finally consented, but she refused to drink wine with them, allowing that only good English stout agreed with her English constitution.

234

"Tell me, Tucker. Honestly, mind. Have you ever tried French wine?"

"No, sir."

"Do try a little, Tucker," urged Jane.

"Nay, miss, ye'll not tempt me."

"Very well, but when we marry, Tucker, I shall expect you to join in a toast with French champagne," said the viscount.

"Oh, champagne, sir! That's different!"

Drew was still chuckling as he rolled up the rugs and returned to the carriage.

"How much longer, Drew?" asked Jane as they set off once again.

"These roads, these animals? Another five hours, at the very least. But you must admit, we haven't met a soul."

"That's true. The day is so beautiful, I could almost forget why I'm here."

Tucker's gentle snore caused Jane to smile, and Drew leaned close to her ear.

"Perhaps you could make believe we are on our wedding trip. Do you remember the night we met?"

"How could I forget? Your behavior was shocking!" Jane's teasing tone robbed her words of offense.

"And your behavior was not? What a paradox you were. Prim and proper, cool as ice one minute; leaping off the terrace and kissing a total stranger with wild abandon the next."

"I had no choice! I was taken by surprise!" she whispered fiercely.

"So you would react the same if any man took you by surprise?"

"No!"

"Only me?"

"Yes, wretch," she admitted. "Only you."

Drew stole a quick glance at the sleeping maid before pulling Jane against his chest and kissing her lips. He released her, declaring his intention to sleep away the last part of their journey.

235

Jane, however, remained alert, staring out the window, building a fairy-tale future in her mind.

"Jane, I have decided it would be best if I stay somewhere else in Paris and resume my true identity."

Drew's announcement was at odds with Jane's daydream, and she turned her raised brows on him in question.

"Then," continued Drew, "I can go about in society freely and locate Cherry. As Mr. and Mrs. Davies we wouldn't have the entree into high circles. And neither of us wants to risk meeting acquaintances accidentally."

"True, but how will you convince Cherry of the error of her ways?"

Drew was blissfully unaware of the tartness of her tones as he considered her query. As far as he was concerned, everything had been settled between them and he no longer needed to tread warily. Jane had agreed to be his wife; she would naturally look to him for guidance in any important decision.

"I suppose I will invite her to join me for a drive and bring her to you."

"As simply as that, hmm? Don't you think Lord Pierce will have something to say about you stealing her away?"

"I daresay I can convince her; that's all that matters."

"And what am I to do while you are conducting your search?"

"I suppose you may do as you wish. With Tucker along, I see no reason why you shouldn't shop and visit museums. You will, after all, be wearing your mourning garb. No one could recognize you beneath that hideous veil."

"You have thought of everything."

Now he noticed the biting edge to her voice, and he frowned. "Is something bothering you, Jane?"

"Why, what could possibly be the matter? I am visiting Paris for the first time. I am accompanied by the man I am going to wed, and before we even reach our destination, he has decided to rid himself of me."

"Jane, you are acting childishly."

While Jane might merely have been speaking from weariness at first, his calm, condescending words pushed her into acting just as he had accused.

"You must forgive me, Lord Devlin, for troubling you with my childish views."

"Jane, my dear, be reasonable."

There! He had just sounded the death knell on any reasonable response she might have made. Instead, responding in a manner she would normally have derided, Jane turned her back on Drew and refused to say another word. Drew's own patience snapped. Had he not ridden to her side, *ventre à terre*, so that she wouldn't have to endure this insane journey alone? Had he not taken care of all the arrangements, down to a place for her to stay in Paris with Jean-Francois's aunt? Was he not prepared to search throughout the city for her silly chit of a cousin?

Devil take her and all women! Let her sulk! He turned and gazed out the window as they entered the gates of the city.

Tucker, who had slept through the altercation between her mistress and her newly acquired fiancé, was perplexed by the coolness of their parting. Drew remained at the home of Madam DuClaire only long enough to satisfy himself as to the comfort and suitability of the dwelling. Jane remained silent during the viscount's quick conference with their hostess. Bidding Drew a chilly farewell, Jane and Tucker followed Madam upstairs to the second floor.

"What has happened between you and his lordship, Miss Jane?" asked Tucker as soon as the Frenchwoman had left them alone.

"I don't know what you mean."

"Now then, Miss Jane, I've been with your family since I was but a child myself. There's no need to act the

237

haughty mistress with me."

Jane shook her head and said, "I really don't see why I bother to try and have a private life. It is impossible with old family retainers about."

"Never you mind, miss. I've followed ye all the way to this godforsaken country where no one understands me and I understand no one. I've not uttered a single complaint, and I have thought it all worthwhile since it seemed you and his lordship were coming to a point. So, Miss Jane, I'll not pry, but if I can be of help, ye've only t' ask."

Tucker turned her back on Jane and began unpacking one hideous black gown after another. Jane nibbled at her lip a moment before coming up behind the maid and putting her arms around Tucker, saying, "Please forgive me. I can't explain what happened between me and his lordship; I don't understand it myself."

"So ye've had yerselves a little spat."

"I suppose so, but I can't say why. I get upset and lose my temper over the least little thing; it's so unlike me. But he's so very overbearing, Tucker. Are all men like that?"

"Most of them, Miss Jane. My Henry, rest his soul, was forever telling me what t' do. It bothered me at first. Then I learned to just smile and go about my own way."

"Didn't that make him angry?"

"Sometimes, but it was better than trying to change him. And you can always make up later."

Jane nodded, digesting the older woman's sensible advice. She wasn't certain she could even pretend to agree with Drew when she didn't. It seemed dishonest, but there was no denying she was unhappy as things now stood between them.

"I'm going to go downstairs and take a turn about that lovely courtyard. Would you have tea sent to me there?"

"Yes, Miss Jane. Best take yer shawl; it'll be cool in the shadows."

Jane woke to a rainy day. With her morning chocolate,

Tucker delivered an envelope from Drew. Jane set it aside as she sipped the hot liquid; she was in no hurry to read any missive from him, she told herself firmly. She watched Tucker pull out yet another repulsive black gown. Idly, her eyes fell on the envelope again.

There was something oddly familiar about the handwriting. Jane shrugged and picked up the envelope; she supposed she had seen numerous other notes written in Drew's hand, but she hadn't noticed what a scrawl he had. She tore open the paper.

Dearest Jane,

I have found lodgings at the Hotel St. Jacques in the Rue d'Honore. If you need me, you may send for me there. I had the misfortune of meeting Mr. Tuttle once again; he is staying here, also.

I have been invited to a breakfast al fresco at Versailles today, so I will not have the time to come to you at Madam DuClaire's. Hopefully, I will meet the missing cousin at the breakfast and can restore her to you this evening.

I trust you slept well and are rested from our arduous journey. I am told that a Madam Arnot is the best couturière in Paris. On my way out of the city, I will stop by her shop and arrange for her to visit you this afternoon. Perhaps you would wish to order a Parisian wedding gown.

Ever Yours,
D.

Jane pitched the offending paper onto the rumpled sheets and proceeded to drink up her tepid chocolate. Parisian wedding gown, indeed! While he is out having the time of his life dancing with French beauties and English tourists! And he expected her to sit in the house with only a visit from the dressmaker to enliven her day! She would just see about that!

"Tucker, we're going out! Lord Devlin has written to tell

me the name of the best dressmaker in Paris, and I intend to visit her posthaste!"

"Yes, Miss Jane," said Tucker doubtfully.

Jane paused outside the shop of Madam Arnot, gazing in the window at the enticing display of rich silks and satins.

"Look at the red silk, Tucker. Can you imagine that at our next Valentine Ball?"

"Oh, miss, you'd be ever so beautiful in it with your coloring. And your green eyes would shine like emeralds."

"I must have it."

Jane was treated like royalty; clearly, Madam Arnot had no difficulty dealing with France's former enemies. Jane's senses were assaulted with a dizzying array of fabrics and fashion plates. She finally settled on two morning gowns, one in blue cambric and the other in a peach wool crepe, a carriage dress of royal blue serge, and the ruby red silk for a daringly cut evening gown.

Madam Arnot's shop was unique; she stocked an entire range of hats and headdresses to compliment her creations. Her shop was also connected with a shoemaker next door, so her customers could complete their ensembles without leaving the premises.

While Madam and her senior seamstress removed to one side to confer, a young shopgirl served Jane tea.

Jane smiled at the timid girl and asked, "What is your name, child?"

"I am Marie, madam."

"Do you enjoy working here?"

"Oh yes, madam. Someday I hope to be allowed to sew dresses for the beautiful ladies." The girl blushed at her own enthusiasm.

"Did you make your own gown?"

"Yes, madam."

"Then I'm sure you will be able to sew for Madam Arnot one day. Your gown is very well made."

"Thank you, madam."

Madam Arnot turned, and the servant curtsied hastily and scurried away.

As Jane watched her go, an idea began to form in her mind. She wouldn't dare ask Madam Arnot for information about Cherry; madam held the ear of too many influential ladies. But a shopgirl? No one spoke to or listened to a lowly shop girl. Jane could question her with impunity.

"Madam Davies," began Madam Arnot, "we can promise to have the dresses for you in four days, three perhaps. If it will be convenient, I will send Madam Lefevre to you tomorrow for a final fitting on the evening gown."

"That will be fine. Shall we say eleven o'clock?"

"Very good, madam."

"Oh, and send the girl Marie along. I have a fondness for young people."

Madam Arnot masked her surprise admirably. "*Bien*, madam. I will see to it."

Jane was smiling as she and Tucker left Madam Arnot's. She couldn't wait to tell Drew that she had discovered a way to locate Cherry. She knew her cousin; if everyone said Madam Arnot's gowns were the best in Paris, then that was where Cherry had gone.

"Well, well," muttered the dapper little gentleman watching their departure with great interest. "It seems Paris has been blessed with yet another English heiress. There's a mystery here."

A huge wagon rattled through the narrow street. Mr. Tuttle dusted off his brocade coat and settled his wig more firmly on his head. Resolutely, he set off down the street, following the shapely figure dressed in black and her sturdy maid.

Once he had verified the identity of his quarry by peering through the salon's window, Mr. Tuttle retired to the nearest café. Resting his chin on the knob of his cane, he took an occasional sip of wine and waited for a suitable recipient of his latest on-dit to appear.

He had not long to wait.

"Mr. Havelock! You are well met."

The rotund Roland paused and looked down cautiously. While a conversation with Mr. Tuttle would be amusing and would not harm his consequence, he had no desire to unwittingly become the man's next on-dit. He would need to exercise extreme caution.

"Tuttle. Didn't know you were in Paris."

"Yes, yes. You may always find me where the *ton* is most plentiful. Have a seat, my good fellow. *Garçon,* another glass for my friend."

Roland lowered his considerable bulk onto the wrought-iron chair. Mr. Tuttle smiled, his crumbling teeth rendering such an action repulsive.

"I had no idea you and your family were in Paris either."

Roland looked around, expecting to see his mother. She was the only one in the world he truly considered "family." "Family? You must be mistaken. M' mother's an invalid. She'd never come to Paris."

"No, no, not your mother, old chap. Your cousins, the beautiful Misses Lindsay and Pettigrew. I suppose they came to Paris together?"

Roland, who had spied Cherry strolling in the park, wasn't surprised by this news. But Jane was another matter! Jane—in Paris! Mr. Tuttle's eyes shone with excitement.

"You are surprised! You didn't know they were here?" said the man, running his tongue across his lip in anticipation.

"Cherry, yes," said Roland, dropping his guard. "But Jane? I'd no idea."

"Yes, it is true. I, too, must admit to being surprised. Miss Lindsay is reputed to be a bit of a homebody."

"Perhaps, but she's hardly a recluse. Must have decided to come over with friends now that the Continent has opened up again. I'd like to call on her; I don't suppose

242

you know where she's staying." Roland tried to hide his burning curiosity about Jane's whereabouts from Tuttle's inquisitive scrutiny.

"Of course I do. Perhaps we could pay her a call together right now."

"Can't right now," said Roland nervously. The last thing he wanted at this point was to alert Jane to his presence. First he needed to decide on a course of action. Getting to his feet, he added, "Pressing appointment. I'll call later."

"Ah, very well, if you must go. Miss Lindsay is staying at number eight, Rue Voltaire."

"Thank you, Tuttle. Must dash."

Roland Havelock was not a patient man, but when it came to making an easy profit, he could be very patient, indeed. And profit he would, he vowed, as he waited outside the DuClaire home for someone, preferably a servant, to leave. It was dusk before his patience was rewarded by the appearance of Jean-Francois's son, Jean-Luc.

Havelock was not a man of great ambition, but he was intelligent. He could speak four languages fluently; French was one of them. Silently, he followed the youth to a nearby café. As if by random, Havelock chose the table beside the country lad and struck up a conversation. Jean-Luc was intrigued to find an Englishman so capable of speaking his own tongue, especially one who was so interested in what he, a mere boy, had to say. Soon the youth was telling his life history in answer to Havelock's gentle probing.

Finally, Havelock asked, "Then this is your first visit to Paris?"

"Yes, monsieur."

"And you are staying here alone?"

"Ah no, monsieur. I am staying with my aunt Madam DuClaire."

"How did you travel? On horseback?"

The young man puffed out his thin chest. "No, I drove a

243

fine carriage for three of your countrymen. At least, two were women and one a man. A lord, I heard the maid call him."

"So you drove for a lord and his wife?"

"No, she was not his wife, though they pretended to be when they stayed at our inn in Dieppe." Jean-Luc winked and attempted to sound worldly. Kissing his fingertips, he said, "The lady had a figure to tempt any man. She is also very nice, but the lord wouldn't stay with her. He had me drive him to the Hotel St. Jacques. It was very strange. Me, I would not have left such a one as Mademoiselle."

"Nor would I, my young friend. Nor would I," said Havelock, his devious mind already scheming on the best way to turn this bit of knowledge to his own advantage.

Drew stared at the huge pavilion erected on the smooth lawn. Tent was perhaps the more accurate word for the gaudy red and white monstrosity. A wooden floor upon which the gaily dressed visitors stood covered the green grass, and an orchestra began to tune up in preparation for the dancing.

What a crashing bore this breakfast is, thought Drew for the hundredth time. He should have spent the day and evening at Madam DuClaire's with Jane. No, he reminded himself, also for the hundredth time, he and Jane were not on the best of terms at the moment. He wasn't even certain she was speaking to him. And no matter that he had vowed to wipe her vagaries from his mind, she had a peculiar habit of invading his every thought. That girl over by the rose bush, for instance—she was wearing that pale shade of yellow that looked so bewitching on Jane. Even the females who did not put him in mind of Jane by their mannerisms or appearances managed to inspire thoughts of Jane as he contrasted how she would have responded to his conversation.

If it were not for his promise to find Cherry, Drew would have left before dark. As it was, in his taciturn mood, he avoided contact with as many acquaintances as possible. Really, he thought cynically, almost all of England's beau monde was in Paris. Who was left at home?

"Lord Devlin! I had no notion you were coming to Paris! How delightful to see you!" Drew whirled around and stared at Cherry who was busily searching the crowd on the makeshift dance floor. She looked up at him once more, her china blue eyes wide and inquiring.

"What are you doing here, Cherry?" What a little jade she was, ruining her reputation by appearing in public with her lover. He looked behind her for Lord Pierce.

"I was invited," she laughed. Then, seeing his frown, she said, "Oh, I suppose you mean in Paris?"

"Yes, in Paris," he answered, holding his temper in check.

"It was a last minute decision, really. When Peter told me—"

"Ah yes, Peter. Where is the lucky man?"

Cherry now frowned, perplexed by his sarcastic tones. "Why, he's not here tonight. He was invited to a cockfight or some such thing. But, of course, his mother and sisters are here, except Mary, who returned to Bath several weeks ago."

"Wait!" said Drew in astonishment. "You mean to tell me you're here with Peter and his family—his entire family?"

"Well, of course! Are you feeling quite the thing, Lord Devlin?"

He grinned, causing Cherry to reconsider her opinion that Lord Devlin was too old and staid.

"I am fine, Miss Pettigrew; I am better than fine. Would you care to dance?"

"Yes, thank you, Lord Devlin."

During their dance, Cherry was disconcerted by Drew's tendency to laugh out loud at her every comment. Cherry wondered at this since she wasn't known for her great witticisms. When the music ended, Drew returned her to Lady Pierce and proceeded to entertain the dowager with his pithy remarks on the passing crowd.

Drew began to enjoy himself. The irony of Jane's rescue mission to France struck him as laughable. He wanted to hug Cherry, to thank her for creating this unique opportunity to be alone with Jane.

At midnight, a sumptuous buffet was served. Champagne flowed freely, and Drew was in his cups. He had planned to leave directly after supper, but Lady Pierce's youngest daughter, Margery, scandalized her mother by asking him to dance, and Drew laughingly led her onto the floor. After dealing with this silly young damsel, Drew led a giggling and delighted Lady Pierce into the next waltz.

Finally, he led Cherry into the Boulanger. His purpose quickly became obvious to his partner; he had decided to be stuffy again.

"Miss Pettigrew, how is it you've come to Paris without your mother?"

"She wished to return to the country."

"Then she gave her blessings for you to travel with Lady Pierce?" continued Drew when the dance brought them together again.

Cherry nibbled at her lip, reminding Drew of her kinship with Jane. "Not precisely, but I knew she wouldn't mind once she realized."

"So you have, in essence, run away."

"No!" exclaimed Cherry before they were separated once again. A moment later, she explained, "That is, I left her a note explaining all. We're only staying a month. When we go home to Heartland, I'll make it up to her."

"Your mother is not at Heartland."

"Then London."

"Nor is she in London."

"Where is she?"

"I believe she has gone to visit her sister. She was quite agitated, I understand."

The steps of the complicated dance sent them apart once more.

"But why?" asked Cherry when she took Drew's hand again. "Surely she understood!"

"I'm sure I couldn't say. Perhaps you would be wise to send her a note again, explaining the situation."

"Yes, I shall! And Jane, too! If Mama is upset, she will have dragged Jane into it as well!"

"Good!"

The music ended. Drew had the satisfaction of seeing Lady Pierce and her charges leaving shortly afterwards; Cherry was hurrying them along. Quite satisfactory, he told himself. He would have good news for Jane on the morrow.

Driving back to town in the rented gig, Drew had trouble keeping his eyes open. He began to talk aloud in order to stay awake.

"Well, my dear fellow, you've done it. You've taken care of all of Jane's worries and fears. Now she can go home."

He pulled back on the reins sharply; the rented horse came to a jarring halt.

"Damn fool!" he muttered. "Now Jane will go back to Heartland and things will be just as before. She'll shut herself up in that house with Pipkin guarding the door, and she won't even speak to you. Yes, you've done a proper job of it!"

He lifted the reins and urged the horse forward again.

"We'll just see about that! First I'll get things settled between us. Then I'll tell her I've found Cherry and that there can be no scandal attached to Cherry's name since she is in Paris under Lady Pierce's protection. After that, Jane can go home, but I'll be with her!"

Jane rose early, anticipating a busy day. She took special care with her dress, selecting a simple morning gown in powder blue since she had no plans to go out. She wore her hair down, straight and shining, held off her face by a white grosgrain ribbon. She studied her finished appearance complacently. She looked positively demure, she decided. And dressing in such a fashion, she reasoned, would

247

help her keep her temper with Drew when he called.

As Jane descended the front staircase to the breakfast room, the knocker sounded. Jane opened it, a tentative smile on her lips.

"Cousin! How fortuitous to find you in!"

Jane frowned at the immense figure of her Cousin Roland. He was the last person she expected to see! "How did you know I was here?"

"Please, Cousin, won't you allow me inside? No need to tell the world our business," he simpered.

Jane grimaced but stood aside. Havelock entered the foyer with a jaunty stride.

"Have I disturbed your breakfast?" he asked, sniffing the air.

"No, I hadn't reached the dining room yet. Why are you here, Roland?"

"Tsk, tsk, my dear," he intoned, looking at a servant who was dusting the banister.

"Oh, very well. Won't you join me for breakfast?"

Jane made sure she was ahead of her cousin as they filled their plates from the sideboard. She was thankful Madam DuClaire prepared too much food at every meal; as plentiful as it was, Roland emptied every bowl and platter, piling the food onto his plate until it resembled a feed trough in the stables. Once they were seated, a servant poured out two cups of Madam DuClaire's strong, black coffee and then left them alone.

"Now, Roland, how did you know I was here, and what do you want?"

He chewed a moment longer and swallowed noisily before speaking. "Mr. Tuttle told me. Really, Cousin, you should be more careful if you wish to remain incognito. Mr. Tuttle is a sad rattle."

Jane ignored his taunt and said sharply, "Never mind that. What do you want?"

"I merely wanted to see you, a member of the family, a familiar face in this foreign land and all that."

"Hmpf!"

"Cousin Jane! You wound me!" She glowered at him, and Roland was so moved by her expression that he actually put his fork down. "Oh, very well, Jane. I hesitated because the topic of my visit is so unpleasant."

"Roland, I have no money to spare while I'm in Paris. I must save enough to get home."

"No, no, you persist in misunderstanding me."

"Then it isn't for a loan that you've come?"

"Certainly not! No, I have come to warn you."

"Warn me? About what?"

He had her attention now. Jane sat forward expectantly. "I wanted to warn you about Lord Devlin. I spied him yesterday. I didn't think anything about it until Mr. Tuttle told me about you being here in Paris."

"So?" asked Jane warily.

"I couldn't tell you when we were in Bath, but now I must. Devlin is a cad. He's done everything possible to earn his nickname Devilish Devlin."

"Rubbish!" said Jane resolutely. "That is the most ridiculous thing I have ever heard."

"Yes, you would say that. I am ashamed, yes, ashamed, to admit that I didn't reveal the truth about the man from the very beginning. It was inexcusable, but he was blackmailing me."

"Blackmail!" Jane whispered. Closing her eyes, she felt the foundation of her world slipping and sliding beneath her feet. Then her good sense reasserted itself, and she asked, "Why would he do such a thing? And don't tell me for money; I happen to have it from a reliable source that he is very plump in the pocket. Explain yourself, Roland."

"It began innocently enough. When I invited him to join me at the Valentine Ball at Heartland, I had no idea he could be so devious. After the ball, he began to talk about Heartland constantly. It seems he'd gone all over the house that night. He said the house was just what he had been searching for."

"I am aware that he offered to purchase the estate through my solicitor."

"Yes, of course, but when you sent him about his business, that's when the trouble began."

"Roland, you're bamming me, and I'll not be taken in!"

He stood up after swiping at the jam running down his chin. With pompous dignity, he said, "Very well, Jane, if that is how you feel. I have done my family duty. I wash my hands of the affair. Any consequences are entirely on your head. I only hope—"

Jane felt her resolution tremble like the tiny tremors before an earthquake.

"Sit down, Roland. You may as well have your say. I shall then decide whether or not to believe you."

"That is all I ask. As I was saying, he talked of Heartland all the time. I was dining at his house one evening—"

"I had no idea you were such close friends," murmured Jane.

Roland shrugged. "We played cards from time to time."

"Go on."

"We were having our port after dinner, and he asked me, would I sell Heartland to him if I were the master there. I laughed and answered yes, for you know, Jane, Heartland does not hold any special meaning for me," he added apologetically. Jane nodded, impatient for him to continue. Roland had to restrain himself from gloating; he could see she was beginning to believe him. Perhaps he should have gone on the stage; he was really quite good! "Then Devlin asked who stood to inherit the estate should you die childless."

The color drained out of Jane's face; she gripped the edge of the table. She wanted to scream, to shut out her hateful cousin's words, but she doubted she could have produced a sound.

"Yes, I was shocked as well. More shocked when I discovered he'd been questioning a solicitor about the matter."

"Is there anything else?"

"Well, you know about that silly trick at the chapel at Heartland. But I began to wonder about other times. Do you remember when you and he were locked in St. Valentine's vault at the abbey?"

"Yes," she replied with a shudder. "Someone locked us in from the outside."

"Did they? Think, Jane. Did you try the door, or did you just take Devlin's word for it?"

Jane tried to recall, but her memories of that time were blurry. She had been too terrified to think straight at first; then, with Drew's arms around her, rational thought had been impossible.

"And, of course, you know about the notes."

Jane's head popped up, and she asked, "What notes?"

"From some stupid play. I forget the name. It was a joke, at first. Later, I suppose his reasoning was that if you thought someone was in love with you, then perhaps you'd sell Heartland in a fever of confusion."

"Of course," she muttered to herself. "That's why I thought his handwriting so familiar yesterday, that awful scrawling handwriting." She choked down a sob.

"I'm sorry, Jane. I had no idea this news would upset you so. Have you formed some sort of attachment for the man?"

Jane ignored his question and made one last attempt to rebuild her crumbling dreams. "You said he was black-mailing you. How?"

"I am terrible at cards; everyone knows that. We played twice; I lost heavily both times. I have no proof, but I wondered later if perhaps there was some shady dealing. . . . Anyway, I couldn't afford to redeem my notes, so I went to Devlin, like a gentleman, to request an extension. That's when he told me he would keep quiet about my financial embarrassment for a price, for you know a man's honor is at stake when it gets about he had the poor judgement to play deeper than his purse."

Jane waved a hand impatiently. "Yes, yes."

"He promised that he would even tear up my notes when he finally possessed Heartland—one way or the other. I had no choice but to agree. That's why I left Bath; I couldn't stand by idly and watch his duplicity."

"Roland, I think you'd better go," said Jane weakly.

"Jane, dear, I am so sorry for my part in this. I hope you can forgive me."

"It is not your fault."

"If I can be of any further assistance to you, in any way . . ."

Jane shook her head. His objective achieved, Roland Havelock bowed, his corset creaking, and left Jane alone.

Jane wasn't certain how long she sat staring at the cup of coffee in her hand. It was as though she had been asleep for a very long time when the maid came in to clear the dishes. When the servant would have retreated, Jane motioned her forward.

Setting the cup down, Jane got to her feet. It was difficult to move; her legs felt cramped. Pondering over this objectively, she decided she must have been tense during Roland's visit. She wandered out of the dining room and sought the refuge of the cozy sitting room. She settled on the plump sofa, curling her legs underneath her and laying her head on her arm which rested on the sofa's rounded arm.

Perhaps she was jumping to conclusions. She knew Drew better than that. Didn't she? But if Drew were innocent, then that would mean Roland was lying. She'd known her cousin to lie about sneaking an extra muffin from the kitchen, but that had been when they were children. And how could he hope to profit from lying about Drew? If what he had said were true, Roland was risking his reputation as a gentleman by telling her. A gentleman . . . Drew had admitted that first night he wasn't a gentleman. That had been after he had kissed her, after she had found him wandering around upstairs near the nursery, wandering where no other guest would have gone.

And what had been the purpose behind that silly trick at the chapel? He'd been trying to scare her. Had he really thought she would sell Heartland over such a trivial thing. And the falling stones at the abbey? Had he been behind that, too? How could she believe such a thing? He was the one who had pushed her to safety. If his purpose had been to . . .

Jane stood up abruptly. How could she believe any of this about Drew? Drew, the man who loved her, and whom she loved. And he did love her; she was sure of that.

She walked to the window. It had begun to rain, a slow, drenching rain. Who was she trying to fool? the old, sensible Jane asked. She knew nothing about love or men. It was quite possible that Drew didn't have the heart to murder her, so when frightening her hadn't worked, he had realized the only way he would get his hands on Heartland was to marry its mistress. What could be more natural? Marrying for position or money was done all the time.

"Madam, Monsieur Devlin is here. Shall I show him in?"

Jane nodded and wiped away the tear that threatened to spill onto her cheek.

"Good morning, Jane. I was afraid you might still be put out with me and would refuse to see me."

She turned to greet him; he was smiling at her, that winning smile that always made her forget everything else. But not this time. She wouldn't be transparent this time; she would keep her self-control.

"Did you enjoy yourself at the breakfast?" she asked.

"It was a terrible bore. It was like being in London—the same people, the same conversations." Drew frowned. Jane was acting oddly, holding herself aloof.

"Jane, are you still upset with me because I'm not staying here? I did explain—"

"No, I'm not upset at all about that, Drew."

She sounded like she was being truthful, yet her voice held little warmth. "Ah, I see what it is! I told you in my note I would come by last night when I returned to town. It was so late; I knew you would be abed, and since I had no news to report—"

"News?" asked Jane. She had almost forgotten his original reason for attending the breakfast.

"Yes, about Cherry."

"Oh yes. I didn't really expect her to be there. She has put herself beyond the pale, but to appear openly with her lover would be too brazen, even for Cherry."

"How cynical you sound, Jane. Have you given up hope?"

She looked him straight in the eye. "Yes, I believe I have."

He moved to her side and started to place his arms around her. Jane turned away, walking to a narrow, straight-backed chair and sitting down.

"I'm sorry, Drew. I have the headache this morning. It doesn't happen often, but when it does, the pain is unbearable." She lowered her head so he couldn't see her face.

"My poor love, let me send for a physician."

"It would do no good. Only time and sleep can help," she said. "Tucker will make up a potion with laudanum for me."

"Then I'll leave so you can go back to bed. I'll call this evening to see how you are." He placed a gentle hand on her shoulder for a brief moment. Then he left her, never noticing the tears beginning to fall on the tightly clasped hands resting in her lap.

The headache had become a reality by the time Tucker came into the room a half-hour later. "The seamstress is here with yer gown, Miss Jane."

"What? Oh, thank you, Tucker. Is the young shopgirl here, also?"

"Yes. What is it, Miss Jane? Ye've been cryin'."

Jane stood up and squared her shoulders, determined to ignore the pain in her temples and her heart. "It is nothing, Tucker. Come along. I can't wait to see how the red dress is coming."

While the seamstress poked and prodded, Jane stood quietly, smiling at the shopgirl occasionally. Marie held the package of pins and the tape measure, jumping each time she was addressed by the stern seamstress.

"Tucker, why don't you help Madam Lefevre pack her things? Marie can help me out of this," said Jane when they had finished. Tucker nodded and opened the door to the dressing room for Jane and the girl.

When they were alone, Jane said, "You must meet all of Madam Arnot's customers, Marie."

"Yes, madam, almost all of them."

"I suppose many of them now are English."

"That is also true, madam. If Madam will just step out of the skirt?"

Jane complied and asked, "Did you ever see a young lady named Miss Pettigrew?"

"I don't know, madam. There are so many strange English names."

Jane stepped into her blue morning gown. "You see, one of my cousins is in Paris, but I'm not certain where she is staying. Cherry is so thoughtless—"

"Did Madam say 'Cherry'?"

"Yes, have you seen her?" asked Jane eagerly.

"I believe that is what they called her. It seemed an odd name; that is why I remember it."

"Was she beautiful? Petite, blond, and blue-eyed?"

"Yes, that is she!" Marie began to rattle on as she buttoned up the back of Jane's gown. Jane listened in growing amazement. "She was with her aunt. Ah *non*, not an aunt. She called her Lady Pierce. I remember well, now. I was trying to decide who was related to whom. There were two other young ladies. One, I think, was Margery."

Jane whirled to face the girl. "Are you certain about who was with her?"

"Certainly, madam. It was only yesterday morning, not long after you had left. They were collecting their new gowns to wear to the great breakfast at the Palais de Versailles. They were going there straight from Madam Arnot's shop."

Jane held the girl's arm as she sank onto a nearby chair,

255

her legs shaking. She felt dazed by the news she had just heard. Cherry hadn't run away with Lord Pierce at all! She was, quite properly, under the unexceptional chaperonage of Lady Pierce. Her reputation was unblemished. While Jane's . . . ?

Jane began to laugh, a hysterical laugh that sent the young servant scurrying from the room. When Tucker hurried in, Jane was almost falling out of her chair, gasping for breath between bouts of silent giggling.

"She'll be all right. Sometimes things just strike her funny," explained Tucker to the bewildered Madam Lefevre and Marie. "If you've gotten everything, that'll be all."

When they were alone, Tucker said severely, "Here now, Miss Jane. You'll be having those two Frenchies believing all Englishwomen are mad."

"I'm sor—sorry . . . Tucker. . . . I simply couldn't help it. You'll never guess! Miss Cherry is with Lady Pierce, not Lord Pierce. She's done nothing wrong, at least, not in the eyes of society. All she is guilty of is disobeying her mama."

"That's wonderful, Miss Jane! Now we can get her and go home!" said Tucker thankfully.

"No, we can't just go and get her. How would I explain my presence here? I couldn't tell her the truth, and Cherry knows only too well that nothing short of a catastrophe could bring me to Paris when Heartland's Open Day is less than a month away. No, I'll just have to go home as anonymously as I came. Heavens, it will be good to get out of these blacks again!"

"Lord Devlin'll be glad, he will."

"Lord . . . ?" Jane sobered instantly. "Marie told me Cherry attended that breakfast, Tucker—the one Lord Devlin went to yesterday. But he told me she wasn't there."

"Maybe he just missed her. It was probably very crowded."

"Not that crowded. My God, Roland was right, right about everything." Jane sat as still as a statue while the enormity of her mistake permeated her mind. Just as a person whose loved one has died suddenly can feel no further pain beyond that one terrible fact, Jane was too shocked to feel anything yet.

"Miss Jane, Miss Jane! Please speak to me!" Tucker wailed.

Jane focused on her maid and smiled. "It's all right, Tucker. I'm fine. We must pack now. We're going home."

"Just the two of us, Miss Jane?"

"Of course. We'll be fine," said Jane, her voice becoming stronger, more decisive. "We have Jean-Luc to drive us back to the coast where we can spend the night. Jean-Luc's father will see to our passages for the packet. If the weather takes a turn for the better, we can be back in England by tomorrow night."

"But, Miss Jane, what about Lord Devlin? It seems a shame, after all he's done, to punish 'im for one little lie."

"Yes, for all he's done," murmured Jane, staring off into space again. "Very well, I shall leave him a note with Madam DuClaire. But she is not to give it to him until tomorrow morning. I've put up with all I intend to today. With a little luck, we'll be back in England before he realizes we have gone."

Tucker shook her head, a worried frown on her forehead. She would try one other device to stall her mistress's hasty retreat. "But Miss Jane, what about your new dresses? They won't be ready until tomorrow."

"True, I hadn't thought of that. I have it! I'll leave the payment for the dresses with Madam DuClaire, also. Then she can ship them to me at Heartland. You see? Everything is taken care of. Now, you go downstairs and tell Madam to have the carriage brought around in an hour. We should be packed by then."

Jane's preparations were interrupted a half-hour later with the unwelcome news that Roland wished to see her. Handing Tucker the gown she had been folding, Jane hurried downstairs.

"What is this I hear, Jane? Leaving Paris in such a hurry? Why?" Roland was enjoying acting the part of the concerned relative. He had been watching the house all morning. He'd seen Lord Devlin come and go; he had been pleased by the brevity of that visit. After the seamstresses left, he had watched a flurry of activity as a footman was sent to find Jean-Luc. How clever he felt to have guessed the reason Jane needed her young coachman.

"It's time to go home, Roland. Paris simply doesn't agree with me."

"But surely you're not traveling alone?"

"I have Tucker with me."

"A maid. Hardly protection."

"And my pistol," she added coldly, causing her cousin to shiver.

"Ah, good. I say, Jane, I hope I'm not being forward, but do you think I might go along—at least as far as London? I'm rather tired of Paris myself."

"I don't know. We're almost ready to leave." Jane hesitated. She didn't care for Roland, but sharing the carriage with him would give her someone to talk to and would also keep Tucker from becoming too inquisitive. And while she was conversing with him, she couldn't be thinking about . . . "How soon can you be ready?"

"I shall be back here within the hour."

"Never mind, we shall pick you up in a half-hour."

"Good! Here's my direction," he said, taking out a stubby pencil and scribbling on a soiled calling card.

♡   *Chapter Nine*   ♡

After Drew left Jane, he drove back to his hotel. What he had wanted more than anything on this rainy day was to spend some time with Jane. The long hours would have flown by in her arms. Instead, he was going to spend a lonely afternoon, just waiting for evening when he could return to Madam DuClaire's and see Jane.

The rain stopped late in the afternoon, and Drew left his hotel, making his way to a nearby wine shop. As he sipped the dry white wine, he watched the passing world through a single murky window. He grinned as a haughty young lady went storming past, a handsome youth on her heels, obviously begging her forgiveness for some transgression. Drew felt a spark of sympathy for the hapless man; it was rather like what he'd felt lately with Jane.

"Lord Devlin, we meet again."

Drew looked up sharply. "How was your journey, Tuttle?"

"Impossible! Utter tedium. You should have joined me as I suggested."

Drew smiled slightly, but made no comment. Tuttle stared at the empty chair, and Drew finally said, "Won't you be seated? I have an appointment in a moment, but we have time to share a glass of wine."

The fussy little man flipped up the long tails of his unfashionable coat and perched on the edge of the chair.

Just like a baby bird hoping for a worm, thought Drew.

"It seems everyone is in a rush to some appointment lately. Why, only yesterday, Mr. Havelock—" Drew came to attention at the mention of Jane's cousin, and Mr. Tuttle's eyes began to dance. "Do you know Havelock?"

"To a degree," said Drew.

"It is the same with me. We shared a bottle of wine at one of those charming outdoor cafés yesterday, but Havelock and I are not on intimate terms. Rather a sordid fellow, though I can't put my finger on it. Comes from a good family, though."

Drew nodded, pulling out his timepiece to check the hour. He wouldn't want to be late for his fictitious rendezvous.

"Actually, our conversation was about his family," continued Tuttle. "All of them are here, you know. Odd thing is, Miss Lindsay isn't staying with Miss Pettigrew. As far as I can tell, she, Miss Lindsay, is here on her own. Are you acquainted with Miss Lindsay?"

Drew reflected that Tuttle had an annoying habit of asking questions to which he seemed to have the answer already. Cautiously, he admitted, "I am acquainted with Miss Lindsay. My mother's home is in Bath, so I have met Miss Lindsay upon occasion."

"Ah yes, now I remember. You and Lady Cynthia were quite the talk of London after she danced with you three times at the Assembly in Bath."

Drew laughed. "I had no idea such trivial news would be worth repeating."

"Yes, indeed. A peer of the realm? You are always newsworthy, my dear Devlin. But the thing that intrigued me so very much, being somewhat a connoisseur of on-dits, was the news of your entrance at this same Assembly with a voluptuous beauty on your arm. My source was unable to put a name to the lady, but from his description, I would guess it was Miss Lindsay."

"Your source was probably correct. My mother and Miss Lindsay are quite the best of friends. Now, I really must go. Oh, tell me, Tuttle, where is Havelock staying? I'd rather avoid him."

"Of course. He has taken lodging on Rue de Havre, number six, I believe."

"Thank you."

"Just one more thing, Devlin. You never did tell me who your traveling companion to Paris was."

"No, I didn't, did I?" Drew nodded and walked slowly away.

He proceeded to Madam DuClaire's house by a circuitous route, entering by the back gate near the stables. He doubted that Tuttle had followed him, but he couldn't be too careful with Jane's reputation.

Drew had decided to tell Jane about Cherry immediately. They needed to leave Paris before the inquisitive Tuttle discovered their secret.

Drew entered by the kitchen door, startling Madam DuClaire, who was consulting with the cook.

"Bonjour, madam. It has turned into a fine evening, hasn't it?" he commented, removing his fashionable beaver hat.

"Yes, monsieur," replied the matron.

Drew frowned, wondering at her nervous state. "I have come to see Madam Davies."

"I am sorry, sir. She is ill and has asked that no one be admitted."

"Jane, ill? Has she sent for the doctor?"

"It was unnecessary; it was only the headache. She will be fine tomorrow. Her maid gave her laudanum. She will sleep through the night. Why don't you call again tomorrow?"

Drew looked uncertain. Madam DuClaire held her breath. She had liked the polite Anglaise, and the maid, as well. She didn't wish to lie to the handsome lord, but she had promised not to give him the note until morning.

Drew settled his hat back on his head. He went out through the kitchen door and stood for a moment in the yard, the fragrant scent of garden herbs filling the air. He turned, staring at the darkened upstairs windows, wishing he knew which was Jane's.

With a sigh of disappointment, he retraced his steps to the street to wend his way back to the Hotel St. Jacques. Once back in his room, he sent down for a deck of cards and a bottle of brandy. It seemed dulled senses and a game of patience would be his only company on this, his last evening in Paris.

The weather cooperated for the journey, and Jean-Luc made excellent progress on the main roads. Jane was tired but pleased when they reached Dieppe by ten o'clock. Jean-Francois greeted Jane warmly, looking past her for his friend Drew.

Jane quickly took the landlord aside and explained, "Lord Devlin decided to remain in Paris. My cousin agreed to escort me home. I would appreciate it, Monsieur DuClaire, if you wouldn't speak of me being here with Lord Devlin."

The shrewd Frenchman nodded after a moment. "I will put you in the same rooms as before. Fortunately, they are available. Do you desire a supper?"

"Yes, thank you, monsieur. We hope to set sail tomorrow, weather permitting."

"I will send Jean-Luc into Dieppe to purchase passage for you before breakfast in the morning."

They rejoined Roland, and Jane introduced him to the landlord.

Roland turned up his nose at Jean-Francois's extended hand and said haughtily, "Show us to our rooms immediately."

The landlord turned on his heel and led them up the narrow flight of steps.

When they were alone, Jane rounded on her cousin, saying, "Really, Roland, was it necessary to be rude? The French despise class distinctions. They held a revolution

262

about that very thing, you may remember."

"Yes, and then we beat them when they got out of hand," he retorted, examining the mantel and its figurines for dust. "Really, you would think these people could keep the rooms clean."

Jane shook her head and turned away in disgust; it was impossible to make him understand. When she looked back, he was exploring her bedroom, or rather the one she had occupied on the way to Paris.

"I'll take this room. There's only one window, and I am susceptible to drafts. You can have the other one; it's a corner room. It has three windows. I know you won't mind; you're so robust!" With that, he disappeared into his chosen room.

Jane toyed with the idea of storming in after him. But he would wonder at her vehement protests, and Jane didn't feel strong enough to answer his questions. Silently, she entered Drew's bedchamber. She wished she could laugh at such an absurd notion; after all, he had only spent one night in this chamber, she told herself, looking around the room. A small fire burned in the grate; it was a warm, inviting room. Her green eyes traveled to the bed where she had lain with Drew. She closed her eyes, swaying as she recalled the exquisite pleasure of his touch.

The door opened, and Tucker entered. Jane gave the maid a weary smile.

"Poor lamb, you're worn to the bone. I told Mr. DuClaire just to send up a tray to your room. You'll feel better once you're all tucked up in bed," crooned the maid, helping Jane off with her bonnet and gloves.

The maid, Jean-Francois's eldest daughter, struggled to open the sitting room door while balancing two trays precariously. Roland, hearing the noise, opened the door, saving one tray as it slid out of her grasp.

"Merci, monsieur!" exclaimed the girl, smiling at him.

"You're quite welcome, my dear. But what's this? Two trays?"

"Yes, monsieur. The maid requested one for madam's room. And here is yours, monsieur."

She set the heavy tray on a table and proceeded to lay the covers for one. With the girl's back to him, Roland slipped a small vial from the pocket of his scarlet brocade dressing gown and lifted the top off the pot of hot water on Jane's tray. Three, four, five drops. That should do it. Silently, he replaced the lid.

"Voilà, monsieur. I hope you enjoy your dinner."

Roland's thick lips formed a sweet smile. He was feeling good! Invincible! He reached for the girl and pulled her against him. Groping her backside, he lowered his head for a wet kiss. She cried out, struggling against him; he held her tighter still.

"Mr. Havelock!" growled Tucker indignantly, after shutting the door to Jane's room.

He released the frightened maid who fled the room.

"Just a bit of fun, Tucker."

"That child is not one of your village wenches! She is the landlord's daughter, and he is a respected businessman."

"And you, woman, forget yourself! Get out of here and take that tray with you! Next time you dare to question me, you'll feel the back of my hand!" He loomed over her, but Tucker never flinched. With great dignity and composure, the maid moved past him, picked up the tray and returned to Jane.

Less than an hour later, Jane was tucked into bed, her stomach full, her stiff limbs warmed and relaxed.

"Yer sure ye won't have some more tea?"

"No, it just doesn't taste right."

"It's th' way these Frenchies make it. They must use sweetened water in th' pot." Tucker blew out the last candle before she left. "Good night, Miss Jane."

"Good night, Tucker."

With the room bathed in mellow firelight, Jane was left alone in the soft bed. An aching loneliness settled over her. She wished she were a little girl again; things were simpler then. But now, even in the darkened privacy of her room, she struggled against the tears. Her eyes burned, and her temples throbbed, but she refused to give in to her despair.

It was the bed, she decided. Abruptly, Jane climbed off the thick mattress. Dragging the counterpane behind her, she curled up in the overstuffed chair by the fire. Mesmerized by the orange flames, she drifted off to sleep.

But Drew haunted her, even in her dreams. Jane was riding Sinbad across the green lawns at Heartland. Her hair streamed behind her, fanned by the cool breeze. Suddenly, in the distance, she saw another figure on horseback. It was Drew, calling her name as he came closer. Behind him were two other riders, slower than he because they rode ponies. Jane dismounted, waiting for Drew to pull up and jump to the ground. He took her in his warm embrace, kissing her tenderly until they were thrust apart by eager little hands. She looked down to see two dark-haired children, a boy and a girl. She knelt and put her arms around them, hugging them to her bosom. Drew laughed and pulled her to her feet, enfolding her with one strong arm while he picked up the little girl with the other. Jane tousled the dark hair of the boy, and he giggled.

Jane opened her eyes slowly; she focused on the windows, wondering if the dim light were moonlight or the beginnings of dawn. She realized she was back in bed, though she couldn't recall how she had gotten back there. She stretched, smiling as she recalled her dream. How, she wondered, could she have such a sweet dream about such a villain? How could she believe the terrible things Roland had told her? And yet, being a realist, Jane reflected that it was impossible not to believe her cousin.

Shivering, she reached out from under the thick coun-

265

terpane and took her grandmother's timepiece from the bedside table. Holding it up to the dim light, she read the time; it was six o'clock. Too early to expect her cousin to be awake. Resigning herself to an hour of inactivity, Jane burrowed back under the covers.

What she needed more than anything was to be back home. Once there, she would be able to make some sense of the confusion troubling her. At Heartland, she would find peace.

Drew was up early also, though he had no idea of the shock he was about to receive. He breakfasted in his room, then dressed hurriedly. It was only eight o'clock, but he wanted to reach Jane early, even if it meant waking her.

He settled his bill before stepping out into the crisp morning air. The sun was up, brightening the world as servants hurried along the streets, shopping bags under one arm. Drew tipped his hat to an industrious matron sweeping her front steps. He even whistled quietly, assured that such a lovely morning could only be the beginning of a wonderful day.

He tripped up the front steps of Madam DuClaire's house and beat a confident tattoo with the knocker. No back steps for him this morning; he and Jane would shortly be leaving Tuttle and his prying eyes behind.

"Yes, monsieur?" asked the downstairs maid as Drew walked past her.

"I wish to see Madam."

"Of course, monsieur." The maid hurried away and returned with Madam DuClaire.

Drew said, "I'm sorry, madam. I meant for the maid to get Madam Davies." Madam DuClaire looked very grave, and Drew asked anxiously, "What is it? Madam Davies hasn't taken a turn for the worse, has she?"

"No, monsieur. Please come into the salon. I have a note to give you."

Drew did as he was bade. Madam DuClaire watched as he digested the contents of Jane's note.

Dear Drew,
    I find that after many hours of reflection I must admit that I have mistaken my feelings for you. It would be unfair of me to pretend otherwise, so I have decided to return to Heartland without further interchange between us. I hope you will forgive my rather callous farewell, but I think it is for the best.
                                                Best Regards,
                                                        Jane

"When did she leave?" he asked, his voice hollow with resignation.

"Yesterday, monsieur. Madam was emphatic that I not give you the note until this morning. I hated having to deceive you last night. I'm sorry."

"Thank you, Madam DuClaire," he said, reaching into his pocket and producing his purse.

"Ah, *non!* I will accept nothing from you, monsieur. Perhaps Madam will come to her senses," said the romantic matron. Drew shook his head, and Madam DuClaire protested, "She is very much in love with you, monsieur. A woman can tell these things. If the other gentleman hadn't come—"

Drew's polite expression vanished, replaced by flaring nostrils and piercing brown eyes. "What gentleman?"

Madam DuClaire retreated a pace before the fierce Englishman. "A cousin, one of my maids said. He came to see her twice yesterday. Once at breakfast, and when he left, Madam was very distressed. Then he came again while she was packing to leave. I overheard them."

"What did this man look like?"

"He was a huge man, tall and big. He wore an unpleasant expression, as though he was smelling some old poultry."

"Havelock! Tell me, madam, it is of extreme importance. What did they talk about the second time?"

"The gentleman wanted to know why she was leaving. I don't remember what she told him, but he asked if he might go with her."

Drew took a deep breath, bracing himself for the horrible truth. "And she answered?"

"She said she would pick him up at his lodging on her way out of town. What is wrong, monsieur? You are as white as a ghost!"

"Pray God that that is not what I find. If he harms one hair—Exactly what time did they leave? Could they have reached your brother's inn last night?"

"Easily, monsieur. Jean-Luc was excited about the prospect of driving on the main roads. He was anxious to test himself and his horses. Wait, monsieur! You're going after her?"

"Yes, I'm going after her."

"I have a package you may give her. The dressmaker sent it over early this morning. You will see that Madam receives it?" she asked, handing him the large package.

"Yes. Tell me, madam, where can I hire the fastest team of horses?"

"At the hotel, monsieur, where you stayed."

"Thank you."

"Good luck, monsieur!" Madam DuClaire almost shouted as Drew rushed past and out the door.

Jane had little appetite for breakfast, and when they set sail on the choppy sea, she was feeling wretched indeed. Tucker, occupied with her mistress, forgot her own queasiness as she tried to make Jane comfortable.

By the time they landed at Brighton, it was evident that Jane was suffering from more than seasickness. As they disembarked, Roland hurried ahead to book them all rooms for the night.

Tucker, helping her feverish mistress along the crowded dock, muttered, "Like as not, 'e's absconding with th' money ye gave 'im for th' room."

"Nonsense, Tucker," Jane managed to say.

"Hmph! Well, ye'll notice 'e couldn't be bothered to find ye a carriage. Afraid yer catchin'. Just like a man!"

"Please, Tucker."

The maid suppressed further comments as she hailed a hackney and hustled her mistress into the musty carriage. Moments later, they were set down in the yard of the Ship's Inn. Tucker paid off the driver and followed Jane inside.

The same landlord showed them upstairs. In no time, Jane was smiling weakly at her maid before closing her eyes and falling into a restless sleep.

"How is she?" asked Roland several hours later. He glanced up from his empty plate and was surprised to see a look of loathing on the maid's face.

"She'll do, Mr. Havelock."

"Yes, but will she be ready to travel in the morning? I can't stay here forever!"

"Since it's Miss Jane's carriage and coachman, I don't think ye'll have much say in the matter. Tom Summers wouldn't think of setting off if Miss Jane's not fit."

"How noble of him," sneered Havelock.

Tucker said daringly, "Why don't you hire your own carriage and leave . . . sir?"

"I would, but I can't abandon my dear cousin when she is ill. Let me know when Jane wants to leave in the morning. I feel certain she will be well by then."

Tucker withdrew, neglecting to curtsey.

"Damned servant," muttered Roland. He sat back in his chair; it creaked under his weight. Slowly, he licked his fingers, savoring the feeling of repleteness.

Jane hadn't cooperated and died, but she was ill. That was some compensation for the risk he had taken in Dieppe. He would need to be careful; Jane was quite good with a pistol. He didn't dare confront her, especially with that pesky maid around.

Slowly, he smiled. Yes, he thought, an accident could be arranged after he had parted ways with her at Reading. That would soon take care of his dear, dear cousin — and her insolent maid as well!

But Devlin . . . Havelock sat up straight and glanced at the door as though this thought might produce the viscount in the flesh. Then he relaxed. Devlin couldn't possibly be in England yet. He would be waiting to cross the channel, probably on the morrow.

Roland decided abruptly that he would be forced to pay Jane a visit first thing in the morning. A word or two from him about Devlin following them would soon see Jane ordering out her carriage to continue their journey.

How fortunate Jane hadn't sent her coach and servants back to Heartland. Her carriage would be much more comfortable than a hired one. Of course, it was a shame the carriage would need to be damaged. But he could easily order a new one, a better one, when he had all the money from Heartland.

He wouldn't sell the estate, of course. There would be no need. And somehow, life would be even sweeter knowing he had deprived the cunning Lord Devlin of Jane and Heartland!

By morning, Jane was feeling better. She no longer had the fever or queasiness, though she remained weak. When Tucker came in with the breakfast tray, Jane was seated at the dressing table, daydreaming as she brushed her long hair.

She set the brush on the table and said, "Is my cousin awake yet? I want to reach Heartland tonight, so we must leave as quickly as possible."

"Yes, Miss Jane. I 'eard 'im bellowing for 'is breakfast not fifteen minutes ago. I think 'e's as anxious to be off as you are." The maid sighed.

"What is it, Tucker? You may speak freely with me."

"No, miss, I can't, for what I want to tell ye is not mine to tell. I just hope ye'll be careful and use your head. It could be the wickedness yer running from is closer than you think."

"Now, to what are you referring?"

"I can't say any more. But ye want to be careful who ye trust these days," said the maid enigmatically.

Jane decided to ignore Tucker's prophecies of doom and began to pick at her breakfast. A bite or two of biscuit, a cup of good English tea, and her stomach rumbled a protest. She pushed the tray away.

"I think I'll dress now, Tucker, and take a turn outside before being cooped up in that carriage all day."

"Just as you say, Miss Jane."

"It is so good to be back in England!" said Roland as the carriage rattled down the streets of Brighton.

"I must agree with you. Perhaps someday I would like to go back to the Continent, but not any time soon."

"I couldn't agree more!"

They fell silent, staring out their prospective sides of the carriage. Scattered houses gave way to green meadows, and Jane yawned.

"I have a deck of cards, Jane, if you'd care to pass the time with a friendly game of piquet — penny stakes, of course."

"What a good idea, Roland."

Roland's mouth started watering when Jane picked up her square jewelry case and placed it on the seat between them.

Jane laughed and commented, "I knew my medicine case would come in handy."

"Medicine?"

"Yes. It is meant for jewelry, but since I rarely travel, I use it for emergency medical equipment — bandages, bacillum powder, and such. I leave it in the carriage in case

271

there is an accident along the road."

"How clever of you," said Roland, beginning to deal the first hand.

They played for two hours. Jane knew that Roland was a terrible card player; if anything, she was worse. At the final tally, she owed him one pound six. He waved away her efforts to pay him.

"No, no, Jane. It is too gratifying to find someone worse with cards than I am. I wouldn't dream of taking your money. We'll have a rematch another time."

Jane was surprised at his magnanimous attitude. It was a side of her cousin she had never seen.

Roland smiled and put the cards away. "I suppose I'll be leaving you before long. We should be in Reading in an hour. I'll be able to hire a gig there and drive on to London. I appreciate your letting me tag along like this."

"It's been very pleasant, Roland."

He extended his smile to Tucker who was eyeing him with distrust.

The closer they came to London, the denser the population of houses. They left the main road at Leatherhead to swing southwest of London. By noon they were pulling into the yard of The Crown, one of Reading's best inns.

Tom Summers supervised the ostlers who came running out to unhitch the team while Jane was escorted to a room to freshen up.

Roland took a short stroll in the yard, seemingly uninterested in the bustling activity swirling around him. He stopped by the stable, pretending a great interest in the horses while he watched Tom Summers inspect the carriage. Next, the coachman spoke to the ostlers, assuring himself they would harness only the best team to his mistress's carriage when it was time to leave.

Then he and the groom entered the common tap for a bite to eat and a tumbler of French milk, a popular drink with the mailcoach guards. The milk was sweetened with a lump of sugar, two fingers of rum, and a hint of nutmeg grated on top.

Roland came into the tap room just as they were sitting down to their drink and a steaming dish of pigeon pie.

"Mind if I join you? At least for a drink."

"O' course not, Mr. Havelock," said Tom Summers respectfully. The young groom, not as adept at masking his feelings, glowered at the huge man. The coachman jabbed the youth with a boney elbow, making him more cheerful.

Roland took a long pull on the potent liquid and said, "I was hoping you'd do me a favor, Summers."

"Aye, sir," said the older man cautiously.

"Yes, you know I'm no judge of horseflesh. I was hoping you'd go out to the stables and pick out a decent team for me to drive to London. Nothing too racy, mind. I'm not as good with the ribbons as you are," Roland said with a self-deprecatory laugh.

"Be glad to, Mr. Havelock. What did you have in mind, a chaise and four, or just a pair?"

"Handling a pair is as high as I aspire, Summers. Thank you." Roland stood up and paid the reckoning for himself and the two servants.

Young James watched him leave with wide eyes. He shook his head in wonder and commented, "What d'ye think o' that, Mr. Summers? I never knew 'im t' be so polite and all."

"Nor 'ave I; still, it's no wonder," said the wise old man. "Just shows 'e knows 'ow t' behave if 'e wants somethin'."

When Jane entered the private parlor, Roland was already wiping his chin. He speared a last elusive bite, finishing this before he stood up.

"Must apologize for eating without you, Jane. I really

273

must be going. I don't drive as fast as your man, and though I've less distance to cover, I do want to be settled in some lodgings before dark. Besides, the thought of traveling across Hounslow Heath at dusk makes me shiver. I've no desire to make some highwayman's fortune."

"That's quite all right, Roland." She extended her hand, and he bowed over it. He held out a chair for her, choosing one that faced away from the yard.

"Good-bye, Jane. Thank you again for bringing me this far. Oh, I've already settled the reckoning for this and for your people, so don't let the landlord tell you otherwise," he advised.

"Thank you, Roland. How thoughtful of you. And remember, send me your direction when you get settled in London. I want to be sure you receive your invitation for Heartland's Open Day."

"I will!" he promised as he left the room.

Jane looked at the table before her; it was still overflowing with food. How odd that Roland had left her so much from which to choose. Perhaps he was sickening with the same fever she had had.

Jane selected her food carefully and was relieved she was able to consume a normal quantity. Evidently, whatever bothersome little illness she'd experienced was gone.

As she ate, she listened to the muffled shouts of coachmen and ostlers as carriages arrived and departed the busy inn. The noise was constant, rather like a gentle rainfall, almost lulling one to sleep. Her back to the window, she only listened. Watching such endless activity might have been tiring in itself.

It was into this sleepy atmosphere that a frantic Lord Devlin burst. The door flew open, slamming against the wall; the landlord shouted his protests; Drew and Jane stared at each other.

Drew's appearance was shocking. His driving coat with its modest quantity of capes was open, revealing a stained shirt. He had torn off his cravat and removed his

coat; his waistcoat hung open limply. His face was un-
shaven; his black hair was truly windswept.

Jane got to her feet; with a wave of one hand, she dispersed the landlord and the small knot of curious specta-
tors. Slowly, she walked to the door. Drew watched in
silence as she shut it.

"You look terrible," she said bluntly.

"You're looking a trifle pale yourself," he answered.

"I've been ill," she said simply.

He walked to the table and sat down, helping himself
to a dish of kidney pie. Jane watched as he devoured the
remainder of it, draining her cup of tea to wash it down.

"Where's Havelock?" he asked finally.

To Jane, who had no knowledge of Drew's suspicions
about her cousin, his question meant only one thing.
Drew had been blackmailing Roland and finally wanted
revenge.

"He's already gone." Jane was surprised how calmly she
spoke.

"Are you all right? He didn't do anything to hurt you?"

"Hurt me?" asked Jane, her voice rising slightly. Oh
no! she wanted to shout. He only told me the truth—a
truth so painful I will never trust another man again! Instead, she said flatly, "No, he didn't hurt me."

Drew's relief was so great, he buried his face in his
hands. He looked so vulnerable, so rumpled and dear.
Jane wished with all her heart she could go to him, but
knowing what he had done, she couldn't allow herself to
take one step closer. He raised his head.

"I have been traveling since yesterday morning to get
here in time. Now I find you well and apparently out of
danger. It makes me feel foolish, Jane."

"I don't know why you would do such a thing. Didn't
Madam DuClaire give you my note?"

"Yes, I got that piece of rubbish. I must have read it a
hundred times during the night while crossing the Channel."

"You crossed at night?" she asked, distracted by this

particular revelation.

"Yes, at night. Had to give Jean-Francois's friend a bloody fortune to take me over!"

"That is unfortunate. At least, you are here, though I'm not sure I understand why."

"Not understand? The devil, you say!" He reached into his pocket and flung a grimy, crumpled scrap of paper onto the table. "And how was I supposed to feel when I read this? Well, let me tell you, Miss Lindsay, I felt bloody awful! And then to find out you're traveling with that snake in the grass!"

Jane put her hand to her ears and screamed, "STOP!"

The silence following this eruption was deafening; even the carriages in the yard were still for a moment. Jane listened, appalled at her freakish outburst. The usual inn sounds resumed, and she expelled a pent-up breath.

Drew stood up and began walking in her direction. Jane circled behind a chair and warned, "I shall scream if you touch me."

"Do you think I care what people will think?"

She knew he meant it; he had no respect for society's opinion. But she did. "You profess to care for my opinion. I can't bear the thought of you touching me."

He winced, but he moved farther away.

"I have reason to believe Havelock may have been trying to kill you."

Jane gripped the back of the chair and shook her head.

"It's true. The accident at the abbey, the shelf in larder, all of that."

Jane circled the chair and sat down; she covered her face with her hands and her shoulders began to shake. Drew took a step toward her, then stopped. She didn't want him to comfort her.

"Jane, I realize it may be hard for you to think a relative capable of this, but he is a desperate man; he will do anything to get his hands on Heartland."

She raised her face. He expected to see tears; instead,

Jane was laughing. This was more frightening than tears.

Between spasms of laughter, she gasped, "The most amusing thing, Drew, is that he says the same thing about you!"

She continued to laugh, and Drew waited patiently for her to regain control.

"Jane, you know I wouldn't lie to you."

"Do I? How? You've been sending me those silly notes and lying about it. They nearly drove me crazy, especially when I realized Cherry wasn't behind them. You must have known they would upset me. I'm hardly the type to have a secret admirer."

"You are exactly the type, with that frigid facade you put on for the world."

"You do have a way with words, Lord Devlin." He watched her walk toward the door. She opened it, holding it open for him to pass. "You'll forgive me if I don't fall into your arms this time, Lord Devlin. I fear I've had enough of men and passions to last me a lifetime."

"But Jane . . ."

She shook her head, and Drew realized suddenly it was useless. He might persuade her, but somewhere, deep inside, she would always wonder. He didn't want a wife who couldn't trust him implicitly.

He strode past Jane and out into the yard. He found Tom Summers by the carriage where they were harnessing a new team. One of the new horses was proving restless. He reared, moving back and forth in the traces. Standing beside the carriage, Drew heard a strange cracking sound.

He bent down, looking carefully at the tongue of the vehicle. Not wanting to sound a general alarm, Drew called to Jane's coachman.

"Yes, my lord?"

"Summers, I think you better check the carriage. Looks as though someone has tampered with it."

"Impossible, my lord. Except for a quick bite, either me or James has been watching the carriage," replied the old man indignantly. Nevertheless, he, too, bent to inspect the tongue. He straightened up and shouted, "Here, you! Get that horse out of harness!"

"Wot's yer problem, mister?" yelled one of the ostlers.

"Get that beast out o' th' way, I says. There's somewhat wrong wi' the carriage." Drew, Summers, and young James inspected the wooden tongue. Summers shook his head. "This here tongue's been cut. See where the ax took out chips of wood?"

"Who'd do such a thing?" asked James.

"Who, indeed?" said Drew quietly.

They stood up. "Mr. Havelock," whispered James, not realizing he was voicing the thoughts of his two companions. "That's why 'e was being so nice. 'E wanted to get you an' me away from th' carriage and into the stables!"

"You're no doubt right, my boy, but I don't think your mistress is in any mood to hear such a tale at this moment."

"So ye'll just keep mum about it, d'ye hear?" said Summers.

"O' course, Mr. Summers. I wouldn't upset Miss Lindsay for the world," said the young man stoutly.

"Good," said Drew. "I must prove to myself whether our suspicions are correct. Did either of you see Mr. Havelock leave? Did he go in the direction of London?"

"Yes, my lord. 'E might double back, if 'e was wishful to see if 'is dirty work paid off. With a cut like this, 'twould probably hold past Newbury. It's flat going till after that. 'Twould take some pulling and lunging, like up a 'ill t' make it break in two."

"In other words, the tongue would snap where it would do the most harm."

"Aye," said Summers slowly. "When ye catch that young beggar, m'lord, give 'im one for me."

"I'll give him several for all of us," promised Drew. "You may as well let them repair this, Summers. That way, if Havelock intended to backtrack and intercept you, he'll wonder what's become of you."

"Then 'e would end up 'ere."

"True, and I've no worry but you'd know how to handle him. Just keep a close watch on your mistress—now and later. When I meet Mr. Havelock, I intend to persuade him—forcefully, if I'm lucky—to leave the country again. This time, for good."

"Amen to that, m'lord." Drew's rented phaeton was brought into the yard with two fresh horses. He swung up easily and waved to his two coconspirators. "Good luck t' ye, m'lord!" called Tom Summers.

Jane watched this exchange with interest from the darkened doorway of the inn. When Drew was out of sight, she joined her coachman beside the damaged carriage.

"What's the problem, Summers?"

"Just a bit o' trouble wi' th' carriage, miss. Don't you worry about it. It'll delay us 'bout an hour; we may 'ave t' put up for th' night somewhere, but we'll put most o' th' ground between 'ere and 'ome behind us before nightfall, never you fear."

"What happened to it?" asked Jane, peering past the coachman.

"Just a weakness in th' tongue, miss."

"May I see it?" she demanded. He stood aside. Jane, who was as knowledgable as most men about carriages and horses, took only a quick glance to determine that someone had tampered with the vehicle. She turned to her coachman. "When did this happen? Is it possible Lord Devlin had access to the carriage while you were eating?"

"Lord Devlin?" asked the incredulous groom.

"James!" warned the older man.

"But Mr. Summers! If 't weren't for Lord Devlin, we might never 'ave seen the thing! We'd 'a been killed!"

"I'm sorry, Miss Lindsay, but what th' boy says is true. Lord Devlin thinks it might 'o been done by yer cousin."

"Yes, he would think that," murmured Jane. "Do whatever you must to get us on our way, Summers."

Jane wandered back inside; she returned to the private parlor, her thoughts uncomfortable company in view of all that had passed.

Perhaps she had been too hasty, and yet, she was too weary to try and make sense of all that had happened. If Drew were to be believed, she had been traveling with a man who wanted her dead. Then why hadn't Roland tried to kill her somewhere along the road?

She had no answer to this question, except the unpalatable thought that Drew should not be believed. Oh, perhaps Roland had been partially correct. Perhaps Drew had wanted Heartland so badly that he would consider marriage to its mistress. But that fact held no comfort for her. To marry a man whose true object of desire was her estate? Never!

"Miss Jane, the landlord wondered if you'd like a room upstairs to rest in until our carriage is fixed," said Tucker, poking her head in the parlor's door.

"No, Tucker, I'll just wait here."

"Miss Jane?"

"Yes."

"About Lord Devlin . . ."

"Tucker, I know you are partial to his lordship, but I'd rather not discuss either him or my cousin, not now, not ever."

"As you wish, Miss Jane."

"Just call me when the carriage is ready to go."

♡ *Chapter Ten* ♡

Drew pushed his cattle as fast as possible. He knew Havelock was a ham-fisted driver, so he felt certain he could overtake the man. But he failed to take into account Havelock's cowardice. The last thing Roland Havelock wanted was to have Drew Devlin catch up to him, so he drove his team as he'd never driven one before.

Havelock reached London by four o' clock and soon had secured lodgings at a modest boarding house near St. James Street. He sent the carriage to a nearby inn which agreed to return them to The Crown in Reading. Next, he changed his coat and made his way out of doors, determined to enter the first gambling den he came across.

"Why the hurry?" asked a smooth voice from behind.

Havelock wheeled to face his nemesis, his beady eyes bulging in their sockets.

"Devlin! How the devil . . . ?"

"That's how I earned the nickname, Havelock. Always turning up at the most devilish moment."

Roland Havelock looked to his left — a dark alley lay that way. To his right? A busy street. He took a step back, preparing to flee.

"Not so fast, old boy," drawled Drew, grabbing the mountainous man by his lapels.

"Here now, Devlin," protested Havelock.

"Precisely. Here and now," replied Drew with a deadly calm. Exhibiting a physical strength that had frightened much braver men, Drew yanked Havelock into the alley and threw him against the brick building, making the big man's teeth rattle.

"What do you want of me?" Havelock squeaked.

"A bit of truth and a promise." Drew pulled a pistol from his pocket and stepped away from Havelock, keeping the firearm leveled at his prisoner's ample girth. "Tell me all you have done to Jane; tell me how you've tried to kill her."

"You're mad, Devlin!" cried Jane's cousin. "Why would I do such a thing?"

"We both know why, though I regret having to admit I probably put the idea in your head."

"So you admit to being a party—"

"I only admit that I didn't realize how dangerous you would become. Now, tell me." Drew could see Havelock's brain churning, wondering exactly what Drew already knew. He would be loathe to admit anything he didn't have to.

"Actually, it wasn't all that much. Just a scare or two."

"Tell me," barked the viscount.

"Well, Sims did most of it," whined Havelock. Then he added with acerbity, "But he never succeeded."

"Ah, yes, Sims. He was responsible for the larder shelf. And the abbey stones?"

"That was Sims, too!"

"But your hands are not entirely pristine, are they? The chocolates?" Drew was fishing now; he had never been convinced there had been anything wrong with that box of sweets. The moon came out from behind the clouds, its light falling on Havelock's face. The man was obviously in the agony of indecision. Drew waved the pistol and demanded, "Well?"

"All right! Yes! Yes, I poisoned the chocolates and the tea, as well! Just let me go, Devlin! Please! I'll leave the country, anything!"

"The tea? Now that would have been . . . ?"

Too late had Havelock recognized his mistake. Devlin

hadn't known about the tea. But it didn't matter now, thought the big man, nothing did except escaping from this man and his pistol. Havelock's shoulders sagged and he confessed, "In Dieppe, but I gather Jane didn't like the taste of it. She must not have drunk it, except a little; she only became ill."

Hearing the details, Drew wanted to pull the trigger, ridding the world of one of its evildoers. Instead, he said coolly, "And then we come to the carriage."

Roland Havelock's head jerked up; he had counted on Drew not being aware of his latest attempt. Until that very moment, Havelock had clung to the hope that even as he spoke, his cousin might be lying dead in a ditch. Now, all was well and truly lost. Jane would live; his mother would never inherit Heartland, and its income was lost to him forever.

He nodded and said, "Yes, and the carriage."

"One more thing, Havelock."

"No! I swear! There was nothing else!"

"I beg to differ. Where did you get rid of the Heartland pendant?"

"I . . . I don't know what you're talking about now! The last time I saw it, it was on the table beside Jane in the gold salon."

"You'll forgive me if I wonder why you would bother to remember such a trivial detail."

Havelock was panting like a trapped animal. Those beady eyes slid back and forth searching for an escape that would not materialize.

Drew cocked the pistol. "I am always amazed at the hair triggers the gunsmiths put on these dueling pieces."

Havelock wiped his brow on the sleeve of his coat, staring at the pistol all the while. Finally, he began to tremble and confessed. "Fleet Street. Number twenty-three. But it won't be there anymore!"

"You had better pray that it is," said Drew. He yanked the cravat from Havelock's neck and tied his prisoner's fleshy hands behind his back, securing it to a pipe that ran

283

the length of the building. Then he pulled out his own handkerchief and gagged him.

"Now I will send word to a couple of friends about where to find you. They are sailors on one of my ships. They will take you on a healthful sea voyage to the Americas. Try to be thankful for this because I promise you, if I ever set eyes on you again, I will gladly put a bullet through your temple."

With this, Drew left. He made his way to the shipyards and arranged Havelock's voyage. Next, he went to the nearest posting inn. Here, he hired a fresh pair and turned his rented phaeton back toward Bath.

He changed teams at The Crown in Reading and continued on to Newbury. Here, his inquiry brought the news that Jane's carriage had passed some three hours earlier. Waving his thanks to the young ostler in the yard, Drew continued on until he reached the George Inn in Hungerford.

It was after midnight, but the ostlers in the yard were quick to come running as he halted his phaeton.

"Will ye be stayin' th' night, sir?"

"Yes. Tell me, did a lady and her maid stop here several hours ago? Her old coachman was driving."

"Aye, sir. Ye'd be thinkin' on Miss Lindsay of Heartland, Bath."

"Yes, that's the one," said Drew eagerly.

"Aye, they stopped an' stayed, sir."

Drew threw the young man a coin and hurried inside.

He was greeted by a rather sleepy landlord who was anxious only to return to his bed. Still, the proprietor knew quality when he saw it. He perked up more upon learning that his late-night arrival was a peer.

He lighted Drew upstairs and showed him to a room. Lighting several candles, he apologized for its meager size.

"It's fine. Tell me, where is Miss Lindsay's room?" asked Drew.

"Now, m'lord, I don't hold with. . . ." He winked and pocketed the gold crown Drew had slipped into his out-thrust palm. "Last room on the left at the end of the hall, m'lord."

Drew waited until the landlord had shuffled back down the steps. Then he changed his riding boots for slippers and eased out of the room and down the hall, a single candle providing a small pool of light.

Damn the foolish chit! he thought as he tried the door and found it unlocked. Jane must have lost her mind! A solitary female traveler to be so trusting in a public inn.

Silently, he crossed the bare floor; he raised the candle to light the bed; yes, that was Jane's long, glorious hair fanned out across the pillow. He set the candlestick on the bedside table. Leaning over the bed, Drew whispered, "Jane, wake up."

Jane stirred, groaning as the horror of her nightmare hit her. Drew had been in it; Roland, too. She was torn between them . . . Jane heard someone calling to her; she told herself to open her eyes, but she was so very tired.

"Jane!"

Drew! It was Drew! She opened her eyes. The shadowy candlelight lent his face a ghoulish cast. Closing her eyes, Jane reached beneath the pillow. She sat up, shoving the ghoul away with one hand while she produced her tiny silver pistol and fired.

Drew staggered back; one hand flew up to cover his cheek. His voice strangely clear, he said, "Why does the woman I love want to shoot me?"

He collapsed onto the floor as the padding of bare, running feet ended with the door being flung open. Tucker, candle in hand, pushed past the inn's interested occupants.

"Miss! Sweet Lord! It's his lordship!" she breathed.

The landlord, shocked rudely awake this time, elbowed his way inside, a wide-eyed maid following in his wake. He knelt beside the fallen viscount, made sure he was still breathing, and clambered back up on his feet. "An accident, my dear patrons, a mere accident!" announced the landlord loudly, his deep voice restoring normalcy to the nightmarish scene. He shut the door and the knot of people dispersed. Quickly, he lighted all the candles he could find.

Jane, who had been frozen since the gun discharged, came back to life, dropping the weapon and beginning to shiver. "Is . . . is . . . he . . . dead?" she asked, her teeth chattering.

Tucker glanced up from her position on the floor. Her white nightcap was soaked with blood where she pressed it against the side of Drew's head. "No, Miss Jane, not dead."

"But . . . the . . . blood?"

"Head wounds always bleed mortal bad."

"What happened, Miss Lindsay? This man arrived not more than twenty minutes ago. He claimed to be Lord Devlin."

"And so he is," said Jane, regaining her sense of competency. "You must send for the doctor immediately."

The landlord nodded to the silent servant who hurried from the room.

"We'll need to get him into bed," said Jane doubtfully. She stood up and pulled on her wrapper.

"His room is down the hall, miss," said the landlord, who was also judging the wounded man's weight against his own strength.

"It would take an army to carry him all that way," said Jane. "We'll put him in my bed."

"Very good, miss." With Tucker continuing to staunch the flow of blood, Jane and the landlord pushed and pulled until they had Drew settled in bed. Tucker lifted the cloth, but the bleeding continued.

"Miss Jane, send someone t' th' carriage for th' medicine case."

"In a trice, Miss Lindsay," responded the landlord.

By the time the doctor arrived, the bleeding had stopped. The physician cleaned and examined the narrow, ugly gash that ran along one side of Drew's head.

"He'll do. I'll just bandage his head again. He'll be fine in a day or two, though he may have a headache. He's a very lucky man. A half-inch to the right and he would be blind, or dead."

Jane shut her eyes and sent up a small prayer of thanksgiving. The doctor departed, and Jane sent Tucker away to get whatever rest she could for the remainder of the night.

Jane pulled a chair over to the bed and sat down. She stared at Drew, willing him to wake up, if only for a moment.

Why had he been in her room? Had he followed her all this way, waiting for dark when she would be asleep so he could come into her room and smother her? What had he wanted? That awful nightmare she had been having had clouded her sound judgement. If she had been completely awake, she wouldn't have shot him. Would she? And so, the question remained: what was he doing at this particular inn, inside her room?

With a sigh, Jane admitted she would never know the answer to this question. She would always doubt her ability to discern truth from prevarication when listening to a man, especially when her heart was engaged.

Oh! And it was definitely engaged, she concluded, her soul filled with despair. She was in love with this fierce, unconventional man! But where there was no trust, love would moulder and die.

The sun rose. Outside, it would be another beautiful day. Her eyes red from lack of sleep, Jane sat by the bed, waiting.

Drew opened his eyes, wincing at the discomfort this caused him. He focused on the blurry figure by his side. It was Jane, her troubled green eyes never faltering.

"The doctor says you'll soon be fit again." Jane's voice was devoid of emotion.

"That's certainly good to know." He watched her a moment longer before saying resignedly, "It's over, isn't it, Jane? We both must admit it and get on with our lives. I can see it in your eyes. I had hoped . . . But last night proved to me—rather forcefully—" he added, a glimmer of a smile lighting his eyes, "that we can never again completely trust each other. Thank you for staying with me through the night." He raised up on one elbow and extended his hand for her to shake. Jane looked at it for a moment before putting her hand in his. One firm shake of the hand, and he released her.

Without another word, Jane left the room.

Tucker came in twenty minutes later to collect Jane's clothing. She flashed the viscount a look of frustration, but said nothing.

After helping Jane dress, Tucker hurried back to Drew's bedside for a brief farewell. "Now then, m' lord, I only 'ave a moment before we leave. D'you need anything?"

"No . . . yes! My valet. Tell him to come here and bring my groom, my curricle and team, my clothes. Just everything. I'm going back to London from here."

"Very good, m'lord." Tucker turned as she heard Jane call her from the yard.

"And Tucker, tell our confederates that I've taken care that Mr. Havelock is out of the country. Still, I'll feel better knowing you, Pipkin, and Mrs. Brown are keeping an eye on her."

"God bless you, m'lord!" said the tearful servant, taking his proffered hand and pressing it warmly.

Jane's carriage entered the front gate of Heartland in the late afternoon; Tom Summers sounded his yard of tin to announce their arrival. Jane eagerly peered out the carriage window, anxious for that first glimpse of home. There it was, like a haven of peace! She sat back in the seat, folding her hands in her lap very properly.

Tucker, watching Jane through half-closed eyes, wondered what strange thoughts went on inside her mistress's head. Here they were, returning after a week spent on a wild goose chase, during which Miss Jane had become betrothed (albeit unofficially), then unbetrothed, and had finally ended by shooting her former fiancé. And there she sat, as prim as a preacher, seemingly untouched by any of her adventures.

Jane's next words seemed to bear out Tucker's thought. "Remind me, Tucker, to send for extra domestics to help clean in the next two weeks. And, of course, I must send out the invitations tomorrow. I fear it will be a late night."

"Yes, Miss Jane," said the maid, her amazement at her mistress's imperturbation growing by the minute.

"But first, it is imperative that I send a note to Aunt Sophie. I must set her mind at ease. Then I can resume my preparations for our Open Day celebration."

The carriage stopped and James let down the steps and opened the door. As Jane descended from the carriage, she smiled. Not only could she feel the house welcoming her, but Pipkin had assembled most of the first-floor staff by the front door.

"Welcome home, Miss Jane," intoned the butler.

"Thank you, Pipkin. I am so delighted to be home," said Jane.

Pipkin bowed his head and said, " 'Go home to thy friends, and tell them how great things the Lord hath done for thee, and hath had compassion on thee,' said our Lord."

Jane grinned; it was good to be back home where she belonged! As she entered the house, a feeling of contentment settled over her. She made her way upstairs, lingering at the landing to look down at the marble entry with its crystal chandelier.

Mickey followed, loaded down with her things; he waited patiently for her to proceed.

Jane turned to him and asked, "Did you miss me, Mickey?"

"Yes, Miss Jane."

"I missed everyone here, too." She noticed a large, unfamiliar box he carried. "Where did that come from, Mickey?"

"Th' boot, Miss Jane, along o' all th' rest."

Jane continued up the stairs to her room. When Mickey had put down his burdens, Jane said, "Go and ask Mr.

Summers who put this box in the boot of the carriage."

"Yes, Miss Jane."

Jane placed the plain box on the bed and opened it. The red dress! And the others, too! But how? She picked up the deep red evening gown and held it against her. How excited she had been at the prospect of wearing the daring dress for Drew. Jane walked over to the cheval glass to study her reflection. It would be every bit as revealing and appealing as she had hoped. Abruptly, she returned it to the box. The other dresses she would wear, but not the red one; it had been made for someone else, someone who was alluring and exciting—not plain Miss Lindsay.

"Miss Jane?"

"Yes, Mickey?"

"Mr. Summers says Lord Devlin gave 'im th' box t' put in th' carriage."

"I see. Thank you, Mickey."

"You're welcome, Miss Jane." The footman lingered and said, "Miss Jane?"

"Yes," sniffed Jane.

"You're not goin' away again, are you?"

"No, Mickey, I'll not be going away."

Jane slept like a baby, her spirit untroubled by dreams, either good or bad, such was the influence of being at home.

She had not written out invitations the night before, being too tired, so she rose early, spending the morning at her escritoire penning invitations to all of her acquaintances, from the dowager duchess of Wentworth to the poorest family in the village. Sending these off with Mickey, she returned to her writing desk and wrote several more invitations, one of which was to her old school friend, Sally.

Sally hadn't made an appearance at Open Day for several years due to babies and other family obligations. But perhaps this year she would come. Jane hoped so; she

290

would dearly love to have a long, comfortable coze with the gay and worldly Sally Cumberland. Perhaps Sally could advise her. . . . No, Jane told herself, she needed no advice. She was managing superbly on her own. Still, it would be wonderful to see Sally again.

Despite the physician's recommendation to Drew that he rest for two or three days before returning to London, Drew left the inn the next morning. His head continued to ache, but his vision had cleared.

Most of the *ton* had already left for country homes or the seashore, so Drew had no difficulty securing rooms on Bond Street. The rooms were not elegant, but would do until he found something permanent. He had decided to make London his home, and if his mother wished to see him, she could come for a visit.

Though his head was aching abominably by evening, Drew decided to go out to his club. He was dressed impeccably, his cravat and coat pressed to a nicety by his finicky valet Crispin. His dark hair had been carefully arranged to cover the healing wound.

After entering White's, Drew nodded Mr. Ambrose, bowed to Sir Thomas, and finally settled across from Lord Wharton for a few hands of piquet.

Sir Thomas stopped by Drew's table and said, "Didn't know you were back in London, Devlin. Here for a long stay?"

"Yes, as a matter of fact, I'm planning to purchase a house once I find one that is suitable."

"Why would you want to do that, my boy? Your uncle's got a perfectly good town house on Grosvenor Square. They don't get any more suitable than that."

"True, but that is his house," said Drew, continuing his play.

"So what? He's got an agent in the city. Go to him and get the key. Lord knows your uncle will never know."

Lord Wharton placed his cards on the table, pushed

back in his chair, and said slowly, "He's right, you know. Besides, it'll be yours soon enough. The man must be over seventy if he's a day!"

"I'll think about it," promised Drew.

"You do that," said Sir Thomas. "And since you're staying in town, I'll tell my wife you're here. She'll get the word around in no time. All the hostesses are crying for eligible men at this time of year. By tomorrow, I predict you'll be up to your ears in invitations!"

"That's kind of you, Sir Thomas."

"Think nothing of it. Good evening."

Lord Wharton nodded to himself before observing, "Now that the Season's over, my wife encourages me to invite my political friends to the house. Keeps us from getting dull, don't you see. We get into some rather heated discussions from time to time, but if you'd care to come, I know Lady Wharton would be delighted."

"Thank you, Wharton. I should like that very much. As a matter of fact, one of these days I plan to sit in the House of Lords."

"Really, Devlin! Most interesting, most interesting. How do you stand on the Corn Laws?"

Drew slept later than he had planned. A moderate drinker as a rule, he had taken wine too often with the hard-headed Lord Wharton. Sitting on the edge of the bed, he cradled his head as Crispin pulled back the window curtains. Drew silently promised himself he would refrain ever after from trying to "keep up" with any politician.

"Your coffee, my lord," said the very proper valet.

"Hmm." Drew took the cup and saucer and took a quick gulp of the strong, hot liquid. Better, he decided after a moment; he then continued to down the fortifying brew.

With his wiry tiger Piglet hanging on the back of his curricle, Drew drove into the city. Farther and farther he went until he reached Fleet Street, Number twenty-three.

When he entered the pawn shop, a dignified older man came forward. He was dressed like a respectable lawyer, though the fabric of his clothing was frayed.

"My name is Mr. Armstrong. What may I do for you, sir?"

"Mr. Armstrong, I am looking for a piece of jewelry, something for a lady of my acquaintance."

"I have many beautiful things."

"My friend is particularly fond of rubies—large rubies. You see, I would like to prove to her that my heart is truly engaged."

"I see, I see." The man hesitated. Clearly, he was on the horns of a dilemma. It was obvious to Drew that the shop-keeper did know about the Heartland pendant. He must still have it, but he was afraid of being caught selling stolen goods. Drew could see him vacillating as he weighed one side against the other.

Finally, greed won.

"I believe I have just the thing." The dapper old man vanished into his back room. He emerged moments later clutching a velvet box. With a flourish, he opened it.

There it was! The Heartland pendant. He hadn't sold it because he hadn't dared. There wasn't another like it in the world.

"How much?" asked Drew, lifting the heavy pendant and turning it this way and that.

"It is very valuable, sir. Only notice the size of the heart-shaped ruby in the middle of the setting. And the diamonds surrounding it? There are at least twenty."

"Agreed. How much?"

The man took the pendant and studied it thoughtfully before returning it to the box. "Let me think, Mr. . . . ?"

"It's 'my lord,'" said Drew. "Not 'mister.'"

"My . . . my lord?" The shopkeeper's boney fingers closed around the velvet box. Drew grabbed the hand, forcing the man to drop the box.

"Tell me how much, Mr. Armstrong. But remember, I could easily arrange for Bow Street to come here and take

293

an inventory. That would prove most enlightening. Now, Mr. Armstrong, you were saying?"

"Fi—five thousand," stuttered the old man.

"One," countered Drew.

"One? But I paid—"

"Then make it two thousand. I am weary of all this bartering."

"Very well, my lord, you win. Two thousand it is!"

Drew left the pawn shop and went straight to his bank. With a sigh of relief, he gave the pendant over to the safekeeping of one of the senior partners. When his mother came to London for a visit, he would let her return it to Bath and its rightful owner.

The two weeks until Open Day flew by. Jane was tempted several times to postpone the entire event, but she had managed to accomplish all that needed to be done.

Aunt Sophie had returned within a few days after receiving Jane's missive. Cherry arrived a week before the festivities. She received a chilly greeting from her mother, but they were both too good-natured for it to last. Cherry produced a charming, rose-colored dress from her trunk and presented it to her mother, who was very shortly hugging her daughter and exclaiming over every ribbon and flounce on Cherry's new Parisian wardrobe.

Jane was hurrying along the upstairs hall when Cherry called to her. "Jane, please come here; I have a present for you, too."

"How thoughtful of you, Cherry," said Jane as she unwrapped the package; inside laid a beautiful comb and brush with handles carved out of a delicate crystal. "They are beautiful, Cherry! Thank you so much!"

Cherry's face lit up like a sunbeam. "I'm so glad! It took me days to decide what to get you, Jane. I knew our tastes were dissimilar in fashions, so I didn't want to choose something you would consider hideous. And though you love to read, a book seemed too impersonal. Then I saw these. You have such beautiful hair, I knew they were perfect for you!"

"Thank you, Cherry, for the brush and comb, as well as the compliment." Jane's eyes suddenly filled with tears, and she quickly excused herself. Shutting the door to her own room, she indulged in a fit of crying. When the tears had been spent, she bathed her face and picked up her schedule of tasks.

The day before the gala event, Jane received a letter from her friend Sally. Jane had hoped Sally would simply arrive on her doorstep since she had yet to receive a letter of regrets. But as she read, she discovered she was doomed to disappointment.

Dearest Jane,

I must apologize for waiting so long to reply to your kind invitation, but I was so hoping I could come for a visit. Little Andrew has had the chicken pox, so I was waiting to make sure he was recovered enough for his mommy to leave him. Yesterday, I decided he was indeed restored to health after he took his pony out for a ride without permission — in the streets of London, if you please! His father says the boy is like me!

So, I had the maid pack my clothes while I tended to the hundred and one last details. Then I went to my room to dress. I sat down before the glass and looked at my face. I saw six red dots on my cheeks! Chicken pox! Can you imagine? Let me tell you it is not amusing! I have spent the morning trying not to scratch, but it is impossible! And, my dear Jane, they appear in the most *shocking* places!

So, I fear Heartland will be forced to have its Open Day without me. But enough about my ailment. I'm beginning to sound like my great-aunt Penelope.

Now, I must catch you up on all the latest on-dits. First of all (since you wrote me not long ago to inquire into the gentleman's background), you'll be interested to know that the former Lord Devlin is now earl of Cheswick. He and his mother are on their way to York even as I write.

Also, do you remember Geraldine, that hateful, red-haired girl at school? You'll never guess who she has just married! A bishop, no less! It seems that . . .

Jane finished reading the letter quickly. To be sure, she told herself, the only fact that interested and distressed her was that Sally wasn't coming. And Mrs. Peterson? Her journey to York explained why Jane hadn't received a response to that invitation. She was relieved to know it wasn't because Drew's mother had discovered Jane tried to kill her son!

Still, Open Day had lost some of its sparkle for her. Sally's silliness and *esprit de vivre* made everyone feel like laughing. Without her, Jane would just be the most proper Miss Lindsay. And while she would be hostess to a veritable army, she would still be alone.

Finally the big day came. The guests began arriving in the morning. Jane wore one of her Parisian gowns, a pale peach crepe. When Cherry saw it, she exclaimed over its cut, demanding to know if Jane had discovered a new dressmaker in Bath.

Jane smiled enigmatically. "No, Cherry, I still patronize Mrs. Warner's shop." That was true enough. She had been in Bath only two days earlier and had stopped in to speak to Mrs. Warner about a new hat.

Jane turned to greet their first guest. The remainder of the morning was filled with games and relays for the children. Men of all social stations participated in foot races, and some of the young bucks organized a horse race. The ladies played croquet or set a few stitches on their needle-work, their gossiping tongues keeping time with their needles. The dowager duchess of Wentworth shared a comfortable coze with a farmer's wife as they discussed topics ranging from the best type of apple for baking to raising children. Sir Humphrey and the squire discussed politics with the village smith. And here and there, groups of fashionable and not-so-fashionable young people laughed and teased, entertaining themselves with childish games like tag and spillikins.

By late afternoon, the lines between the classes became apparent once again. After dark, there was to be dancing under the trees, as well as a huge buffet. In preparation for what many considered the highlight of Heartland's Open Day, everyone was resting—ladies in the bedchambers, farmers' wives on quilts spread on the green lawn. Napping children shared their pallets with nannies or mothers. The gentlemen played piquet or billiards while sipping port or brandy. The tenant farmer joined the village shopkeeper for a cooling glass of ale.

The sun met the horizon. The lawns were once again busy as the Heartland servants set out the plentiful buffet before joining the merriment.

The orchestra, hired from the Bath Assemblies, began to tune their instruments. Like magic, the guests assembled for the first dance. Following a tradition begun so long ago no one living remembered its origin, Pipkin bowed in front of the elegant Miss Lindsay and requested her hand for the country dance. Anyone not acquainted with the couple might have mistaken them for grandfather and granddaughter, so handsome they were together. At the end of the first refrain, the other guests joined in.

Jane noticed Cherry clinging rather too closely to a young man she didn't know. "Pipkin, who is that with Miss Cherry?"

"I believe that is Mr. Pope-Jones, miss. He is staying with the squire. I understand Miss Cherry made his acquaintance during her recent sojourn to Paris."

Before the next dance began, Jane sought out her cousin. Cherry was still in Mr. Pope-Jones's company, but her mother was also present.

"Jane!" exclaimed Aunt Sophie. "Please! You must tell me what to do!"

"Mama! You act as if we have done something wrong!" whispered Cherry indignantly.

"Mrs. Pettigrew, I assure you . . ." began the young man.

"Excuse me," said Jane, breaking into the babbling. "I don't believe I've had the pleasure."

"Where are your manners, Cherry?" asked Aunt Sophie.

"Jane, this is Mr. Reginald Pope-Jones. My fiancé," she added defiantly. "Reggie, this is my Cousin Jane."

The handsome young man made her a creditable bow and said, "Charmed, Miss Lindsay."

Jane hardly noticed, so shocked was she by Cherry's revelation. "How do you do?" asked Jane automatically. Before Mr. Pope-Jones could evince a response, Jane took Cherry by the arm, saying, "I want a word with you." She led her reluctant cousin away from the other guests. They settled on a stone bench at the edge of the gardens.

"I know what you will say," pouted Cherry.

"Good, then you probably have already thought of the answers. Tell me about your fiancé."

"Reginald comes from an excellent family." Jane nodded, and Cherry continued, her defensive words coming faster. "He is the eldest of three. He will inherit an agreeable estate on his father's death. He already receives a yearly income of two thousand from his investments."

"Investments?"

"Yes, it is the most fascinating thing, Jane, but he knows exactly what and when to buy and sell. He is really brilliant," said Cherry in awe-struck tones.

Jane smiled; if she hadn't heard it with her own ears, she wouldn't have believed Cherry would look beyond the surface at anyone. And here she was, describing Mr. Pope-Jones's brilliance at the first opportunity. Jane began to listen more keenly.

"Mother thinks we haven't known each other long enough. Jane, you must persuade her; she will heed your advice."

"About what, precisely, do you need me to persuade Aunt Sophie?"

"That it is quite proper for us to become betrothed so quickly and that we may announce our betrothal this evening!" Cherry's eyes shone like diamonds; her face radiated happiness. Jane nodded her assent and received a crushing hug.

The guests were gone or sleeping in one of the many bedchambers. The house was silent as the ormolu clock on the mantel in her room chimed four o'clock in the morning. Jane forced herself to close her eyes and rid her mind of all thought. Gradually, she relaxed, and sleep overtook her.

Jane slept late; many of her overnight guests had already departed for their homes. She ignored the morning gown Tucker had laid out; instead, Jane donned her oldest, most comfortable riding habit. She paid a quick visit to her old nurse; though Nana refused to leave her room, she still expected to hear all the details about Open Day. Jane remained only a few moments, promising to return that evening.

Jane tripped lightly down the back stairs and out to the stables. James threw her into the saddle and prepared to mount his own horse when Jane waved him away, insisting on riding alone like old times.

She rode to the abbey. Though she was careful to stay clear of the high, crumbling walls, she renewed her acquaintance with every nook and cranny, except, of course, for Brother Valentine's tomb. Like an exorcist, she resolutely banished her memories of Drew from the ruins.

An hour later, she rubbed Sinbad's velvety nose and fed him a carrot before climbing on a fallen stone and remounting.

"Well, old fellow, it's just you and I now. Or soon will be. Cherry will be married next spring. Aunt Sophie will probably go and live with her and Mr. Pope-Jones when they return from their wedding trip. I'm not complaining. It is quite peaceful at home by myself. And I certainly have interests to pursue and friends to visit. But sometimes, I wonder . . ." The big horse never did learn what his mistress wondered, for Jane dug in her heels, and off they went.

Drew shut the last drawer with a sigh of relief.

"That should do it, Lord Cheswick," said the lawyer, straightening the small mound of papers on the old desk.

"Good! I never realized what a prolific letter writer my uncle was."

"Oh, yes indeed! That's how he kept abreast of all the latest details in society. Now, I must be going, unless you have other questions?"

"No, Mr. Pender. I want to thank you for all your help these past weeks. Not being familiar with my uncle's business affairs, I'm afraid I would have made a sad botch of matters."

"Not at all, my lord. I have every confidence that the Cheswick estate will remain in prime case. And please, let me know when you will arrive in London. The house there has been shut up for so long, it will take an army of maids to clean it. I'll go ahead and hire the main staff; then you may make any changes you wish when you arrive."

"Good. I won't keep you: I know you are anxious to begin your journey." Drew shook hands with the solicitor.

Sitting back down behind his uncle's—no, he reminded himself, *his*—desk, Drew felt a great rush of relief. Finally, it was over. There would be no more funeral visits, no more solicitors. He could relax now in his own home.

A moment later, he was drumming his fingers on the

smooth desktop. Then he stood up and took a turn about the room. Idly, he studied the titles of the books on one shelf. He moved to the window; a steady rain was falling. If only he could go for a ride, this restlessness would leave him.

Drew returned to the desk forcing himself to sit down. The dark, shiny surface was vacant; all evidence of his uncle's affairs had been neatly summed up and stored. The estate was in excellent condition; the house was in no need of repairs. Drew thought, even if I could go for a ride, there would be nothing to do, nothing to accomplish.

"Drew, dear? Has Mr. Pender gone?" asked his mother from the doorsill.

"Yes, we have finally finished."

"Good, I know you are glad of that. Luncheon is ready."

"At least that will give me something to do," grumbled the new earl.

Faith Peterson cocked her head to one side and studied her son carefully. "You are bored!" she exclaimed.

"Am I? Perhaps you are right, Mother," he said, escorting her to the small dining room. A large tray of cold meats and cheeses occupied the center of the cozy table. A tureen of steaming rarebit stew and a basket of hot scones completed the simple repast.

"The signs are obvious, my dear."

"I ask you, Mother, is it any wonder? I must admit I misjudged my uncle in one respect. He may have treated us badly, but he was an excellent landowner. His tenants prosper, his land is well tended, his house is in perfect repair. Mr. Pender told me that even the house in London receives a yearly inspection from the handyman."

"Yes, Rupert managed everything and everyone. Still, the house in London has been empty for fifteen years or more. In that time, carpets fade: upholstery grows brittle. I'm afraid we will have a great deal of work to do there."

"Do you think so?" asked Drew eagerly.

"Oh, yes. I would be happy to help. Besides, now that you have inherited the title, you will want to take your seat

301

in the House of Lords. I understand that any man with political aspirations simply must have a wife to act as his hostess, so you will want the town house ready for her."

"This is one politician who won't. You'll just have to act as my hostess," he sad, grinning at her.

"What? You mean I am to be denied my grandchildren?"

"Mother! Please, the servants!"

His mother, who had not so long before been little more than the housekeeper at Cheswick House knew very well that the servants were probably listening. But she also knew these servants; they would never allow what they overheard to leave the house.

"Drew, I have heard enough! You have been moping around this house for the past month. You are depressing to be with, my dear."

"Thank you so much," he snapped.

His mother patted his hand and said, "You're welcome, for only someone who cares would dare tell you these things. Drew, go to London. I'll come along, too. We'll trick the town house out in the finest style. And then you may drive me back to Bath, return Jane's pendant, settle down together, and give me a houseful of grandchildren!"

Drew stood up so abruptly that he knocked over the heavy chair; the sound reverberated through the walls. He picked it up; gripping the back of it, he asked, "Do you think it would be so easy? For God's sake, Mother, she shot me!"

"And so would I if you appeared all of a sudden in my bed!"

"Mother! I was not in her bed!"

"Very well then, *on* her bed. The poor thing had just come to realize someone wanted her dead. How could she be thinking straight?"

"Ha! Poor thing? Jane?" he scoffed. Then he was silent, thoughtful.

"It will take at least five months to redecorate that monster of a house. Jane will have thought things through by then; she will be missing you, Drew. We'll return to Bath, and . . ."

Drew smiled, a tentative expression, neither full of despair or hope. "And she will fall into my arms," he said.

"If she doesn't, my dear Drew, you'll just be forced to pull her into them!"

♡   *Chapter Eleven*   ♡

Jane smiled and waved until the carriage was out of sight. Pulling her shawl closer, she hurriedly returned to the warm house. As she set a chair closer to the fire, she reflected that December had been a cold, dismal month to this point, far colder than usual.

As a matter of fact, the Christmas season promised to be different, too, and the weather suited her mood. She would be alone for the first time in her life on Christmas. Oh, not truly alone. Friends would drop by, or she could call out the carriage and pay visits to neighbors—by herself.

"What on earth is the matter with me?" Jane asked out loud. She looked around sheepishly. Good! She had closed the salon door: it would not do for sharp-eared Pipkin to think she'd taken to talking to herself. "Which you have," she added aloud once more.

Jane laughed. Now she was being maudlin. Perhaps she should have gone with her aunt and Cherry to the Pope-Jones's for Christmas. But somehow, it hadn't appealed to her. Was she jealous of Cherry's happiness? She didn't think so. Rather, it was the fact that Jane felt Christmas should be a time for family and close friends, not an excuse for an awkward social institution like a house party.

So here I am, she thought, looking around the empty gold salon.

Enough of this! Jane stood up and pulled the bell. "Pipkin,

tell the stables to send round the carriage. I'm going shopping."

"Very good, miss."

Jane spent the remainder of the morning and the early afternoon searching for little gifts for every staff member at Heartland as well as each tenant's children. With Tucker's wise council, she felt she acquitted herself very well. She selected a new Bible for Pipkin, who tended to wear them out, Tucker told her. She purchased a box of sweets and some handkerchiefs for Nana, and for Mrs. Brown, a journal of blank pages, so the cook could record her recipes. For the maids and footmen, she selected small tokens. Finally, Jane shopped for the children of her tenants. She bought lengths of soft rope to make jump-ropes for the girls: Tom Summers offered to add painted wooden handles to the ends of each one. For the boys, she had wooden tops, and for the babies, warm blankets. And for all of them, she had an ample supply of sweets. Shopping for the children was the most fun of all, decided Jane.

With her purchases loaded in the carriage, Jane said, "Now, Tucker, I have one more gift to select, and you cannot be with me."

Her maid smiled. "I was thinking th' same thing, Miss Jane."

Maid and mistress parted company on Milsom Street. Jane lingered where she was, peering into the pastry shop window. When Tucker was out of sight, she stepped two doors down and entered the linen draper's shop. She had just settled on a blue shawl of the finest weave when a familiar voice interrupted her train of thought.

"No, I wanted a navy blue. That is too light."

Jane followed the sound and soon found the voice's owner. "Mrs. Peterson, I didn't know you had returned to Bath!"

"Only yesterday, Jane. How nice to see you again. You look wonderful! I must ask you about Miss Pettigrew." Faith Peterson turned to the clerk and said, "I shall come back another time, young man. Let's go have some tea, Jane."

"I would love to." She handed the clerk her selection. "Wrap this up tight for me, please. I'll come back for it later."

"Very good, Miss Lindsay."

When they were settled at a dainty table at Jolly's pastry shop, Mrs. Peterson said, "I saw the notice in the paper about Miss Pettigrew's betrothal. She must be very happy."

"She is. I believe it is truly a love match. It rather shocked my aunt and me: Cherry has always been such a flibbertigibbet. But she is quite devoted to Mr. Pope-Jones."

"A good family, the Pope-Joneses, I mean."

"Yes, she and my aunt are spending Christmas at their country home."

"Were you not invited?" asked Mrs. Peterson.

"Yes, but I declined. This is Cherry's moment. Besides, I can't think of anything worse than spending Christmas with strangers."

"Spending it alone is definitely worse. I know," said the observant older woman. "Well, it shan't be! You will come to my house for Christmas dinner. Then neither one of us will be alone."

Jane hesitated, wanting to ask if Drew would be present, but not daring. She knew Mrs. Peterson was not above matchmaking, but she wouldn't lie if asked a direct question. Finally, Jane mustered enough nerve to ask, "Will Drew be there?"

"No, I'm afraid not. That is why you coming would keep me from becoming moped. I do so hate to be alone at Christmas."

The sorrow in Faith Peterson's tones made Jane ask anxiously, "He's not ill or anything, is he?" What if he had died from the pistol shot? she thought desperately.

Chuckling, Mrs. Peterson patted Jane's hand and said, "Of course he's not, my dear. He's in York, and he has recovered completely."

"I . . . you mean Drew told you about. . . ?"

"Yes. He couldn't hide it from me. When first I saw him, I noticed his hair was combed strangely. I soon had the whole story. I do hope it taught you not to sleep with guns under your pillow."

"No. That is, I don't usually do such things, but it was a strange inn, and I was traveling alone."

"And someone had tried to take your life," whispered Mrs. Peterson, after looking around to be certain no one was eavesdropping.

"Not someone," said Jane quietly. "It was my cousin Roland. I have come to realize that in the past months."

"Have you?" asked the matron, her tone incredulous. Jane returned a puzzled look. "Then why on earth haven't you written to Drew, you foolish child? He has been the worst bear, always cross!"

"I didn't suppose he would care. If you could have seen the look on his face before we said good-bye, you would agree."

"Nonsense, Jane!" Mrs. Peterson stopped. Lowering her voice, she added, "He had just been shot, Jane. How should he have looked? Never mind, you will write to him today."

"No!"

"Then I will."

"No, please, Mrs. Peterson! I couldn't do such a thing! And neither will you! The circumstances have changed!" Jane whispered frantically.

"Changed? In what way?" Faith Peterson crossed her gloved fingers, praying Jane hadn't found someone else.

"Drew is now the earl of Cheswick. He will think it strange that I've changed my mind now. He and everyone else will think I am marrying him for his title."

"Jane, I can't argue with you about what the world will think. You are no doubt more versed than I am in the ways of the *ton*. But you must ask yourself if the opinion of the world is worth losing a lifetime of happiness. Drew loves you: he would gladly give up his title and the estates if you would be his wife. Has he not spent the last five months putting up with tradesmen and workers, trying to get his town house ready for you?"

"He has? But why? Why would he simply assume I would come running at the drop of the hat? I haven't heard a word from him!"

"And you won't. Drew is a proud man, very dictatorial. He is more like his late uncle than he would care to admit. You know what he is: he takes charge of the least detail of one's life. I tell you, I wouldn't choose such a man. But there is a depth of feeling in him that is so precious, so out of the ordinary. And, I suppose, all of his overbearing ways are worth this—at least for someone of your strong character: you will be able to stand up to him. I daresay you'll lead him a merry dance."

Mrs. Peterson's eyes had grown misty, but Jane was growing impatient. "But I cannot simply write to him!"

"No, but I can."

"It's anthrax, my lord. No doubt about it. We'll have to destroy the entire herd and burn the carcasses."

Drew stared at the field of cattle: most of them appeared healthy still, but he knew it was only a question of time before each one sickened and died. "Then do it," he said. Turning on his heel, he climbed on his horse and rode away without a backward glance.

When he had been summoned back to York by his capable estate manager, he had hoped the man was mistaken. But after viewing a bonfire of dead livestock as he passed one of the neighboring estates, he knew the worst had come true.

For the gentry, the epidemic would mean a loss of income: for the laborers, it spelled death. If their milk cow died, they faced starvation. And worse, perhaps, the workers themselves could contract the deadly disease.

When Drew reached the manor house, he shut himself up in his study and composed a letter to his mother, explaining that he would be remaining in York for several weeks. He knew she would be disappointed he would be away for Christmas.

For Jane, Christmas was indeed different, but in a delight-

308

ful way. Drew's mother had exaggerated when she had told Jane she would be alone on Christmas. She had invited twenty-six people to her dinner. Guessing games and singing were the entertainment of the afternoon. After dinner, guests were invited to participate in an exchange of gifts. The gifts had to be created, however, for Faith Peterson hadn't warned anyone about this plan.

Everyone drew names: they then had a half-hour to find a gift. Jane had drawn Giles Stanton's name. She thought and thought and was about to give up when her frustrated gaze fell on Lydia Ashmore. Slowly, a smile formed on her lips. Quickly, she took Miss Ashmore aside and asked permission to write on a card the gift of one kiss from Lydia. The young lady blushed, but laughed and agreed.

When they reassembled in the drawing room, the merry exchange began. The dowager duchess of Wentworth began by handing a card to her friend and hostess. Faith began giggling as she read it aloud.

"I give you, my oldest friend, a piece of advice. Never accept an invitation to a dinner unless you first discover if the hostess has planned some inane form of entertainment."

"I protest, Your Grace," said Giles Stanton. "I think this a very good sort of game."

"I suppose so, since you cheated and drew Miss Ashmore's name," said the dowager.

"You next, Giles," said Jane.

He grinned. From his pocket, he produced a small velvet box. Lydia Ashmore gasped and looked to her parents for guidance as she opened it.

"Well, what is it, girl?" asked the dowager.

"A ring, a pearl ring," she whispered.

"Will you accept it, Miss Ashmore?" asked Giles.

"I . . ." She looked at her father.

"Go on, Lydia. I've spoken to your young man."

Giles placed the ring on her finger and might have kissed her in front of everyone if Jane hadn't interrupted. "I should give you your present now, Giles." He was none too pleased, but he took the card with a smile.

Reading it aloud, he said, "With the young lady's permission, your gift is a kiss from Miss Ashmore."

Everyone started laughing as Giles claimed his present.

Next, it was Jane's turn. Faith Peterson also brought out a velvet jewelry box. As she handed it to Jane, she explained, "I cheated, also, Jane. I had this for you all along. Actually, it is not from me. It is something Drew found."

Jane opened the box gingerly. "Hurry up, girl!" snapped the dowager.

She stared at the contents of the box. The pendant. The Heartland pendant. It could be no other. "How?" she whispered.

"He found it at a pawn shop. Someone told him where it might be found," explained Drew's mother softly. "Let me put it on you."

"No, no. Not now. I am too overwhelmed. Thank you." Holding the box tightly in her hand, Jane watched the rest of the gifts being exchanged. She would look up suddenly and discover Drew's mother watching her, but she still was too stunned to seek an explanation.

When all the guests were taking their leave, Jane found a moment to be alone with Mrs. Peterson to ask, "Was there any message?"

"Only that he hoped this would make you happy until he could speak to you again, face to face."

Impetuously, Jane hugged her. Then she hurried out to the waiting carriage.

Drew settled back against the comfortable squabs of the carriage. Had the weather been better, he would have taken his curricle, but not across York, not in the winter. Still, there was something to be said for being driven. He would arrive in Bath feeling jostled, but not exhausted.

He had been anticipating this journey for six weeks, from the day just before Christmas when he had received his mother's encouraging letter. He had been like a lion caged, unable to leave immediately. But the epidemic of anthrax

310

had spread throughout the region: entire herds of sheep had been slaughtered, and still it spread. Then the terrible blizzard had hit. Food was scarce: people were starving, his people. Drew had been obliged to remain, even after the roads had become passable once more. Finally, the crisis had passed, and he had been free to leave.

He had received numerous letters from his mother, each containing glowing pictures of he and Jane's future together. Being a realist, Drew had taken this with a grain of salt. He was unwilling to trust his optimistic parent in this. She was probably exaggerating, he had cautioned himself more than once. Jane may have realized he hadn't been behind all her accidents, but that didn't mean she was ready to spend the rest of her life with him.

So he had determined to journey to Bath at the earliest opportunity to gauge for himself Jane's feelings. Unfortunately for Drew's patience, this earliest opportunity was the second week of February.

Jane began to avoid Drew's mother. She knew Mrs. Peterson meant well, but Jane doubted her veracity after receiving neither a visit nor a letter. The older woman's continuous promises of Drew's devotion had begun to ring hollow as the weeks passed.

Jane threw herself into the preparations for Heartland's Valentine's Ball with a feverish energy. Cherry helped, but her fiancé was staying with the squire again, and she was often to be found in his company.

Two days before the ball, Jane sent Cherry to inspect the hothouse flowers with the head gardener. Two hours later, Jane set out to search for her cousin. She discovered her and Mr. Pope-Jones holding hands in the summerhouse a cozy fire keeping them warm.

Her Aunt Sophie was also proving elusive. With Cherry's nuptials scheduled for the first week of April, little else interested Sophie Pettigrew. Jane would set her to making a list of chores for the maids, and would return an hour later to discover a list of additional guests for Cherry's wedding.

Jane threw up her hands in defeat. Then an inspiration hit her. She had been so busy, she hadn't found any time to make up the anonymous valentines for the wallflowers. Jane gathered up all the necessary materials in a box and carried them to the summerhouse.

"Cherry, I have another chore for you, I'm afraid."

"Oh, Jane! I'm sorry, I forgot about the hothouse flowers! I'll take care of that right now."

"No, no. I have something much more important for you to do." Jane smiled at Cherry's fiancé and said coyly, "And perhaps you would care to assist her, Mr. Pope-Jones."

"I will be happy to be of service, Miss Lindsay."

"Good!" Jane stepped outside and returned with the box of papers and laces and ribbons. Mickey followed her, carrying a small, sturdy table. "You see, Mr. Pope-Jones, we always have a good supply of anonymous Valentine cards to give the poor ladies who have no, or few, admirers. That way everyone can enjoy our little tradition and not feel left out. Cherry and I have been taking care of this particular project since we could write a legible verse. It is rather fun to think up romantic sayings when you have no idea who will receive the card. Then we dress them up with lace and ribbons."

"I see. I'm not very good with lace or ribbons, Miss Lindsay, but I have tried my hand at poetry at one time. It was not very good—"

"I'm sure it was wonderful," protested Cherry.

"I have every confidence you will be able to create a verse or two—now that you have such a beautiful inspiration."

"Inspiration?" he asked. Jane nodded to Cherry who was gazing at her slow-topped fiancé with adoration. "Oh, yes! By Jove, don't I just!"

Satisfied that they would manage to produce a mountain of very bad, but very sentimental verse, Jane hurried back to the main house. Her next objective was her Aunt Sophie. She discovered her still pondering over the distant wedding's guest list.

"Aunt Sophie, I need you to do something for me."

"Of course, Jane, you know I am here to help you."

Jane managed to refrain from laughing and said seriously, "It has occurred to me that if we use too many of the hothouse flowers for the ball, there may not be enough blooms to decorate the house for Cherry's wedding breakfast. I have sent the head gardener out to check, but he knows nothing about the number of flowers it takes to do an appropriate arrangement. If you wouldn't mind—"

"Say no more!" exclaimed her aunt, jumping to her feet. Sophie Pettigrew whisked out of the room and down the hall, never realizing how her niece had bamboozled her.

At five o'clock on the day of Heartland's famous Valentine's ball, Jane was awakened from her nap by an excited maid. Tucker stood back, a pleased expression of anticipation on her face. Jane frowned and tried to burrow underneath the pillow.

"No, miss. You must wake up: something just arrived for you."

Jane sat up slowly, afraid to think what or who had arrived. But Tucker had said "something." Jane held out her hand, and the maid placed the elaborate card in her palm. Jane frowned. Valentine cards were always saved for the ball.

"Open it, Miss Jane," said the maid, unable to contain her excitement.

Jane caught Tucker's impatience and tore through the sealing wax. The verse was written in the most beautiful scrawling hand she had ever seen.

My dearest love,

I would ask your forgiveness for the long delay in writing. And I will let Hastings plead my case, just as he does Marlow's to his Miss Kate Hardcastle. Do you remember the scene?

"Come, Madam, you are now driven to the very last scene of all your contrivances. I know you like him, I'm sure he loves you, and you must and shall have him."

313

Since it seems I was so inept at persuading you, perhaps Hastings's words will soften your heart, and you will look upon my suit with favor, my one and only valentine. I will know your answer if you will meet me at the summerhouse at seven o'clock.

Forever yours,
D.

"Well, what does 'e say, Miss Jane?" exclaimed Tucker, unable to restrain her curiosity a moment longer.

"I am to meet him at the summerhouse at seven o'clock." Jane felt dazed, unprepared: she had given up hope, and now this. What should she do?

"DO?" demanded the maid.

Jane focused on the servant: she hadn't realized she was speaking her thoughts aloud. Suddenly Jane smiled, and Tucker clapped her hands with joy. "Tucker, where did you put the red gown? The one from Paris?"

"It's still in th' box, Miss Jane, tucked away in th' spare wardrobe. I'll have it pressed and freshened before you can say St. Valentine!" Tucker hurried away.

Jane opened the door to the dressing room where Mickey was filling the copper tub. He gave her a queer look as she grinned at him and vanished back into her room.

Tucker returned half an hour later, the red dress draped carefully across one arm, a warm towel in the other. She hung the dress in the wardrobe and took the towel to her mistress.

Jane said quickly, "You didn't tell my cousin or aunt, did you?"

"No, Miss Jane. Though if I would 'ave seen them, I might 'ave. They're dressing, too."

"Good! I wouldn't want anyone to know, Tucker. If things should go awry—"

"Don't talk that way, Miss Jane," said the maid.

"Very well, but you understand, don't you?"

"Yes, I understand. But don't you worry, this time will prove the charm."

* * *

Jane agonized on how to wear her hair, finally deciding to tuck the long, heavy locks into a red net snood. Then she stepped into the dark red gown: the silk shimmered in the candlelight. When Tucker had finished fastening the tiny row of buttons in back, Jane bit her lower lip, hesitating before she went to stand in front of the cheval glass. The old Jane, the Jane of last year's ball, wouldn't have dared to wear the gown she wore. But Jane failed to be either shocked or embarrassed as she scrutinized her appearance in the glass: instead, she grew warm at the mere thought of Drew's reaction to the ivory expanse of uncovered flesh. It was tasteful and certainly not as daring as many of the ladies wore. She nodded to Tucker who had remained silent. The maid thought she had never seen her Miss Jane so radiant, so beautiful.

Jane glided down the stairs for one last inspection of the ballroom. Just as she was pleased with the red dress, she was also happy that she had chosen red and white roses for the decorations this year. For once in her life, she would truly feel like the belle of the ball, if all went well in the summerhouse. The phrase repeated itself in her mind, keeping time with the ticking of the clock. If all went well . . . if all went well . . .

And then it was time. Jane arranged her shawl, and like a soldier leaving for war, she squared her shoulders and let herself out onto the balcony. This time she walked around to the stairs. She wanted to run, but she forced her stride to remain slow and steady. She opened the door.

Stepping inside, she stopped to let her eyes adjust to the gloom of the single candle. There he was, studying her, his expression hooded, impossible to read. Jane felt breathless: she had forgotten how handsome he was, especially in his black evening clothes.

"I'm glad you decided to come, Jane. I wasn't at all certain you would."

"I couldn't stay away, Drew."

"I meant to write you, to tell you that Havelock had been persuaded to leave the country, but I doubted you would believe me."

"I would have. But I already knew. My aunt, Roland's mother, wrote me. He hadn't told her why he was leaving, only that he was."

"So, now you know I was telling the truth?"

"I have known that almost since I . . . shot you," said Jane, dropping her gaze. This was going all wrong! They were speaking like strangers: where was the fire, the passion?

"I didn't blame you: it was rather stupid of me. Did Pipkin or Tucker tell you about our plan to protect you?"

"Plan?" asked Jane, her voice rising. "No, perhaps you should tell me."

"Some other time," said Drew, beginning to relax.

But Jane would have none of it. If he hadn't asked her to meet him in the summerhouse to make love to her, then she might as well argue about the past! "I don't appreciate the idea of you and my servants conspiring and scheming behind my back!"

"Come now, Jane, our only scheme was to insure your safety. Be reasonable," said Drew, frowning.

Jane turned her back on him. "Hmph!"

"Now, see here, Jane, I didn't ask you to join me out here just so you could treat me to another of your shrewish scolds! The last time you nearly killed me!"

"You'll never forgive me for that, will you?"

Drew opened his mouth to protest this unjust accusation when he noticed her shoulders were shaking. He stepped up behind her and handed her his handkerchief. "Please, Jane, I didn't mean to upset you. Don't cry," he said, tenderly turning her to face him.

Jane looked out from behind the serviceable handkerchief and grinned up at him. His brows came together, and he grabbed her, shaking her heartily. "You minx! You jade! Making me think you were upset!" he complained. "I should shake you till your teeth rattle!"

Jane's grin faded as she touched his smooth jaw. "I would

much prefer to be kissed, my lord," she whispered.

His hands slipped down her arms, and he pulled her closer, bending his head for a lingering kiss.

Abruptly, he released her: Jane staggered, and he put out a hand to steady her. Leading her to the sofa, he sat down beside her, but made no attempt to embrace her again. Jane held her breath, frightened by his silence.

"Jane, I am proud and arrogant," he began.

She smiled again and teased, "You have been talking to your mother."

He allowed himself a slight smile before continuing seriously, "I am often overbearing. I am forever forgetting to ask what other people's wishes are: I make the decisions for them."

"I have known that since the last Valentine's ball, Drew. It didn't stop me from falling in love with you."

"Yes, but I nearly destroyed that love with my peremptory manner."

"Drew, if you are going to continue in this manner very much longer, I'm afraid I will be forced to leave you here. I have guests arriving in forty-five minutes," said Jane in her usual, straightforward fashion. "And if you expect me to confess my many faults, you will have an even longer wait."

He turned his charming grin on her. "That is certainly true."

Jane laughed, taking no offense at his quip. "So?" she said, cocking her head to one side as she waited.

"Very well, if you won't let me unburden myself, I shall simply continue as I am accustomed to doing. Jane, you will marry me without any further delay. I have already spoken to your Rector Hall, and he has agreed, reluctantly, to perform the ceremony this very evening."

"But the banns?"

"I took the precaution of securing a special license before coming here this evening."

"And if I would prefer a lavish church wedding, Lord Devlin?"

"I had thought of that. We can always have it in the little

chapel beyond the garden," he said.

"Oh no! You'll not lure me back out there with the ghosts and ghoulies!"

"Then it is settled?" he demanded.

"Yes, Drew."

Finally, he took her into his arms, kissing her mouth passionately. Jane locked her arms behind his neck, her fingers twisting his dark hair. He lifted his face and looked deep into her eyes. "I love you, my one and only valentine."

"And I love you, dearest Drew, but please, don't stop kissing me," whispered Jane.

He laughed—a short, snuggly sound as he lowered his head against her luscious breasts. He lips returned to her mouth while his hands began to stroke and explore: Jane slipped down until she was reclining on the sofa. Drew stopped kissing her and got to his feet, walking gingerly about the room.

"Cramp in my leg," he explained. Jane sat up, grinning at him.

"Your rheumatism?" she asked solicitously, not bothering to conceal her giggles.

"Very possibly, after driving over a hundred miles in the past two days," he snapped. "Most of it, I might add, in the freezing cold."

Drew straightened up and raised a brow. He approached her slowly, his smile holding a promise and a threat.

"Shrew!" he taunted.

"Overbearing cad!" she returned, rising to meet him.

His hand shot out, but he clasped only air as Jane sidestepped him. He reached for her again, but this time Jane entered his embrace willingly.

"We should go in," she breathed into his hair after several minutes.

"Forever worried about what the world will think," said Drew, between kisses.

"Drew, the guests will be here soon. Do you really think I'm in any condition to greet them?" He tasted her lips one last time before holding her away from him and saying hon-

318

estly, "The only thing you are fit for at this moment is bed—my bed."

"Oh, Drew! I am ruined! My hair . . . my dress . . ."

"You look beautiful. Your color is high: your lips a rosy shade of red. Tucker will set your hair to rights in no time. Come on, my love, let's go inside. It is time for our ball, and for you to shine."

She paused before leaving the summerhouse and said, "You really didn't need to use quotations from *She Stoops To Conquer*, Drew. You are quite poetic."

"Ah, but the story of the taming of a shrew seemed so appropriate."

"I would take offense, but I know how like the domineering Marlow you are," said Jane, clinging to his arm as they wandered toward the house.

When they entered the ballroom, Pipkin came forward, an unaccustomed smile on his face. He made a deep bow to Jane and said, "Miss Jane, on behalf of the staff, I have been asked to give you our best wishes."

"Thank you, Pipkin. Thank you all," she added as she realized every servant was assembled in the ballroom, smiling on her and Drew.

"Thank you," said Drew.

"Nana?" asked Jane, her voice trembling from the shock of seeing her old nurse out of the nursery. She took one gnarled hand in hers and said, "Why?"

"Ye didn't think I'd let ye marry without me, child. Now, where is this man who's goin' t' be yer husband?"

Drew joined Jane and smiled at the old woman. Jane held her breath, praying Nana wouldn't take one look at Drew and start screaming about piskies and faeries.

"Well, do I meet your approval?" he asked.

"Hmph! What did yer ol' nurse tell ye last year on th' night o' the ball?"

"I'm not sure I remember," said Jane.

"I told ye 'e would steal yer heart, I did." The old woman

319

laughed. "Let's get on wi' it. I can't be stayin' out all night."

"Rector Hall is waiting in the library, Miss Jane. Shall I bring him in here?" asked Pipkin.

"Yes," said Jane, looking around the gaily decorated ballroom with its cupids looking down from the ceiling.

As they waited for the parson, Jane said softly, "There is only one thing missing."

"That is?"

"One of my fondest memories of the ball was watching Grandfather place the Heartland pendant around Grandmother's neck."

"I would do so, but you have the pendant, remember?"

Jane signaled to Tucker to bring the velvet box. Standing in front of a gilt-framed mirror, Jane watched as Drew fastened the heavy pendant around her neck. Then he turned her, and Jane said, "I love you, Drew."

"And I love you, my one and only valentine."

TRAPPED!

John Slocum ducked as the lead beat off the top of the rock like angry hailstones. He waited a few seconds after the last shot had whined into the distance, then swung around, rifle ready. He fired four quick shots.

One bullet found a target. He heard a man yelp in pain. The cursing that followed told him that he hadn't hit the man in a spot where it would take him out of the gunfight. If anything, it might make him even madder—and even more dangerous. Slocum didn't much care one way or the other. If they got to him, they'd lynch him. Dead was dead . . .

JAKE LOGAN

SLOCUM AND THE ARIZONA COWBOYS

BERKLEY BOOKS, NEW YORK

SLOCUM AND THE ARIZONA COWBOYS

A Berkley Book/published by arrangement with
the author

PRINTING HISTORY
Berkley edition/February 1987

ISBN: 0–425–09567–3

A BERKLEY BOOK ® TM 757,375
Berkley Books are published by The Berkley Publishing Group,
200 Madison Avenue, New York, N.Y. 10016.
The name "BERKLEY" and the stylized "B" with design are trademarks
belonging to Berkley Publishing Corporation.

PRINTED IN THE UNITED STATES OF AMERICA

1

Even in the Arizona desert, the fall of 1881 was cool and wet and threatened outright rain. John Slocum hardly noticed as he rode into Tombstone. The wind blowing off the Sonora Desert might chill the bones and promise a real winter, but what happened in the city streets proved enough to freeze his very soul.

He reined in and curled one leg around the saddlehorn, leaning forward slightly to watch the drama unfolding in front of him. Two men stood less than twenty feet apart in front of the saloon, hands poised over their gun butts.

"You son of a bitch!" shouted one at the other. "I'm gonna blow your damned face off!"

"Do it," came the cold command from the other. Slocum estimated chances. The man all hot and bothered stood little chance against the other's calm. He fumbled in his shirt pocket and pulled out fixings for a cigarette. He patted his horse on the neck and soothed the skittish ani-mal. Gunfight finished, the horse might bolt, but he doubted it. The mare didn't cotton to other humans. When the guns went off, the horse would like it even less.

Slocum curled a rolling paper and tapped out enough tobacco for a moderate smoke. A toss of his head and the pouch string pulled tight once more. He ran his tongue along the paper and expertly rolled. All the while he worked, he kept his eyes on the men in the street. The one wanted to shout more curses rather than fight. Slocum saw that this tactic would only result in the man's death.

The man's opponent widened his stance slightly. His hand didn't shake. His lips curled slightly in a sneer. He didn't bother with insults.

Slocum struck a lucifer, held the flaring stick away from his face until it settled down to a cheerful blaze, then lit his cigarette. He tossed the lucifer into a water trough, then firmly tugged on the reins in time to keep the horse from bolting.

The gunfight had finished the way Slocum had thought it would. The man who had kept his head saw his chance, drew, and fired twice before the insult-shouting man could pull his six-shooter free of his belt.

Slocum puffed deeply. The tobacco was stale but the smoke warmed his lungs and reminded him that he hadn't come to Tombstone to sit in the biting wind and watch men being slaughtered.

He put his heels into the horse's flanks and rode slowly past the fallen body. Slocum never glanced back as he rode on and stopped in front of the Broken Spur Saloon, a small establishment hardly wider than the doors leading into the main room.

Dismounting, he brushed off trail dust, took a deep drag off the cigarette, then tossed it to the dirt. It had left a stale, lived-in taste in his mouth that couldn't be banished with anything less than a few shots of rye.

Slocum looked up and down the main street of the small mining town and shook his head. This Cochise County boom town didn't appear any different from dozens of others he had ridden through. Given the chance, he'd get lucky at the gaming tables playing poker, and win enough to be able to drift on farther west. Or maybe north. It didn't matter much to someone like John Slocum.

The War and its aftermath had taken too much out of him to ever call any place but horseback home. He had been a sniper and one of the best, a marksman sitting on hilltops and waiting for the flash of gold braid on Yankee officers' hats. A tour with Quantrill had left him gut-shot by his own side and sickened with the carnage tearing the country apart.

But returning to the family homestead in Calhoun County, Georgia, had proven even worse for Slocum than anything that he'd done or seen during the War—and that included the death of his brother Robert. Slocum had returned to the farm on the grassy hill, his parents dead and the future filled with nothing but the promise of loneliness. He had taken to the work with a will, fixing up the farm, making it the kind of place for others to envy. And envy it they did.

A carpetbagger judge had taken a shine to the farm and declared it confiscated because of nonpayment of taxes during the War. Slocum remembered the day that the Reconstruction judge and his hired gunman had ridden up to the farm. That evening Slocum had ridden away, two fresh graves on the knoll near the spring house.

He'd never been back to Georgia and didn't intend to go back. The law had a long memory when it came to judge killers, even no-account carpetbagger judges. Slocum had dodged his share of lawmen over this ever since, and had done enough more to make those same lawmen hunt him down for other crimes.

Now all John Slocum wanted out of Tombstone was enough whiskey to wash the foul taste from his mouth. He intended to move on, having no interest in the silver mining activities that made the entire of Cochise County a suddenly prosperous area.

Before entering the Broken Spur, Slocum reached down and slipped the thong off the hammer of his ebony-handled Colt Navy. He didn't even realize he'd done it; such unconscious habits kept him alive in a town where men were gunned down on the street and no one paid no never mind to it.

Arizona Territory had the reputation for being tough. Slocum was tougher.

He glanced up and down the length of the stained bar. Only four miners bellied up. The rest of the clientele clustered around a table where the man who had shot down the other boasted of his feat.

Slocum sneered and went to the bar. He didn't like men who bragged about their skill with a gun.

"How much for a half bottle?" he asked the barkeep.

"You got a powerful thirst there, mister," the bartender observed. He cocked one eyebrow as he assessed Slocum's ability to pay. "That'd be five dollars—gold."

"How much in greenbacks?"

"Ten. Ain't worth shit out here. Nothing but gold. 'Less you got silver."

Slocum knew the price was exorbitant but doubted he would be able to find any other saloon in Tombstone charging less. He fumbled in a vest pocket and found a half eagle freshly minted up in Carson City. He dropped the tiny gold piece onto the bar. Before it had stopped its melodious ringing, the barkeep's quick hand swept it up and secured it in his own pocket. In the same motion, he pulled out a bottle half-filled with brown sludge.

"Don't want trade whiskey for that kind of money," said Slocum.

"Take it or leave it, mister. I got other customers who're willing to buy it."

Slocum had been on the trail all day and the biting desert wind had taken its toll on body and patience. He reached out and took the barkeep by the front of his apron and tugged. The man slammed into the back of the bar.

"I'm sure you can find a bottle of better quality rotgut." Slocum jerked on the apron strings and brought out a yelp from the man.

"No need to get testy, mister. Most folks around here think this is fine." He reached under the bar. The bartender's eyes widened when they came level with Slocum's Colt. Slocum had drawn the pistol and laid it on the bar.

"Better come back with whiskey, not a bung mallet."

"Sure thing. Here." He put the new bottle down on the bar and straightened. Slocum pushed the trade whiskey across, then nodded curtly. He replaced his Colt and took the half bottle and a shot glass to a table in the corner of the room.

Settling down with his back against a thin wall, he drank slowly, letting the pungent whiskey burn away random aches and pains, the taste of dust and tobacco in his mouth, his cares about getting on with his aimless drifting.

The man who had been the victor in the gunfight pushed away some of the ardent admirers and said loudly, "I'm feelin' lucky today. Who's up for a little wagerin'?"

Slocum didn't pay as much attention to the man as he did the crowd around him. A few shuffled their feet and began moving away. Others were more direct, almost running for the bar. Only two remained at the table. They exchanged looks and a quick, secret smile.

"Well, sir," said the one on the gunman's right. "I'm up for a friendly little game of draw poker."

"Reckon I am, too," chimed in the other. Slocum noticed how well they worked together. They were card sharps preying off feckless miners and anyone else too stupid or too drunk to know better. Slocum waited one heartbeat . . . two. Then the first spoke again.

"Betting for straws don't appeal to me none. Let's make this a friendly game . . . but for small stakes. Just enough to make it interesting. Call it table limit of five dollars?"

"Ten," spoke up the second. "'Lessen our friend here don't want to go that high."

Slocum saw that they had their fish hooked. The man still rode the emotional wave of killing another. He still felt lucky, invincible. Slocum knew what it was like, and fought hard to avoid the feelings. They only got you into bigger trouble.

"Five!" the gunman cried. "Make it ten!"

Only Slocum saw how hard the two gamblers worked to keep the smiles from their faces. He watched and thought and decided. They weren't very good card players. Just good enough to cheat drunken miners.

"Room for another in the game?" he called out.

"Why, certainly, sir. Be honored to have you join in," said the first gambler.

Slocum brought his bottle and sat down opposite the gunman. He glanced at the deck and saw that they'd shaved it from the way one gambler stroked the edges with his forefinger. So obvious.

"Don't remember seeing you around here before," said the gunman.

"Don't remember seeing you, either," said Slocum.

"High card deals." He cut and got a queen. The card sharp to his right got a king of spades, high for the table. He dealt slowly, deliberately.

Slocum knew the procedure well, having seen it a hundred times—having even worked it a few times himself. The first hands would go the way of the gunman and himself. Then the sharps would begin to gamble in earnest and the tide would turn drastically, a few hands wiping out all the gains and more. No man walked away after one bad hand or even two. By the third, he would vow to get back all he'd lost, rationalizing the loss by saying that it still wasn't his money, that he played on winnings. A minor win of a few dollars, then two devastating hands that would wipe out any poke brought into the game.

That was the way it was done. That was the way these two gamblers intended to do it.

Slocum let them feed him the pots, coming out of the opening hands about fifty dollars ahead. The gunman across had twice that in neat stacks on the table in front of him.

"Whiskey!" the gunman bellowed. "For the entire bar!" He paid for it. Slocum paid no attention to the happy cries and noisy drinking at the bar. The two gamblers exchanged glances and inwardly seethed. They wanted that money so easily spent. But they were professional enough at their work to realize that this was a cost of doing business. Let the gunman play the big man. That would only make it harder for him to resist betting on a losing hand later.

Slocum took in another five dollars and began to wonder if he should stop. The gamblers would go for the kill on the next hand or the one following.

"You, Frank McLaury!" came a loud voice from the door. "Keep those hands of yours on the table where I can see 'em or I'll blow your goddamn head off!"

Slocum turned and saw a portly man with a big handle-bar mustache stalking across the saloon. He held a sawed-off shotgun that, if fired, would take out everyone at the table and half a dozen bystanders. He didn't seem to care as long as this Frank McLaury didn't do anything stupid. Slocum looked at the two gamblers. The dark expressions on their faces told which one was McLaury.

Slocum looked across the table at the gunman. Although more than half drunk, the man didn't show any sign that he'd go for his gun. If anything, he seemed amused.

"Sheriff Behan, how good of you to come by and pay your regards."

"You no-good, thievin' son of a coyote." Slocum saw the battered star on the mustached man's chest now. The sheriff swung the shotgun and caught McLaury on the side of the head. The gunman tumbled out of the chair and fell onto the floor.

"Go on, Frank. I want to plant you beside Kincaid. As God is my witness, I want to blow your fuckin' head off!"

McLaury froze, hand no longer inching toward his pistol. Slocum calmly pulled in his winnings and pocketed them, not knowing what went on between the sheriff and McLaury and not caring one whit. It had something to do with the dead man in the street. What more than this, Slocum didn't know or much care.

"Don't go leaving, mister," came the sheriff's sharp command. "You in cahoots with the Clantons? You got that look about you."

"The Clantons?" asked Slocum, seeing that the sheriff meant him. "Don't know anything about the Clantons. I just stopped for a drink and a friendly game of poker before passing through."

"You two," the sheriff said, motioning to the two gamblers. "You clear out of here. I told you I don't want your kind bilkin' honest miners of their earnings." The sheriff spat. "Though I can't rightly say either of these two varmints is honest."

The two card sharps were torn between raising a fuss and meekly obeying the sheriff—and his sawed-off shotgun. They made their silent, quick decision and left the money. There would be other suckers to cheat, and poker games with shaved decks and marked cards. They almost ran from the Broken Spur Saloon.

"You, come along with me." The shotgun rose and pointed in Slocum's direction, the barrels looking big enough to crawl into. As the shotgun shifted, Slocum saw McLaury awkwardly going for his gun.

"Look out!" Slocum shouted, diving to one side. The sheriff caught the motion of McLaury's gun hand from the corner of his eye. He jerked back around, one barrel discharging as he moved. The other barrel he fired in the gunman's general direction, but McLaury hadn't stayed still. He was rolling, shooting and raising hell in the saloon.

Men dived for cover as McLaury shot wildly. The sheriff reloaded and emptied two more barrels at the gunman. By this time, Frank McLaury had vanished into the back room. The sheriff rose and reloaded, tossing the smoking shells onto the floor.

"Still got you by the short hairs," he told Slocum.

"There's no need," Slocum said, pointing to the way the sheriff's knuckle turned white as it curled around the double triggers. "I don't mean you any trouble."

Slocum felt the man's hot, dark eyes studying him, working to firm up the quick judgment he'd made as he'd stormed into the saloon after McLaury. The bleakness in the sheriff's eyes told the story. He thought Slocum and Frank McLaury belonged together—buried at the edge of Tombstone in the cemetery.

Slocum backed away, hands in front of him in plain sight. If the sheriff meant to murder him, he'd have to do it in front of a dozen witnesses. But Slocum knew that wouldn't mean spit to him if that scattergun tore out his guts.

Dead was dead, no matter what rained down on the sheriff's head later.

"Put that gun of yours on the table. There." The sheriff indicated which one using the muzzle of his shotgun. Slocum obeyed. For several seconds the sheriff said nothing, eyeing Slocum coldly. Then he said, "Don't remember having seen you in these parts before. You must be one of Clanton's new recruits."

"I don't know what you mean, Sheriff," said Slocum. "I just rode into Tombstone. Saw McLaury, if that's his name, gun down that other man. Came in here for a peaceful drink and a game of cards."

"You was winnin'." The sheriff made it sound like an accusation of guilt.

"It happens," Slocum said cautiously. "Usually someone wins and someone loses. That's why they call it gambling."

"Don't go getting smart with me." The sheriff jammed the jagged edge of the scattergun into Slocum's belly. Slocum involuntarily backed away and came up hard against the wall. "I'm Sheriff John H. Behan and I don't take to nobody smartin' off in Tombstone. Not since I been sheriff here, I don't."

"I rode in from down south."

"Mexico?"

"Dropped down south of the border for a time," Slocum allowed. "Heading up to Salt Lake City."

"You not one of them Mormons? Have nothing but trouble with them."

"No."

"That gun looks like it's been used a sight more'n most folks'."

"Could be," said Slocum. "But it doesn't get used for no reason."

"You're not one of Ike's boys?"

"Ike Clanton?" Slocum shook his head. "Heard the name. Who hasn't? But I've never laid eyes on the man in my life."

"That was one of his backshooting cayuses you were playing cards with. That Frank McLaury and his brother Tom think they own this goddamn town. All of Clanton's men do, ever since Old Man Clanton died."

"Old Man Clanton?"

"Newman H. Clanton," said Sheriff Behan, looking at Slocum with narrowed eyes. "You're either one damn good liar or you never heard of the Arizona Cowboys."

"Heard of cowboys," said Slocum.

"When Old Man Clanton died, his son Ike took over the cattle rustlin' in this part of the territory. Not a cow, not a steer, not a bull, not even a damn piece of jerky is safe from his rustling. The Arizona Cowboys they call themselves." Behan spat again, a huge dark gob finding its way directly into a spotted brass spittoon at the end of the bar.

"But you wouldn't know anything about that, now would you?"

"Nothing," Slocum said. He noticed that Behan hadn't taken the shotgun from its position just under his navel.

"You're just passin' through, don't have any permanent

business here, now do you?"

"That's right, Sheriff Behan. Just on my way to the north."

Behan spat again. "You ain't in cahoots with Clanton. You're a damned Republican."

This caught Slocum by surprise. Politics had never meant a great deal to him. Most of the carpetbaggers had been Republicans, sent into the South to watch over their onerous Reconstruction laws. But that had been a piece back. Slocum listened harder to Behan's words and detected a familiar twang.

"You from Missouri, Sheriff? Seem to hear it in your voice."

"Where I come from don't mean squat to you, mister. All you need to know is that I was sheriff up in Yavapai County before Governor Fremont appointed me sheriff of Tombstone. I got the backing of the town in whatever I do, and I ain't going to let your kind turn this city into a stinking hellhole!"

Behan had turned red in the face from his speech. The tips of his mustache quivered and made Slocum worry that the trigger finger might tighten. He'd seen what a sawed-off shotgun did to a man. At the range of a few inches, Slocum knew he wouldn't have any middle left if Behan took it into his mind to shoot.

"Didn't meant to rile you," Slocum said. He knew that McLaury getting away made it even worse for him. Behan wanted someone to parade through the streets and maybe even hang for whatever crimes remained unsolved in Tombstone and Arizona Territory.

"Not with the Clantons," Slocum repeated, hoping this would pacify the sheriff. If anything, it made him madder.

"Damn it, of course you ain't. Don't you think I know better? Clanton wouldn't have anything to do with cross-eyed swine like you! You're one of *his* backshooting road agents."

Slocum started to protest, then clamped his mouth firmly shut. Anything he said now would be wrong. Better to wait and listen and maybe find out what was going on in Tombstone and in Behan's mind—if he lived long enough to use that information.

"No, you ain't one of Ike's Cowboys. You're one of *his*. Wyatt Earp thinks he can send his spies down into my town any time he wants. Well, no sir, he's wrong! You're going to go back and tell that horse-fucking son of a bitch that!"

"Wyatt Earp? The deputy marshal?"

"You know who he is. That, that . . ." Behan's wrath rose to the point where he couldn't even speak. When he calmed a mite, he said, "Bet he's writing another of those damned hate letters to Marshal Dake. Listen up, mister. It ain't going to do him one whit of good. You tell him that. *I'm* sheriff of Tombstone and him and his brothers can't do a damn thing about it."

Slocum saw cunning replace anger in Behan's eyes. He wasn't sure this wasn't more dangerous for him.

"No, you ain't going to carry my message back to Earp. Not directly. McLaury may have gunned down Abel Kincaid out in my street, but you'll stand trial for it. By God, you'll stand trial and I'll see you sent off to Detroit Penitentiary!"

Slocum saw his chance and took it. Behan turned slightly, the shotgun muzzle swinging away slightly from Slocum's midsection. Slocum batted the short barrels with the palm of his left hand while he reached for his Colt Navy with his right. He felt blisters spring up as his palm touched hot steel; Behan fired twice, trying to get Slocum in front of the muzzle again.

Slocum found his Colt and smashed it hard into the side of the sheriff's head. The barrel glanced off the top of the moving man's skull. The impact was solid enough to drive Behan to the floor, eyes rolling up in his head.

Slocum considered putting a bullet in the fallen sheriff. That would solve some problems, he knew, but it would create a sight more. No matter what differences there were between Earp and this sheriff, killing a lawman seldom paid anything but a rope around the neck. He looked up and leveled his six-shooter at the bartender.

"Don't go thinking you're a hero," Slocum said to the man, backing from the Broken Spur Saloon. Total silence had fallen inside the room. He unhitched his horse and swung up into the saddle. He groaned slightly as he settled down. He'd hoped for more than a few drinks. A bath and some time on a soft feather mattress would have been nice. Even a whore for the night would have improved his disposition some. But he had no time to spare in Tombstone.

From inside the saloon he heard Behan mumbling and thrashing about. As John Slocum wheeled around and started out of town, he heard Behan shout, "Get a posse. Get some men and form a posse. He ain't gettin' away from me!"

2

John Slocum threw back his head and laughed harshly. Inside the Broken Spur Saloon, Sheriff Behan still shouted for the townspeople of Tombstone to saddle up and ride with him in a posse. The sheriff wanted to lynch Wyatt Earp's no-good, lying spy.

Slocum didn't laugh at the sheriff's belief that he had been sent by the deputy marshal for some unknown and nefarious purpose. He laughed at the notion of the man forming a posse. In the Arizona Territory it took an act of Congress to get a posse mounted and riding.

The sheriff first had to contact the territorial marshal. In this case, Slocum reckoned, that would be Marshal Crawley Dake up in Tucson. The marshal had to telegraph the request for funds to Washington, D.C. Slocum wasn't certain who in the nation's capital had to authorize the money to pay the posse. Either the Attorney General or the Secretary of the Interior had to approve the request before it was sent to the President himself for action.

Slocum didn't worry. Before the restrictive *posse comitatus* law could be invoked, he might be all the way to Salt Lake City. Or even back down into Mexico. All the sheriff had done was blow off some steam like a giant pufferbelly locomotive.

He might decide to not even leave Tombstone, which suited Slocum just fine.

Slocum pulled up the lapels of his coat to protect himself from the frigid wind. He had wanted to spend the night in a bed and maybe even find himself a woman willing to warm it with him. But he couldn't complain much. He had gotten out of the crooked poker game with his life and almost sixty dollars of the two card sharps' gold. That more than made up for the half eagle he'd wasted on the Broken Spur's gut-searing imitation whiskey.

The sun shone warm in his face, helping drive off the cold from the northerly winds gusting around him and kicking up occasional dust devils. That strong breeze hinted at early snow in the mountains to the north around Tucson. Slocum wondered if his trail might not be better to the west rather than to Salt Lake. He didn't know if Behan had got so riled that he would patrol the roads going north. Slocum doubted it, but then how many men laid the sheriff out like that? Getting pistol-whipped wasn't something most men forgot easily.

Sheriff John Behan seemed prouder than most.

Slocum kept heading west.

As he rode along, he thought about all the sheriff had said. The Clantons were a tough bunch, no doubt about it, but Slocum had no fear of them. He'd ridden with tougher. Bloody Bill Anderson and Quantrill and Quantrill's wife Cattle Kate all carried killing to extremes, shooting instead of talking when it suited them. Ike Clanton couldn't hold a candle to them.

But then Quantrill and the others were far in Slocum's past. Ike Clanton was here and now and might pose a problem, if the Tombstone sheriff was any indication. Slocum's eyes narrowed when he saw the sudden glint of metal in the setting sunlight. He swung his horse around and headed due south, thinking to avoid whoever rode ahead.

In less than a mile he crossed the twin ruts of a road hacked through the Sonoran Desert by sheer repetition. Coach after stagecoach had driven this road, steel-rimmed wheels cutting into the sun-baked earth until a crude road formed.

Slocum dismounted and knelt, studying the track more carefully. Definitely stagecoach tracks. The width, the depth, the hoofprints from many horses all told the tale. He stood and squinted into the sun now hanging low in the west. Although it might have been a coach that had given that single reflection, he doubted it. Wells, Fargo and Company drivers didn't cotton much to the idea of driving at night through such terrain. They usually found themselves a place to hole up and rest both team and drivers.

He walked a dozen paces, looking at the ground, trying to decide if a stagecoach had come by recently. He thought it likely but couldn't tell for certain. The dirt was too firmly packed and baked dry by the sun. Slocum smiled grimly as he turned up his collar to the cold wind. It was hard to believe this land boiled in the day and froze at night—until moments like this.

Slocum swung into the saddle and rode slowly to the west, sometimes following the track and sometimes avoiding it. He guided his horse to the top of a small rise and sat there staring at the barren landscape. Its starkness matched the desert inside Slocum's gut. He wanted to take some time from his endless traveling and stay in one place, just for a while, But it never worked out that way. Remembering the reception he'd gotten back in Tombstone only reinforced his feelings of desolation. So many small towns were like that. The sight of a stranger brought out the law, ready to run any troublemakers out of town.

Tombstone was worse than most. He hadn't even been able to get a bath before Sheriff Behan ran him off.

A small sound, not of the desert, alerted Slocum. He bent forward slightly—and this saved his life. The sharp report from the rifle and the whine of a bullet came long after the hot lead grazed the lobe of his ear and sent his hat flying forward.

Slocum reacted instantly, tumbling in the direction taken by his hat. The bullet had come from behind. A backshooter was at work.

He picked himself up from the ground and tried to soothe his jittery horse. The skittish animal reared and pawed at him with her hooves. Slocum got her quieted down, then listened hard for some clue to the man responsible for shooting at him.

Shouted words came on the night breeze. ". . . son of a bitch is hit, I tell you. Let's go get 'im!"

"Careful, Lucas," came another voice. "He didn't move right. I watched and he didn't fall like you really nailed him. I think you just winged him."

"I shot him square in the back of his rotten head. Don't give me any of your lip. Let's get him and collect the bounty."

Slocum swore. Then he began to wonder. Had Behan succeeded in forming a posse this quick? That seemed outrageous for all that had happened between him and Behan, even if he *were* one of Deputy Earp's spies. Or did this political war run deeper than he thought? Slocum couldn't figure it out and he didn't try. Staying alive meant more than knowing the bloody details of the Behan–Earp feud.

He led his horse downslope so that he was no longer silhouetted against the blood-red disk of the setting sun. He found a waist-high cholla and wrapped the reins around it, then pulled his Winchester free from the saddle scabbard. He didn't want to face bushwhackers with just his sidearm.

Quieter than a shadow sliding across another shadow, Slocum worked his way around the bottom of the small rise until he came to the north side. From here he looked down a rocky arroyo. He worked the well-oiled action on his rifle, wincing at the loudness as it cocked. Slocum fell belly down and aimed down the arroyo, waiting for the men he knew were going to come sooner or later.

He waited less than five minutes before two figures came down the sandy bottom. One tugged at the other's sleeve and pointed to the top of the rise. The other shook his head, indicating that they should split up and circle the rise.

"Hell, Lucas, he's dead!" blurted the taller of the men.

"Shush!"

"He ain't in no condition to hear us, I tell you."

"You know what the boss said. We're not supposed to take no chances. These sons of bitches are dangerous."

"You don't have to go tellin' me that!"

Slocum frowned. Who were these men? They didn't talk like lawmen, and why would bandits come after him? Clanton and his Cowboys specialized in Wells, Fargo shipments and rustling cattle. No need to bushwhack a solitary rider on the desert. There was hardly any money in that and the risk could be immense.

Just how big, Slocum was getting ready to show them.

Slocum's finger tightened around the Winchester's trigger, then eased back. Curiosity began to get the better of him. Who in hell *were* these owlhoots?

"Damn," he cursed under his breath. He had to be careful. If they were part of Clanton's gang, there might be a dozen more backing up these two.

Slocum sank down into deep shadow when one man came directly toward him. The man's progress told that he had no idea of Slocum's hiding place, that anyone was within a mile of him. He stumbled on the loose rock and cursed loudly, cut himself on a mesquite thorn and cursed even more, then blundered past Slocum. Slocum followed, trying to see the man's vest and if a star gleamed there.

Slocum didn't think he was a lawman and when he didn't see a badge, this confirmed his suspicions. Bounty hunter? Slocum didn't think he had a bounty on his head. Behan didn't have that kind of money around—and any reward had to be approved by the Arizona Territory governor, which might take weeks.

Or was Behan angry enough to promise a bounty and then hope that it would be approved later, after Slocum was either locked up or dead and buried? That didn't set right.

Slocum became even more curious. He followed on feet so soft that the man ahead heard nothing. All the time, Slocum kept his rifle leveled and ready for action.

"Lucas!" came the cry from around the hill. "I found his horse. No sign of him. Be damn careful!"

Lucas—the man in front of Slocum—called back, "You sure? I coulda swore that I got him dead center."

"Don't even find any blood."

"Too dark," said Lucas. The man stomped forward, not even trying to walk quietly.

"You make more noise than a war party of Jicarillas," Slocum said.

"Keeps away the rattlers," Lucas said. Then the man

realized that the voice had come from behind and wasn't familiar. He spun but Slocum took two quick steps and swung his rifle, aiming to catch the man on the side of the head and stun him.

Lucas had moved forward half a pace; Slocum's rifle butt connected harder than anticipated and directly on the point of the man's chin. Lucas's head snapped back, his body jerked upright, and he fell to the ground.

Slocum knelt and began going through the man's pockets for some indication of why Lucas and his partner so willingly backshot him. The man's vest pocket yielded a battered two-dollar watch. Slocum squinted at it. From what he could see, the watch ran at least an hour slow. Holding it to his ear, he knew why. It sounded as if gravel had been dropped inside the case. He stuffed the watch back into the man's pocket and continued his search.

A sweat-soaked bundle of greenbacks went into Slocum's pocket. From the size, Slocum guessed that the roll amounted to less than ten dollars. He continued to dig but found nothing more. No warrant for arrest, no papers of any kind. If Lucas belonged to a *posse comitatus* he certainly hid his authority well.

Slocum took the man's six-shooter and stuck it into his belt. Lucas hadn't carried the rifle he'd used to backshoot Slocum. Slocum left the man unconscious and went to find his partner. Questions still burned bright in Slocum, and he wanted some answers soon. He was rapidly tiring of this hunt.

He retraced his steps around the slope and then worked his way uphill again. He saw where he'd hitched his horse. The animal snorted and jerked hard at her reins, trying to pull free of the spiny cholla.

Slocum lay still, keen eyes looking for any sign of movement. Something spooked his horse. He thought it might be the other bushwhacker lying in wait nearby.

He smiled slowly when he saw the brief bright flare of a lucifer. The man worked on a cigarette while he waited impatiently. John Slocum instinctively brought his rifle sights to bear on the spot where the careless man's chest would be. He paused for a moment, considering how easy this shot would be. That wouldn't satisfy his curiosity about the identity of his victims, though.

It was getting colder and Slocum wanted to put this to a quick end. A bullet would do it, but wanton killing had lost its appeal to him long before the Lawrence raid and being gut-shot by Quantrill for protesting the slaughter of innocent women and children.

He moved back downhill until he came within a few yards of the man hunched down behind a low bush, trying to smoke his cigarette without being too obvious. To Slocum the man might as well have lit a signal fire.

"Go for your gun and you're a dead man," Slocum said.

The man tried, anyway. Slocum fired. The man shrieked—nothing too serious, Slocum guessed.

"I can see you pretty good," Slocum said. "Don't make me kill you."

"You thieving son of a bitch!" the man shouted. Then, louder, "Lucas, he's got the drop on me!"

Slocum spat out a bit of desert sand that had accumulated in his mouth, then said, "Lucas decided to take a little nap. He'll be fine, but not for an hour or two. *Drop your gun!*"

The man refused to give in easily. His rifle came up and spat foot-long tongues of bright orange flame as he fired out into the night. He had no idea where Slocum was, but one bullet came close enough to force Slocum to the ground. He hefted his own rifle and sighted in on the black mass of the bushwhacker.

A single shot silenced his assailant. Slocum waited for a few minutes, chaffing at the delay but knowing he had to wait. If the man only play-acted that he'd been hit, Slocum would be in a world of woe trying to approach before the man tired of it.

A good five minutes went by and Slocum detected no movement. He inched forward until he reached out and touched the man's boot.

Slocum stood, rifle covering the man—and instantly knew he hadn't waited long enough before advancing. The same hard boot he'd touched lashed out savagely and knocked away the rifle's muzzle. Slocum's bullet dug a path down into sand even as the man surged to his feet, fists swinging.

Slocum could either retreat or attack. His powerful legs gathered under him and he drove forward, rifle barrel slamming hard into the man's chest. Somewhere in the jumble of flailing arms and legs, Slocum lost hold on the rifle and caught a fist on the side of his head that turned him dizzy for a second.

"You backshooter!" the man snarled. "You think you can rob and kill and nobody'll do a damned thing about it. Well, mister, you're wrong. *Dead* wrong!"

Slocum saw the man going for the six-shooter stuck in his belt. Slocum turned on the ground and tried to get to his Colt slung in its cross-draw holster. He couldn't reach it but he did find the butt of Lucas' pistol. Slocum dragged it out and fired at the same time the other man did.

Slocum knew instantly that he had missed. The feel of the gun was all wrong. His shot had gone up and to the left. But the other man hadn't done much better. He sat down heavily and moaned. His gun had blown up in his hand. Bloody shreds of flesh dangled.

"Go on, kill me," the man moaned. "That's about all

you know how to do, ain't it?"

"Don't know who you think I am, but you're wrong." Slocum tossed away Lucas' gun. The balance was wrong for him and the man obviously tended to it too seldom for it to be in good condition. He preferred his own well-balanced, precision Colt Navy.

"You're one of Clanton's men. You got to be."

"Who are you? You and Lucas?" Slocum asked the question, wondering if he'd get any answer without beating it out of the injured man. The sheer hatred boiling from the man's eyes was almost enough to bore through mortal flesh and bone.

"Special agents for Wells, Fargo, and Company," the man said between clenched teeth. The pain got to him and he wobbled until Slocum wondered how he kept upright. "You know that, you, you . . ." Words weren't enough for the company man to express his hatred.

Slocum pulled his hat down to keep his face in dark shadow. Behan wanted a piece of his hide. It wouldn't do letting the Wells, Fargo man get together with the sheriff. If they joined forces, they might make life damned miserable for him until he could get far enough away so that it didn't matter.

"Let me see your hand." The man tried to resist. Slocum jerked hard enough to give the man a shot of pain that made him clench his teeth and turn pale. Slocum looked at the hand and decided it wasn't too bad. Some skin had been burned off and a couple of fingers didn't work right and proper, but no serious, permanent damage had been done.

"Should keep your pistol in better condition," Slocum said. He ripped away the man's bandanna and wrapped it around to protect the wound.

"Why're you doin' that?" the man snapped. "Just being

nice to me ain't enough. I'll see you swinging at the end of a rope for the way you been shootin' up our stages. You bastard."

"You got the wrong man," said Slocum. "I'm just passing through. I don't much care about robbing Wells, Fargo or killing you or your friend." Slocum gestured in the direction where he'd left Lucas unconscious on the ground. "But I don't like men who get idiot ideas into their heads and then hang onto them come hell and high water."

The man grumbled.

"I'm not one of Clanton's gang, but consider this a friendly warning. The next time your path crosses mine, you'd better be a sight more civil. If you're not, you're going to end up buzzard bait."

The man fell silent and just stared. Slocum saw that he hadn't convinced the company man.

Slocum stood and backed off, then turned and went to find his rifle. As he bent down, he heard movement behind him. He forgot the rifle, hit the ground, and rolled, his Colt Navy coming into his hand in one smooth motion. He cocked and fired. The dull grunt told him he'd found his target.

The man had crawled over to where Slocum had discarded Lucas' pistol and had tried to use it. Slocum's bullet caught him high on the shoulder and knocked him back.

"You're not dead, but you will be next time. That's a promise," Slocum said, angry.

He found his rifle and went directly to his tethered horse. He jerked the reins free of the cholla, got a few spines out of the leather, then climbed into his saddle. From behind the nearby creosote bush he heard the man alternately moaning and swearing up a blue streak. When he started yelling for his partner, Slocum put his spurs into the horse's flanks and trotted off.

He didn't like backshooters. But more than this, he had a real loathing for stupid men. The ones he left behind were too stupid for their own good. They hadn't given him a chance to identify himself, to show that he had no larcenous intentions toward their damned stagecoaches. They'd just shot at him from behind.

That thought festered and made Slocum even angrier. He'd given them the chance to admit they were wrong. He might have identified himself if they hadn't been so set on shooting someone down. They might have a blood feud with Ike Clanton or others in his gang of rustlers, but that didn't give the Wells, Fargo agents any call to shoot at everyone out in the desert.

Let them ride guard and protect their shipments. Slocum saw nothing wrong with that. But to go manhunting and backshooting anyone they found . . .

By the time he found the twin ruts left by the Wells, Fargo and Company coaches, he seethed at the stupidity and viciousness shown by the two agents.

A slow smile came across his face when an idea hit him. Wells, Fargo owed him for what their men had tried to do. And he wasn't above becoming the very bandit they'd accused him of being.

The next stage that came along would fall to him. John Slocum vowed that he would get something to pay him back for what they'd done to him up on that rise.

A small silver shipment might go a long way toward soothing his ruffled feathers. A very long way. And the best part of it was that Ike Clanton and his Cowboys would get the blame.

3

The more Slocum thought about robbing a Wells, Fargo stagecoach, the more he liked the idea. Sheriff Behan hadn't treated him very civilly back in Tombstone. Thinking the worst of a person might not be too smart, Slocum reflected. That person might get ideas.

The real clincher came when he thought about the two company men Wells, Fargo had patrolling the road. Lucas and his partner had done more to incite crime in Arizona Territory than to deter it. At least, that was true when it came to John Slocum. He wasn't a man who felt that anyone owed him a living.

He did feel that you paid for what you did, one way or the other. Lucas and the other man had taken the bottom off his ear. This was a minor wound, hardly a scratch compared to the way that gun had blown up in the agent's hand. But their actions had produced a debt. Slocum fig-

ured a few bars of silver being shipped from the mines
south of Tombstone might make his trip a mite easier and it
would certainly even the score with sheriff and shipping
company.

Slocum poked fitfully at the cooking fire, then looked
up over the haze-purpled mountains far to the east. The sun
poked above them, promising warmth and lying. The night
hadn't been too bad; he'd spent worse on the trail. But he
worried about the two company agents following him.

"All the more reason to lighten the load of a stage," he
said aloud. If those two were the best Wells, Fargo could
put into the field to protect their shipments, he had nothing
to worry about.

He finished his breakfast and scattered the cooking-fire
ashes before breaking camp. In the saddle he felt a sense of
purpose that had been lacking in recent weeks. Slocum had
drifted aimlessly, not knowing or much caring where he
went. Although he didn't intend to make a living out of
robbing stagecoaches, this robbery brought him back to
full life. He felt a vitality and sense of purpose surging
through his veins that had been absent too long.

He *wanted* to rob that Wells, Fargo coach.

Slocum rode along the twin-rutted dirt road, eyes sharp
for a likely spot to ambush the stage. The flat desert didn't
afford good opportunity, so he kept riding. Not knowing
the stage's schedule put him at a small disadvantage, but
Slocum didn't care. He had nowhere better to be and nothing better to do.

The road turned up slightly, heading into the foothills.
He rounded one and stared at the army of saguaros march-
ing along the lee side of the hill. A man could stand behind
one of those giant cacti and never be seen. But he put this
ruse out of his mind. The cacti only grew some distance
away from the road and weren't of much use to him.

He reined in and stared when he saw a cloud of dust in the far distance. Many riders, moving fast and hard. Slocum craned his neck but failed to make out any details. From the direction they came, he knew it couldn't be anyone pursuing him from Tombstone.

Slocum pondered this new development. With Wells, Fargo and Company so eager to string up outlaws, this might be an entire band of agents riding hellbent for leather to—where? Slocum didn't know. But as long as they moved in a direction away from him, he felt confident that their company's stage would fall an easy prey to him.

He wheeled his horse and rode farther along the road until he found a spot where the road switched back so that whoever rode shotgun wouldn't be able to see the right side of the road too well. The sharp bend and steep grade made it necessary for the stage to slow down, also. That would be the time to make his move.

Slocum rode back and forth along a mile of road, hunting for the exact spot for his robbery, deciding on the quickest way to make his escape. Not wanting to kill anyone needlessly had its drawbacks. That left angry company men behind him, determined to bring him to frontier justice. Most drivers couldn't care less about being robbed, if they came through with their hides in one piece.

The guards were a different breed, though. Slocum had ridden shotgun a time or two in his day to earn a few extra dollars. It always came as a personal insult to those men when they were held up. He shook his head as he remembered the feelings. Not too many guards survived a stickup, either. That might have something to do with how nasty they always got after a robbery.

String up a road agent and maybe save themselves from being robbed again was their philosophy.

"So," he said, patting his horse on the neck. "That

boulder's where you'll be, old girl. Just waiting for me to come back with a load of gold and silver bars. Then it's off to Mexico." His eyes turned toward the south. The desert wouldn't be hospitable but it had to be an easier path than trying to get on through the mountains to the west or heading north up past Tucson and enough lawmen to catch any robber.

Slocum played out what would happen over and over, seeing it slightly different each time. He didn't want any mistakes. A solitary robber was at a disadvantage. That made this all the more exciting for him. He owed Wells, Fargo something for the way their two agents had treated him.

Hell, he thought, the entire Arizona Territory owed him. Sheriff Behan had jumped him, too. Let Wells, Fargo and the sheriff go after each other like fighting cocks in the ring. Slocum smiled at the idea. Behan caught merry hell for the way Clanton operated so freely, of that he was sure. If Deputy Marshal Earp had any say-so, Behan would be under continuous scrutiny.

That might even be the festering source of dispute between Earp and the Tombstone sheriff.

By midday, Slocum had worked through any problem that might come up. He pushed some large rocks down onto the rutted track to slow the stage, then climbed up atop a large boulder and stretched out, hat pulled down over his eyes. Like a lizard in the sun, he dozed most of the day. Only when the distant clatter of harness and wheels rose from the desert floor to his vantage point did he come fully awake.

Standing gave him a good view of the road. The cloud of dust rising from the trail told of a heavily laden stagecoach. He smiled at that. He doubted passengers would be plentiful this time of year. That meant the stagecoach creaked and strained under a full load of bullion.

His only problem would be getting away with it.

Slocum hefted his rifle and adjusted his sweaty bandanna over his face. Pulling down his battered, dusty gray Stetson so that he peered out from under the rim, his features totally hidden, he crouched down beside the boulder and waited.

Less than five minutes later, he heard the wheezing horses working to pull the heavy stagecoach up the slope. When the second horse came even with his position, he rose and aimed his Winchester directly at the dozing guard.

"Lose that shotgun or I'll blow your head off!" he shouted.

The driver tried to whip the horses into a run. At this angle of incline, around that bend, it proved futile. The guard jerked alert, eyes blinking. For a moment the sunlight blinded him. When he could see clearly he looked directly down the barrel of Slocum's rifle.

"Don't," Slocum cautioned.

"You damned . . ." began the guard. He spat, then tossed his shotgun over the side of the box. It landed in the road, discharging one barrel. Slocum thought his heart was going to explode at the sound; he almost pulled back on the trigger to shoot the guard.

"Wait!" cried the driver, putting on the brake. The stage tried to roll back down the hill. Without the brake it would have started dragging the horses with it.

"Toss down the strong box," Slocum ordered.

"You won't get away with this," the guard said, courage returning. "We'll track you down, by God. Every agent for Wells, Fargo will be after you. There'll be a reward. You'll be a wanted man."

"You'll be dead if you don't shut up." Slocum had no desire to listen to futile threats. Before he had done anything to warrant it, the company agents had been after him. He might as well be shot for a wolf as a lamb.

"There's nothing in the box you'd want," said the driver.

"I'll look." Slocum heard a ring of truth to the driver's words. The heavy iron box sailed through the air and landed heavily in the road to the side of the coach. Slocum cautiously circled around and went to the strong box. He used the butt of his rifle to knock off the rusty padlock. A quick look inside confirmed what the driver had said.

"Only U. S. Mail," the driver said.

"Something's weighing you down. Maybe back in the boot." Slocum motioned for the men to get down. They complied with ill grace, the guard muttering under his breath and scratching furiously at his beard.

As Slocum walked to the back of the stage, he pulled open the door and ordered, "Everyone out."

Only one passenger emerged—and she almost cost Slocum his scalp.

Momentarily distracted as the woman climbed out, exposing one dainty ankle, Slocum took his eyes off the guard. The man let out a bull roar and charged, meaty arms reaching out to encircle Slocum. They tumbled backward, going a short distance down the hill and into a rocky ravine. Slocum winced in pain as the rocks tore at his back and side, but he came to his feet before the guard.

Setting his feet, Slocum gauged the distance between them and swung a haymaker that would have thrown him flat on his face if he missed his target. The wild, hard punch landed squarely on the side of the guard's head. The man went down like a buffalo shot with a .69 caliber Sharps.

Slocum spun, Colt flashing from his holster. He got the drop on the driver just as the man picked up Slocum's fallen Winchester. They stood facing one another for a heartbeat, each trying to decide who had the advantage.

The driver looked down into Slocum's cold green eyes. He dropped the rifle and stood, hands in the air.

"You just made the right decision," Slocum said. He glanced at the guard. Blood trickled from the corner of the man's mouth and his eyelids pulsed. Slocum guessed the guard would be out for at least fifteen minutes, maybe more.

He climbed back up the ravine slope and stared at the woman who had distracted him. She showed no fear. Her cornflower-blue eyes boldly challenged him, daring him to say and do his worst. Light brown hair floated out from under a large-brimmed hat like an angel's halo to frame an oval face so perfect and beautiful that it took Slocum another second to pull his attention back to check the driver.

The driver's spirit had been broken. He stood as docile as a cow chewing its cud.

"Sorry to inconvenience you, ma'am," Slocum said.

"Does this mean you're not going to rob me?"

"More interested in what might be riding at the back of the stage." Colt on the driver, he edged around and unfastened the canvas. He almost laughed at his good fortune. Four heavy boxes had been stashed here. Levering one out, he let it fall to the rocky roadbed. He had to shoot off this lock; it was brand new and showed no hint of rust. Slocum kicked open the lid and stared inside. Ten small silver bars gleamed.

"Each box carrying the same load?" he asked. The driver shrugged.

Slocum's mind raced. He couldn't possibly get away with four boxes—forty bars of silver bullion! His horse wouldn't stand up under the load, not with the hard riding he'd have to do to get down into the interior of Mexico. As much as he hated to pass up such bounty, he could take only a few bars of silver.

No wonder Ike Clanton and his Cowboy gang preyed on Wells, Fargo! With treasure such as this being transported out to the coast, everyone could get rich.

"This is all I need," he told the driver. "Get your guard into the stage and drive on."

The woman looked startled. "You're not going to shoot us?" she asked.

"No, ma'am. No need. I have what I need right here."

"You're not even going to take the rest? The other three strong boxes?" she pressed.

"Ma'am, during the War I saw a lot of plundering. Told myself then to just take what I need and leave the rest. Can't use any more than this," Slocum said, indicating the ten silver bars at his feet.

"You mean you don't have pack mules to move any more," said the driver.

"How bad do you want to get back in and keep on driving?" Slocum asked in a low, level voice that carried so much menace that the stagecoach driver took a stumbling step backward, his hands going even higher in the air.

"That is a strange philosophy for an outlaw, sir," the woman said. She turned slightly and Slocum got a good look at her figure. It was even prettier than her face. He licked his lips beneath the bandanna. It had been a powerful long time since he'd had a woman, and this one was both pretty and feisty.

She turned back and studied him again. "You *do* want me, don't you?" she asked in a voice so low that only Slocum could hear.

"Get back into the stage, ma'am. You might have to tend to the guard."

"You did hit him rather powerfully," she said, a smile

dancing on her lips. She showed no fear. Slocum found himself liking her spirit more and more—and there was nothing to dislike about her face or figure.

"Go fetch him up here," Slocum ordered the driver. The frightened man slipped and stumbled down the steep rocky slope, shaking the guard to get him awake.

"You're not like any outlaw I've encountered before," the woman said.

"Don't reckon you've come across too many, then," Slocum said. He watched the guard and driver carefully.

"I've seen my share. Arizona Territory is rife with them," she said. "My name is Ruth Macabee."

"Don't expect me to introduce myself," Slocum said. The driver moved to one side at the bottom of the ravine, his hand out of sight. Slocum didn't like that one bit.

"Here," Ruth Macabee said, handing him his fallen rifle. He almost snatched it from her. She started to laugh, then held it back and only grinned widely. He couldn't help noticing her perfect teeth.

Hell, everything about Ruth Macabee was perfect, as far as he could see.

"Don't go pulling out a gun," Slocum said to the driver. The man turned, hands high.

"The guard!" Ruth cried.

Slocum swung about in a smooth motion, his Colt homing in on the guard who had recovered. The guard had the hideaway gun. The double-barreled derringer exploded at the same instant that the Colt Navy spat its leaden death. The guard jerked, flat on his back in the ravine.

"You killed him!" cried the driver.

"Try anything that damnfool stupid and you'll join him!" snapped Slocum. He cursed the guard's stupidity.

Turning to the woman, Slocum said, "Get my horse. She's up in the rocks. Bring her back."

"Aren't you afraid I'll ride off and escape?" The tone Ruth used was teasing, taunting, challenging.

"You got to come downhill past me. Now get the horse!"

"Yes, sir." Slocum watched as she made her way upslope. He shook his head. Even from this direction she looked damn good.

He turned back to the driver and guard. The driver bent over the guard. "Throw the hideout gun away," Slocum called. The driver obeyed. He saw that the guard stirred. He had wounded him but he hadn't killed him outright. For that he was glad. He had no grudge with the man, though the guard certainly would with him after this.

Slocum glanced back upslope to see how Ruth Macabee fared with his horse.

To his surprise, the woman handled the horse with ease. Slocum had found the horse skittish. Ruth had no such problem.

"Here you are, Mr. Robber," she said. She looked down at the driver and guard. "I suppose I shouldn't say anything, but . . ."

"What is it?" Slocum asked, transferring one silver bar at a time into his saddlebags. The stitching threatened to tear open. He might not be able to carry all ten bars.

"I'll make a deal with you. I give a piece of important information, and . . ." She let her words trail off again.

"And what?"

"And you let me come along with you."

Slocum stopped and stared at her in disbelief. "You're joshing me," he said.

"Not at all, sir. I have my reasons. Oh, don't worry about your plunder. I have no designs on the silver."

"No!"

"Then I really shouldn't tell you about the posse riding

up the road toward us," Ruth said in a superior tone.

Slocum took a few paces down the road so that he could look around the sharp bend. Although he failed to see the riders, he saw their dust. Straining, he could even hear the pounding of their horses' hooves.

"You didn't have to say anything. They would have caught me with my pants down," he said, wondering about the woman's motives.

"I suspect I'd be more interested in you in that condition," she said, bright blue eyes twinkling. "But I am quite serious about wanting to join you."

"Does the sheriff want you?" Slocum asked.

"The sheriff? You mean that posse? I have no idea who they might be. I chanced to see them when I was higher up the slope fetching your horse."

"Sheriff Behan from Tombstone," said Slocum. That seemed the most logical choice for the posse's leader. But it might also be Lucas and his injured Wells, Fargo agent friend. With John Behan, he might get a trial. If the Wells, Fargo company men caught him, Slocum knew he'd be lynched on the spot.

"I suppose it's of interest knowing your pursuers," Ruth said.

"Why come with me? They're after me. They'd think you were an accomplice." Slocum hazarded a quick look at the driver and guard. Both were quiet and hadn't moved an inch.

"I have my reasons. Not the least of which, you seem to be a strong, intelligent man. And a gentleman. I like that. I like that a great deal."

The last thing Slocum wanted was a woman, even one as beautiful as Ruth Macabee, slowing down his escape. But he knew he had little time to argue with her.

"My horse is carrying all the load she can. Unless you

can run a damn sight faster'n I think you can, I'm afraid you'll have to stay here with them." He indicated the driver and the guard. "You'll be safe with them. Just tell Behan that you were a victim, too."

Slocum found himself talking to empty air. Ruth had spun about, her long skirts stirring up a cloud of dust as she went to the lead horse. Her fingers worked expertly on the harness. In less time than he'd imagined possible, she had the horse free.

"If you can ride bareback, you can come along," Slocum said. He didn't think he'd have anything to worry about. There was no way she could ride without a saddle. Ruth Macabee looked and spoke like a lady whose exposure to horses might be one of those fancy English riding saddles and a groom to help her up.

Slocum looked with some longing at the three untouched boxes of silver and the four bars he had to leave in the one he'd opened. Six weighed down his mare to the point of her balking.

He put his heels to the horse's flanks and urged her forward, uphill, along the road and to a crossing arroyo. With luck he could follow the path he'd scouted earlier, confusing any pursuit with the tracks he'd left searching out this route.

Slocum pulled down his bandanna and leaned forward to assure his mare that everything was fine. Then he put the spurs to her. He wanted to get away from the coach as fast as he could. If Behan's posse had tired their animals charging up the road, well and good. That would give him another ten or fifteen minutes' headstart.

Slocum jerked around in the saddle when Ruth Macabee said, "Where are we heading? South to Mexico? Or west? Heard tell that the Cowboys have a hideout in the White Mountains."

He rode at a good clip, and Ruth paced him easily. She had hiked up her skirts and straddled the horse taken from the stage team, riding with the easy grace of a born horsewoman.

"Close your mouth. You'll catch flies," she chided. "Now, where are we heading? South or west?"

"South," Slocum said. He only hoped that he'd be able to keep up the pace that Ruth Macabee set as they wended their way through the torturous arroyos and then out into flat desert once more. The woman rode as if she'd been born on horseback.

What had he gotten himself into?

4

John Slocum felt his mare weakening under him. The weight of the six silver bars, his own weight, and the strain of picking her way through the loose gravel and soft sand took its toll on the mare's stamina. He reined in and dismounted.

"What's wrong?" Ruth Macabee asked. She looked as fresh as a daisy, and the horse she sat astride carried her with no effort. "Oh, your horse is tired."

Slocum wiped off some of the foam from his mare's sides. It wouldn't do to run the horse into the ground. He would be afoot and at the mercy of the sheriff and his posse.

"Damn the man," he swore.

"Do you mean the sheriff from Tombstone?" asked Ruth. She swung down and landed lightly beside him. She took hold of her horse's bridle and led the animal as if it were the most natural act in the world for her. Slocum was beginning to suspect that, for all her Eastern finishing school manners and speech, Ruth was more at home with a horse than a teacup.

"We had a small run-in," Slocum said. "Nothing that should have gotten him this riled." He thought back to Lucas and the possibility that the Wells, Fargo men had gone into Tombstone and put up the money for the posse.

He should have left both men for the buzzards.

"You do seem to be dangerous," she said, casting a coy sidelong look in his direction. "But looks can be deceptive."

"What's that supposed to mean?"

"You could have killed both those men back there. Heaven knows they deserved it. You would have robbed them and let them be. Anyone could see that."

"You could?" Slocum said, more amused than he let show.

"Of course. You're dangerous, yes," she said, her voice turning husky and low. "But only when necessary. You wouldn't harm anyone just for the thrill of it. You're not like so many of the men out here."

"Which school did you attend?" he asked.

Ruth smiled and said, "The Groton Women's School of Refined Manners. Do you find me . . . refined in manner?" Again the coy look, the batting of her long dark eyelashes, the gleam of merriment in her wondrous blue eyes.

"I find you something of a problem," Slocum said. "My horse isn't going to keep going much longer. That means the posse will overtake us. What am I supposed to do then?"

"I might be able to use a rifle."

"Did the Groton Women's School teach you that?"

"There are many things Miss Peony and the other instructors didn't teach me, but which I know very, very well."

"Sheriff Behan might not cotton to you being with me. He's the kind of lawman who will shoot first and think about things later. You might be better off parting from my company."

"I will not!" Ruth Macabee sounded indignant at the suggestion.

"What do you want from me? The silver?"

"I am not a liar," she said. "I don't want six bars of silver. It doesn't even look to be high grade, though it might fool me. I'd have to examine it more closely."

Slocum shook his head. The woman rode bareback like an Apache, had the manners of European royalty, and considered herself a judge of bullion metal. Even worse, she had attached herself to him, and that made even more questions about her rise.

"What's your name?" she asked. "If we're going to be traveling companions, I'd like to know what to call you."

He considered this. If Behan overtook them, Slocum wasn't sure he wanted Ruth being able to put a name to his face. He laughed harshly when he thought a bit more on that. Behan knew who he trailed. Putting a name to the face meant nothing.

"You can call me John," he said.

"You're trying to say that as if it's a lie. I don't think it is. Very well, John. I believe your horse is rested enough so that we can ride once more. Would you like me to ride her for a mite? My weight isn't as great as yours and this horse is a sturdy brute."

Slocum silently nodded. What Ruth said made sense, and he was sure she couldn't steal his silver by trying to outrun him. That silver weighed down the mare more than he'd thought. But then he'd found more booty on the stage than his wildest dreams. All he'd really wanted was to strike back, to show the sons of bitches that they couldn't get away with pushing him around.

He hadn't expected a king's ransom to be laid at his feet like this. Slocum only wished that he'd had a pair of pack animals and maybe a partner. With that combination and some luck, he could have gotten free of any posse.

Now he'd have to depend more on luck than skill, and still he would only end up with six bars.

He rode bareback easily, occasionally glancing over at Ruth Macabee. She was quite an enigma. She showed either great courage or stupidity. He hadn't decided yet if she were a spoiled Eastern heiress out West to add a tad of excitement to her dull society life, or if some other motive drove her.

He had to believe that something more made her such a willing accomplice. Even if they were caught and she pleaded for mercy, claiming that he'd kidnapped her, she might not get gentle treatment at the posse's hands. She was so damned beautiful that someone in the posse would get the notion in his head to have a little fun with her.

For that matter, how did she come to be traveling alone? Wells, Fargo and Company had a good reputation for delivering their passengers alive, but the trip had to be especially dangerous for a lone woman.

"Where were you going?" he asked.

"Nowhere in particular," Ruth said, slowing her pace to ride alongside Slocum. Her knee brushed his. He tried to hold down the sudden thrill he felt at this brief contact. "I left Groton—that's in Connecticut, you know—and wanted to see the country I had read so much about."

Slocum heard a faint tremor in her voice. She hid great emotion well. And he was sure she was lying through her pretty, pursed lips.

"Perhaps, once I got to the Pacific, I would take a train north to San Francisco. That seems such a fine city. Have you ever been there, John?"

"Once or twice," he allowed. "Seems like a dangerous way of checking on what you've read. Those penny dreadfuls don't tell the real tale. You can get killed out here and nobody really much cares."

"That's the sort of thing I am interested in finding out for myself. You see, John, I want very much to become a newspaper reporter. There's a newsman in St. Louis, Mr. Joseph Pulitzer of the *Evening Post-Dispatch,* who is willing to give a woman a chance at the job."

"Never met too many reporters that knew their a— Excuse me." Slocum looked straight ahead. The reporters of his acquaintance were little better than confidence men. He couldn't see a woman in such a job. And Ruth's voice carried that small quaver that he took to mean that she was lying again. She had contrived this story to cover some other motive for her trip through the Arizona Territory.

He rode along for a spell, thinking hard. The route into Mexico wasn't going to be open to him, he decided. And with a woman along, even one like Ruth Macabee who managed to keep pace with him, he wasn't going to be able to cross the border before Behan's posse caught up. The pace was too slow and his horse was too tired. Those heavy silver bars weighed the mare down too much.

"You can always leave the silver," she said suddenly.

"What?" He glanced over at her. He had been thinking that Ruth wanted only the silver. This didn't set well with his ideas. "You wouldn't mind if I just dropped them and rode off?"

"As long as I got to go along."

"What is it that you want from me, if it's not the bullion?"

"Why, John, don't you think a woman can want you for yourself? I don't have to *want* anything from you."

"You don't leave a stage to ride with a stranger—a robber. What do you really want?" he demanded.

"Such suspicion, John. I'm disappointed in you." She chided him as she might a small child. It only increased his feeling that she wanted something from him that he might not be able to deliver.

"We've got to pick up the pace. The sheriff will be coming along after us soon enough. Don't know how good a tracker he is, but once we get into the desert, he'll be able to spot us from any rise."

Ruth squinted into the sun. "Be dark soon."

"It won't be dark for another four, five hours," he said glumly. In the twilight he stood a chance of losing the sheriff. But in the afternoon sun, Slocum saw no way of doing it.

"What about yourself, John?" she asked. "Where do you hail from? Not these parts. You've got a slight accent."

"It doesn't pay to know much about me. If the posse catches us, you're a kidnap victim, nothing else. I don't reckon I'd buy that story if I were Sheriff Behan, but we can try it. The less you know about me, the better."

"We won't be caught." Ruth Macabee spoke with such determination that Slocum looked at her anew. Something drove her. He just couldn't figure out what it might be.

They rode for another two hours, taking only brief rests before Slocum pulled up and pointed. A dust cloud in the distance warned of riders. He peered at the roiling dust, trying to judge how many might be in the posse. Slocum couldn't think of any reason for any other large band to be out on the warm desert sands.

He pulled the mare to the west and rode at a brisker pace. As they traveled, the horse tired visibly, stumbling often. Slocum finally reined in and dismounted.

"We've got to rest."

"That group of riders," Ruth said. "Do you think that was the posse? How could they get in front of us like that? They were riding from the west."

"That's why we're heading to the west," Slocum said tiredly. "Don't want to be where they're going, want to go where they've been. Safer."

"The White Mountains might give us a chance of losing them. Those mountain canyons are all twisty and turny," Ruth said with some animation. Slocum studied her. The woman's cheeks had flushed with color and a feel of excitement made her even more beautiful. She wanted to go to the mountains. He wondered why.

"Heard tell that Clanton and his Cowboys are holed up there. Might be even more dangerous than letting the sheriff find us."

"Ike Clanton is a fiend," she said with heat. Ruth turned and stared at Slocum, realizing she had reacted too strongly. "I've read everything I can about him. He would make such a good subject for an interview. That would surely get me a job on Mr. Pulitzer's newspaper."

Again Slocum had the feeling that she lied. He shrugged it off. There would be a parting of their ways soon enough. His horse wasn't strong enough to continue another day without collapsing under the burden of the bullion bars.

"We can reach the mountains by sunset," Ruth went on. "They're not that far."

"They are," said Slocum. "Desert air makes distances seem shorter. The White Mountains may be a two-or-three-day ride."

"Oh, no, they're not. We can reach the foothills in another two or three *hours'* riding."

Slocum didn't argue. He lay back and tipped his hat across his eyes. He needed rest as much as his mare did. But he didn't relax. He stayed keyed up and as jumpy as a long-tailed cat near a rocking chair.

The posse always rose to the top of his thinking. He hadn't expected them and only luck and a bit of planning on his part had allowed him to escape. Sheriff Behan wouldn't spend much time following the false trails near the site of the robbery. He would fling out a few scouts to find where the real trail lay. Slocum guessed that he had less than a day before the posse overtook him.

The other men he had seen riding in the distance bothered him, too. It wasn't a posse. Not unless there were two riding across the Sonora Desert. He reckoned those must have been Ike Clanton's men. Although he didn't expect it to happen, the posse might find the Cowboys and chase them into Mexico. That would take the heat off his tail.

Slocum knew there were two kinds of luck in the world, ne kind that just happened and the kind that you made. The first wasn't much good because it happened so seldom. He had to depend on the latter.

"John," Ruth Macabee called softly. "Come here for a moment. I'm not sure what I see."

Slocum looked out from under the brim of his battered and dusty gray hat. She stood on an arroyo bank staring back in the direction they'd just ridden from. He heaved himself up and took long strides until he stood beside her.

"What you're seeing is the posse," he said. The way they fanned out left little doubt in his mind. When he saw the sharp reflection of sunlight off a badge, he was positive. "Let's ride."

"John, your horse isn't going to make it. Put the saddlebags on my horse. It's stronger."

"Not much to anchor the bags to," he said.

"I'll put them in front of me." She looked at him, a small smile crinkling even her nose and the corners of her eyes. "Unless you think I'm going to steal your booty."

"Take it for all I care now. My hide's the only thing worth saving." He looked at the saddlebags weighing down his mare. "Though it'd be a real shame to just dump the silver."

"You would, though, wouldn't you?"

"If it meant my life. There's always more silver, other stagecoaches to rob. Don't know what it'd be like in the Promised Land and don't want to find out for a good long time."

Ruth laughed. Slocum unhitched the saddlebags and tossed them over the shoulders of her horse. She mounted in one quick jump with an ease that bespoke long practice. Whoever Ruth Macabee was, she wasn't an Eastern girl looking for a reporter's job.

They followed the meandering course of the sandy arroyo for almost a mile. Then Slocum motioned for the woman to get to higher ground. They struggled up a gravelly bank and onto rockier terrain. He hated to admit it, but Ruth had been right about the foothills. These rises and gulleys were part of the White Mountains. They hadn't been the long ride away he had believed.

"Where do we go, John?" she asked.

He looked over his shoulder and saw that the sheriff had taken the scent and now raced along like a bloodhound on the spoor of a fox.

"We find a place to do some shooting. You go on and I'll take a shot or two at them to keep 'em honest."

"No!"

"Why not? You've got the silver."

Ruth's mouth opened, then closed. She couldn't come up with a reasonable answer and hadn't expected to need to lie. Slocum knew now that she didn't want the silver. She wanted something more valuable. It was beyond him to guess what that might be.

He dismounted and led his mare to a ravine with several large boulders that would provide some measure of safety when the posse opened fire. He pulled out his Winchester and shook his head. He didn't have that much ammunition. Less than a dozen rounds, he discovered. To fight off Behan and his men with this and a Colt Navy didn't seem too likely to him. But he'd have to try. It meant his life.

"Higher, John. We can go higher."

He saw that they had time to do as Ruth wanted. Barely. Already he heard the excited cries from the sheriff and the men with him. They knew the end was near for their prey.

Another hundred yards up the ravine, Slocum had to take cover. A bullet ricocheted off a rock to his right and went singing off into the distance.

"Get down!" he called to Ruth Macabee. The lovely woman had already led her horse to safety behind a small dam of rocks.

He levered a shell into the chamber of his Winchester and sighted down the ravine. He cursed when it became apparent that none of the posse was overzealous enough to poke up their heads so he could shoot them off.

"Give it up," came Behan's shout. "We got you now, you mangy son of a bitch."

"I got a hostage with me," Slocum yelled back. "You don't want her getting hurt, now do you?"

"Don't make no never mind to us who you got!" another man in the posse shouted.

Slocum found out how much having a hostage meant. A

fusillade of bullets drove him down. He waited until the firing had died down, then poked his head up to look. Another hail of bullets forced him back. They were willing to blow the mountainside apart with their gunfire, he saw.

John Slocum wasn't going anywhere—except to the nearest tree to have his neck stretched by the posse.

5

John Slocum ducked as the lead beat off the top of the rock like angry hailstones. He waited a few seconds after the last shot had whined into the distance, then swung around, rifle ready. He fired four quick shots.

One bullet found a target. He heard a man yelp in pain. The cursing that followed told that Slocum hadn't hit the man in a spot where it would take him out of the gunfight. If anything, it might make him even madder—and even more dangerous. Slocum didn't much care one way or the other. If they got to him, they would lynch him. Dead was dead, whether it was done by someone only doing their duty or someone who was pissed off.

Slocum checked his ammunition supply and didn't like what he saw. He ran perilously low. When John Behan and two others tried to be heroes, Slocum used another four rounds. That kept the Tombstone sheriff at bay—for the moment.

Slocum ducked back behind the rock and started up the ravine. He found Ruth Macabee hunkered down less than fifty feet from where he'd made his stand. She gave him a level look that lacked any hint of fear.

"No more ammunition?" she asked.

"A few rounds, but not many more," he admitted.

"We can get deeper into the canyon, but we're going to have to get up some steep slopes to get out. This is a box."

"Damn." Slocum took a quick shot at one of the posse members who was trying to get to higher ground. The well-aimed bullet knocked a stone out from under the man's boot and sent him sliding face down along the rocky slope. Slocum wasn't up to his usual good marksmanship today. But the posse was getting the idea that they had to hang back or maybe get hurt. He'd have to use that—fast.

He motioned silently to the woman. They led their horses deeper into the canyon, the stony walls rising sharply on both sides. He couldn't see the end of the canyon but he took Ruth at her word that this was a box canyon.

"There, John. We can make it." Ruth pointed to a narrow gulley hardly large enough for their horses to pass through.

"They'll corner us if it doesn't cut through the ridge and lead to the next canyon," he said. But Slocum saw no other choice. They had to run. Standing to fight was a quick way to death. They were outnumbered and outgunned and he was running short of ammunition.

"I looked about fifty yards into the gap," Ruth said. "That far, at least, wasn't a dead end."

Dead end. The words rang in Slocum's brain like a cracked church bell.

"Get going. I'll hold them back."

"How many rounds do you have left?"

Slocum checked. He had only three shells for the Winchester. His Colt Navy held six. He dug in his gear and pulled out a matching Colt. That added five more shots, since he always carried it with its hammer on an empty cylinder. Fifteen bullets to hold back half that number of men. He should have been able to do it, but he knew that luck entered into it—and those men wouldn't make easy targets for him. They hadn't so far; they wouldn't now if they thought they'd trapped him.

A cornered rat always fights more fiercely.

Ruth started up the narrow gap, her horse protesting. She soothed the animal and got it moving. Slocum hurried his own mare into the gap and let it follow Ruth's. He had no time to tend to skittish animals. He was fighting for his life.

New attacks mounted from down the canyon he'd just left. The sheriff and his men shot at random, not having a distinct target, but it was enough to force Slocum to keep his head down.

He glanced over his shoulder and saw that Ruth had gone some way into the gap. He waited, then saw a target present itself. He fired. The man rose up, clutched at his chest, and fell backward. The way he moved told Slocum that he'd gotten a clean, killing shot. He felt no elation. He had just killed a man who had wanted to kill him. No emotion was attached to the act.

He fell into the deadly calm that he'd always experienced in battle. Before and after a fight he might show nerves, but never when he worked. His rifle fired twice more, finding one man's exposed arm. The Winchester's hammer fell on an empty chamber.

Slocum began retreating slowly, his eyes studying the

rocks on either side of the narrow gap. Nothing looked too promising. He'd hoped to find loose shale that might be brought down by a well-placed bullet or two. He saw nothing. If he had been on the rim of the canyon, he might have been able to roll boulders down the slopes just as Cochise and his Apaches did in Canyon de Chelley. But he had no chance to scale those sheer cliffs to get onto the rim.

"There he is. After him, men!" came the cry. Slocum used a few rounds from his Colt to keep Behan and the posse back.

"Hurry, John," came Ruth's urgent words from deeper in the rocky notch. "There's a crossing canyon. We might be able to get free if we reach it!"

Slocum joined her and saw instantly that they had no chance. The distances were too great to get deeper into the confusing array of canyons. But one chance did present itself.

"There," he said, pointing to a small arroyo. "We might be able to ride down that. If we get away from the rocks on the canyon floor, it'll let us ride." The only hope Slocum had was mounting again and riding hellbent for leather and dropping the silver bars. The rocky floor presented too many obstacles for easy riding. The horses had to pick their way carefully. Even so, they stumbled often. Too often.

But in the sandy-bottomed, steep-sided arroyo, they might have a chance.

Slocum started to pull the saddlebags with the silver bullion free from his saddle, but a bullet put a crease in his hat and forced him to duck. He knew any more delay would result in him being plugged, and maybe the mare as well.

He jerked hard on the reins. The horse protested, then

bucked as another bullet sang its song of death. This convinced the animal to move, silver bars weighing her down or not. Slocum barely kept up as the mare pranced and danced and made her way to the arroyo.

"Ride!" Slocum called to Ruth. "We can get out the mouth of canyon before . . ." His words trailed off. Toward the mouth of the long canyon he saw a cloud of dust rising. Part of the posse had backtracked, left the other canyon, and had now entered this one, cutting off retreat.

"Up the canyon, John," the woman gasped. "We might be able to get away in a crossing pass."

Slocum didn't know the White Mountains too well but that notion didn't strike him as being too likely. Canyons seldom had more than a handful of ways out. They had entered through a narrow gap. Was there another one they could use to escape? He doubted it, but they had to find out. They had no other chance.

He wheeled his mare around and guided her deeper into the canyon. Already came the posse's jeers and shouts of triumph. Those men had to know this country better than Slocum. They knew he rode into a box canyon, a trap, his capture and death.

"Stay low," he ordered Ruth. She already hugged the neck of her horse. A bullet danced off a nearby rock and opened a shallow groove on the animal's flank. It reared on her. Ruth Macabee did her best to keep control, but without a saddle and stirrups, she lost her balance and fell heavily. Slocum came level with her and reached down. Her blue eyes shone with gratitude as he pulled her up behind him.

The mare sagged under the added burden. They wouldn't be able to race away. The horse could do little more than stumble, but her pace was better than Slocum could have made on foot.

"There, there, old girl. You'll get oats for this—when we get out of here."

The horse looked back over her shoulder and let out an incredulous snort. Then she simply stopped. No amount of urging on Slocum's part could get her to move. The animal reached the limits of her endurance. To push her more would be to kill her.

"We fight," said Slocum. "For all the good it'll do us."

"We can—" Ruth began. He silenced her with a wave of his hand.

"There's no chance for me. You can plead for mercy from them. Sheriff Behan didn't strike me as a real bastard. He might not even lock you up."

"Listen to them," Ruth said, shuddering. "They sound like a pack of hunting dogs. Vultures, all of them! I'd rather die than let them take me."

Slocum didn't argue the point. The thought had occurred to him that the posse might consider raping such a beautiful "outlaw" part of their reward. He emptied his Colt, then switched to his spare. Six shots, no more. Then they'd overrun his position. He wondered if they would even put a cross on his grave.

Would they even bother to bury him after they hanged him, or would they leave his carcass for the buzzards?

Slocum knelt and slowly fired, each shot winging its way toward one of the posse. He hit one in six that he aimed at. Then he ran out of ammunition.

A sudden explosion from behind startled him. Slocum spun and saw the telltale white smoke from a rifle rising from behind a saguaro. A second shot pulled him in the other direction. This shot could only have come from behind a boulder at the far side of the arroyo. Still another

shot from halfway up the wall of the canyon brought a
scream of pain from someone in the posse.

"We got those sons of bitches!" came a cheerful cry
from even deeper in the canyon. "They'll learn better'n to
come after Clanton's Cowboys!"

"Do you see where they are?" Slocum asked Ruth. She
shook her head. He turned back to the posse. They had
stopped their steady advance and now took cover along the
arroyo banks, but it wouldn't do them any good, he knew.
Not if more of Clanton's men were stationed along the rim
of the rocky canyon. From the high ground they could
shoot anyone moving in the canyon.

Slocum's keen eyes worked along the rim. Twice he
saw the glint of the setting sunlight off rifle barrels. Along
the canyon floor the day died with an abruptness that
always startled him. Everyone moved in twilight now, the
long tongues of orange from the rifles providing dazzling,
blinding illumination.

"You up there, Ike?" cried Behan. "You there?"

"Ike's not with us, Sheriff," came a rough, bass voice.
"Don't matter none. Curly Bill Brocius knows how to treat
lawmen right. Everyone, open up on 'em!"

Slocum grabbed Ruth and carried her to the sandy arroyo floor as a dozen riflemen started shooting.

"They're as likely to kill us as the sheriff," Slocum said.

"I'm not complaining," said Ruth, snuggling closer.
The woman made quite an armful. Slocum had to admit
that this was the only bright spot on an otherwise tarnished
day.

"The Cowboys are driving off Behan and his posse.
Listen." Hooves pounded from the mouth of the canyon.
The sheriff had decided not to face up to Curly Bill and his
superior firepower and position.

"That's good! The posse would have hanged us!"

"Me, maybe. Not you. But what's a band of road agents going to do to us? To you?"

"You worry so, John. You shouldn't. Clanton has a reputation for being fair with other robbers. He'll listen to our story. We've made it! We're going to get away from the sheriff!"

Slocum didn't share Ruth Macabee's enthusiasm for riding smack dab into the arms of the outlaws.

Dead was dead. No matter if a lynch mob did it or Clanton's Cowboys plugged him between the eyes.

Slocum pushed the woman away and stood, hands high, when he heard the crunch of boots in the sun-baked sand as the outlaws came down to see who they had rescued.

6

John Slocum slipped his Colt into his belt. The other ebony-handled pistol weighed down his left hip in its cross-draw holster. Neither would serve him against so many rifles.

"John," Ruth Macabee said breathlessly, "these are Ike Clanton's men!"

"So it seems."

The men came down from their positions on the cliff faces and from behind protecting boulders. Slocum had guessed that a dozen men might have been in the band. More than two dozen came to form a circle around him and Ruth. He pushed their crude comments about the lovely woman out of his mind. Just staying alive would prove the hard part.

None of these desperadoes had the look of the good samaritan about them. Most would as soon shoot their grandmother for her gold teeth as look at her.

"What we got here?" asked a short, squat, burly man with bushy brown handlebar mustaches. He wore a dusty black bowler that had seen better days and a brocade vest with large rents in it. A thick gold chain dangled across the front, clicking every time he moved. Slocum figured that a stolen watch was fastened onto the end hidden away in a torn vest pocket. A heavy Colt bounced on the man's right hip and in his gnarled hands he held an ancient Henry rifle with a revolving cylinder. Everything about the man bespoke death.

"Thanks for helping out," said Slocum. "The sheriff wanted a piece of my hide."

"And why would John Behan come all the way from Tombstone after the likes of you?" the man asked. He stopped in front of Slocum and peered up at the taller man. Slocum stood stock still, his cold green eyes boring down into the man's watery ones. He looked Slocum up and down critically, then walked around him. Slocum sized up the others while he was being scrutinized. Too many rifles pointed in his direction for him to do anything but die if he tried to escape. He stood quietly, waiting for the challenge he knew would come.

"You don't look like a big enough fish for Behan to go fishin' for, not with that many paid hands in a damned posse. How'd you get him all riled up?"

"Ran into a pair of Wells, Fargo men. They mistook me for someone else. Reckon I left them wanting to get some revenge. It was them that got the sheriff after me."

"Behan don't cotton none to them company sidewinders," the man said. He spat. The dry sand sucked up the juice and left a dark, hard spot. "He wouldn't cross the street to kick 'em in the balls. No, you done something to him."

"Might have left Tombstone in a hurry," said Slocum.

"You're a cool one. You know who we are, don't you?"

"You're with Ike Clanton!" cried Ruth Macabee. "You're the famous Cowboys."

"Famous?" laughed another. "Hear that, Bill, we're famous. Or so the lady says."

Slocum wished that Ruth hadn't drawn their attention. Men living at the edge of the law seldom had enough of what a woman could offer. A lady as lovely as Ruth would be a prize second to none. Yet Slocum had to wonder at her reaction.

She seemed delighted to have been rescued by some of the worst of the Arizona Territory bandits. If she didn't have the sense God gave a mule, there wasn't much Slocum could do about it. But it set him to thinking that Ruth Macabee played a hand very close to her fine chest. He just couldn't fathom what it might be.

"You're a good-lookin' one, ain't you?" said one man, moving closer to peer at Ruth in the dim twilight. "You and me're gonna be good friends, ain't we?"

As he reached out to touch her cheek, he grunted and doubled over. The outlaw fell to the ground clutching his belly.

"Don't *mo*-lest the lady," the stocky man said. He tipped his bowler in Ruth's direction and said, "I'm Curly Bill Brocius, the one responsible for riding herd on these mangy owlhoots. Forgive Josh, there. He gets himself into an uproar over the damnedest things."

"Looks worth gettin' into an uproar over," another man observed. He fell silent when Curly Bill fastened his watery-eyed stare on him. Slocum wondered how much it would take to push Brocius over the edge and turn him kill-crazy. He spoke politely to Ruth and hadn't done anything to give the opinion of being close to a mad-dog killer, but Slocum had seen the type before.

Cross Curly Bill Brocius and die. It was that simple.

"Now we come to why you folks are out on the desert being chased by our good friend Sheriff Behan."

"We robbed a stagecoach!" blurted Ruth.

"Oh, you did now, did you?" Curly Bill said sarcastically. He cocked his head to one side. The twisted brown locks that give him his nickname worked out from under the bowler and bounced in springy coils. "What booty did you take off the Wells, Fargo coach? Nothing but a few pieces of U. S. Mail, is my guess."

"No, Mr. Brocius," Ruth said, her face aglow with excitement.

"Ruth," cautioned Slocum. The Cowboys would find out sooner or later, but he wanted to use the six silver bars as a ransom. If they merely took the bullion, there'd be no reason to leave either Slocum or Ruth Macabee alive.

"We didn't get much," she rushed on, ignoring Slocum. "The posse almost caught us at the stagecoach. We could only get away with a part of the cargo."

"Ain't no bullion being shipped now," said Josh, pulling himself to his feet. He stayed bent over, every line of his body showing pain and the desire to strike out. Slocum became warier. Josh couldn't touch Curly Bill without getting more of the same.

That didn't leave too many people in his power.

Slocum crossed his arms, ready to fight if Josh wanted to make a play.

"Now, what Josh here says is true. No Wells, Fargo and Company shipments are being made for a month or more. We were too good at stopping them, it seems. While Ike and a few others was off rustling cattle, me and the boys took it to Wells, Fargo and cleaned them out."

"Silver bars," Ruth cut in. "We were only able to get

away with a few silver bars."

Curly Bill Brocius motioned. Two of the men went to Slocum's mare and rummaged in the saddlebags.

"How damn, Bill. They got six silver bars. Six of the damn things!" cried one.

Curly Bill's eyebrows rose. "Looks like we been lied to. Our source of information in Tucson said that Wells, Fargo wasn't gonna be transportin' any bullion."

"There were three other strong boxes," said Ruth. "Ten bars in each box. We had to leave four."

"That so?" said Curly Bill. His pale eyes fastened on Slocum. "Tell me that's the way it happened," he challenged.

"Just as she said. Behan and his posse came up before we could do anything with the rest."

"Are you a lucky son of a bitch, or are you just a lyin' snake in the grass?" Curly Bill asked in a tone that showed he hoped that he could gun down Slocum.

"Mr. Brocius, it's true. Every word of it," said Ruth. "Whoever's supplying you the information on the shipments may have been wrong—or he might have been found out. What if those Wells, Fargo agents lied to him? It might be their way to sneak the shipments past you."

"It might, it might," said Curly Bill. "It might also be a sneaky way of getting one of the company agents into our camp."

"I'm not a Wells, Fargo agent," Slocum said coldly.

"Neither of us is," said Ruth.

"Lady, I don't think you are, but this one's got the look about him." Curly Bill's eyes flashed to the worn ebony handles of Slocum's Colts, to the way he stood, to the hardness in his eyes.

"You got all six of the silver bars. Doesn't matter where it came from," said Slocum. "Take it and be damned.

We're not asking anything from you."

"You'd just let us take the bullion?" goaded Curly Bill.

"Not much I can do about that, is there?" asked Slocum. Most of the rifles still pointed straight at him. "Reckon that's an expensive price to pay for getting Behan's posse off my trail. But not as expensive as getting lynched."

"Behan was after you for something else. How'd he know you was going to rob the stage, unless you told everyone in town? You don't seem the type to do that."

"We got into a fight," Slocum said with some reluctance. "He ended up with a gun barrel alongside his head. I left Tombstone rather than wait for him to get up and ask me to dance."

Curly Bill Brocius threw back his head and laughed, the echoes ranging up and down the canyon. "That's rich! You knocked out old Behan, he comes after you and spoils what may have been the best damn robbery this month. You sure have had a turn of bad luck, haven't you?"

"Is my luck going to get any worse?"

Curly Bill Brocius studied Slocum again, took off his bowler and used an elbow to polish the dusty dome, then settled the hat squarely back atop his head.

"You got us all wrong, mister. We don't steal from others in our line of business. No, sir."

"You're not letting me keep the silver?" Slocum asked suspiciously.

"Well, sir, not that. Let's say five bars of that is for services rendered. Seems a fair enough price to pay."

"We . . . we don't want to just go riding after the sheriff," Ruth cut in. "Can we go with you? For a little while?"

Brocius laughed at this. Slocum simply stared at the woman.

"Ma'am, you can ride with us anywhere we go. Reckon you earned the right. None of us has much liking for Wells,

Fargo and you hurt them bad, leastways their pride. Damn, but I wish we coulda taken the rest of that silver."

"So do I," said Ruth, her eyes going unfocused at the thought of so much bullion. This convinced Curly Bill Brocius.

"You're welcome to come back to camp with us."

"Bill . . ." Josh started. "I don't think Ike's gonna like havin' visitors."

"Can we join you?" asked Ruth. "Haven't we proved we can do anything you can?"

Ruth Macabee fell silent when Brocius shot her a cold look. The outlaw said, "This silver don't prove nothing, just that you got lucky—once."

He stared at Slocum, then back to Ruth. "You can ride up to camp with us. Josh might be right about what Ike'd say. But the two of you don't look like that much trouble till he decides."

"We'd prefer to just ride on out," said Slocum. He didn't want to find himself a prisoner in the center of the White Mountains. The Cowboys obviously had their camp well hidden. Once they rode into it, no one left alive who wasn't approved by Ike Clanton. Slocum couldn't figure it would be any other way.

"No!" cried Ruth. "We'd like to see the camp."

Slocum stared at the woman. She wasn't stupid. Far from it, if everything Slocum had seen of her meant anything. Ruth Macabee had lied repeatedly to him, of that Slocum was positive. But what lay behind her desire to see the Cowboys' camp? It wasn't the need for a newspaper article to impress a St. Louis editor.

"We'll just head on up into the canyon," said Curly Bill Brocius. "We can reach camp before it gets much darker."

Slocum started to speak. A rifle cocked behind him. Any chance for getting away from the outlaws lay behind

him now, dashed by Ruth's insistence on learning more—
too much—about the Cowboys.

"Lead the way," he said to Curly Bill. The man tipped
his bowler in Ruth's direction, waited for his two captives
to mount up, and then summoned a man who held the reins
to his horse.

Brocius rode a few yards to the rear, letting others
choose the path through the White Mountains and into their
camp. It was as if he wanted to be sure of having a good
shot at Slocum's back should any trouble develop.

For the hour they rode, a spot itched between Slocum's
shoulder blades, just about the spot where Brocius stared.

As Slocum rode down the long, narrow canyon, he looked
up and saw the silhouettes of armed guards in the rocks.
An occasional spark from a fire rose and lived a brief life
before dying against the darkness of the rock and sky. The
canyon took a sudden bend to open on a large valley. Even
in the darkness, Slocum got the impression of open spaces.

He inhaled deeply and caught the scent of animals, of
piñon fires, of things recently growing and now harvested.

"We got a real town here," said Brocius from behind.
"Don't go thinkin' you can get away from us. You'll have
a couple hundred men on your heels before sunup."

The number of fires Slocum saw scattered throughout
the valley told him that Brocius might have underestimated
the manpower gathered here. Ike Clanton had assembled a
small army. No wonder that they were able to rustle cattle
and hold up stagecoaches and keep the entire southern half
of the Arizona Territory in constant turmoil.

"You that worried about a posse finding you?" Slocum
pointed to more guards along the rim of the canyon. Although the darkness prevented him from getting a good

count, fifty sentries on duty wouldn't be too high a number.

"There's more'n Behan to worry over," said Brocius.

"You mean Marshal Dake?" asked Ruth.

Brocius laughed harshly. "Old Crawley Dake's got his head stuck up his ass most of the time. Must tickle, what with that bushy mustache of his." Brocius enjoyed his own joke for a few more seconds, then said, "Wyatt Earp's our real worry."

"Heard that he's not much for keeping to the letter of the law," said Slocum.

"He's not above taking a little illegal money here and there," said Brocius. "That don't bother us none, but it's his damned ambition that's got us spooked."

"If he clears out your valley, he might be able to make political hay, is that it?" asked Slocum. He'd heard this story before, seen it played out in a dozen places. A man got the hankering to be more than he was. No amount of killing and backstabbing was enough until he got the power he sought. No reason to think Wyatt Earp was any different.

"He wanted Behan's job bad," said Brocius. "Got crossed up in the politics. Behan's a damn Democrat! Imagine that, them givin' the sheriff of Tombstone's job to a Democrat when Earp's a good Republican. Been friction ever since."

"You could hold off an army with that number of men," said Slocum.

"Didn't say you was right about Behan and Earp comin' to visit. We might have to hold off a damn army."

Curly Bill Brocius said nothing more. Slocum settled down in his saddle and rode, thinking hard. The Cowboys prepared for a major battle. The way they had worked the rock to fortify this valley showed that. But if the territorial law wasn't their concern, what was?

Ranchers didn't take kindly to having their livestock stolen. Wells, Fargo had men patrolling their road to stop plundering. But could these two groups threaten Clanton's security when the law didn't?

Slocum didn't think so. Something else worried the outlaws and kept them jumping at shadows.

He turned when Ruth laid a hand gently on his shoulder. He looked through the murk and imagined that he saw her bright blue eyes glowing with intense inner fire. Some passion he didn't understand burned high in this one.

"John, don't think badly of me for jeopardizing your life in this manner. I *had* to get in here. I just *had* to!"

"Why?"

"Please. We can talk later."

He didn't ask her why she thought that there would be a "later."

"Rein in, there, mister," ordered Brocius. The outlaw trotted past and stopped at a narrow neck in the canyon. He spoke rapidly to others hidden, then motioned for them to advance in single file. As Slocum rode past the boulders, he saw ten or fifteen men gathered around, rifles ready. They looked able to hold off a siege to their mountain fastness.

"Wait," called Brocius. "You can't just ride into our town without paying duty."

"Duty?" asked Slocum. He smiled without humor. He knew what the man meant. "Would your entry fee just happen to be a bar of silver?"

"The man's got good sense," crowed Brocius. "I told you he wasn't nobody's fool." Brocius reached out and took the bullion bar. If nothing else, it allowed the mare to travel with less weight on her hindquarters. But Slocum didn't see how to make an escape, either in the darkness or in the bright light of day.

"Get off and lead your horse from here on," commanded Brocius. The man had already dismounted himself. Slocum followed his lead, Ruth's arm brushing against him as they walked.

"This is home," said Brocius. "You're free to find yourself a place to stay. We got some empty tents at the edge of town that might do you till something better's available."

Slocum looked down the rutted, muddy main street. A crude planking saloon seemed the center of activity. Of a boarding house or hotel he saw nothing.

"Need a stable for my horse. Got one to recommend?" Slocum asked.

"Ain't none. Most all take care of their own animals."

He knew Curly Bill Brocius played with him now, like a cat pinning a mouse by the tail and carefully batting it with the other paw. Slocum looked around. All the others had gathered in a circle, leaving him and Brocius in the middle. The onlookers seemed to enjoy the spectacle more and more.

"No rooms available?" Slocum asked.

"Not for you. For the lady, hell, I'll be glad to put her up." Brocius's arm circled Ruth's waist and pulled her close. He kissed her before the woman had a chance to resist.

When her predicament finally hit her, Ruth yelped and kicked and tried to use her fists against the outlaw. Brocius held her easily, seeming not to notice her struggles.

Slocum heaved a deep breath and turned, feet planted slightly wider than his shoulders, legs bent and right hand turning cold in reaction to what must be done. He didn't fear Curly Bill Brocius. He only worried about what would happen once he killed the outlaw leader.

"So? Reckon you got some fire in your veins, after all," said Brocius. "Or do you mind if the lady learns what it's like to be screwed by a real man?"

Slocum checked the move that would bring out his Colt. Ice gushed through his veins when he realized that both his pistols were empty. He hadn't reloaded after fighting off Behan and the posse. And after the sheriff had left, there had not been a chance to clean and reload his brace of guns.

He faced down a murderer with only empty pistols.

7

John Slocum pulled his hand back a mite from where he held it ready for instant motion. Drawing down on Curly Bill Brocius would be instant death. In a flash, he ran through the scene in his mind. His hand going for his Colt, beating Brocius by a frenzied heartbeat, his hammer coming back, trigger releasing it—and the dull click as it fell on a spent chamber.

"Go on, mister. Draw," said Brocius. "Unless you don't think she's worth fightin' for." He sneered and his mustache bobbed up and down.

Slocum reached up slowly, his steady fingers working on the gunbelt buckle. He dropped the holster to the dirt. Brocius frowned. Slocum slowly took out the Colt stuck in his belt and tossed that after his other pistol.

"What you doin', mister?" Brocius' hand jerked spastically now, itching to go for the butt of his pistol.

"You're talking about being a man. Let's see just how good you are." Slocum took three quick paces and swung. His fist struck the side of the man's head, not hard enough to hurt Brocius but hard enough to knock his bowler off.

"No, Bill, don't!" Josh cried when he saw Brocius going for his pistol. "Give him what he wants. Beat the bastard's head in!"

When Brocius hesitated to think this through, Slocum had the chance to wind up for a real punch. He struck Brocius square in the belly. Slocum grunted, his hand going numb from the impact. Brocius's stomach and the granite cliffs surrounding this valley had much in common —both were damned hard.

Brocius staggered back a pace, still working at getting his sixgun into play. Slocum lowered his head and charged, his shoulder catching the outlaw squarely and driving him backward. They went down in a pile of flailing arms and legs. After two short, hard punches, Slocum knocked the man's gun out of his hand.

At least they were on an even footing.

Or so John Slocum thought until Brocius let out a bull-throated roar and bodily picked him up. The outlaw tossed him away. He fell heavily. From flickering light from a nearby campfire, Slocum saw the dark cloud of fury that had descended over Brocius. Before this moment, the man's mad dog killer instincts had been submerged. Now they blasted to the surface. It wasn't hard to see why Curly Bill Brocius commanded the Cowboys in Ike Clanton's absence.

Brocius advanced, heavy arms hanging down in front of him, swinging slightly from side to side. But it was the man's watery eyes that Slocum watched. Brocius' eyes had narrowed to slits. Slocum felt the hatred burning behind them. Hatred and stark madness.

"Argh!" roared Brocius as he charged. Slocum dodged to one side and kicked as hard as he could. The toe of his boot found a berth in the pit of Brocius' stomach. Slocum stumbled back, his leg tingling from the impact. He had decided to keep hammering away at the man's belly to soften him up. It didn't seem to work. Brocius might as well have had real rock in his guts.

"What's wrong, Bill? Slowing down?" taunted Slocum. He swung a hard fist that connected with Brocius' upper arm, missing the target of a large nose but landing on a bicep.

"You—you're gonna die," grunted Brocius. The man charged. Slocum tried to sidestep but slipped in the mud created from the overflow where the outlaws watered their horses. Brocius wrapped his strong arms around the small of Slocum's back.

The outlaw applied immense pressure. Slocum gasped as the pain mounted. He felt himself being bent backwards, his spine threatening to snap.

The world swung in crazy circles around Slocum. He had only seconds before Brocius succeeded in breaking his back. Slocum swung the flats of his hands together, bringing the palms down hard on Brocius' ears. The bull of a man shrieked in pain.

The instant his grip weakened, Slocum brought a knee up. That failed to do any damage but gained him enough leverage to kick free. He landed in a heap, gasping for breath.

"John," he heard Ruth Macabee call plaintively. He didn't have time to look at her. "I'm sorry," she said. "I didn't think this would happen."

His world again filled with Brocius' heavy panting and the groping hands. Slocum knew he couldn't outpower the outlaw. He caught a meaty hand, separated the fingers, and caught the pinky and ring finger in his own strong grip. He jerked hard, bending Brocius' fingers back at an unnatural angle.

"You son of a bitch!" Brocius screamed.

Slocum swung around, driving his elbow hard into Brocius' face. Blood spurted from a broken nose. Slocum remembered the arms, the way his back still hurt. He dared not give Brocius another chance at him.

He wondered how many men Curly Bill Brocius had killed with his bare hands. John Slocum was not going to be another.

Again he drove his elbow into Brocius, this time finding the pit of the man's stomach. Softness hinted that the powerful man weakened a mite. Slocum kept up his punishing attacks to the midriff. When Brocius reached down with both hands to protect his gut, Slocum kicked one leg out from under the outlaw.

As Brocius stumbled and fell to one knee, Slocum laced his fingers together and swung his hands as if they were an axe of flesh and bone. He caught Brocius directly under the chin.

The impact sent Slocum reeling. Curly Bill Brocius fell forward into the mud.

For a long minute no one moved, no one spoke. It was as if the world had frozen. Then Ruth Macabee broke the silence. She ran to Slocum and threw her arms around him.

"John. I'm sorry. I never meant for this to happen. I didn't think it ever would."

Slocum awkwardly put his arms around her, wincing at the pain. He worried that he had broken his hands, his arms, his back. Everything hurt like hell.

"We might be in real trouble now. What are they going to do now that I beat Brocius?" He looked around the circle of men, their expressions uniform. All were stunned that anyone could beat the bull-like Brocius in a fair fight.

Brocius stirred, lifting himself up from the mud. He wiped some of the blood and dirt from his face and shook all over like a wet hound dog.

"Your gun. Use your gun!" Ruth whispered urgently. He held her back. It wouldn't do to go for the useless pistols.

"You," groaned Brocius. "You son of a bitch." Brocius got to his feet and lumbered forward.

Slocum hurt all over. He couldn't even dodge when Brocius' arms circled him once more. But to his surprise Brocius tossed him into the air and caught him, then pounded him on the back.

"Goddamn, that's the best fight I been in for months. None of these pantywaists can stand up to me. You're all right, mister. What's your damn name, anyway?"

"Slocum." He thrust out his hand. Curly Bill took it and pumped hard.

"Yes, sir, Slocum, you're all right. Damn good fight. Josh! Get your worthless butt over here. See that Slocum has a place to stay. Nothing fancy, but enough."

"What about me?" asked Ruth.

"Hell, we settled that. You're with him. Leastways, for the night." Brocius laughed heartily and walked off, favoring one leg and rubbing his hand across his damaged nose.

Slocum sagged with relief. He stiffened in time to keep from going to his knees. It never paid to show weakness, especially in front of murderers like these. He motioned. Ruth retrieved his pistols and gunbelt. He slung them over his shoulder. His fingers refused to work on the belt buckle.

"We'll be needing something to eat," he said. "Trail rations get old mighty quick."

"I'll see if Miz Green can't scare up somethin' for you," said Josh. The man stared at Slocum as if the man had just walked on air. He turned and hurried off, muttering under his breath, "Never seen *anybody* whup Curly Bill before. Never! Don't reckon even Ike could, even on a day when he's feelin' his meanest."

"Suppose we should follow him," said Slocum. He straightened painfully and began walking. Ruth Macabee looked at him curiously, then grabbed up the horses' reins and followed.

"You!" she called to Josh. "Wait. We need a hot bath. Can you arrange for it?"

Josh turned and started to say something, saw the expression on Slocum's face, then swallowed hard. "We can get some water heated up for you, I reckon. Be puttin' you in the spare tent at the far end of the camp. Don't have no decent beds in town right now. Not for a lady, at any rate."

"A tent will do," Slocum said.

Josh bobbed his head up and down like a bird pecking at corn and motioned them toward a tent set apart from the others. Slocum bent painfully to enter. Inside there wasn't much in the way of furnishings, but it looked like the Palmer House to him. He sank to the thin blankets tossed over a pallet of straw.

"You look poorly, Mr. Slocum," said Ruth. She stared at him. "That *is* your real name?"

"John Slocum," he said.

"Good," she said. "I'll see to the bath."

Slocum stretched out. His back gave a twinge that brought him up to a sitting position. More cautiously, he lay down. His tortured muscles protested, then began to relax. His eyelids were drooping when Ruth returned. Josh pulled a huge galvanized tub behind and put it in the center of the tent, almost filling the space.

"Now, the hot water," she said almost primly. She stood there like a schoolmarm as Josh fetched the hot water.

Buckets of steaming water went into the galvanized tub. The last bucket poured, Josh stood by the tent flap and looked nervous.

"That will be all," Ruth said, dismissing him as she might a servant.

"You surely do move in and take over," observed Slocum. He stared at the woman, marvelling at her beauty. In spite of all they had gone through that day, the chase by Sheriff Behan's posse, the fight in the canyon, the rescue by Clanton's Cowboys, the fight with Curly Bill, in spite of all that Ruth looked like an angel.

Her hair had come undone from the way she had fixed it up. Soft drifts of light brown hair floated around her head as if the clouds had come down from the heavens just to decorate her. Dirt smudged her face, but this only accentuated her high cheekbones and the fine, straight nose and full lips.

"I have to," Ruth said. "That's the only decent way of accomplishing anything."

Slocum closed his eyes and tried to force away all the pain in his body. It was disappearing slowly. What he needed more than anything else was a good night's sleep.

"Well, Mr. Slocum, are you just going to lie there?"

"What?" He forced his eyes open. "Sorry. You go on. I'll keep my eyes shut, though in this light I won't see enough to embarrass you." The only illumination in the tent came through the opened flap from distant campfires.

"You were the one who so gallantly defended my honor. You should go into the bath first. It's only fair." Ruth stood, hands on her flaring hips, staring down at him. "But there are just two things I must know first."

"Two? What are they?" Slocum sat up again and began unbuttoning his shirt. The movement made him giddy with pain.

"The first is why you didn't use your pistol. You have the look of a man who is quite capable. Curly Bill Brocius moves like a big old bear in comparison."

Slocum told her about not reloading. "I'll remedy that as soon as I can get my gear out of the saddlebags. Providing they left me my spare ammunition," he said.

One tiny hand covered those red, full lips in horror. "Your pistols weren't loaded? Oh, John!"

He winced as she hugged him.

"I'm sorry. Here, let me." She pushed his hands away and finished the job of stripping off his torn shirt. Ruth's agile fingers worked over the buttons on his longjohns and she skinned those down from his shoulders. Bruises covered his upper arms and shoulders were Brocius had hit him.

Soft lips brushed over those wounds, kissing and teasing.

"You taste like . . . a man," she said in a low voice. Her hands worked lower, finding the buttons on his denim trousers.

"You said you had two questions. You asked the first," Slocum said. "What's the second?"

"How often do you bathe?"

"Often as I can," he said, startled.

"You didn't let me finish my question." She nuzzled at his neck. "How often do you bathe with a woman?"

"Not often enough," he answered. He reached out and took her in his arms, pulled her close and ignored the stabs of pain that danced along his arms. The crush of Ruth Macabee's lips against his soothed away all discomfort.

Slocum tried to unfasten the complicated ties on Ruth's blouse and failed. His hands felt like wooden clubs, clumsy and unable to do much more than shake and give him pain. He had been too effective against Brocius.

"No, wait," she whispered. Ruth stood and began undressing. In the faint light she turned into an angel come to earth. One by one, she got free of her garments. She daintily discarded them until she stood naked in the dim firelight filtering in from outside.

Slocum reached out for her. The soft, milky smooth skin rippled with gooseflesh.

"Close the damned tent flap," he said. Ruth Macabee obeyed, then returned.

Her arms circled him and drew him closer. Together they awkwardly sat down in the large galvanized tub. There didn't seem to be room for the pair of them.

"Let me get some of the trail dust off you," Ruth said, stepping out.

"But . . ." Slocum's protest vanished when he felt her quick, agile fingers working across his body, soothing and stimulating as she laved away the dirt and tiredness. She knelt behind him, outside the tub. Her hands crossed his hairy chest, then worked lower, lower, lower until Slocum let out a tiny gasp of pure pleasure.

"That surely does feel good," he said.

"What? What feels good? This? Or this?" Rush kissed his neck as her hands found the growing hardness between his legs. The warm water lapped gently against his bruised body but it was the heat within that brought Slocum fully alive. It had been too long since he'd had a woman. And he wasn't sure he could remember ever having one this caring or beautiful.

"My turn," Ruth said. Her hand dipped lower in the tub and cupped his balls. She lifted him right out. They exchanged places.

Slocum shivered with the cold in the tent but had to admit he didn't think much about it when he got the chance to run his hands over the woman's lush body. Naked, she

was even prettier than with her clothes on. Never had he
seen such feminine perfection.

He cupped those two marvelous breasts, now buoyed by
the warm bath water and bouncing slightly. He worked his
way down to the matted triangle between her thighs,
dipped in briefly and teasingly, then raced along her long,
slim legs. He felt the play of Ruth's strong muscles. Here
was one woman who rode often. No Eastern lady from a
fancy ass finishing school had such strength.

Slocum couldn't wait to feel those legs locked around
his waist. Just the thought made him even harder, needier.

He reached down and cupped her buttocks, lifting her
up. Those fleshy globes made more than a handful. By the
time Ruth got out of the tub, all soapy and clean and
flushed with excitement, Slocum was about ready to bust.

"So nice, so big!" Ruth cupped his balls in one hand and
pulled him closer to the edge of the tub. Her full lips closed
around the tip of his steely shaft.

Slocum gulped. The pleasure surging into his loins
turned his legs to rubber. He sank down, Ruth following
him, her mouth working hungrily at the spire rising from
his groin.

"Don't, no more," he pleaded. "That's so damn fine.
Too fine."

Ruth looked up, a wicked grin on her face. This was no
prissy lady. She was lusty and knew what she wanted, too.

"Back into the tub," she said. "Get your legs up and
over the rim."

"But . . ." Slocum pointed to the blankets and the straw
pallet.

Then he understood what Ruth Macabee intended. He
swung around and gently lowered himself into the bath
water. By the time his rear touched the bottom of the tub
Ruth had swarmed up, her feet on the either side of the tub.

Slocum looked up and saw heaven descending on him. They were in almost total darkness now, but enough light came in from campfires outside to throw shadows across the wanton woman in wondrous ways. Her breasts bobbed and swayed. And her legs parted as she came down, the divine province Slocum had explored earlier now opening its soft gates and taking him in fully. They both groaned as he sank deep into her steamy interior.

"Musta died and gone to heaven," Slocum said. He was pushed down to the bottom of the tub by Ruth's weight— and he enjoyed it more with every passing second. The curve of her fine ass fit perfectly into the curve of his groin. Best of all was the warmth around his throbbing length. He felt the pressures mounting within him and fought to hold the tide back. He wanted this to last for as long as possible.

Slocum gasped repeatedly when Ruth put her hands on the sides of the tub and lifted herself up a few inches. The movement was clumsy but it had its effect on him. She lowered herself again and immediately rose once more. This slow up and down movement caused Slocum's hips to jerk in response.

"Relax," she said. "Relax and enjoy it. You deserve this. You saved my life tonight. I want to repay you."

"You make it sound like this is just duty," said Slocum. "Don't suppose you're enjoying it, too?"

"I *love* it!" Ruth Macabee cried.

Slocum reached out and cupped her large breasts, tweaking gently, moving his fingers across the lust-hardened nubs of her nipples. He guided her up and down with these two warm handles in the motion that excited him most.

The water began sloshing over the sides of the tub. Neither noticed. Their arousal had reached a point where there was no turning back for either of them. Slocum couldn't move, pinned in the bottom of the tub. Ruth did it all. She rose and dropped, slowly at first, then faster, with more power, with more passion.

Slocum clutched down hard on her breasts when he felt the hot rush of his seed fountaining into her moist, tight channel. Ruth bent forward and wiggled her ass around and made Slocum's pleasure all the more intense. Then she gasped and went stiff, throwing her head back.

He pulled her close, his face buried between the soft mountains of her breasts. He licked and kissed and sucked on the turgid nipples while the woman rocked through her own bout with desire.

They sagged against one another. Ruth finally straightened and managed to get herself out of the tub.

"That was incredible," Slocum said.

"Stand up," she ordered. He obeyed silently. She began toweling him off, using her skirts. The woman paid special attention to the sleeping giant dangling between his legs. By the time she had finished, she had reawakened lusts in his groin.

"Didn't think I wanted to do anything but get some sleep," Slocum said, marvelling at the miraculous resurrection Ruth had performed.

"Suppose we should try out those blankets," she said, shivering deliciously.

They sank to the thin blankets, then wrapped them around each other. And again they found a way of getting even more warmth into the cold night.

It was almost dawn before Slocum finally got to sleep. He didn't mind at all.

8

The sounds of the camp awakening around him brought John Slocum to a groggy awareness of the world. He stretched, winced at the pain in his tormented muscles, then stretched again more cautiously. The pain vanished and he felt almost human again. He reached over beside him to find Ruth Macabee.

When he didn't find her, he sat bolt upright. The galvanized bathtub still dominated the tent but of the woman he found not a trace. Her gear was gone and he had no hint about how long it might have been since she departed.

Squinting at the bright light, Slocum looked out the tent flap. The sun just poked above a peak at the far end of the valley. He had no idea how tall the peaks in the White Mountains might be, but it could be damn near nine o'clock. He smiled, remembering why he had been so long in getting to sleep.

"Need more nights like that," he said to himself. Slocum pulled himself from beneath the warmth of the blankets and into the chilly morning air. After dressing quickly, the first order of business he tended to was the cleaning and loading of his two Colt Navys. He made mistakes. Everyone did. But Slocum stayed alive by never making the same mistake twice. If he had to face Curly Bill Brocius again, he wanted to do it with loaded pistols.

Fastening his gunbelt securely around his middle, he ducked through the tent flap and went outside to see what the camp looked like. The view he'd had the previous night hadn't been too good.

Slocum stood stock still and stared. He let out a long, low whistle of astonishment at what he saw. The Cowboys didn't have a camp. They had a full-fledged town hidden away from the law.

No wonder they were so touchy about having sentries guarding this place. They had a lot to lose if Earp or Sheriff Behan took it into their heads to raid it.

Slocum had been in many towns far smaller than this one. Large enough to support two streets running parallel, it stretched for a goodly way to small farms ringing the town. Stores did a moderate business and he saw enough women and children about to realize that Ike Clanton had a lot at stake in this town.

Slocum began walking. No one paid him any mind. They must figure that anyone getting past the sentries had to be accepted. One or two men nodded in his direction, recognizing him from the night before. As he walked, Slocum felt the ripple going down the street ahead of him. By the time he reached a small clapboard building with the word "Saloon" crudely scrawled on the front wall, everyone stared at him.

He entered the saloon. Even at this time of morning,

four men bellied up to the bar.

"Howdy, Slocum," greeted a man Slocum didn't know. He might have been one of the riders with Curly Bill Brocius. Or he might have just heard about the fight.

"Morning," Slocum acknowledged. "Let me have a shot of whatever's handy. But no trade whiskey." Slocum didn't feel like burning his guts out with the cheap whiskey made from black powder, rusty nails, and anything else lying around.

"Don't have much else. Can get you a bottle of champagne," said the barkeep. He smiled at Slocum's skeptical expression. "Damn fine stuff. Ike got a case of it off a Frenchie what was ridin' the stage into Tucson. Said he brought it all the way from France with him."

"Never mind," said Slocum. "Anything."

He sipped at the liquor and winced. This wasn't the way to drink it. He knocked back the entire shot of the vile-tasting whiskey. It burned its way down his gullet and puddled in his belly, but it warmed him and brought the world into focus.

"That's a dollar," said the barkeep.

"A mite steep for a shot of horse piss," said Slocum. The barkeep only shrugged, as if saying, "Can't help it."

Slocum dropped the money onto the bar, nodded to the other four patrons, and went back into the street. A cafe across the street drew him. The whiskey gurgled on an empty belly. He needed something more than the beans and peaches he'd been living on out on the trail. To his surprise, the meal he got was edible. Even more to his surprise was the five dollars asked for it.

"Are all the prices in town this high?" he asked the owner. The man, who looked as if he could take Curly Bill on for breakfast and best him twice before noon, nodded.

"Hard to get supplies up here. Have to sneak everything

in. The law's been tryin' to find this place for well nigh a year now. Can't do it. We're growin' by leaps and bounds."

"And have to charge high prices," finished Slocum. He paid the bill, checked his pocket, and found that he still had a goodly sum left from the poker game back in Tombstone. But at a dollar a drink and five dollars a meal, even a hundred in gold wouldn't last much longer.

Then there was Ruth Macabee. He had to find her. He had no idea how she'd be faring in this high-priced outlaw hideout. Slocum stood under a wooden roof overhang and looked down the muddy main street, smiling. Maybe he shouldn't worry about the woman. She had a way of getting what she wanted.

This set him to thinking in other ways. What did Ruth Macabee want? Silver wasn't it. She'd had the chance to drygulch him and take the six silver bars. She had gladly turned them over to Curly Bill in exchange for entry into this valley.

Slocum lifted his gaze to the White Mountains all around the town. The valley walls were dotted with mine tailings where earlier settlers had bored into the rock hunting for minerals. Slocum guessed that these were mines that had petered out. Could that be what Ruth sought? A silver mine?

He spat. There were easier ways to get silver mines. Safer, too. He didn't believe her story about wanting to prove herself as a reporter for a St. Louis newspaper. But it might be easier to swallow than Ruth coming into the heart of Clanton's town to do some prospecting.

"Hey, Slocum," came a voice he recognized all too well. Without being in a hurry about it, Slocum slipped the thong off his Colt's hammer and turned to face Curly Bill Brocius.

"Want a word with you." The stocky man trailed two others Slocum didn't recognize. He didn't want to cross them. From the way they moved he knew they were quick with their sixguns—and wouldn't hesitate to gun him down if Curly Bill gave the nod.

"What can I do for you?" Slocum asked.

"Want to know your plans. You got to earn your keep around here. Nobody gets a free ride."

"Been paying my way so far," Slocum pointed out.

"You got some gold," said Brocius. "I been talkin' to the barkeep and some others around town. But we got high overhead here. You're gonna have to decide soon on how you're gonna earn your keep."

"Didn't figure to stay forever in the tent."

"That was a gift, sorta," said Brocius. "Ain't many men that can best me like you did last night. If you're interested, maybe you can ride with me. You got a weird mix of luck about you."

"How's that?"

"We done some checkin'. You had good luck in robbin' the only stagecoach leaving Tucson in the past month with any bullion. But you had bad luck in that Behan was so close by. He wasn't on your trail. He was out after some Mexicans what snuck across the border and were raisin' hell nearby."

Slocum nodded. That made him feel a mite better. Behan might hold a grudge, but the grudge wasn't *that* big.

"So if I'm that unlucky to have a posse on top of me, why want me along?" Slocum asked.

Curly Bill Brocius laughed heartily. "Hell, that's the kind of luck we need. We don't care about no posse. We can handle them without even tryin'."

"Might be," said Slocum. He looked toward the valley rim. Now and again he caught the glint of sunlight off metal pinpointing the location of the sentries. "But you don't have a young army up there in the hills for nothing."

"Damned *Pronunciados*," grumbled one man. Brocius silenced him with an angry look.

"We can hold our own against any damn posse, no matter what goes on between Ike and Wyatt Earp."

"How's that?" asked Slocum.

For the first time, Brocius looked upset at his big mouth. Then disgust replaced the uneasiness. "Ike's a good man—the best. But sometimes he ain't got the sense God gave a mule. He's been screwin' the same dancer what Earp's sweet on. That bitch Emma ain't gonna keep her mouth shut too much longer. When it gets out, Earp's really gonna come lookin' for Ike."

Slocum shrugged. How Clanton and Earp spent their spare time mattered little to him. But he didn't think the preparations in this valley had anything to do with Wyatt Earp getting angry over Clanton seeing his woman.

"What are those *Pronunciados* you mentioned?" he asked, looking at the man who had made the muttered comment.

"Nothing much to bother your head with, Slocum. South of the border, they got a hot revolution going. Some of the rebels sneak north to get away from the Mexican Army. The *Pronunciados* cause more hell for us than any posse. The army don't care if they shoot up a rebel or one of our boys."

Slocum didn't have to ask why Sheriff Behan had been out on patrol with so many men. He had been chasing elements of the Mexican Army back south of the border. Slocum remembered the dust cloud he had seen out on the desert. It hadn't been raised by any posse or even Clanton's Cowboys. It had been either the Mexican Army or the rebels. Nothing else fit together right for him.

"We got different bands of men, each under a different captain," said Brocius. "I got about thirty men at my back. Ike's brothers, Billy and Phin, got about that under them. Ike oversees the whole operation."

"I can choose any of the groups?" Slocum asked.

"You can but you'd be a damned fool to do it," Brocius said. "Phineas Clanton is as crazy as a stewed hoot owl and Billy, well, he ain't been right in the head since he got shot last August. The only bunch where you'd make any money's with me."

Slocum eyed Brocius. The man had an air about him that Slocum had seen on the battlefield. Men died for lesser commanders.

"How's the loot split up?"

"Ike takes half to keep this place runnin'. The other half is ours. I take ten percent and the rest is divvied up even-steven with everybody who helped out."

Slocum did some quick figuring. If a robbery brought in a thousand dollars—and this was almost beyond even the best bank robber's imagination—and ten men went along with Brocius, that netted only forty-five dollars a head.

"Don't leave much," Slocum said.

"I made damn near five hundred dollars in the last year," said the man just behind Brocius. "Can't match money like that punchin' cattle. Or doin' much else, for that matter."

"Money seems to be in rustling them," agreed Slocum. He immediately saw where only Ike Clanton came out ahead. Even the princely sum of five hundred dollars wouldn't last long in this high-priced town—and Slocum reckoned that Ike took a healthy cut of all business within the township, too. He might work it from all directions, supplying as well as taking a cut of the sales.

"Then you're in? I can always use a good man and any

man what can whup me like you did last night's one hell of
a fighter." Brocius seemed lavish with his praise, but Slocum caught the undercurrent of deadliness to the man's
words. If Slocum didn't agree, he'd end up gut-shot or
backshot and buried where no one would ever find his
corpse.

"My daddy always told me to go with the best," he said.

"Then you're in. Good. Be in the saloon tonight around
nine. We're gonna be plannin' a raid into Tucson." Brocius
slammed a meaty hand into Slocum's shoulder and thrust
out his hand. Slocum shook. This seemed to be what Brocius wanted. He motioned and his two trailing gunmen
hurried to catch up with him.

Slocum knew he had to leave the valley soon. Staying
with Brocius, even in a valued position, wasn't what he
wanted out of life—and life might be damned short with
the Cowboys.

In its way, though, this was exactly what Slocum
needed. The alliance with Curly Bill gave an excuse to get
out of the valley without being shot to hell and gone. Once
outside the rocky boundaries of this mountain fortress, he
could slip away and be in California before Brocius knew
he was gone.

Slocum didn't cotton much to rustling or robbery on a
regular basis, but he did it when the mood struck or he was
in sore need of money. Splitting it with the likes of Clanton
and Brocius was something he'd never do willingly.

The sun had risen entirely above the White Mountains
and gave a cheerful feel to the town. The people looked
happy and prosperous enough and Slocum thought he'd
even heard a school bell ringing earlier. He walked back to
the tent he and Ruth had shared. The woman still hadn't
returned.

Slocum looked around and found where his mare had

been staked. Careful study of the ground showed that Ruth's horse had also been tethered there, but that she had taken it. He found her small footprint clearly outlined nearby in damp ground. He looked down the valley.

"She headed there. I suppose I ought to see what's got her so all-fired interested in this place." Slocum saddled his mare and swung up into the saddle. The horse protested the weight. He patted her on the neck and said gently, "Rest isn't something either of us is likely to get much of any time soon, old girl."

He let the horse set her own pace as he rode along a small trail that led down along the valley floor. Eyes ever watchful, he saw evidence of many of the Cowboys along the rim. They must ride their watch, he decided. Otherwise, every man in the whole Arizona Territory would be needed to keep such a guard posted.

Abandoned silver mines lined the walls. He guessed that Ike Clanton had moved in and taken over a town that had already existed. When the silver mines petered out and the miners left, the Cowboys came in. After counting a full dozen mines, Slocum gave up. He doubted the ore in any of these mines had amounted to much. Certainly not like the mother lodes found south of Tombstone.

Evidence of the hard work was everywhere. And more than one mine site had a small cemetery alongside. Hard work, death, and damned little in the way of riches, he thought.

Now and again Slocum dismounted and walked his horse, as much to give the mare a rest as to study the ground. Not many passed this way. Ruth Macabee's trail crossed back and forth over soft soil. When it did, he checked to be sure he was still tracking her. A large cut in one of her horses's shoes helped identify her spoor.

"Where's that woman going?" he wondered aloud.

"What's driving her to risk her life?"

He couldn't get it out of his head that it must be something special. She had turned down six silver bars—more, if he counted the rest of the bullion carried on the Wells, Fargo stagecoach. If not riches, then what? He almost believed her story about wanting to be a reporter now. Almost.

As he walked along, he heard the sharp click of steel against rock. Slocum stopped and turned slowly, locating the direction of the sound. Somewhere ahead. Slocum turned from the small trail and went directly upslope toward a mineshaft and cabin. There he tethered his horse and climbed onto the cabin's roof. He cursed as one foot slipped through the rotting roof and he almost fell. He pulled himself free and proceeded more cautiously, keeping his feet only on the strongest roof cross member.

Slocum stood up at the peak and cupped his hands around his eyes for better vision. He saw Ruth Macabee leaving the next mineshaft up the valley. The woman angrily threw a rock at a wooden cross in a small cemetery. Her aim was good. The loud crack of stone against wood came to Slocum across the several hundred yards separating them. Ruth, obviously angry, vaulted onto her horse and savagely kicked at its flanks. She headed deeper into the valley.

It took Slocum longer to get down off the roof than it had for him to climb up. He led his horse directly across the rocky terrain to where Ruth had been. At first he thought her anger had been directed at the poor prospector buried under the crude cross.

Slocum couldn't even make out the name. Wind and sun had long since worn off any writing that had been on the grave marker.

"So what's she so danged mad at?" he wondered. He

slowly went to the mouth of the shaft. Slocum hesitated to enter. The timbers holding up the mine roof weren't in any better condition than the cross on the unknown miner's grave. Termites had eaten well and often at spots just inside the mouth.

"Curiosity is going to kill me yet," he grumbled. Slocum entered the mine, wary about cave-ins or sudden shafts in the darkness. He poked his way along a few dozen paces, then stopped. The dust on the floor showed that Ruth had come this far, then halted. He knelt to examine the floor, the walls, the roof.

As far as he could tell, this mine wasn't anything special. Ruth had scratched at part of the exposed rock, as if trying to pry out some of the quartz in a narrow vein. She hadn't done a very good job of it. He couldn't figure out what Ruth's interest was in such a dangerous, mined-out silver shaft.

He backtracked, happy once more to see the light of day. Slocum didn't have any real fear of being in such closed spaces, but the clean valley and the blue Arizona sky appealed to him more than rocks and dust and darkness.

"Only one way to find out what's got into her," he said. He mounted and rode back down to the trail, turned and followed her at a brisker pace that left his mare whinnying and complaining constantly.

"Now you cut that out," he said. "You're not carrying all that silver this time. Just me. And you done that for a good many months. Come on now and be a good girl."

Slocum got to the top of a small rise and spotted Ruth Macabee. She rode slowly, her attention fixed on the mines ringing the valley.

"Ruth!" he called out. He couldn't help but notice the jerk of surprise when she heard her name. At first, he thought the woman would try to race away, as if she'd been caught doing something naughty. But when she saw it was Slocum, she relaxed.

He rode over to her. "Been looking for you," he said. "You should have let me know you were going out."

"I didn't want to awaken you. You were sleeping so peacefully," she said. Her words didn't match her nervousness. He thought she tried to hide something.

"Finding anything worthwhile?" he asked.

"No, nothing." Ruth worked too hard to make her reply seem casual.

"Must have been thousands of dollars' worth of silver taken from these mines not too many years ago," he said.

"It was all low-grade," she said. "I looked in a few just to see what had been left. Some of the ore wouldn't assay out to more than a few ounces per ton."

"You seem to know a lot about mining. How's that?"

"Oh, John, I don't know *anything* about silver mining. Really. It doesn't take a great intellect to see that this was a poor mining area. No wonder they all left."

He started to ask what it was she sought. Ruth Macabee obviously wasn't going to volunteer the information. Slocum found himself growing increasingly curious about the lovely woman and the object of her secret search. Curiosity had gotten him into worlds of trouble before, but it made life worth living.

A woman like Ruth could have anything she wanted in the bigger, more sophisticated cities, yet she had risked life and reputation to worm her way into Ike Clanton's camp.

Why?

Slocum had to know.

"What—" Slocum cut off his question when a mirror flashed high on the valley rim. Another and another and still another came from different locations. Less than a minute later the echoes from a rifle came down the valley.

"What was that?" he asked.

Then all hell broke loose. From the number of shots being fired, John Slocum thought he had been hurled back in time to Gettysburg.

9

A war had broken out. Slocum pulled Ruth Macabee along so fast and hard that she protested.

"John, stop it. We can't do anything if it is as bad as it sounds."

He wasn't certain and said so.

"You'll just get us killed rushing off like this without knowing what's happening. This might not mean a thing. Remember how those ruffians act. They might only be shooting up their town for some enjoyment."

Slocum knew that wasn't so. He had seen the sentries signalling those down in the valley. Someone had attacked —and from the reports from the rifles, they weren't using standard weapons. The sound struck him as familiar, but not like a Winchester.

An explosion shook the entire valley, sending Ruth sprawling and Slocum to one knee. Their horses reared and bolted. His mare ran only a few yards but Ruth's kept running until it vanished back in the direction of the town.

"Come on. No matter how much steam you think the Cowboys might want to blow off, you've got to agree that they're not using blasting powder to do it."

Slocum helped the woman stand up. He caught his mare, mounted, then pulled Ruth into the saddle behind him. He wanted to dig his heels into the horse's flanks and race like the wind back to the town, but he knew the animal couldn't stand it. He worried about the horse's sorry condition. She seemed to be weakening and rest did nothing to help her regain strength.

The gunfire grew more intense. Slocum saw that dozens of mirror signals flashed down from the valley rim now. He had no idea what coded messages they carried, but they weren't reporting all clear.

"Look at that," Ruth said in a low, husky voice. "There must be a hundred of them. But who?"

"Soldiers," Slocum said. "Mexican soldiers. The question's why they crossed the border and came all the way up into the White Mountains to launch an attack against Clanton." He shook his head, not understanding. Conditions along the Arizona Territory–Mexican border were never easy. But this?

"I recognize the uniforms now," said Ruth. "From pictures," she added. The way she spoke told Slocum that again the woman lied. He didn't bother trying to figure out why. He urged his horse forward until they were shielded from the battle raging along the town's main street by a large boulder. He slipped from the saddle, taking his Winchester from its sheath as he went.

Helping Ruth down, he said, "Stay here with the horse. I'll go see what I can do."

"Which side are you going to help?" she asked.

"Don't have much choice. The Mexicans are bound and determined to kill anyone not in their uniform. Since I don't cotton to the idea of wearing a fancy Mexican getup, it looks like I'll be working for Clanton and the Cowboys. Leastways, this time around."

"John." She took hold of his arm and stopped him. He thought she was going to insist on trailing along, as she'd done after the stagecoach robbery. Again Ruth Macabee surprised him. She pulled him close and kissed him passionately. "Don't get yourself killed," she said, pushing away reluctantly.

"We can agree on that point," he said. He tossed his hat to the ground and stuck his head up over the top of the boulder. Less than a hundred yards away a pair of Mexican soldiers closed in on a small child, intent on killing him.

Old training took over for John Slocum. He was carried back to innumerable Civil War battlefields and the methods he had used as a sniper. He leveled his Winchester and watched the drama unfolding. The young child dodged but the two men closed in like the jaws of a hungry coyote closing on a rabbit.

With a single pull of the trigger, the coyote lost one jaw. Slocum's round caught the soldier high in the chest and flung him backward to fall into the dust, arms outstretched. The other soldier spun and yelled something Slocum didn't understand. A second bullet took the right leg out from under the soldier. Before Slocum could finish the man, the child rushed out.

A knife blade flashed in the warm autumn sunlight. Then blood spurted from the soldier's throat. The child had efficiently cut both neck arteries with a single slash.

"Damn," Slocum said. But he couldn't fault the child. You had to survive, no matter what. It still rankled that the child had had to learn that lesson so young.

Slocum waved. The young child returned the gesture, bloody knife held high.

"Sherman may have been a bloody-handed butcher, but he surely was right," muttered Slocum.

Slocum slipped over the top of the boulder and went down into the hell that raged. Fighting went from building to building. It took him several seconds to realize what was wrong with the way the main street looked to him. The saloon had been reduced to a pile of rubble, not from being put to the torch but from having so many bullets shot through it. Wood that looked like a million termites had feasted on it lay scattered on the site. When the walls had been blown away, the roof had collapsed.

Here and there, Slocum saw arms and legs poking out from under the rubble. He skirted the area and moved back toward the center of the small town, where the fighting grew more intense.

"Slocum!" came a cry. "Over here!"

Slocum kept low and ended up diving to keep from being turned into wormwood like the saloon by a score of bullets singing around him. Seldom had he encountered such savage fighting even in the War.

He sat up and leaned against the building. Josh said, "I thought you were a goner out there. I couldn't warn you about the damn Meskins up on the roof of Ike's headquarters."

Slocum looked around the corner, keeping his head down. Even so, he drew fire. A large building across the street had been taken and was being well-defended by the Mexican soldiers.

"Didn't know that was Ike's," Slocum said. "Don't matter much now who had it. The army has it and that's what counts."

"Must be thirty, forty of them in there," said Josh. His

eyes were wide and his face flushed. A tiny spot of red seeped out on his upper arm from a graze.

Slocum hazarded another look. He guessed their number at fewer than twenty, but he couldn't fault Josh any. In the heat of battle, it always looked as if the enemy had more men and you had fewer.

"What the hell's going on?" Slocum asked. "Why's the Mexican Army coming in here? At the first shots, I thought it must be Behan or even Earp."

Josh snorted in disgust. "The Meskins are the ones what killed Ike's pa a few months back. We'd done made a raid down into Sonora and ambushed four of them. Got damn near four thousand dollars off their corpses, but it turned out one of them was Governor Pesqueira's personal envoy. He was on his way to Tombstone."

"So they came after Newman Clanton?"

"Killed him dead," said Josh. "Him and Jim Crane and two others. We thought that'd be the end of it, but the territorial newspapers keep rilin' them up. The *Tombstone Epitaph* and the *Tucson Daily Arizona Journal* both kept harpin' on how we been let have free rein and how the marshal ought to form up a posse and come after us."

Josh spat. Slocum noticed that it was bloody. The man had bit his own tongue somewhere in the fracas.

"Didn't much move Dake or Earp or Behan. Surely did get Governor Pesqueira mad at us."

The politics meant nothing to Slocum. Getting out of here alive did. If it meant taking on the entire Mexican Army, then he'd have to do just that. He dropped into the dust and wriggled forward. He sighted at the roof line and waited.

"Go on, man, shoot! Kill the bastards!" cried Josh.

"Hush up," said Slocum, concentrating. "I don't have

enough ammunition to waste." Even as he spoke, a soldier poked his head over the edge of the coping. Slocum squeezed and knew even before the recoil knocked the rifle back into his shoulder that there would be one fewer soldier facing them.

The Mexican caught the bullet high on the forehead. Slocum saw the soldier topple, carried backward by the force of the bullet.

"We got to do something," said Josh. His voice rose and almost broke in shrill hysteria.

"Just sit tight and wait. Your chance will come."

Slocum heard Josh rising. He rolled over and looked back at him. Panic had finally seized hold of the man. Josh let out a shriek and ran out into the street, firing his six-shooter up in the air, hitting nothing and drawing attention to himself.

Slocum cursed. He knew he should let the man get his damn fool head blown off, but he couldn't. He shot twice —fast—to keep a Mexican marksman on the roof down. By the time he got to his feet, another one had sighted in on Josh.

The man tumbled head over heels and lay shaking in the dust. Tiny puffs of dust rose around him showing where the bullets missed. Slocum took a deep breath, then dashed out, firing from the hip as he went. The slugs only added a cloud of splinters to the battle scene. He knew that he was missing every single Mexican by a country mile.

"Hang on," he called to Josh. He slid on his knees and emptied the Winchester's magazine, grabbed Josh by the collar, and began pulling him back.

"Help me, damn it," Slocum called. "Use your good leg to help." Bullets smacked into the wood hitching post and destroyed it. Other flights of hot lead ripped apart the wall behind which Slocum had taken cover with Josh earlier. He hunkered down and pulled even harder. He felt the man's shirt ripping.

Slocum had to get a better grip or risk leaving the man exposed to gunfire. When he turned to work his hand further into the collar of Josh's shirt, a hot flash along his side jerked him upright in pain. Slocum had been wounded before and knew this wasn't serious. With any luck, he might live to risk his neck again.

A second bullet dug away at the flesh along his thigh. But by this time he had dragged the unresisting Josh back under cover.

"You son of a bitch," Slocum said. "That was dumb."

He looked down at Josh, eyes wide and staring up at the bright blue Arizona sky.

"You dumb son of a bitch," Slocum repeated, his voice lower and his tone different now. He reached over and closed the dead man's eyes. Slocum had seen more than his share of death but one thing he never got used to was a dead man with his eyes open.

He rummaged through Josh's pockets and found a dozen rounds for his Winchester. He put them into the magazine and turned back to the battle raging in the street. The time to mourn Josh would be later, if he could muster enough sympathy for the man then. He hadn't really known him.

But he had been someone personal to Slocum, not some faceless sniper or child killer. Slocum settled down and began the methodical destruction that had been his trademark during the War. Six more Mexican soldiers fell before he ran out of ammunition for his rifle.

Slocum tugged and pulled free his Colt Navy. For this kind of fighting it wasn't nearly as good as a rifle, but it would do.

"Slocum!" came a cry. He turned and looked down the

alley. Curly Bill Brocius ran along, bent double.

"How's it looking from outside?" Slocum asked.

"Not so good. They got a colonel in charge. Must have promised him all the women in Sonora for his own if he cleaned us out." Brocius laughed harshly. "Ain't even that. I think they was looking for *Pronunciados* and chanced on us. Damned bad luck, nothing else."

"They send that many men out to catch their rebels? These *Pronunciados* must be a real thorn in their side."

"Ike was out scouting a week or two back," said Brocius, "and he found a den of them not ten miles from here. They was passin' on through so we didn't do anything about them. Should have, if they drew an entire goddamn company of soldiers."

Brocius looked down and saw Josh. He said nothing.

"There're still about a dozen holed up over there. Josh said that was Ike's headquarters. What's it like inside?" Slocum asked.

"You ain't thinkin' on burnin' it down, are you? Ike wouldn't like that one little bit."

"Might not have any choice in the matter. What's happening elsewhere around town?"

"About fifty of us dead," Brocius said. "The sentries warned us, but we didn't believe 'em, not when they said a full hundred soldiers was ridin' down on us."

"How many Mexicans dead?"

Brocius smoothed out his bushy mustache. Bits of wood and dirt had weighed down the ends. "Don't know. I counted four or five."

"I accounted for eight." Slocum remembered how one had died at the hands of the small child. "Seven," he amended. "Seen eight die."

"You sure been a busy bastard, ain't you?" said Brocius, smiling broadly.

"Whether they're looking for *Pronunciados* or us isn't going to matter much. We can't let them set up shop over there."

"Hmm, hadn't thought on it. You're right. They get a foothold, get a message back, and next thing we know, they got reinforcements drivin' us out of here."

"If any of them escape, they'll be back, if they stay or not," said Slocum.

"Makes sense. The last I heard, the guards along the rim have kept 'em bottled up. But that won't last long if we get the shit kicked out of us. Them guards'll head for the heart of the mountains first sign of us losing."

"I saw an officer inside Ike's headquarters," Slocum said. "You sure it's a colonel in charge? I think that might be him."

"He's got a powerful lot of firepower in there," said Brocius. "Ike liked to keep a couple hundred rounds of ammo stored against emergencies. Never thought we'd lose it like this."

"Where is Ike?"

"Him and a dozen others are over toward Tucson raisin' a little hell. Can't count on them. Don't think he's due back for another couple days. Might be even longer."

"We might have to burn the place to the ground to get the soldiers out," said Slocum.

"Too risky," said Brocius. "The places on either side'll go up like tinder. Might as well set the whole town on fire—that's what you'd be doin' if you tried burning them out."

Slocum had to admit that Curly Bill Brocius looked to be right.

"They cut down the saloon with gunfire. Maybe we can do the same to them. I need more ammunition."

Brocius shook his head. "What you got is what the rest

of us have. If it's in your pocket or in your gun, that's it."

"The rest is stored inside the headquarters?" Slocum asked angrily.

"That's the way Ike wanted it."

Slocum had to admit there was a certain logic to that. With a gang of highwaymen like the Cowboys rubbing shoulders in this hideout town, keeping ammo from them might contribute to everyone's safety. Not even Ike Clanton could keep all ammunition away, but restricting it might prevent needless fights.

Now that lack of ammunition meant that they might have to abandon the entire valley.

"Whatever we do, we're going to have to do it fast," Slocum said. He took a couple of shots at soldiers ducking and dodging and making their way to the headquarters. If the colonel continued to reinforce his troops with the remnants of his command, he might be able to make a stand for days—or longer.

"Looks like we're driving all of 'em into the building," said Brocius. "Reckon that's a good sign. We're winning everywhere else but here."

Slocum said nothing about winning the battle and losing the war. Burning the entire town to the ground might be the only way to root out the Mexicans.

"How many men do you have?"

"Can't say," Brocius said, glancing over at Josh. "We're scattered to hell and gone. Might be able to round up a dozen or so. What you got in mind, Slocum?"

Slocum had nothing in mind, but he had to know what resources were at hand before coming up with any ideas at all. Nothing would take the place of a battery of cannon aimed at the headquarters building. If Ike Clanton kept a tight check on ammunition, Slocum didn't think the outlaw would let a cannon sit around untended.

"Let's get the men together and see if anyone has any notion what we might do. But keeping the soldiers bottled up seems a good place to start."

Brocius nodded. "Be back soon."

Slocum fired sporadically at any soldier moving across a shot-out window or poking his head above the roof coping. He didn't hit anyone, nor did he get any of the men running like Satan himself was on their tail to reach the dubious safety of the building. Slocum counted another four soldiers making it back to their colonel. Without exaggerating their numbers any, Slocum thought there might be as many as twenty still inside the building.

Brocius returned, eight men following along behind. Most had been wounded and none could be counted on to obey orders, Slocum saw. Even if Ike Clanton himself had been here, these men might not obey.

"Here's a present." Brocius tossed him a box of cartridges. Slocum reloaded his Winchester and made sure the others had their magazines filled. Ten against at least twenty. He didn't like the odds, even with the Mexicans inside and pinned down.

"I got some of the younger kids going around countin' the corpses," said Brocius. "We took it pretty heavy in the first assault, then we gave a good accountin' of ourselves. I figure we lost damn near seventy men. Not many casualties since that first attack, though."

Slocum blinked in surprise. That about wiped out the town, except for women and children.

"Yeah," said Brocius. "What you see might be all that's left in town to fight."

Slocum put his hand up to shade his eyes. Someone on the valley rim signalled. Brocius turned and watched for a minute, chewed at the ends of his mustache as he deciphered the message, then let out a whoop of joy.

"Hot damn! Phin's comin' back in and he's got five men with him."

"Five?" Slocum sank down and drew up his legs to rest his rifle across them. That made it fifteen against at least twenty soldiers. When it came to training—not to mention desperation—he had to favor the Mexicans.

"When's Phineas Clanton going to get here?" Slocum asked. The words were hardly out of his mouth when he heard gunfire at the end of the street. Phin Clanton and his five men rode full tilt down the center of the street, rifles blazing away left and right. Slocum wished they'd hold off until they had a Mexican in their sights, but that wasn't the way Phin did things.

Slocum saw instantly what would happen if an all-out attack wasn't mounted against the Mexicans. Phin Clanton and the five men with him would be slaughtered.

"Attack!" Slocum screamed, getting to his feet and firing as he ran forward. He felt his left shirt sleeve jerk several times as Mexican bullets tore at him. This was the dumbest thing in the world to do and Slocum knew it—but the unexpected attack might work. It might take the Mexican troops by surprise.

Phin Clanton wheeled his horse around and jumped from the saddle. He had a sixgun in either hand. Both blazed as he shouted incoherently and ran to the door. The man to his right died in a fountain of blood as a bullet took off the left side of his face. Phin didn't even slow down as he kicked open the door and dived into the room.

Slocum was only a few seconds behind. He fired at anything moving in the room. He didn't care if he hit Phin Clanton or not. The madman had started this; he might already be dead.

Slocum got two soldiers, then felt Curly Bill Brocius and the others crowding in behind. He sidestepped and let them in. When his rifle ran out, he went back to his Colt. Three more soldiers died before he ran out of ammunition and had to reload.

By the time he had the percussion pistol reloaded, the fight was over. Phin Clanton strutted like the cock-of-the-walk, wearing the dead Mexican colonel's heavily braided hat.

"By damn, that was a good fight," Phin said. "A damn good fight. You surely do know how to welcome a man home, Curly Bill."

Brocius was grinning from ear to ear. They had won and that was all that mattered. Slocum looked around the large room. Bodies were stacked like cordwood. Already flies came to claim a free meal. He didn't want to think about the worms.

Slocum went outside and stood in the middle of the street. Women and children came out of hiding to survey the ruin caused by the soldiers. It amazed Slocum that such an unorganized group as the Cowboys could defeat an entire company of trained soldiers.

Bad luck had been on them when the Mexicans found their valley. Good luck had been on the outlaws' side after that.

"Joe Bob up on the hill said that the guards kilt damn near forty of them Meskins as they rode in," Phin Clanton said. "I'm gonna ask Ike to give everyone a fifty-dollar bonus."

A cheer went up from the survivors circled around Phin.

Slocum jerked when he heard soft movement behind him. Ruth Macabee hurried over to him and threw her arms around him.

"Oh, John, I was afraid you would be killed."

"Been through worse," he said. "Just can't remember when."

"You done good, Slocum," came Brocius's hearty, booming voice. He slapped Slocum hard on the back. "I'm gonna tell Ike personal about how you led the charge right behind Phin."

"Thanks," Slocum said dryly. He couldn't care less if he got any credit or not. He had saved Phin Clanton's life. Why, he couldn't really say.

"Why did those soldiers come into the valley?" asked Ruth.

"They were huntin' *Pronunciados*," said Brocius. He explained about Ike's scouts finding a small encampment of the rebels a week back.

As Curly Bill talked, an idea formed in Slocum's head. He watched Ruth's reaction. If she wasn't after silver or a story for a newspaper, maybe she had taken it into her head to help the rebels. It was something an idealistic young woman might think was romantic.

"*Pronunciados*," Ruth said carefully. She looked up and down the main street. "If the Mexican Army is so intent on following these *Pronunciados* up from Sonora, maybe you ought to do something about them."

Slocum waited for her to suggest forming an alliance, the *Pronunciados* and the Cowboys. Again she surprised him.

"You should track down the sons of bitches and kill every last one. Then the army wouldn't have any call to come into the White Mountains hunting them."

Curly Bill Brocius nodded, then walked off muttering to himself.

Any thought of Ruth entertaining romantic notions about rebels trying to overthrow a dictator left Slocum's mind.

What *did* Ruth Macabee want? He was farther from answering that than ever before.

10

John Slocum tried not to think of the work he did. The bodies were stacked head-high by the time both Mexican soldiers and outlaws were removed from the buildings and crudely prepared for burial. Slocum's shoulders and back ached as he worked to dig one grave after another in the rocky soil along the slopes of the valley rim where the cemetery marched endlessly.

He wiped sweat and dirt from his face and stared. Over a hundred new graves had been dug in the past two days since the assault. The stench from those bodies still unburied rose and gave strength to his back to dig just one more grave.

Slocum had been through battles in the War that had been costlier in lives, but seldom since had he seen such savagery on both sides. The Mexican soldiers had given no quarter when they rode through the pass into the valley.

Deguello. No quarter asked or given. That accounted for so many of them being slaughtered by the guards Clanton had stationed along the rim of the canyon. But they had fought well. Slocum finished another grave and moved on. Someone else had the responsibility of deciding which body went in each grave. They had finished burying all the dead Cowboys first before working on the Mexicans.

As he dug he thought hard about his position. Slocum knew that he couldn't stay here, caught in the middle of the Arizona Territory politics. The Mexican governor wanted all the Clantons killed because they had robbed a Sonoran silver mine and killed his envoy to Tombstone. Behan wanted to capture or kill the Cowboys because that would solidify his position as sheriff in Tombstone. Wyatt Earp had a personal grievance against Ike Clanton because the man was sweet on the woman the deputy marshal wanted.

And the Clanton gang preyed indiscriminately on rancher, Wells, Fargo shipment, and anyone who happened along the Arizona roads.

Those were the players in this deadly game—them and the lovely Ruth Macabee.

Slocum stopped to wipe sweat from his eyes. What about Ruth? Just as soon as he decided he knew what made her tick, the woman did an about-face that confused him all over again. He had really thought she was a romantic young thing out to help the downtrodden *Pronunciados* against their oppressive masters.

No one hotly suggested to Curly Bill Brocius that he exterminate the rebels who wanted to help them. Brocius was the kind of man who would seriously consider such an idea—and carry it out.

Slocum wiped more sweat away. Seeing the carnage wrought by the Mexican soldiers in their hunt for the

Pronunciados made him want to agree. Get rid of anyone bringing such death to the White Mountains. But he had to admit that the Sonoran governor would have been just as happy having Ike Clanton's ears for decoration as the deaths of the rebels.

Slocum leaned against the shovel and peered across the valley. He saw a moving figure. He watched, noticing the rhythm and gait of the horse. It was the animal stolen from the Wells, Fargo stage.

"Ruth," he said. "She's out looking for . . . what?"

Whatever the woman sought, she returned to the sloping valley walls to continue her meticulous hunt. Slocum didn't think it could be a usable silver mine. None of these had the look of prosperous mines about them. The silver veins had petered out quickly. Gold? He didn't think so. The quartz didn't look good enough for that. Besides, he had tracked her into one mine. All she had done was walk in, scratch a bit at the rock, and then leave.

She was looking for somethng in the mines, and it wasn't a mother lode of gold or silver.

Slocum threw down his shovel and called it a day. He had lost count of the graves dug. There might be enough. Maybe not. If nobody objected, they could always put two or three of the soldiers in a single grave. Most were nameless and the Mexicans weren't in any condition to protest such unChristian treatment.

He walked back down the hill and into the main street. Hammers flashed in the warm autumn afternoon and buildings were being repaired with almost indecent speed. Only a day ago he wouldn't have thought any of the buildings would have been fit for human habitation any time soon— if ever. Now only the saloon lay in total ruins. Given a good supply of the cheap whiskey served at the saloon, any place might be turned into a proper establishment.

"Slocum, lend a hand," called Brocius. The stocky man wrestled with a large barrel.

"What's in this?" Slocum asked. The contents gurgled.

"Get it over to Ike's headquarters. We're settin' up shop there. A new saloon."

Slocum had to laugh. The town was again complete and functioning as it had before the Mexican raid.

"Ike's gettin' in tonight and we want everything to be right as rain for him."

"Any word how it went with him?"

Brocius spat. "He got some money. But he's bringin' back that dancer woman with him. Only cause trouble."

Slocum nodded. Wyatt Earp wouldn't take kindly to this.

"She's tourin' with a medicine show. If a couple of the others hadn't had a talk with Ike, he'd of liked to bring the whole damn medicine show in here. Talk about following one disaster with another. We just get cleaned up from the Meskins and then we'd find ourselves fightin' off a whole damn posse."

"It'd be quite a chore for Earp to clean out this entire valley," observed Slocum.

"Why'd he want to clean it out?" asked Brocius. "The son of a bitch would keep it for himself. Anyone what wanted to stay alive would be ridin' for him instead of Ike."

"You're saying the deputy marshal is inclined to rob coaches and rustle cattle, too?"

"You don't know nothin' about how lowdown the Earps can get, do you, Slocum? Virgil's a deputy marshal, too, and as mean a son of a bitch as ever walked the face of the earth. Ugly man, ugly as a mud fence, and vicious."

Slocum stared. Brocius was calling Wyatt Earp's brother vicious?

"The pair of them—and maybe includin' their brother Morgan—are the worst thing what ever happened to the Arizona Territory. Damned Republicans."

Slocum and Curly Bill Brocius got the barrel of whiskey up the steps and into Ike's headquarters. The bullet holes in the walls had been patched and the place fixed up after the Mexican colonel's occupation. Phin Clanton sat on a chair, feet up on a table, hat tipped forward. He snored loudly.

"Don't pay him no never mind," said Brocius. He tapped the side of his head to indicate that Phin was a trifle on the loco side. Slocum didn't have to be told. The man had charged straight out into the muzzles of the soldiers' rifles.

"God looks after drunks and madmen," he said.

"If that's true," said Brocius, "Phin will live to be a hundred. He's both. Here, let's sample this to make sure it hasn't spoiled none." Curly Bill knocked the lid off the barrel and exposed the sloshing contents. The vapors rising from the whiskey made Slocum take a step back.

"Good stuff," he said. Brocius passed him a tin cup. Slocum took a healthy swallow and let it warm his gullet.

"You know how to fight. You didn't lose your head when the bullets started flyin'," said Brocius. "I'm tellin' Ike about you. I reckon he's got an important place for you in the gang, 'specially now that we lost so damn many men."

"How many?" asked Slocum.

"Counted over forty, then got tired and stopped." Slocum didn't want to ask Curly Bill if he could count at all, but the number sounded about right. The soldiers had taken heavy losses getting into the valley, then had inflicted heavy casualties on the Cowboys.

He took another deep drink of the harsh, biting whiskey. Damn near a hundred and fifty men had died in that raid, and he'd heard rumors of fourteen women and three children dying, too.

"Hell of a way to get promoted," observed Slocum. Brocius shrugged. Death held little meaning for this man.

Slocum looked up when he heard the clatter of hooves outside. A tide of cries rose that told of Ike Clanton's return. Slocum hurriedly finished the whiskey and moved to one side of the large room. He wanted to see what sort of man Clanton was.

He found out immediately. Ike Clanton burst into the room, trailing his men behind like flies falling off a mangy horse. For the world, Slocum thought that Phin Clanton had a twin, both in looks and action. The only difference between the brothers seemed to be in a low cunning that kept Ike alive and running this town. He entered his headquarters and immediately took a quick look around.

"Who's that?" he demanded, instantly singling out Slocum.

"Newcomer, Ike," said Curly Bill. "Damn good fighter. Helped us get rid of the Meskins. Followed right behind Phin when he came rushin' in to get 'em."

Clanton and Slocum stood two paces apart, as if they were squaring off for a fight. They eyed each other, appraising, thinking, considering, maybe even each one wondering about his chances against the other. Clanton broke the deadlock.

"If Curly Bill says you're all right, you're welcome any time with the Cowboys."

"Thanks," Slocum said.

"You got the look about you. Deadly, hungry. You want to go along with me on a job?"

Slocum pondered this. If he said no to Clanton's invitation, he might never see the light of another day. Clanton tested him. Fail and die. For all that the outlaw said about

being so readily accepted by the Cowboys, Slocum knew
that was so much bullshit. Only when Clanton *really* said
so would the rest of the gang treat Slocum as one of their
own. Brocius was a trusted lieutenant; he could never
speak completely for Ike Clanton.

"On one condition," Slocum said.

"What's that?" Clanton moved, his hand resting near the
butt of his Colt.

"The job's got to be worth it. I don't waste my time
with penny-ante holdups."

Clanton stared at him, then roared with laughter. "By
damn, I like you, Slocum. There's nothing cheap about
you, no sir. Come on over. Let's talk about this."

Clanton motioned. Brocius hurried to furnish tin cups of
whiskey for both his leader and Slocum. He joined them
only when Clanton made an impatient gesture. Slocum saw
that Curly Bill Brocius was terrified of Ike Clanton. Any
man who inspired such a reaction in Brocius was a man to
watch carefully—and never turn your back on, Slocum
decided.

"Been scoutin' up near Tucson," Clanton said. "This is
going to be *the* bullion shipment of the year. Wells, Fargo
is moving damn near a ton of silver day after tomorrow.
Been savin' up to get it through with one sneak move."

"But you ain't gonna let it, are you, Ike?" asked Brocius.

"Hell no!" Clanton downed the cup of whiskey. Brocius
refilled it for him. Clanton looked around the large room as
if making sure no one overheard his plans. Of the men who
had entered with him, only two remained, guards at the
door standing with arms crossed. Ike stared hard at his
brother Phineas, but the sleeping Clanton snored loudly
and without interruption. Ike shook his head in disgust and
took another swig of the potent whiskey.

"It's like this. We're gonna need a minimum of ten men. Fifteen might be better."

"You make it sound like a war. We already fought one battle," said Slocum.

"Yeah, heard about that. Saw what happened as I was ridin' in. Don't want to let word of it leak out, neither. Might give that son of a bitch Earp a hint that we can't defend ourselves." Clanton hunched forward, drawing a map on a tabletop with a whiskey-dipped finger. "Here's the terrain. I figure we set ten men here in ambush. There's gonna be a hefty number of Wells, Fargo agents riding guard. These ten take them out. The rest of us—five'll be enough—hit the wagon here." His finger stabbed down with a wet *plop!*

"We just take the silver, wagon and all?" asked Brocius.

"Might have to uncrate it and get it onto pack mules once we get deep enough into the mountains. Don't want to bring the wagon into the valley. Leaves too deep a track."

"We can leave to intercept the shipment," said Slocum. "And you can have the pack animals follow at the same time. By the time we finish with the wagon and get it heading back in this direction, they can meet us. Saves time all around."

"Good idea." Clanton frowned. "That makes it closer to twenty men in on the robbery, though. Fifteen to do the robbery, another five to get the mules down."

Slocum asked what the problem was with that.

"Don't want to leave the valley too weak after the raid. That damned Pesqueira might send out more troops to find what happened to this dead company."

"And there's Earp," Brocius spoke up eagerly, wanting to help. "He might have a posse roamin' around huntin' for you."

"Screw Earp."

Slocum noticed that Clanton didn't deny the possibility. He inhaled deeply and caught the faint scent of a woman's perfume lingering on Clanton's trail-dirty clothes. What Curly Bill had said about the dancer being with Clanton might be true. If he'd brought her into camp, Earp might be on the trail with blood in his eye.

"You don't have to pay a full share if you let me lead the mules," came a voice that spun them all around. Standing in the door between Ike's two guards was Ruth Macabee.

"Who the hell's this?" demanded Clanton.

"A friend," spoke up Slocum. "My friend."

"She's got sass. Can she get the damn mules down to us in time? She'd only have a day or two to do it. Those pack animals don't get there, we might have a world of trouble on our hands."

"If she says she can, she can," said Slocum. Ruth shot him a look of gratitude.

"Some of the other women might help, too. Their men got killed in the raid and they're sore in need of money. This would be a good chance to help you and help themselves."

"Can't give you much," said Ike Clanton, leering at Ruth. "You and four other women would only be in for one share. You'd have to split it among yourselves."

"I'm sure that even a fifth of one share will mean a great deal," she said.

Slocum leaned back and wondered anew at Ruth Macabee's motives. She had turned down a considerable amount of silver to gain entry into this valley. Now she made it sound as if silver was all she wanted. And the strange glow in her eyes told Slocum that victory burned bright within her breast.

That could mean only one thing. She had found whatever it was she sought hidden here in the valley.

"Settled," said Clanton. "We ride at dawn the day after tomorrow. Curly Bill, you get the extra men. Slocum here'll be one. I got six. Find six more." He moved close enough to Brocius so that only the outlaw and Slocum could hear. "And leave Phin out of this. Startin' a frontal assault like he done on them Meskins was damned stupid. I don't want him or us gettin' killed if he takes it into his head to do it again."

With that, Ike Clanton swung out of the room. His two bodyguards followed.

Slocum looked from Curly Bill Brocius to Ruth and contrasted their expressions. Brocius anticipated another successful robbery. But Ruth looked as if she had already committed the theft and waited only to spend the loot.

11

John Slocum hooked one leg around the saddle pommel
and rested from the hard ride as he watched the empty
desert blossom in color as the sun rose. The sunrise came
peaceful and lovely, but his gut-level feeling about Ike
Clanton's robbery didn't match the scene stretching in front
of him. In his head, he had gone over the plan a thousand
times and it looked good.

It looked damned good. But it felt wrong.

He remembered leaving Ruth Macabee. Her eagerness
for this robbery had nothing to do with him going. It rested
on getting control of a dozen mules. She had never handled
pack animals before and had carried on about how much
she would learn on the way through the winding canyons
and down to the desert floor where the Cowboys would
join up after their successful robbery.

She had been passionate in her farewell. He smiled and warmth rose within him as he remembered just how passionate. No man could leave a fine woman like Ruth Macabee and the way she'd bid him goodbye and not want to return rich and hankering after more of her and her loving ways. Slocum drew his forefinger over his lips. She had bruised them with her lustful kisses.

"What's she found in that valley?" he muttered. Whatever it was amounted to more than she figured to get from leading the pack animals down to take the stolen bullion back to Clanton's hidden valley. That wouldn't amount to much for Ruth.

Slocum's mind turned back to the robbery coming up as surely as the sun rose. A ton of silver. Half went to Ike, the other half would be divvied up into fifteen equal portions. A thousand pounds of silver—sixteen thousand ounces.

"What can I do with damn near seventy pounds of silver?" He smiled. He could think of something. It made up for the six bars he'd lost to Curly Bill Brocius as payment for getting into Clanton's gang.

That sobered him. For over a thousand ounces of silver bullion, there wasn't a man in the Cowboys not willing to shoot him in the back. For all of Curly Bill's hearty good humor, Slocum trusted him the least. Slocum was the newcomer to the gang and that made him prey to anyone who thought getting another sixty ounces was worth the price of a lead slug through Slocum's head.

But that wasn't the cause of his uneasiness. Something didn't set well with him, and Slocum couldn't put it into words. He had lived a long time relying on his feelings.

"Ready?" came Brocius's voice from his right. Slocum glanced in the man's direction. Brocius had his carbine out and ready for action. He had pulled a red bandanna up to hide his face, though Slocum wasn't sure why Brocius bothered. The plan didn't call for any of the Wells, Fargo guards to be left alive.

"Reckon so," said Slocum. He wanted to ride off and never look back, but doing that would only bring the murderous, killing shot all the sooner. "That them over there? Just round the bend?"

Brocius squinted. "That's them. They ought to take care of the guards any time now. Yeah, there! Look!"

The distant drama unfolded according to Ike's plan. The ten Cowboys struck savagely and without warning from ambush, their rifles aimed only for the guards accompanying the heavily laden wagon. The wagon's driver would spur his team on, tiring the horses in his futile escape attempt and making it easier for Ike, Brocius, Slocum, and two others to overtake. They didn't want the driver overturning the wagon. That would strand them miles and miles away from their pack mules. In that case, their booty would be only what they could carry.

"Looks to be six, seven guards. That's a lot fewer than you thought, Ike." Brocius looked at the leader of the Arizona Cowboys. The man rubbed his hand over the worn butt of his pistol.

"Let's get them bastards!" Ike Clanton shouted. He spurred his horse forward, kicking up a cloud of dust. Brocius quickly followed. Slocum hung back, letting the others go on. His gut rumbled with uneasiness now. Things were going well. Too well.

"They finished off the guards," crowed Clanton. "They'll be able to help us out in a few minutes."

Slocum saw that Ike was right. The ten who had ambushed the guards had finished them off. Of the original ten, eight still rode. Trading two for six seemed a fair price to pay to attack a helpless wagon.

Slocum sped up, not wanting to be left too far behind. That would attract unwanted attention. They followed the wagon up a short incline, then down the other side.

As they topped the hill, Slocum thought the world had exploded around him. Huge gouts of flame leapt up from the ground, spooking his horse. He fought to stay in the saddle as the mare wheeled and bucked at the unexpected noise and flame.

He caught sight of the other four who had gone ahead. By hanging back a ways, the explosion had been in front of him. For Ike and the others, it had come from behind them. Rocks blew far into the air, then came cascading down on them, taking their horses out from under the robbers like a scythe cutting through autumn grain.

Slocum got his mare under control and saw what had happened. Ike Clanton had ridden ahead, throwing caution to the winds. He had ridden past pockets of dynamite planted by the men now rising from cover to gun down the outlaws the way they might shoot ducks from a blind.

Curly Bill Brocius jerked when a slug ripped through his arm. He slumped forward, barely avoiding being stepped on by his horse. Ike Clanton's horse screeched in pain; Slocum saw that the rocks had broken both its back legs. Clanton fought to pull his rifle out from under the animal.

One bullet meant for Ike Clanton put the injured animal out of its misery.

Clanton dived down behind the horse's carcass, dragging out his pistol and firing wildly.

"We got 'em, Wyatt," came the call from Slocum's left. "We got the scurvy sons of bitches!"

A man wearing a six-pointed star badge rose. He tipped his stovepipe hat back on his head and lifted his rifle. All

Slocum saw was the way his mustache interfered with his aim. The rifle jerked and there was one less survivor of the dynamite trap.

"Damn you, Earp, you won't get me!" shrieked Clanton.

"What's the matter, Ike, can't you take it? Come on out. Don't fight it. Let me make it clean. I don't owe you that much, but I'll kill you with one good shot. If you get me riled and make me come for you, I'll bury you up to your eyeballs out in the desert. It'll take you days to die that way!"

"The Yaquis tried that on me, Earp. Didn't work for them, won't work for you!" Ike Clanton fired until his six-shooter hit an empty cylinder. He ducked back behind his dead horse to reload.

"Virgil!" called another. "There's one of them owlhoots to your left!"

Slocum bent over his horse's neck just as Virgil Earp sighted him and fired. Slocum urged his mare forward. She stumbled in a crater left by the dynamite. Slocum fell off to the side. As he went, he fumbled his Winchester from its scabbard. Against the Earps and their deputies it wasn't much, but it would have to do. Slocum didn't think they'd stop and let him explain how he really wasn't one of the Cowboys.

Slocum worked the lever and fired with deadly accuracy. By the time he had emptied the magazine, he had driven the lawmen under cover and given Brocius and Clanton a chance to retrieve their own rifles. He quickly slid down the rocky slope on his belly, cutting himself to ribbons. Slocum hardly noticed. If they couldn't hold off the Earps, they were going to be dead.

"Surrender, Ike. Give up. We'll let you stand trial before we hang you. Ain't that fair?"

"That Virgil Earp," muttered Brocius. "Always was a kidder. They'd never give us a trial."

"How much ammunition you got?" demanded Slocum. "Except for my Colt, I'm out."

"Here," said Clanton. He had pulled one saddlebag out from under his horse. In it was a box of cartridges. But try as he would, he couldn't get his rifle free. it remained securely pinned beneath his horse's dead carcass.

Slocum used his reloaded rifle with deadly effect. He kept the Earps at bay.

"Damn, what happened?" muttered Brocius. He lay beside Slocum, his entire side soaked in blood. "Why'd they plant those charges? It was like they knew we'd be coming."

"They did," Slocum said bitterly. "They knew exactly where we'd attack and how. They laid a trap for us. I don't reckon there's a nickel's worth of silver on that wagon."

"How could Earp have known?" muttered Clanton.

Slocum didn't bother to ask if the dancer Ike was sweet on had stayed in the valley. He knew different. Clanton had spent the night with her and she'd left a day before the outlaws. She had had plenty of time to meet with Wyatt and tell him the Cowboys' plans.

Slocum knew he could worry about who the traitor was and how to tell Clanton later—if they got out of the trap the dancer had fashioned for them. Slocum felt as if he'd just shoved his head willingly into a noose and now the Earps had pulled it tight.

He rose to a squatting position and fired with deadly accuracy. Another deputy sank behind a rock without making a sound. Slocum knew he'd got the man in the head. But how many were left? He tried to remember the scene as he'd gotten caught in the explosions. There were the two Earps. At least five others. The wagon driver.

"Can you see the wagonbed?" asked Slocum.

"Yeah, so?" called Clanton.

"What of the canvas cover? Is it back or is it still over their fake load?"

"Pulled away. The wagon's empty."

"Damn," swore Slocum. "I think they had three or four deputies hiding under that canvas, just waiting to pounce. We got a dozen men facing us. Maybe more."

Slocum settled down and let the lawmen shoot at them. Before too much longer, they'd have blown away most of the flesh on Clanton's horse. Slocum hoped they would be long gone before that happened.

"Can you get to the wagon? It may be our only chance for getting out of here."

"We can try," said Clanton.

The outlaw leader got his feet under him and said, "Cover me while I try for it."

"Wait. We can't leave him." Slocum indicated Curly Bill. The stocky outlaw had turned pale from loss of blood. He couldn't even stand; they would have to carry him.

"Leave the bastard," snarled Clanton. "He shouldn't have got himself shot like that."

Ike Clanton said nothing more. He shot away, bent low and dodging from side to side. Puffs of dust kicked up by bullets rose around his feet as he made his way to the wagon. Slocum tried to cover him but against a dozen men he had little luck. He thought he might have winged a careless deputy, but he wouldn't bet his life on it.

"Made it, Slocum!" called Clanton. The outlaw climbed into the box and caught up the reins. He whipped the team and turned them back toward where Slocum finished off the last of his ammunition.

Slocum tossed down his Winchester and worked his arm

under Curly Bill's shoulders. He helped the man sit up. Watery eyes stared at him and he tried to say something to Slocum. Only a weak gurgling came from his lips.

"Damn it, get in!" ordered Clanton. "They're gonna blow this damn wagon apart if you don't hurry!"

Slocum heaved and rolled Brocius into the wagon bed. The man fell heavily and lay face down, not moving. Slocum figured he'd done all he could—more than either Clanton or Brocius would have done for him. He vaulted up beside Clanton.

A flying bullet took his hat off and sent it sailing out over the desert.

"They're going to shoot the horses," Slocum said. "Get it around and make it harder for them."

Slocum and Clanton went flying from the wagon when a stick of dynamite exploded under the wagon. Slocum landed heavily, the wind knocked out of his lungs. He lay on the cold desert sand staring up at the blue sky he had thought so lovely. He was going to die under this sky now.

Slocum waited for death.

And waited and waited. Air came back painfully into his lungs. He sputtered and rolled to one side. From uphill came frantic gunshots, a sound he'd heard thousands of times during the War—the same fusillade of bullets he'd heard a few days earlier when the Mexican soldiers had invaded Clanton's valley.

He pushed himself to his hands and knees and saw salvation. The eight surviving Cowboys who had been decoyed had arrived, guns blazing. But the eight quickly became six, then four. Even as he stood, that number was reduced to two.

Slocum staggered off, unable to do anything for them. They had diverted the lawmen's attention for a few seconds. He had to make that time count.

"Help me," came the weak cry. "Help me, Slocum. Damn you, help me!"

Slocum turned toward the plaintive cries. Ike Clanton lay on the ground ten yards away, clutching his arm to his chest. Even at this distance Slocum saw the bright bone poking through the skin. He was injured enough to make fighting almost impossible.

He staggered to Clanton, helped him up. "What now?" he asked. "They got us surrounded."

"No, no!" cried Clanton. "Horses. Two of 'em from the team. Blast didn't kill them. Get them." Clanton tried to point with his broken arm and instantly regretted it.

Slocum saw the horses. Two stood stock still, as if they'd been turned to stone by some arcane spell. Slocum saw that the blast had stunned them. He made his way over and jerked at the pieces of bridle dangling down. He pulled the reins in and led the horse to Clanton. He helped the Cowboy leader up.

"Ride like the very devil," Slocum said. "Git!" He slapped the horse hard on the rump and it took off.

Slocum took cover then and waited. The Earp brothers saw Clanton making good his escape. Within minutes, more than a dozen lawmen pounded hard after the fleeing outlaw. Slocum rested, hidden between two rocks, regaining his strength. Only then did he venture forth to find a stray horse.

He got into the saddle and sat there for a moment, looking at the carnage. Not one of Clanton's men had survived. Slocum wasn't sure that Clanton would elude the posse either, nor did he care.

But when he started to turn toward the south and head for Mexico, something stopped him.

Ruth Macabee. He couldn't ride off and leave her, let her think he was dead.

Slocum laughed without humor. Hell, he couldn't leave her and never find out what it was that she had found in that valley hidden away in the White Mountains. He pulled the horse around and started back for the Cowboys' hide-out.

12

John Slocum rode with his head down, every muscle in his body hurting. He must have been this bone-tired before, but it was too much effort to think back to that sorry time, whenever it had been. He got lost a few times, back-tracked, made sure that Earp and the lawmen weren't on his trail, then found a narrow gulley that seemed promising. He rode up the arroyo for over an hour. The canyon walls took on a familiar look. Slocum looked up now, scanning the walls for Clanton's sentries. He didn't want to get gunned down by a trigger-happy lookout.

He saw the flash of a signal mirror before he saw any of the guards. He reined back and rode slower until the challenge came ringing down from the high ground.

"Who is it?"

"Slocum!" he called back. "Has Ike returned yet? We ran into an ambush. All dead except Ike and me."

He got no response, but he really hadn't expected one right out. The guard would have to check with somebody down in the town, and that might take a while. Rather than riding on, Slocum dismounted and sat on a rock in plain sight. No need to give a guard an itchy finger that might pull back on a trigger. Slocum stretched on the rock like a lizard in the warm sun. He tipped his hat over his eyes and rested.

The scrape of horses' hooves on rock awoke him. He blinked and looked at the sun. He had slept for almost an hour. Slocum sat up and saw a tight knot of riders coming toward him. He almost hoped that Ike had returned. It would make the explanations easier—explanations he was in no mood to give.

Phin Clanton led the small band of men. Ike's brother swung a leg over his horse and dropped hard to the ground. He stalked over to where Slocum sat. "Where'n the bloody blue hell's Ike?" Phineas Clanton demanded.

Slocum started into a lengthy description of all that had gone wrong with the plan. "Even the Wells, Fargo wagon was a decoy," he finished. "There never was any bullion. It was all a trap to kill us. I got Ike on a horse and laid down covering fire." Slocum decided this lie might go over better than the truth. He had used Ike Clanton as a cat's-paw to help in his own escape.

"How'd you get away?" one man asked suspiciously.

"By being damned lucky," said Slocum. "I got to a horse that was running loose. Its owner wasn't needing it any, so I took it. Bullets were flying everywhere. The horse reared and threw me. I landed flat on my back and hit my head so hard that it knocked me out. The Earps must have thought I was dead."

Slocum looked down at his shirt. Hardly an inch of it remained clean. The rest had blood soaked through and through—almost all of it Curly Bill Brocius' blood.

"You don't look that bad off," said Phin Clanton.

"I'm alive. That's about all I can say." Slocum studied the men gathered close by to get an idea if they believed his story. He decided to attack rather than be questioned further. "Why the hell are you all sitting around here on your fat asses? Ike's out there somewhere. He likely needs your help. If Wyatt Earp's caught him, he might be hanging from some tree."

"Couldn't find much more'n a saguaro out there," said Phin. "But you got a good point." He turned and spoke quietly to several men. They grumbled, not liking to take orders from Phin. Phineas Clanton knocked one to the ground. The others mounted and rode farther down the canyon, their search for Ike none too eager, since the Earps promised to be hot on the robber's trail.

"Don't reckon you'd be so hot for us to go lookin' for Ike if you had anything to do with the ambush," said Phin Clanton.

"Wouldn't have even come back if I had."

"Course, you might be a spy. Ike might be dead and you might be leadin' the Earps into the town."

Slocum made an elaborate pose of looking around. "Don't see any posse. Damned stupid of me to take on the entire town alone. Especially in my condition."

"You got a point there, too, Slocum. But then, from what I hear, you always do. Let's get on back up to the valley. You might be wantin' to rest up 'fore Ike gets back."

"That I do," said Slocum. His belly rumbled with hunger. He had ridden a long way without decent water. He was filthy from the fight and the long, dusty ride. Most of all, he wanted to rest.

And to see Ruth Macabee, if she was still around. As he

got nearer and nearer to the valley and the town huddled at the edge of it, he worried that the woman might have taken the pack animals and kept on riding. He had no assurance that what she sought had been found within the valley. It might have been something in one of many crossing canyons that turned the White Mountains into a deadly maze.

He felt some of the tiredness flow from him when they rode down the rutted main street of town and he saw Ruth standing in front of the Clantons' headquarters. She rushed out to him.

"John! You're safe!" she cried. "The guards signalled in that there was a lone rider—one of them who went with Ike. I prayed that it was you."

"It was," he said, dismounting. His aches began to vanish. When Ruth threw her arms around him and gave him a passionate kiss, he forgot all about his minor wounds.

But Ruth didn't. She backed off in a hurry, apologizing. "I didn't mean that. I mean, I didn't want to hurt you. Oh, the blood. You're a mess! How badly are you injured?"

"Not too bad off," he owned up, "but I'm in need of some fine doctoring."

The smile Slocum got from her combined both relief and wickedness. "I'm certain I know what can cure what ails you," she said.

"You, Slocum," Phin Clanton said. "Don't go gettin' yourself lost. When Ike gets back, we'll want to all have a long talk."

"Let me know when he gets back, Phin. I got some ideas who it was doublecrossing us."

Phineas Clanton spat. His eyes turned colder and he got an out-of-control look about him. "I got me some ideas on that score, too. Her name's Emma and she dances."

Slocum nodded that he agreed. He had worried that Phin Clanton might take it into his crack-brained head to

blame Slocum. Whatever had scrambled up the younger
Clanton's head didn't affect him too much now. Or maybe
it was just too obvious that the woman both Ike and Wyatt
screwed had turned in the outlaw to her lawman lover.

"Are you sure she did this?" asked Ruth in a low voice.

"Couldn't be anyone else. Or if it was, Earp double-
crossed them and left 'em dead out in the desert."

"Brocius?"

"He's dead, too." Slocum looked down at his shirt.
"This is mostly his blood. I'm not too bad off."

"Good. I want to make this a proper greeting," Ruth
said, tugging on his arm and steering him toward the tent
they still occupied at the edge of town.

Slocum sank down to the straw pallet and began stripping off his shirt. He tossed it aside. No amount of cleaning would turn it into anything he wanted to wear again.

"A few scratches," Ruth said, eyeing him with real appreciation. She dropped to her knees. Her fingers began to
draw tiny circles in the hair on Slocum's chest. She bent
over and kissed him, her tongue teasing and her long hair
falling forward to tickle and stimulate him even more.

"That's nice," he said, slowly leaning back until he
stretched out. "But we got some talking to do first."

"Later," she said. Ruth Macabee began unfastening his
gunbelt and trousers.

Slocum worked to kick off his boots. But he stopped the
woman from getting him completely undressed.

"I meant it. We got to talk."

"About what?" she asked innocently. Ruth opened her
blouse and exposed those fine, firm mounds of tits. They
bobbed slightly as she moved to discard her blouse and
begin working on her skirt. "If you want to talk about
about these, why not do it closer?"

She took each of her breasts in the palms of her hands

and bent down, offering them to Slocum. The woman
moved slightly, drawing each turgid nipple across his lips.

"I can feel your hot breath on them. That's so good! Oh,
John, take them into your mouth. Suck on them!"

With those wondrous breasts so close to his mouth, Slocum couldn't do anything but what the woman wanted. He
reached up and began kneading her tits, moving them in
tiny circles, then widening it until he could bury his face
into those pillowy mounds and lick and kiss the valley between.

"I . . . I've never felt like this with a man before, John.
You do things to me no one else does. You thrill me so
much! Oh, yes, more, do that more!"

He continued suckling while he let his hands roam over
her bare back and down to the compact globes of her behind. Ruth shoved herself forward, her breast quivering at
his lips.

Slocum had wanted to find out what the woman had
sought—and found. Since she had stayed in the valley,
that meant what she had discovered was hidden away
somewhere nearby. And it must be large or heavy or she
would have taken it with her as she led the mules down to
the rendezvous site—and kept on going.

If she had gotten free of Clanton's valley with her treasure, Ruth Macabee would have been long gone. Slocum
didn't delude himself into thinking that she had stayed for
him.

"You're such a man, John. So big, so goddamn big!"

She skinned his pants off and exposed his groin. The
fleshy shaft between his thighs rose until it was so stiff that
it pained him.

Ruth pounced on it like a hunting cougar. Her slender
fingers wrapped around the thick stalk. She began stroking.

Slocum moaned and pulled in even more of the woman's teat. His arms reached up and around her body, pulling her down on top of him. He almost smothered in the warmth of her softly yielding flesh. Together, they rolled over, Slocum ending up on top. They moved slowly, deliberately. Ruth's hand maintained a firm grip on his throbbing erection until they had shifted position, she on her back, legs wide and Slocum poised and ready to slip forward.

He looked down into her cornflower-blue eyes. They twinkled as she stared back. He bent forward, kissing her softly. The passion mounted and the kiss deepened.

Ruth began thrashing around under him, her body lurching and heaving. She tightened her grip and pulled him insistently to her.

"Please, don't torment me this way, John. I need you so, I need you, *in* me!"

He allowed her to pull him forward. He slipped into her moist depths. It took away his breath. For a moment he hung suspended, balancing on his hands, his eyes fixed on her. Then he drove forward with all the power and need locked up within his loins.

Their bodies merged into one as their passions soared. Slocum tried to restrain himself, but the fiery tide would not be denied. He stroked forward, felt the woman's body tense and heard her gasp, then spilled his seed. They rocked back and forth, locked in the ages-old rhythm until they collapsed, arms around each other.

Sweat turned their naked bodies slippery against one another. Slocum slipped to one side and lay, his face just inches from Ruth's. If her eyes had been bright and glowing before, now they blazed with a radiance that dazzled him.

"It's never been like this for me before, John. Never."

He kissed her gently. To his surprise, she pushed him away and sat up, chastely slipping back into her undergarments and skirt.

"That's it?" he asked.

"You men are all alike. So greedy."

He lay back, his body drained of all energy. He wasn't exhausted, just sated. He watched as she dressed. Finally Slocum said, "Why did you want to lead the mules out to pick up the silver we were supposed to get from Wells, Fargo?"

"I wanted to be of service. I feel I owe this town something."

"And?" he prompted. "What else?"

"Why should there by anything else?" she said, her face a neutral mask.

"What did you do when we didn't arrive? Just come back?"

"Of course."

"What happened to the mules?"

"They're in a corral." She shrugged. Slocum reached up and grabbed her shoulder. Ruth looked irritated that he pursued this matter. "Well, not *all* of them. I took a fancy to some of them. They're quite cute animals."

"We're talking about mules, not kittens. Mules are ugly, long-eared, and cantankerous."

"Yes, they are," she said. He saw her mind spin and turn as it worked over secret thoughts. "I'd never handled very many before. None, actually. But I learned."

"What use can you have for . . . how many?"

"Four," she said without thinking.

"What are you going to do with four mules? That's enough pack animals to carry damned near twelve hundred pounds. I saw you searching the mines. You haven't found that much silver ore that's worth anything. What have you found?"

Ruth Macabee thought hard, came to a decision, and smiled. "I think I can trust you not to doublecross me, John."

He said nothing. Simply agreeing wouldn't make her decide one way or the other. Such decisions had to be from the heart, not the head.

"It's a long story. Back in Connecticut I came across a map. Buried treasure."

"Bullshit," he said. He saw her recoil, then smile even more than she had before.

"No more lies. I *was* in school in Connecticut. But my parents raised me over in New Mexico Territory, up near Farmington. My pa was rich. Had a big spread."

"Was?"

"He and Mama are dead," she said, an edge of steel coming into her voice. "A Ute raid." Ruth heaved a deep breath and Slocum felt the memories of her parents drifting like shadows across the sun. This was the truth.

"Anyway, Pa owned a big spread, ran a lot of cattle. When they died, I wasn't left with much. Actually, I wasn't left with anything. Seems everyone got a piece of the ranch, most of it going to the banker. They were in with the Santa Fe Ring and the judges all sided with the banker in stealing it. But one thing they didn't get."

Ruth turned and fumbled as she searched through her meager belongings. She pulled out a yellowed envelope and held it up as if it were the most precious religious relic in the world.

"This is the last letter my pa sent me before he died. I think he realized something bad was going to happen, but I'm sure he believed the source of his woe would be the banker and the judges. He hid this information from them, and only I have it."

"This is a long way from northern New Mexico to be hiding part of his wealth," observed Slocum.

"He didn't hide anything. Pa wasn't the type. No, he befriended an Apache, one who had been in one of Victorio's raiding parties."

"And the Apache, for the price of a bottle of whiskey, told him where Victorio had hidden all the booty he accumulated over all his years of raiding," Slocum said. She missed the sarcasm in his voice at such an absurd notion.

"Victorio went far down into Mexico," Ruth said, eagerness causing her words to tumble out so fast that Slocum could hardly follow what she said now. "He robbed the white man, he robbed the Mexicans, he stole from the Yaqui silversmiths, he robbed the Navajos and Apaches not of his tribe. He stole from everyone. And he hoarded it all!"

"I've heard the stories," Slocum said, sinking flat on his back and staring up at the tent roof, now gently flapping in the afternoon breeze. "It's like the Lost Dutchman Mine and a dozen other legends. Myths. There's no truth to it."

"There's not?" Ruth sounded crushed.

Slocum had to laugh at her gullibility. "You worked those mules just to get into practice?"

"Well, yes."

"And you've got four of them hidden to get the treasure out of the valley? You expected to find that much?"

"Yes."

"Ruth, I'm sure your papa didn't hoax you on purpose. Or maybe he thought he was just passing along an interesting story and didn't think you'd ever take it as the gospel truth. However it was, Victorio probably never had much in the way of a treasure. Maybe nothing at all."

"Do you really think so?" she asked.

"How can a raider like Victorio carry that much from Chihuahua to here? Or from all over Arizona Territory, with the soldiers hot after him? Doesn't make sense. There's no lost Apache treasure."

"Oh," she said in a small voice. "Then how do you explain the three caves filled with gold and silver that I found?"

Slocum jerked upright and stared at her. The smile crinkling the corners of her eyes and dancing across her lips told him that she wasn't lying.

Ruth Macabee had found a king's ransom in precious metals.

13

John Slocum stared at the woman. He said, "Are you certain that you found gold? Silver?"

"Both, John. I'm sure of it. I may have been back East for several years, but I know good metal when I see it. My papa always said that in this day and age a woman has to know more things than ever before. He took me panning for gold many times." Ruth Macabee smiled ruefully. "I never found more than a few flakes, but he made it seem as if I'd discovered an entire mine filled with it."

"Is it Victorio's trove?" Slocum asked.

"Does it matter? It was exactly where Papa's letter said it would be. I found this valley—he mentioned the possibility that it might be the Clanton's hideout. Then I checked the signs left by the Indians. The Apache was a good friend. Papa had saved his life, and I don't think he would lie about this."

Slocum shook his head in disbelief. Ruth may have been from the northern part of New Mexico Territory and her parents might have been killed in a Ute raid, but she seemed to know little about Indians and the way they lived. No matter what her father had done for this Apache, even saving his life, the Indian would never reveal the location of Victorio's stolen treasure. If the Indian chief ever discovered that a brave had spoken of such a thing to a white man, that brave's life would be worth less than cold spit.

Slocum had seen what the Apache did to one another for tribal crimes. The stark viciousness of their punishment and tortures ensured silence in such matters.

But was Ruth lying? It would be too easy to check out. Or was she just deluding herself, hoping against hope that her pa had left her some legacy to take the hurt out of the loss of both her parents and the family ranch? Slocum thought this was the most likely explanation.

"I want you to see it, John. I need your help." She dropped her eyes and looked away from him. He saw a shy smile flutter across her lips. "The fact is, I need *you*. You've become very important to me. I swear, I almost fainted with relief when I saw that it was you riding back from the robbery."

"Getting anything out of this valley without Clanton's men seeing us is going to be hard. With or without pack animals."

"I know that. I never thought this would be easy—not until I saw you holding up that stagecoach. That was the luckiest day of my life. I just *knew* I could depend on you."

Slocum snorted. "Depending on a road agent is risky."

"I knew you weren't like the other outlaws. I could see that. You could have killed the stage driver and guard. You went out of your way not to."

"The Wells, Fargo agents hadn't riled me enough to

shoot down any of their employees." He thought back to Lucas and the other company man who had waylaid him. Maybe he should have killed them. It might have ended a long string of bad luck. If he had, his first thought would have been to get as far south into Mexico as he could. Leaving the Arizona Territory would have meant that he'd never have robbed the stagecoach, met Ruth Macabee, gotten involved with Ike Clanton and his Cowboys, or any of the rest of that sorry story.

"See?" Ruth pressed. "You're not like Curly Bill Brocius or Phin Clanton or even Ike. They kill because they enjoy it."

"You're saying that you can trust me to help you and not kill you once we get away?"

"No, John. It's more than that. Much more. You know what I mean." She lay back beside him, her clothed body rubbing seductively against his nakedness.

"I want to see the cave with the bullion," he said.

"You don't believe me." He thought she was going to cry.

"It's not that. If I don't see how hard it will be to get out, there's not much I can do to plan our escape."

"Then you'll help!"

"What's my share?" he asked.

She tipped her lovely face to his and smiled wickedly. "Half the gold, of course, and there can be more."

"How much more?"

"Me," she said. She bobbed forward, her lush lips lightly caressing his. As fast as a snake, Ruth pulled back and got to her feet. "Come along now," she said almost primly. "We'll have to hurry. It'll be dark in another hour. I don't like being about in the nighttime. It's too easy to get turned around and lost."

"Too many sidewinders come out then," he said, not

referring to more than fanged reptiles. Slocum began pulling on his clothes, his mind working over all Ruth had told
him. Victorio's legendary treasure? Could it really be? The
Apache chief had raided throughout the Territory for damn
near ten years, accumulating a vast hoard of gold and silver
and jewels. Over a bottle of whiskey, the tale grew until
Victorio was responsible for every burned-down farmhouse, every double eagle lost, every crime in the entire
area.

Slocum smiled. If the Indian chief had committed just a
fraction of those thefts, the wealth would be staggering.
And it had to be stashed somewhere. Why not under Ike
Clanton's very nose? This was a secluded area and had
been abandoned for a decade or longer. There might have
been years between the last miner leaving and Clanton and
his Cowboy gang taking over. Plenty of time for Victorio
to hide the gold.

"How far is it?"

"I'll show you the way," Ruth said. "It's not that I don't
trust you, it's just that people listen in on everything said in
town." She glanced around. No one loitered nearby, but
Slocum understood her caution. The slightest hint of a find
like this would send the Cowboys into a killing frenzy.

"Somebody took the horse I rode back on," said Slocum. He looked around and couldn't find where the animal
had been stabled.

"We can walk a ways," Ruth said. "Then we can ride, if
you don't mind a mule."

"I do," Slocum said with some disgust. But he followed
the woman as she made her way through the tents at the
edge of town and then went past them to a small ravine.
They walked in the bottom of the arroyo for almost fifteen
minutes. Slocum was ready to fold by the time they came
to the small cut in the arroyo's bank where Ruth had teth-

ered the four mules to a mesquite.

"Cantankerous brutes," she said, "but they will do just fine in getting the gold out."

"We have to do a powerful lot of planning before we get to that," said Slocum. He pictured the terrain leading to this valley. Getting by the guards would be well nigh impossible. But an idea formed in his head, one that had great promise because he knew human nature.

Ruth agilely climbed on one mule and got on its back. The mule just stood, refusing to move.

"You have to talk gentle-like to it," Ruth said. She got hers moving, if a bit reluctantly.

Slocum glared at the mule. When it refused to budge after repeated urgings with his boot heels, he bent forward and bit its ear. The mule brayed and took off at a brisk clip, soon overtaking Ruth.

"See?" she said. "All it takes is a little sweet talk."

"You have your ways, I have mine," he said. "Both seem to work just fine."

They rode along the trail he had taken earlier when he followed Ruth on her first searches. Slocum saw the mine cabin where he'd climbed to the roof, then almost fallen through the rotting timbers. They rode on past the mine shaft Ruth had checked and which he had studied, trying to decide what her purpose was.

"There," Ruth said. "See that tiny crevice? It widens and leads back into the mountains almost a mile." She leaned in that direction, applying pressure with her knees. The mule obeyed. Slocum had a harder time convincing his to do the same, but it reluctantly followed after more urging on his part.

At the rocky knife-cut, he called out, "Let me do some scouting." He slipped off the mule's back and turned to look out over the valley. An autumn haze formed, turning the far side of the hills a muted purple in the afternoon sun. But it wasn't the serenity that Slocum appreciated as much as the emptiness.

No one had trailed them. He waited for almost ten minutes, watching closely, and saw nothing.

Only then did he turn his attention to the rocky cut. Slocum noticed straight out a faint white smear of paint high up on the stony face. Scrambling on the rock cleft, boots slipping, he climbed until he came even with the paint.

"What is it, John? An Indian symbol of some kind? I hadn't noticed it before."

"Can't make it out. The weather's eroded the rock something fierce. Reckon it's been here a long, long time to wear down like this." Slocum ran his finger over the symbol, trying to decipher it. It might be an eagle symbol —or it might have been any of a dozen others. But he didn't doubt its Apache origins.

That didn't answer the question of who had placed it here. Victorio? Some earlier Indian shaman?

From his vantage point, Slocum looked once more out at the valley. His heart rose in his throat when he saw a tiny cloud of dust moving from the far side in their direction.

"Keep the mules quiet," he called down to Ruth. "There's someone down there, moving fast."

He slid down the rocky face and landed in a crouch, his eyes never leaving the rider below.

"Where, John? I don't see anything."

He pointed out the dust cloud to Ruth.

"Are you sure? It looks like a dust devil."

"Then it's the only one to form all day. It's a rider. I'll bet you gold to greenbacks on it."

"I've got the gold if you've got the greenbacks," Ruth said.

Slocum smiled. If everything she said were true, she had a mountain more gold than he did scrip.

"The rider's moving down the valley, toward town." His keen eyes failed to make out the details of the distant figure, but he hadn't missed the spot on the far side of the valley where the rider had emerged, seemingly from thin air. They might have been watched by a guard posted there.

Slocum didn't think so. But that was something he'd have to check out later.

"The way looks clear. Let's get moving." He looked up at the rocky crevice and knew they'd be traveling in twilight the entire distance. With such steep, sheer walls, night came fast.

They rode almost a mile along the crevice before Ruth stopped. "There," she said. "See the cave entrance?"

Slocum squinted to see through the shadows cloaking the mouth of the cave. He shook his head.

"Then you'll have to take my word for it. This is the spot. The very spot my papa mentioned in the letter."

Together, they cautiously went up the steep slope to a sharp outjut of rock. Only then could Slocum see the cave. The overhang hid it well from below.

"We're going to need torches," he said. "I'm not blundering around in a cave without light."

Ruth fumbled in her skirt and pulled out a half-used candle. Handing it to him, she found another for herself. Slocum got out the box with his lucifers and struck one. The sudden dazzling flare made him squint. He applied the sizzling end to the candle wick, then lit Ruth's from his. Shielding the candle flame with his hand, Slocum entered the cave, Ruth pressing behind.

"Straight ahead, then take the first tunnel to the right."

He looked carefully at the floor and frowned. The dirt

that had accumulated was muddy from seepage and con-
densation. Any chance to study the floor for indication of
who had preceded him meant little in such muck. Slocum
walked slowly, making sure he avoided the spots where a
rattler might curl up for a little rest.

"This one?" he asked, coming to the branch. He held
the smoking candle up to the wall and saw faint scratches
at waist level, as if whoever moved the treasure in had
been careless and banged strong boxes against the rock.

If Ruth was right. If there was any bullion at all.

"Jesus Christ!" he exclaimed. Slocum stood and stared.
He hadn't gone ten paces from the branch. A cavern
opened around him, its vault easily twice his six-foot
height. Stacked everywhere were boxes. Many had been
opened, their lids ajar to reveal bright silver flashes as he
moved his candle past them.

"Go on, John. Take a good, long look." Ruth almost
crowed in triumph now. "Isn't it everything I said it would
be?"

"More than I imagined," he said honestly. Slocum
opened one box after another. About three-quarters contained silver bars. The other quarter were laden with gold
Mexican coins. "This just might be Victorio's treasure."

Another thought came to him, one that sobered him
quickly. The Apaches might not have left this fabulous
wealth here. This might be Ike Clanton's secret stash.

The bandit had been extorting half of everything taken
by his Cowboys. Nowhere in the town had Slocum seen
any indication of what Ike Clanton did with his wealth.
From all accounts, both from the lawmen and from the
Cowboys themselves, the gang had been exceptionally
successfully in their raids.

"I know," said Ruth Macabee. "This might be Clanton's. The thought *did* occur to me."

"You say there're two more rooms?"

"Go look," she urged. "One—the far one—is incredible. I've never seen anything like it in my life. Even the books we read about the Greeks and their treasure. Nothing compares!"

Slocum moved slowly to keep the candle flame from guttering. The second chamber rivalled the first. But the third one proved that Ruth wasn't exaggerating. Indian rugs had been piled waist-high around the edge of the room. In the center, almost as if it were a shrine, stood a large wooden cask. In it sparkled bright gems the likes of which Slocum had never before seen. He thought some might be diamonds, others emeralds, but he didn't know. He dipped his hands in them and let the stones drain like huge grains of sand through his fingers.

Ruth laughed. "That's exactly what I did when I saw them. Isn't this room exciting?"

He looked around. The wealth contained here staggered him. Ruth came up behind him and laid a cool hand on his shoulder. She moved around his body and ran the hand in the front of his shirt, her fingers touching bare flesh.

"It *excites* me," she said. "I've never made love surrounded by so much gold and silver and jewels."

Slocum looked down into her bright blue eyes. He didn't think she had ever looked lovelier. He kissed her.

The woman's tongue darted out to meet his, to run over his lips, then chase his tongue back into the wet cavity of his mouth. Their bodies pressed together, grinding slowly as passion mounted.

Slocum wasn't certain if the woman aroused him or the thought of so much gold. He was sexually excited and Ruth was, too. The source of such lust didn't matter.

Ruth got his gunbelt free; he let it drop to the cave floor. She worked feverishly to get his trousers unbuttoned; they fell around his ankles and exposed his erection.

"I need you now, John. Now!"

Ruth hiked her skirts and stepped in close. Slocum felt himself pressing against her. The woman raised her leg and curled it around his waist. They gasped in unison as she lifted herself on one toe, then settled down, his hot length finding the exact spot they both desired most.

Slocum began a slow up-and-down motion, moving very little but giving them both exquisite pleasure. He knew he should have been totally wrapped up in the woman. He looked around the room, at the gems and gold, and this kept him moving.

Wealth beyond his wildest avarice!

His hands held Ruth close. They began to move slowly, she hopping, he taking short quick steps. But he lost his balance. They toppled over, landing on a stack of the rich Indian rugs. Here they quickly consummated their passion.

The sudden rush, the slow drifting and Slocum relaxed on the rugs, Ruth Macabee held tightly in his arms.

"John?" she said, her voice shaky. "I have a confession to make."

"What? That this isn't all real?"

"No," she said, in a girlish voice. "I wasn't thinking of you while we were making love. All I could see was the gold all around. It excites me so much!"

Slocum had to laugh at that. How closely they thought alike!

"That doesn't matter, does it? What does is figuring out how to get all this out of the cave—and Clanton's valley."

"If we get it all out," she said, now almost breathless, "we can do this any time we want!"

He laughed again. "We can make love in a room entirely lined with gold coins and silver bars," he assured her. "But we've got to get it out."

"You know how, don't you? I can tell from your voice. What's your plan?"

"It starts off hard," he said. "First of all, we have to walk back to the town."

"Walk? But the mules . . ."

"They stay here. When we return, we ride the other two. That gives us four pack mules. I don't think we can risk more than that. And it'd be nice if we could get two horses."

"To ride? Yes, yes," she said, getting excited all over. "We ride the horses and that lets us pack *four* mules."

Slocum started to button up his trousers but he found Ruth's hot hand stopping him.

"We've got to walk back to town, isn't that right?" she said. He nodded his agreement. "That's so very, very far. And I want to enjoy this. Again."

Ruth bent forward and kissed him. In spite of the gut feeling Slocum was getting that speed was more important than caution in getting this trove out of the valley, he relented.

How many men could boast that they'd made love to a beautiful woman surrounded by a million dollars' worth of Victorio's treasure?

14

John Slocum and Ruth Macabee started back to the outlaw town on foot. Ruth said nothing most of the way, keeping a stoic silence. Several times Slocum heard her muttering under her breath. He thought she kept herself going by counting the huge fortune that awaited her.

Slocum had to admit that the gold and silver in the cave turned the loot from his earlier stagecoach robbery into pocket change. Even if he had gotten all four strong boxes laden with silver bullion, it didn't match Victorio's treasure.

He frowned as he considered this. He doubted if the Apache chief had left the bullion and gold coins. More likely, Ike Clanton was responsible. But whoever had left it, they wouldn't be allowed to simply ride from the valley. Even if the treasure was unknown to Clanton and the other

Cowboys, such wealth would draw them like flies to honey.

And if it *was* Ike's, Slocum didn't care to think how the outlaw would reward such a theft. He might be better off turning himself in to Sheriff Behan and confessing to every crime ever committed in the Arizona Territory. They could only hang him once. Ike Clanton might make the torture last for weeks.

"Can we, John?" asked Ruth.

"Get out of here, you mean?" In the darkness he saw the woman nodding. "I reckon anything is possible. This is going to take some doing on our part, though, and we might not be able to get away with everything in those three caves."

"We'll have to leave some?" He heard the plaintive quality of her voice. The idea didn't set well with Ruth. Slocum didn't much cotton to it, either. Such a fortune would set him up with a fine spread anywhere he wanted to settle.

His thoughts turned from getting away with the fabulous loot to trying to settle down. There wouldn't be any more call for him to go gallivanting around if he had more money than he could spend in five lifetimes. Even assuming the worst, even escaping with only a couple of mules loaded down with that gold and silver treasure trove, he wouldn't be badly off. Not at all.

"Settle down," he said softly, rolling the words over his tongue as if they were some fine, smooth Kentucky whiskey. It hardly seemed possible any more. He had done well enough after the War, getting the family homestead back into shape after his folks had died. The image of the carpetbagger judge and his hired gun coming out to steal the farm because he wanted to turn it into a breeding ranch still burned fiercely in Slocum's mind. The judge and his gunman had died, but the notion that others would be willing to steal what he had wasn't anything he could argue.

Hadn't Ruth Macabee gone through much the same? The Santa Fe Ring and their crooked judges had done her out of her legacy. They called it legal, but it had been as legal as the carpetbagger judge wanting phony back taxes. Slocum hadn't wanted to press Ruth on the subject of her parents' death, but he wondered just how much the Utes really had to do with it.

It always proved easy to blame the Indians for an unexpected death, a burned-out farmhouse, stolen cattle. Slocum didn't discount the notion that the judges and others responsible for the legal chicanery robbing Ruth of the ranch might also have had a hand in her parents' murder. When you were the law, when your word *was* the law, killing and thieving became easy enough.

Didn't much matter, either, which side of the law you were on. He saw no difference between Deputy Marshal Earp and Ike Clanton. One wore a badge to kill and steal. The other just killed and stole.

"We can get out with four mules," Slocum said. "Don't see any way of getting out with more."

Ruth walked silently for some time before saying, "We can always come back, can't we? I mean, if we don't get it all out, we can sneak back and finish cleaning out the caves."

"Getting out is going to be a major chore," said Slocum. "Think on the guards. And Ike's been shot up pretty bad. He's not going to take kindly to anyone trying to desert his little army. He's got few enough men left to carry on with the rustling and chasing after real Wells, Fargo stagecoaches."

"I've got some ideas about getting away," said Ruth.

"I've got one or two myself. Let me work on it," Slocum said. "If they don't pan out, then you can try."

Ruth didn't answer, but Slocum thought nothing more of it. He was too lost in the confusing welter of feelings he had when he entered the town. On the one hand, he didn't care if the entire place burned to the ground, taking Ike Clanton, his brothers, and everyone else with it. But there had been so much suffering already. There were wives who had lost their husbands, children whose fathers would never return. For them Slocum held some compassion.

But not so much that he'd let them have the treasure Ruth Macabee had found. And certainly not so much that he'd let anyone kill him to get to the treasure.

"Go and get everything ready to travel," Slocum told Ruth. "When we get to moving, I want to go quick. If we linger, we might be lost."

"What are you going to do?" she asked.

"That was Ike who rode into town," he said. "I got to go talk to him."

"Why? Let's just get the other mules, and—"

"Ruth, if Ike doesn't find me real quick and hear everything he wants to confirming the ambush, he's going to send Phin and the others after me. I'd rather get the questions out of the way."

"Wouldn't do to have them coming after us when we're trying to get out with the gold, would it?" she said sheepishly. "You're right, John. I'm sorry for doubting you, even for an instant." She came to him and rose on tiptoe to give him a kiss proving just how right he was. She stepped a half pace back. Their eyes locked, blue on green. Then Ruth Macabee turned and lightly ran off to the tent.

Something gnawed at Slocum's gut but he couldn't figure out what it was. He didn't think Ruth would double-cross him. She could never hope to make a deal with any of the others in town and not have them rob her blind.

Slocum knew that the woman realized this. But he had the feeling that she was going to try something dumb.

He pushed it from his mind. He had to face Ike Clanton. The sooner he got it over, the better. Slocum settled his gunbelt into a more comfortable position on his hips, checked the Colt Navy and made sure it held rounds in every cylinder—he wouldn't soon again make the mistake he had with Curly Bill Brocius the first time he'd faced the stocky killer—then lightly dropped the pistol into the holster. He didn't bother with the thong over the hammer to hold it in. He might need his six-shooter quick.

Slocum hesitated for a moment just outside the door of Clanton's headquarters. Loud, angry voices came from inside. He recognized both Ike's and Phin's.

He made sure that his pistol hung easy, then took a deep breath and went into the large room. The outlaw leaders sat at a large table in the center of the room. Ten other Cowboys ringed them, looking over their shoulders.

"Slocum," Ike Clanton said. He made the name sound like a curse. He sat at the table, his left arm bandaged and splinted heavily.

"Thought I saw you coming into town, Ike," Slocum said. "Glad you got away."

"You son of a bitch!" yelled Clanton. He shot to his feet so fast that he knocked over the straight-backed chair. His right hand poised over the butt of the pistol stuck in his holster. "I'm gonna shoot you down where you stand."

"Why?" Slocum's voice carried no hint of fear. He stood with feet apart, arms hanging at his side. The cold green eyes bored into Clanton, challenging him.

If there had been even a hint of fear within his heart, Slocum knew that Clanton would have killed him. But the outlaw respected courage—or possibly feared it in another.

"You put me on that horse and used me for a decoy!"

"I tried to follow. I got hit. Knocked out. There wasn't any way I could help you." Slocum eyed the man. He had been shot up something fierce. Blood caked the side of his head. His left arm twitched in spite of the splint. His pants legs had been damned near blown away by a score of bullets. The outlaw had the look about him of a man who had been through a battle and hadn't come out in any too good a shape.

"You're lyin', Slocum. You're the one what set us up for that ambush. You came through it all right."

"Ike," his brother spoke up. "Slocum and me, we been through this. It'd be damned stupid of him to come roarin' back to town like he done if he had anything to do with it. When he got in, he wasn't in too good a shape, either."

"He wants to keep on betrayin' us," declared Ike. His gun hand moved slightly. Slocum didn't go for his gun, but the temptation was great. He held off for only one reason. He could take Ike Clanton. In the man's condition, he could empty all six rounds into the outlaw before Ike cleared his holster.

But that didn't take into account Phin Clanton and the other Cowboys. They wouldn't just let Slocum kill their leader.

To Slocum's surprise, it was Phin Clanton who reached over and grabbed Ike's wrist. He spun his brother around. They looked at each other, eye to eye.

"You're only going after Slocum because you already *know* who betrayed you."

"What are you sayin', Phin?"

"You don't like what I'm sayin' one little bit, Ike, but it's still true. Slocum's not the one who went cryin' to Wyatt Earp. You know damn good and well that it was Emma."

"No!"

Slocum's eyes widened in surprise. Phin hit his older brother, knocking Ike to the floor.

"That won't knock sense into your hard head. Nothin' will. But maybe it'll get the job started."

Slocum had pegged Phin as the one out of his head. Maybe the younger outlaw had healed up a mite. Or maybe all that had happened what with the Mexican soldiers and having most of the Cowboys killed then and at Earp's hand had brought him to his senses.

"You touch me again and I'll blow your goddamn head off!" shrieked Ike.

"Go on, big brother. Try it."

Slocum saw his chance and took it. "Ike, Phin, cool off," he shouted. "Look what's happening. That woman's got you both at each other's throats."

"Emma's got nothin' to do with this," maintained Ike.

"The hell she ain't!" yelled another Cowboy. "Phin's right. It was Emma that did us wrong."

Ike sat on the floor. His face had turned dark with anger, but he didn't draw on Phin. "You're all wrong. Emma wouldn't do this to me. She loves me!"

"She loves her own hide more, maybe," said Slocum.

"What's that supposed to mean?"

Slocum saw the argument that would pour oil on the troubled waters and let everyone walk away. "Emma had to go back to Tombstone, didn't she?"

"Tucson," said Ike. "So?"

"So she was nabbed by Earp, maybe. I'm not saying there's anything between her and the deputy marshal. There might be, there might not be. But if he caught her and knew she'd been here, Emma might have broken under Earp's questioning. I hear tell he's none too gentle when he starts in on a person."

"No, he's not. Killed more'n one of us tryin' to find out where this town is."

"Does Emma know that?" asked Slocum. He directed the question to Phin rather than Ike. The outlaw shook his head.

"She gave Earp all she could to keep from getting herself killed. Motives don't mean much when your life's on the line."

"She betrayed us to Earp. Don't matter why," grumbled Phin.

Slocum stood beside the younger Clanton and whispered, "Keep your damn mouth shut. We both know Emma's the one who set up the ambush. So does Ike, but he needs an honorable way out of this."

"Nothing honorable about that dancer woman," said Phin. But the man subsided. He kicked at a chair and pulled it around so he could sit at the table. Slocum went and held out a hand to Ike Clanton. The outlaw glared at him, refusing the help. He stood and staggered over to a chair and sat down heavily.

Looking up at Slocum, Ike Clanton said, "Well? You gonna sit down and help us work through this or not?"

That was all the thanks Slocum got. It was more than he'd expected when he came in. Emma might not be branded a traitor, but at least there hadn't been any need to leave someone dead or dying on the ground. Slocum reckoned that Ike wouldn't be any too gentle with the woman if their paths ever crossed again, but that was her lookout.

Slocum had weathered this storm and would come sailing through in fine shape.

He sat at the table and looked over the map Clanton had spread out. "What's the plan?" he asked, not sure what he looked at.

"Ike's not liking what the Earps are doing to the Cowboys," said Phin. "We might just try trackin' them down and put an end to them once and for all."

"There're men out there who will join us," said Ike, his voice hard and carrying the full burden of his hatred. "The McLaury boys will join us again. They done it once, they'll do it a second time."

Slocum sat back, thinking hard. He remembered the name from his brief time in Tombstone. Frank McLaury had been the young buck in the card game that Behan had come after.

"Johnny Ringo. We can get him to join up. We got to play this hand real close to our vests," said Ike. "We got to get together enough men to make sure that Wyatt Earp don't have a chance. We can corner him in Tombstone."

"No chance for doing it in Tucson," said Phin. "That's his home ground. No chance, no chance. We heard tell that he's tryin' to get his brother Morgan into Behan's office as a deputy. That would play into our hand. We might be able to get him and Wyatt and Virgil all at the same time."

Slocum nodded, but his mind drifted away. He had no intention of being a part of any revenge.

"He should never have killed Curly Bill," said Ike. "That was one damn fine man."

"He'll pay, brother. We'll get everyone together and make sure Wyatt pays good," said Phin.

"When are you going to go after Earp?" asked Slocum. This might be just the ruse he needed to get free of the valley—with Ruth Macabee and the fabulous treasure. Ike wouldn't leave a dozen or more men to stand guard over the valley. Not for revenge. He might recruit the McLaury brothers and Johnny Ringo and other desperadoes, but Ike would want men he'd ridden with at his side.

That meant there would be only a few guards left. And

they could be gotten around, Slocum was sure. He began mentally spending all the gold he would pack out of the caves.

"Won't be for a few days. Call it a week. I need to mend up a mite," said Clanton. "You're gonna be with us, Slocum. You're gonna be there when I get Earp in my sights." Ike smiled crookedly. "And you can have Morgan."

"I want him, Ike!" protested Phin Clanton.

"All right, all right. You take him out. Slocum, you can ventilate that good-for-nothing Virgil."

"We'll have to see how it goes, Ike," said Slocum. He knew they were just venting steam now. When the real battle raged, there would be no telling who would be on the receiving end and who would be doing the shooting. Slocum had a bad feeling about this and knew he'd best be far away when the Clantons and the Earps collided, whether it was at Tombstone or Tucson or some other spot in the Arizona Territory. This wasn't his fight.

"You're a good man to have on our side, Slocum."

Slocum nodded, rose, and walked out. He felt a dozen pairs of eyes boring into his back. For all the fine talk, he knew that Ike didn't trust him. Deep down, Clanton wouldn't believe that the woman he was sweet on had betrayed them all to Wyatt Earp. It was still easier for the outlaw to believe that Slocum was the traitor. All the Cowboys would be watching closely to see if he tried to warn Wyatt Earp.

Slocum stopped outside and stared at the cold, diamond-hard points of the autumn stars. He fumbled in his pocket and got his fixings out. It took longer to get the cigarette rolled than usual. Slocum had no reason to hurry. He ran the slim smoke between his fingers, then stuck one tip into his mouth. The lucifer cast sudden shadows.

From the corner of his eye he saw a man jump back into an alley. This convinced him that Ike Clanton doubted his loyalty. He had sent a man to dog his tracks, to report back anything out of the ordinary. Slocum hadn't expected to get this far without a fight. He puffed and looked at the stars working their way across the velvet darkness of the night. Only when he had finished the smoke did he turn and go in the direction away from the alley and the man who was spying on him.

Slocum walked slowly and deliberately, then jumped to one side, sliding between the walls of two buildings. He knew how it would look to a tracker not expecting such a move. He would have just seemed to vanish into thin air.

Slocum stood, back pressed against the side of the building. He felt the wood give behind him. Nothing in the town had been fixed properly after the Mexican troops had shot the place up.

Slocum waited and waited until he thought he'd made a mistake. The soft, sucking noise of a boot working through mud alerted him. He slid the Colt from his holster and pressed harder against the wall, trying to turn himself invisible by force of will. He became a brother to the shadows.

A man came even, cautiously peering into the small space between the buildings. Slocum took one step. As he moved, he swung the pistol. It landed squarely on the side of the man's head. He crumpled and fell face down into the mud. Choking noises loud enough to draw attention told Slocum that his victim smothered in the mud. He grabbed the man's arms and dragged him into the narrow passageway between the buildings. Rolling the man over showed that he still lived.

Slocum robbed him of his ammunition and pistol, sticking the weapon into his belt. He never left a sixgun behind if he might need the firepower a spare offered. Slocum hurried back toward Clanton's headquarters. The windows had been shot out; no one had bothered replacing them. He listened to the discussion still going on inside. It verified his suspicions.

"I do admit to the chance that he might be a spy, Ike," Phin Clanton said. "But it's like I said, I got a powerful suspicion that it's that woman Emma."

"It's Slocum. I feel it in my bones, Phineas. He's the one. Emma would never betray me. She's too crazy in love with me. Trust me. I never steered any of you wrong before." He looked around the tight circle of outlaws. Most nodded in agreement.

"Well, that's true, Ike."

"We're agreed that Slocum couldn't have done it by himself. He must have help. Maybe that bitch that came into the town with him. Maybe somebody else. We got to know if there're more traitors in our ranks before we can move against the Earps."

Slocum knew the other Cowboys would do whatever Ike told them. They were a suspicious lot, able to think the worst of anyone. Winning Phin over probably hadn't been that big a chore, either. Getting out of the valley with the gold and silver now seemed less likely than just getting away with his life to Slocum.

And maybe that wasn't too good a bet any more. But Slocum had to try. For all of it, both the gold and being in one piece to enjoying spending it.

He started toward his tent, then stopped and considered. Getting the two mules Ruth still had hidden in the arroyo wouldn't do much but increase the amount of treasure they could take out. Slocum preferred having a horse under him. If things turned against them, he could ride like the wind. But for that he had to have a horse. Not a balky, long-eared, cranky mule.

Slocum got to the corral and made quick choices, a small mare for Ruth and a strong gelding for himself. Saddling the two stolen animals without raising a ruckus proved difficult, but he succeeded. His life depended on both speed and quiet now. He swung up and onto the gelding. The horse took his weight well and proved as strong as it had looked in the corral. Slocum guided the animal toward the tent where Ruth awaited him, leading the mare behind.

"Ruth!" he called softly. "Where the hell are you?" Slocum bent over and pulled back the tent flap. Their meager gear had been packed but of the woman he saw no trace. Cold fear clutched at him. Had Clanton already made his move—had he taken Ruth as a hostage?

"John?" came a small voice. Louder, Ruth said, "I didn't know who it was."

"Where are you?"

"I had an errand to run. But the gear's ready. Did you steal these?" She ran her hand over the mare's sides, ending up patting the wet nose and producing a whinny.

"We've got to get the hell out of here."

"But I—"

"Now!" he said sharply. "No arguments. Clanton's gotten it into his head that I betrayed him to Earp. He's not sure yet, not all the way sure, but he's whipping himself up to get to that point. When he finds these horses gone, he'll be sure I'm responsible. We've got to get out of this valley *soon*."

"The gold and silver," Ruth said. "All that treasure. We can't just leave it!"

"No one found it for many years," he pointed out.

"Only if it really is Victorio's gold. I . . . I might have just gotten lucky and found Clanton's stash, as you said."

"A hell of a time to be agreeing with me."

"But the gold!" she protested. "There's so much of it!"

"Corpses don't care if they have a pine box or a gold casket," he said. But Slocum felt the same gnawing need to make away with some of that treasure. It was such a damned shame to leave it behind without taking a bit of it.

And if he was right, they might have a good chance of getting away with a considerable portion of it.

"Climb up. We can get the other two mules. Four pack loads of gold and silver ought to keep us happy enough wherever we end up."

"Oh, John!" Ruth Macabee stood in her stirrups and leaned over to give him a quick kiss. "I knew I could depend on you."

"On my greed," he corrected.

"We can get out. There's—"

"Ride. We can get to the cave, get loaded, and be on our way before dawn," he said.

Slocum didn't wait for the woman's answer. He put his spurs into the gelding's sides and hastened the animal on its way. Luck would have to ride at his elbow tonight for everything to go right. But if it did—and if his hunch about Ike Clanton was right—they would get away scot-free and rich beyond his wildest dreams.

15

John Slocum and Ruth Macabee rode slowly through the shadow-shrouded arroyos, wishing the darkness allowed them to ride faster. Slocum looked up and guessed that the moon—only half full—would be rising in another few hours. That might be to their benefit.

It might also spell their downfall. If Ike Clanton and the Cowboys decided to come after them, they'd find tracking easier in the bright moonlight.

Slocum decided to worry about that when it happened. Clanton might decide to track them down in the daylight. Or he might not even know of their attempted escape. The man Slocum had struck back in town might not be stirring for hours yet. Remembering the way he'd felt bone crunch when he'd hit the side of the man's head, Slocum wondered if he would ever regain consciousness. He hadn't wanted him to suffocate in the mud, but he had little feeling for the man one way or the other. If alive, the man presented a danger. Dead, he gave an equally dangerous motive to the remaining Cowboys.

Slocum snorted, sounding just like the gelding he rode.

"What is it, John?"

"Just thinking. Don't much matter what we do or don't do. We're in the same stewpot."

"It matters to me," she said. "We'll get away with the gold. Wait and see."

Slocum had to admit that their chances looked good. As long as the thundering of horses' hooves didn't come up behind them, they had a chance. He had seen Ike Clanton riding into the valley from a spot opposite the caves where the treasure had been hidden. That meant the wily outlaw had a secret way in and out.

All they had to do was get the mules loaded, cut straight across the valley, find the secret exit, and take it. Slocum didn't know where it might lead, but he figured that it wouldn't have the dozens of guards on it that Clanton posted on the main entrance. He doubted that Clanton had bothered telling any of the others about it.

"Here, John, here's the track we left earlier." Ruth's voice bubbled with excitement. Slocum saw how hard it was for her to keep from kicking the horse into a full gallop. The two mules they led would have never stood for such a pace, had they been able to maintain it for more than a few yards.

"Keep your voice down. Sounds carry in this cold air." Every movement along the valley echoed and came to Slocum. He listened hard. He didn't hear the sounds of pursuit he feared so.

They went up the rocky draw and came to the spot where Ruth had tethered the other two mules. They stood and glared at the humans for inflicting such torture on them. There wasn't much to eat within easy reach.

"How do we do this?" asked Ruth. "I've never had any experience loading pack animals with gold and silver."

"The gold first, then maybe the jewels in the third cave. Any room we have left, we start loading the silver bars. I don't think there'll be any chance of getting it, though. Too much gold."

"We can use the Indian blankets as padding for the mules."

Slocum studied the animals. They could also use the blankets to wrap the gold coins so they didn't clink and betray them as they made their way across the valley floor. Silence might mean more than speed after they got the mules loaded down.

Slocum dismounted and led the four mules as close to the entrance to the cave as he could. They were the beasts of burden. Just lugging so much gold outside the cave would wear him down. If it came to a fight later, he didn't want to be too tired to do more than put up token resistance.

He and Ruth Macabee went into the cave. Again he used a lucifer, but this time Ruth hadn't brought any candles. They made crude torches from dried weeds and dead ocatillo wood. The sputtering light made it hard to see what they did, but the sight of so much gold glinting magically in the darkness lent wings to Slocum's heart. To get this wealth, he could do anything.

"Where do we start?" Ruth asked.

"That's easy. The boxes nearest the cave entrance go first. No need to wear ourselves down needlessly rearranging all this. We work our way into the cave."

"But the jewels in the third cave . . ."

"They can be brought out with no trouble. They'll be light and can fill any spaces left in the packs. I'll get to work on the bags of gold coins."

Slocum tipped over the strong boxes and spilled out the fortune in gold. Some of the canvas bags had rotted from age, letting the contents fall out. He spread one out flat and tried to read the inscription to see from where the gold had been stolen. The insignia might have been Wells, Fargo and Company but he couldn't be sure. Even the ink on the canvas had begun to flake and peel off.

"It doesn't matter," Ruth called from across the cave. She might have been reading his mind. "It's all *ours* now. No one else can lay claim to it. Not Victorio, not Ike Clanton, nobody!"

"If Ike gets wind of what we're up to, we don't have a ghost of a prayer," Slocum told her. "But we can get out of the valley without much trouble."

"I know," she said, smiling. Slocum looked up, starting to ask what she meant. He hadn't told her of the hidden passage out of the valley. He shrugged it off. She had such confidence in him that she must think he could work miracles.

The only miracle that Slocum wished he could work over the next hour was squeezing even more gold into the packs dangling over the mules' backs. A fortune beyond his wildest dreams rested on those four complaining, angrily braying mules. Even split down the middle with Ruth, Slocum knew he was rich enough never to have to work another day in his life.

He paused to wipe the sweat from his face and think for a few minutes. Ruth Macabee busied herself in the third cave, going through the gems, picking the finest pieces of jewelry. She was about the prettiest thing Slocum had ever seen. She was smart and good in bed and out.

But he wondered what they'd do after they got out of the valley with the riches. Slocum entertained thoughts of settling down, but they were just that—thoughts. The more he worried the subject, the more he came to realize that it would be a living hell for him stopping for more than a few months in any one spot.

Did Ruth see them staying together after they were safely away from Clanton's Cowboys? She'd never mentioned it. Slocum had the feeling that Ruth did. He wasn't sure he wanted it that way, in spite of her leading him to the treasure, in spite of her captivating beauty, in spite of everything.

He couldn't say why, exactly. Wanderlust was a part of it. No woman deserved a man on the trail most of the time. But there was something more that Slocum couldn't put his finger on. It tore at his gut like a splinter, working in and making a worse wound as he worried about it.

He heaved himself to his feet and made a final trip with a heavy bag of Mexican gold coins mixed in with U.S. double eagles. Staggering out, he heaved it up and onto a rock beside the fourth mule. Using the rock as a rest, he transferred the gold into the pack. The mule brayed noisily, protesting the final addition to its load.

"That'll be it. You're lucky," Slocum said to the animal. "I ran out of energy. You got the lightest load."

"No, it hasn't," said Ruth. She dragged an Indian blanket. Working it toward the mule, she got it up and balanced, then began settling the load. The mule complained even more but the woman ignored it. "This is the best of the jewels. It's not *too* heavy, is it?"

Slocum looked at the mule and smiled as he said, "Mule's got bowed legs. Does that mean anything?"

"Oh, John, you are such a joker."

He looked up and saw the half-moon directly overhead. The tiny cut in the rock had turned to silver. The valley would be almost as bright as day. That meant good time getting across; it also meant that any of the Cowboys looking for them would have no trouble finding them.

"Time to be on our way."

Ruth Macabee looked back at the cave entrance with real longing.

"We can't take it all." He hadn't loaded a single bar of silver. An entire cavern room was still filled floor to ceiling with bullion bars. Each mule walked along under the load of three hundred pounds of gold.

Over half a ton of gold coins!

Slocum's heart almost stopped when he realized the total amount of the wealth they took from under Clanton's nose.

"We did it, John," she said. "Getting out of the valley is going to be as easy as falling off a log."

"We still have a ways to go," he said. They stopped at the rocky cleft. He studied the valley floor. No movement. "See that stone spire?" He pointed straight across to the other side of the valley. "That's the marker that will get us out."

"What? What are you talking about?" Ruth demanded. "I arranged for us to get out. We can't go *there*."

Slocum went cold inside. "What do you mean, you arranged for us to get out?"

"I bribed one of the rim guards. He'll look the other way while we go out. I told him we'd be leaving at three A.M. That'll give us plenty of time to get through the town and out along the road leading down the canyon."

"You bribed a guard?" Slocum didn't know whether to shoot the woman or just leave her. He ended up doing neither. "The guards don't bribe. They're too afraid of Ike Clanton and what he'd do to them."

"This one accepted the money without any hesitation."

"How much did you pay him?"

"All I had. Almost fifty dollars, much of it in greenbacks. We won't be needing paper money, not with so much specie."

"He pocketed the hard currency and passed the greenbacks on to Ike to prove his story. Ike may have given him a reward. Damn."

"You're wrong, John. He . . . he wouldn't do a thing like that."

"And why not?" Slocum's anger faded and was replaced with coldness. Ruth Macabee had given the guard more than paper money and coins to insure their escape. That made it all the more likely that the guard would go to Ike Clanton with the story—and the story might not include Ruth. Slocum would be the villain, the traitor, the one trying to escape Clanton's revenge.

The guard would offer protection to Ruth in exchange for continued favors. Slocum saw it all unfolding. Even worse, he saw his chances for geting free of the Arizona Cowboys fading.

"We ride. To hell with the bribe. He's already told Ike about it. We might be in luck, though. Ike may only have extra men at the main canyon."

"Main canyon? What are you talking about?"

"That was Ike we saw riding in the other day. He came in through a hidden entrance. Ike's too smart to get himself stoppered up in a valley, even one this large. Like any good rat, he's got a second way out of his burrow if he needs it."

"The guard wouldn't. He wouldn't betray me. You're wrong, John. You have to be." The shock on Ruth's face confirmed all that he'd only guessed before.

"Then we can go our separate ways. You can get by with a pair of mules, and I'll take the other two."

"John, we can't split up now. I mean, we're a team. We belong together."

"Is it me or the thought of losing half of the gold that bothers you so much, Ruth?"

"That's not fair."

Slocum snapped the reins and got the gelding moving. The mules tried to slow the pace but he wouldn't let them. Slocum refused to look back to see if the woman followed with her two mules. The faint sounds of her mare and the mules on rock and crunching loose gravel told him that she hadn't gone to the mouth of the valley, that she accepted his decision on how best to escape.

"Keep a sharp eye out for riders. No matter who it is, they'll be after us with blood in their eyes. Do you understand?"

"I'm not a child."

"You're not too damn smart, either. You saw how tight a rein Ike kept on everyone. You see that cemetery outside town?"

"Where you buried the Mexican soldiers? And the outlaws killed in the raid?"

"There were dozens of other fresh graves. All were put there by Ike because he didn't like the way they put their Stetsons on or they looked at him cross-eyed or just because it was a Thursday."

"He's not *that* bad," she said, unconvinced.

"You're right. He's worse. The man is a cold-blooded killer. Anybody crossing him gets shot down, no remorse, no second thoughts, nothing. I think that if Phineas Clanton had argued a tad more, Ike would have shot him down."

"His own brother?"

"None other."

"They're waiting for us?" asked Ruth.

"I don't doubt it. I only hope that Ike won't send anyone to watch this pass. He might want to keep it a secret for his own use. But we can't count too heavy on that. Ike's a suspicious bastard."

They rode in silence, the only sounds being the click of stones against the animals' hooves and a gentle sighing of wind coming down from the slopes. The night turned colder. Slocum wasn't sure if it was because of the autumn wind or the way Ruth Macabee treated him now. He might have smoothed out her ruffled feathers, but something inside kept him from doing it.

She was willing to trade her body for free passage out with the gold. Slocum had called Ike Clanton a suspicious bastard, but he knew he shared that with the outlaw. Slocum had to wonder if the bargaining for free passage had included him in the price.

He would make an excellent chip to trade for escape with four mules laden with gold. Ruth might have used him to get the animals loaded, then traded him for her freedom. If Ike didn't know anything about the treasure trove hidden under his nose, Ruth might even get away without having to reveal the contents of the packs.

Slocum shook his head. This was all speculation on his part. Maybe Ruth Macabee hadn't sold him out to gain even more of the treasure. He just didn't know. This much wealth provided a hefty temptation even for a saint.

And Ruth was far from being a saint.

He reined in and held up his hand. "Quiet," he cautioned the sulking woman. Slocum tipped his head to one side and listened hard. Faint sounds came from up the slope. "Men ahead," he said. "At least two."

"How can you tell?"

"I hear conversation. One voice is deeper than the other."

He dismounted and looked at the stony path they followed. It was hardly more than a dried-out riverbed and didn't take tracks. An army might have preceded them up the slopes to Ike's secret passage out and there'd be scant spoor left behind to show it.

Slocum handed Ruth the reins of his horse and the two pack mules. "You're going to have to wait here for a spell."

"Are you going to scout ahead? What if they've set a trap for us?"

"If it's an ambush, well, I'll have to take care and remove it." He fumbled in his pouch and drew out a shining hunting knife, its thick blade flashing silver in the moonlight.

"Do you have to kill them?" she asked.

"Would you rather let them kill you? Slow-like? After the entire gang has raped you?"

"John, you needn't be vulgar."

He shook his head. That Eastern book-learning had given her ideas that didn't set well with survival out in the West. Killing was a part of life. But he didn't expect Ruth to believe that they couldn't simply waltz out past the guards.

"Wait here," he repeated.

"John," she said. Her eyes were wide and innocent in the moonlight. She looked for all the world like an angel come down from heaven. "Be careful. Don't get hurt."

Slocum silently slipped away, gliding along the edge of the arroyo. He paused for a few minutes and watched to see what the woman did. Ruth dismounted and huddled down to avoid the teeth of the wind blowing downslope.

That satisfied him that she wouldn't try to raise a fuss and bargain her way free, using either him or the gold. He might be doing her a disservice, but that mistake on her part kept coming back to haunt him. If Ruth Macabee was capable of whoring to get away with the gold, what else was she capable of doing?

He started up the incline toward the rock spire that marked Clanton's secret pass. Before he got to the spire, he heard the voices again and saw sparks dancing up from under a rock outjut. Slocum skirted the area and came on the men from the side. Wiggling forward on his belly, he kept far enough away to see how many he faced.

Slocum winced as mesquite thorns cut into his back. He pressed himself down into the cold, rocky ground and moved forward a bit more. Three men sat at the campfire, drinking coffee that had been brewed in a pot still sitting in the coals.

"Ike's got a lot of nerve sendin' us out on this wild-goose chase. Why watch the middle of nothin'?"

Another said, "He's just got a wild hair up his ass. Has ever since Brocius got hisself killed." The outlaw shook his head. "No loss to any of us, Curly Bill gettin' shot up, but it woulda been a good robbery if'n that Slocum hadn't sold 'em out."

"Still don't think it was Slocum. He helped us out real good when the Meskins came riding in," said the first.

The third man spat into the fire, producing a column of steam and a loud hissing. "He was just saving his own hide that time," he said. "Who can tell what reward Earp's offering for Ike? Some men'd turn in their own mothers for a few greenbacks."

The second held up for Slocum. "He didn't seem the sort to me. Loyal."

The argument turned to other topics. Slocum waited and watched, hoping to find out if there were others posted nearby or if these three were all Clanton had sent.

The information didn't come. He would have to act soon or lose any chance of escaping. When Ruth didn't show up at the valley's main entrance, Ike would send the Cowboys out to hunt them down. Slocum had done nothing to hide their trail from the treasure caves; there hadn't been any reason to. Speed had counted more than stealth.

And it still did.

He had to kill these three to gain his freedom. He tested the edge of the hunting knife for sharpness. It would slide in easily between the ribs for a quick, clean kill. Rolling to one side, he made sure he still had the six-shooter he'd taken from the man he slugged in town. The extra fire-power might be needed if he made a mistake along the way.

Slocum backed away, used the thickness of the mesquite's limbs for cover, then moved uphill to get above the three. Walking carefully, making sure that every bootstep didn't disturb loose rocks and send them down in a noisy cascade, Slocum got above the three still hunched over the fire and drinking their coffee.

He considered using the pistol. Three quick shots would eliminate all his immediate problems. But the reports might cause more problems than it solved. If Ike got wind of him leaving, the entire gang could be down on his ears in minutes.

One man rose, stretched, and said, "Be right back. Got to take a leak." He vanished in the direction of the mesquite that had hidden Slocum.

Slocum cursed his bad luck. If he'd stayed where he had been, a knife cut across the throat would have reduced those against him by one-third. Still, he need only kill two now instead of all three.

It was dangerous, but he acted rather than thought. He gathered his feet under him and launched himself out into space.

One man caught the blur of motion from the corner of his eye. He jerked around, rolling to his left, reaching for his gun.

Slocum landed with both feet on the other man's back. The impact sent them both into the campfire. The only difference was that Slocum didn't land on his face in the coals. The man screamed as flesh and clothing caught fire. A quick, hard slash with the knife ended his misery. The dying man's blood sizzled and popped as it dripped into the destroyed campfire.

Slocum paid no attention. He sank into a crouch, let the heavy knife spin in his fingers, then launched it in an underhand toss that ended in the second man's belly.

Slocum had acted a fraction of a second too late. The man had dragged out his pistol. His dying convulsion tensed his finger. The gunshot echoed through the still night like a peal of thunder.

"What'n hell's going on?" yelled the man from the bushes.

"Nothing," Slocum said. "Accident."

He had hoped to fool the other man. He failed. The man came out of the bushes with his trousers unbuttoned and a gun in his hand. Slocum dragged the six-shooter from his belt and opened fire. A limb of the mesquite exploded into splinters as a heavy bullet ripped through it. But that slug had been intended for the man's head; he had moved too fast for Slocum.

Slocum went hunting, gun in hand. A shadow moved.

Slocum fired, closing his eyes as he did so to prevent being blinded by the foot-long flame leaping from the muzzle. He opened his eyes and saw that the man had decoyed him by shaking a greasewood with a dead limb.

He started to circle when three quick shots drove him to the ground. His eyes danced with yellow and blue spots from the sudden flashes. Instinct took over. Slocum fired in the direction of the attack until his six-shooter came up on an empty cylinder. He tossed the gun away. Reloading took time, and he had damned little left.

His trusty Colt Navy slipped comfortably into his hand. Slocum rolled and came to his feet, carefully advancing to see if he had removed the problem guard permanently.

"Damn," he swore. Again the man had duped him. Slocum studied the ground and found faint scuffmarks indicating the direction the man had taken. Slocum took off on the trail, moving as fast as he could without causing too much commotion.

The sound of horses ahead made him break into a run. He got into a small clearing in time to see the man mounting. Slocum fired three times. The horse let out a bellow of pain and sank to the ground.

Slocum fired again, aiming for the rider. He missed. The man returned fire and vanished into the low, scrubby brush.

Slocum stopped and let the ringing in his ears caused by the gunfire die down. In the distance he heard the pounding of boots against the ground. The man had given up the notion of riding back to town and had chosen to go on foot.

A decision had to be made fast. Should he try to stop the fleeing outlaw, or should he find Ruth Macabee and get the hell up Clanton's secret pass?

In the far distance Slocum saw bonfires being lit around

the outlaw town. That convinced him that the gunfire had
been heard.

He spun and retraced his steps. Riding like the very
wind was their only hope now. They would have to stay
ahead of Ike Clanton and the Cowboys or die.

16

John Slocum stumbled repeatedly in the dark as he ran back to where Ruth Macabee awaited him.

"John, what's wrong?" the woman cried. She stood and for a moment the image of an angel returned to haunt Slocum. The pale moonlight turned Ruth's soft brown hair into spun gold and highlighted her cheekbones. "I heard shots."

"There were three of them," Slocum said, out of breath. Loading the more than half ton of gold onto the mules had taken its toll on him. Now this. There had to be some point when he could rest, but he didn't know when it would be. Not now. Not with one of the men running like a scalded pig back to Ike Clanton.

"And?" Ruth prompted.

"Got two. The third is on his way to bring the whole

damned gang down on our necks. We've got to ride and ride hard."

"The gold . . . " The wistfulness in the woman's tone told him that she might die rather than abandon her treasure.

"Bring 'em," he said. "We might have a turn of good luck." Even as he spoke, he knew it wouldn't come to pass.

Slocum swung up into the saddle and caught the reins of two mules. He tugged and got the animals moving. They seemed to prefer walking to simply standing. With such a heavy load across their backs, he didn't blame them a hell of a lot.

"Do you know for certain that there's a path?" Ruth asked.

"No."

"But you said—" His cold stare cut off her torrent of words.

Slocum started up the ravine, found where the men had camped, then headed straight for the spire that he had used as a marker to show where Ike Clanton had ridden out into the valley. For long minutes they rode and Slocum felt a sense of desperation rising.

No trail.

Then he saw it. The rock had fallen over the tiny path so that it hid the trail. He urged the gelding forward. The horse's hooves kicked away the rock. The mules followed in their sure-footed manner. Then came Ruth with her pair of mules.

"This is it?" she asked.

"Not much, but it means the difference between life and death for us," Slocum said. He urged his shying horse along the narrow, winding path as fast as he could—as fast

as he dared. The moonlight began to dim. He glanced over his shoulder. The high canyon walls cut off what light there was, making the way even more treacherous. Many times his horse stumbled and almost fell.

Finally, Slocum knew that continued riding would be too dangerous. But not proceeding would be even more dangerous. He dismounted and led his horse.

"John, I hear something behind us."

Slocum stopped. He put his hand over the gelding's nose to stifle the snorting. The sounds of pursuit came to him.

"They're on our trail."

"We can't outrun them! Not in this narrow canyon. It's hardly more than a ravine with high sides!"

Slocum knew the woman was right. This had been cut by swiftly running water through a soft sandstone fault. Wind erosion had helped it along.

"Stop and they catch us. Keep going and we might have a chance."

"You've got a gun. Hold them off!"

"You take the gun and hold them off," he said. "There might be a dozen or more of them. Even if it's just Ike and Phin, we've got big trouble. They'll be more heavily armed than we are."

"We can't fight them off, can we?" Ruth said sheepishly. "That was a silly thing to say."

"Keep riding," Slocum said. "I've got an idea. If there are more than just the Clantons we stand a chance."

He let Ruth crowd by on the narrow trail with her two mules. Slocum went to his rear pack animal and took out his hunting knife. Splotches of dried blood marred its perfection. He wiped it off on an Indian blanket, then slit the side. Gold coins tumbled out to make a mound in the center of the narrow trail. It would be impossible for those tracking him to miss such a pile.

Slocum stared at it, then went and kicked the coins out along a stretch of the path. Then he mounted and quickly caught up with Ruth. His trailing mule thanked him with a loud bray for the lighter load.

"What did you do, John?"

"Just appealing to human nature," he said. If his idea worked, the Cowboys would see the gold and stop to investigate. Which of them could pass up such easily acquired wealth?

He hoped that none of them could.

This might not be much, but it would buy some precious time needed to put even more distance between the outlaws and himself.

They rode in silence for another ten minutes, Slocum thinking as much about Ruth Macabee as he did their pursuit. The woman was beautiful. He could never deny that. And expert at screwing. He'd never have a complaint on that score. But something had gone wrong between them. It might have been the lure of so much money. It might have been the way she tried to buy their passage out of the valley.

Whatever it was, it had turned Slocum cool toward her.

"John, look. We're finally out of the narrow pass."

The ravine split into two segments, one leg running almost due south and the other angling off to the south and west.

They looked at each other, her blue eyes gleaming in the dimness of the night and his own green ones cooler. Without speaking they both arrived at the same conclusion.

"We're going to have to split up if we want to stay ahead of the Cowboys," Slocum said.

"Which branch do you want?" Ruth asked.

"I'm closest to this one," he said indicating the narrower southwesterly path.

"And I'm nearest the one going south."

For the span of a dozen heartbeats neither spoke. Then Ruth said, "We can meet. In a month. In Denver."

"The Palmer House is the finest hotel I ever been in," said Slocum.

"The Palmer House in a month, then," she said.

He nodded. Again they stared at one another. Ruth was the first to move. She leaned over and gave him a light kiss on the lips. "To remember me by," she whispered.

"Until we meet. In Denver," he added.

Ruth Macabee settled down on her mare and spurred the horse due south, the two heavily laden mules following behind.

Slocum listened and heard faint sounds of their distant pursuit. As long as the outlaws were in the narrow pass, they wouldn't be able to make good time. But when they came boiling out and into the delta area, they could speed up considerably.

Slocum thought on this. He could salt Ruth's trail with more gold and lure the Cowboys after her.

He laughed out loud. "So who wants to be rich?"

He wheeled his gelding into the southwest riverbed and began dropping dollops of gold behind. Within a mile the trailing mule's load was entirely gone. He freed the animal and let it go off into the night, braying as it went.

By dawn he had dropped most of the gold carried by the second mule. He transferred what remained into a saddlebag. It made a hefty stake.

"Easier to carry," he told himself.

An hour after dawn, John Slocum had emerged from the

White Mountains and faced the stark desert between him and the Pacific Ocean. He started across it, knowing that he would never show up in Denver. Not in a month or two or even three.

And he knew that Ruth Macabee wouldn't be there, either.

JAKE LOGAN

___	07567-2	**SLOCUM'S PRIDE**	$2.50
___	07382-3	**SLOCUM AND THE GUN-RUNNERS**	$2.50
___	07494-3	**SLOCUM'S WINNING HAND**	$2.50
___	08382-9	**SLOCUM IN DEADWOOD**	$2.50
___	08279-2	**VIGILANTE JUSTICE**	$2.50
___	08189-3	**JAILBREAK MOON**	$2.50
___	08392-6	**SIX GUN BRIDE**	$2.50
___	08076-5	**MESCALERO DAWN**	$2.50
___	08539-6	**DENVER GOLD**	$2.50
___	08644-X	**SLOCUM AND THE BOZEMAN TRAIL**	$2.50
___	08742-5	**SLOCUM AND THE HORSE THIEVES**	$2.50
___	08773-5	**SLOCUM AND THE NOOSE OF HELL**	$2.50
___	08791-3	**CHEYENNE BLOODBATH**	$2.50
___	09088-4	**THE BLACKMAIL EXPRESS**	$2.50
___	09111-2	**SLOCUM AND THE SILVER RANCH FIGHT**	$2.50
___	09299-2	**SLOCUM AND THE LONG WAGON TRAIN**	$2.50
___	09212-7	**SLOCUM AND THE DEADLY FEUD**	$2.50
___	09342-5	**RAWHIDE JUSTICE**	$2.50
___	09395-6	**SLOCUM AND THE INDIAN GHOST**	$2.50
___	09479-0	**SEVEN GRAVES TO LAREDO**	$2.50
___	09567-3	**SLOCUM AND THE ARIZONA COWBOYS**	$2.50

162b